THE
VIRIDIAN
PRIESTESS

KATRINA CALANDRA

The Viridian Priestess

Cover Designer: Franziska Stern, Coverdungeon.com
Editor: normasnookproofreading@gmail.com
For more information visit katrinacalandra.com

To Manda, I just really love you.

CONTENT WARNINGS

Dear Reader,

The Viridian Priestess includes descriptions of anxiety, death/murder, religious trauma, violence, wound care, improvised surgery, injury, mentions death in childbirth (off page), sexually explicit scenes, strong language, manipulation, weapons, bones, dead bodies, family estrangement, prejudice, classism, and alcohol.

Please take care, Katrina Calandra

CHAPTER ONE

66 "Forgive me, First Mother, for I have grown wicked."

The stones on the temple floor are cold this morning. I press my palms flat and lean forward until my lips graze against them. My breath hushes at the surface as I pray, warming it slightly. The temple may be cold, but it is quiet and empty. Two rows of wooden pews on either side of the aisle I'm planted in are barren, waiting for the faithful to rest on them. They will have to wait longer.

I strengthen my words to be less like a plea, but that is what I have been doing every dawn before the temple service. I am pleading, begging that First Mother will answer me and give me wisdom for the coming days.

"Save us from the imbalance of nature that we, your children, commit." The prayer is forged into my memory—second nature, like a greeting. So memorized, the words have almost lost some of their potency. Some are even spoken without thought. I push my palms harder into the stone, forcing the prayer to be steady and more deliberate. "Deliver us from your loving womb like your First Son, the most wicked of all your children. He, in need of the most mercy."

I've completed all my chores: I've changed the flowers and incense on First Mother's statue. The moon water on the altar is fresh and inviting. I should be able to focus on showing First Mother my devotion but my mind still drifts, so I start again, determined to stay focused on every word. If I can just get through it, say it perfectly with full meaning and intention, then First Mother may hear me.

The bells in the tower toll as I finish my last round of prayer. They chime in a steady rhythm, calling the faithful to worship. I can hear the swooshing of long, silken temple gowns gliding up the aisle behind me and catch an accidental glimpse into High Priestess Constance's mind's eye as she steps around me like I am a puddle to be wary of. She unknowingly granted me permission to use my gift on her years ago. Her thoughts zip into my mind like she's thrown her personal journal at me, so scrambled I can only catch glimpses of the images as they fall around me. I wish she would invoke protection wards like every other high priestess in the Estate.

My knees bruise as I sit up on the hard floor beneath them. My thin black temple gown adds little cushion.

"On the floor again, Priestess Ferren?" Thea's temple gown brushes against me, a pool of gray fabric gathering at the hem of mine. She extends a slim hand, her sheer veil cascading from the crown of her head to the floor on either side.

My bones crack as I rise from the abuse I've put them through since before the sun came up this morning. "Blessed morning, High Priestess Thea," I say as she helps me adjust my matte black veil like I'm one of her young students. I admire the intricate beadwork on her neckline as she smooths the front of my dress. It's iridescent against the dark gray of her high priestess gown to show her status, like the other women who sit stiff as a board in the front row. They were born with divine gifts, like me. But First Mother has found them worthy of more: ascension to high priestesshood.

Thea flicks her soft chin to the altar beneath First Mother's statue. I follow just behind her, head bowed and eyes forced on my feet. I cannot fault her for discretion; our friendship is unusual. We care for each other, but that does not take away the facts of our stations and the invisible boundary that exists more blatantly when we are seen by others.

"I'd much rather burn my knuckles lighting the ceremony candles than sit with High Priestess Constance," she whispers as I arrange the main altar for a basic ceremony: a brass bowl of moon water surrounded by three tall white candles.

Thea kisses them with a long lighting stick. I watch as they illuminate her pretty face. Her eyes widen as each flashes with ignition then settles to an elegant flame. The flumes of incense cocoon us in a thin layer of privacy from the now almost full congregation.

Then the ground shakes beneath our feet, and I wince at the slow rumbling bounce of the temple. It has withstood worse, but this tremor makes the rafters above groan and sprinkle dust. I cover the moon water with my palms until it rolls through and then adjust the candles closer to the bowl—three candles to signify the three celestial bodies lining up with First Mother's moon. The planet Frith, the most natural of the three worlds, denies almost all forms of technology. My world, Cosima, where the priestess order was formed, upholds strict standards of worship to ensure First Mother's inevitable return. And the third candle for planet Viathan, which skirts on the new and old world, creating conflict with whoever takes a solid stance in either direction. In the year of our great planetary conjunction, the tremors grow stronger and more frequent as the alignment draws closer.

Thea lets out a long, relieved breath at the stability of the sacred items still in their place, smoothing her hands over the red-velvet cloth they rest on. A hush falls over the soft whispers of the pre-ceremony gathering.

Priestess Eloise enters alone as the chime of the bell fades. She slowly walks down the aisle, straight to the front row. Her eyes are fixed just above my head, on First Mother's statue behind me. My chest constricts at the sight of her wearing a gray temple gown, signifying that she has ascended to high priestesshood. She has had a vision of First Mother, who brought more gifts, more power. For a moment, I forget what she looks like wearing any other color.

I shuffle to Thea's side and accidentally nudge her fingers into the candle she is lighting on the border of the altar. She gasps then presses a finger to her lips. I mouth an apology with an exaggerated, sympathetic look. The odd silence draws her attention to High Priestess Eloise, then it comes back to me. Her wide cerulean eyes narrow in realization as she studies my face. I drop my head to hide my expression, but there is no masking my jealousy. My deep exhale extinguishes Cosima's planetary candle, but Thea relights it with a flat smile and soft nudge on the side of my arm. This will not be a basic ceremony after all.

I rush to the back of the temple, where the gray candles and communion cup are stored. I squat down in front of the wooden credenza by the sacred rooms, using the extra moment to take in a shaky breath, inhaling the special occasion incense stored inside. The carvings in the wood doors seem to mock me; they blatantly depict First Mother showing herself to a priestess, arms extending downward, offering more gifts.

"I am envious, and I am wicked. Please forgive me, First Mother." I quickly unlatch the intricate hinge and fill my arms with the supplies needed for Eloise's ceremony.

"She could be lying," Thea whispers as I return to the main altar with a pile that almost reaches my chin. I smile down at the cup Eloise will drink from. If I knew the moon water would be used by her, I would have left the layer of dust I found on it this morning. I slam down a candle, trying to flush those thoughts from my head in case First Mother is listening. But I can't help it. The last time I saw Eloise, she was gossiping during a ritual; now she has somehow ascended.

High Priestess Constance casts me a judgmental glance over her small prayer book as I slam another candle into place.

"It will be your turn soon enough," Thea says as she pretends to adjust each candle, moving them slightly only to place them back in their original spots. I do the same, desperate to keep her next to me as long as I can. Thea's optimism for my ascension is as unwavering as her faith.

"When does Viathan arrive?" Her voice is lower than any previous whisper.   .

I stare down at a crinkle in the bloodred velvet by my index finger, eyes fixed on the fabric vein that branches under Viathan's candlestick. Soon, representatives from the planet Viathan will arrive in their horrible sky ships to meet with Cosima's chosen representative, to whom I am the unfortunate assistant to, tasked to help her carry out the traditions of the conjunction year. Thea reminds me almost daily of the opportunity this will be to show further devotion, how this is the act First Mother will see and know I am worthy of ascension. But that only makes me feel a bitterness inside, that others can ascend seemingly for no reason and I have to go to such great lengths to prove myself.

"The last message sent through the beacon was not clear. Soon." My own words fill me with a sense of urgency. I did not pray enough this morning. I should have started earlier. I am running out of time to ascend on my own before they arrive, before we must travel to the planet Frith to retrieve sacred stones for the conjunction year ceremony. My small window to prove that I am truly devout without drastic measures is closing.

"When you return, I will set your altar for ascension, Ferren. I just know it." She secretly squeezes my forearm, hidden by our bellowing veils.

When I return. The words seem so easy, almost too casual. I haven't given much thought to returning, just that I must go in the first place. I watch her float on elegant footsteps to an empty seat in the front row, throwing me one last soft look before opening her prayer book.

Priestesses line themselves on the outside pews near the walls. I position myself at the edge of the black border toward the front. I scan the altar from this angle, making sure I have not missed any of the items needed for the ceremony. Having to fetch something once it has started would likely appear like an intentional act of envy.

A young priestess whose face I recognize but name I forgot sits next to me with a smile. I try not to look down the long row of women of the same status as me. I am by far the oldest at 28. I admittedly don't bother learning their names or engage in pleasantries anymore. It makes it easier to hate them when they ascend to high priestesshood before me, which they always do.

"Blessed morning," is all I can muster for her.

I hear her sharp inhale as she sees Eloise on the other side of the room, sitting amongst her new peers like she has been there since her birth. Like me, she was born divine, with a singular gift or a few simple abilities, but now she has been found worthy by First Mother for more, the temple rewarding her with the status of high priestess, a gray veil and temple gown to let others know her new station.

The young priestess's thoughts are loud and unguarded; they trickle in where our shoulders touch, infecting mine with her excitement.

THE VIRIDIAN PRIESTESS

Please don't make me pretend to be happy. Please just leave me alone.

I wish I had another temple duty to complete. I know I won't be able to keep calm during a doe-eyed conversation. In the past, that's all I did: share my hopes and dreams for what First Mother would gift me when she visited. When she decided I was worthy of more gifts and not just the gift of seeing into the minds of others. Thea is the last priestess I let in. She hid her ascension from me for days, not wanting it to come between us. Our eyes meet across the temple aisle. In a sea of gray veils, her face is the first one I see. I knew when she felt like she needed to hide the most important moment in her life, that friendships for me would be too complicated, almost cruel to participate in with anyone else.

The giant temple doors shut with a heavy wooden thud. A final hush falls over the pews as we bow our heads in unison. A long line of elder priestesses hobble to their esteemed places at the front.

Crixa walks with hands clasped, in her usual midnight-blue robe, the attire and color reserved for the most powerful station: the highest priestess. She wears her brown hair pulled back low, frizzy wisps framing her face, unencumbered by a veil. She is regal and statuesque. I bow my head but secretly lift my eyes as she walks toward me. My mood instantly lifts as she passes me with a wink of her powdery blue eyes. She climbs the platform of the altar, and she gives me a beautifully lined smile at the sight of the altar I have set.

She looks over the congregation and raises her long, slender arms, prompting us to stand, reaching out like the statue of First Mother behind her. "Blessed morning to all." Her voice is deep and husky with age. Some have winced at the authoritative timbre, but I find it soothing. "When the high priestesses of old could no longer fight in the war, they set out seeking the stone First Mother had birthed the world upon. They believed if they could find it, they could wake her to save her most devout, to drive out evil forces. With the help of the old gods, creatures from the beginning, they found the stone and woke her."

There is a crackle of static in the room running through like a current. The power in the air feels like its building in a slow hum as Crixa recounts. The hair on my arms and neck stands up at hearing the history of our world spoken aloud. Crixa often lectures at long lengths before we begin any ceremony, but the tone has become more serious as the Viathan arrival draws closer. Every temple member is on edge, anticipating their presence in the city. They are a necessary evil to keep the three worlds' common enemy at bay.

"They pleaded to First Mother, but when she beheld them, she saw how wicked her children had become. They fought and killed each other. They argued over resources they were freely given, made machines that destroyed the soil and killed their neighbors faster, more coldly. At the center of it all was the most wicked of her children, First Son." Crixa pauses in the theatrical way she does when all eyes are on her. "Our First Mother was so tired, and her children were selfish. In her infinite wisdom, she split the once whole world into three—three separate pieces of the birthing stone." Crixa gestures up over her head, like she is cracking a giant egg. "Frith did away with any technology, any tools of First Son. Viathan loosened their rules and adopted a new way of life, skirting the old and new ways. But it was different for us! First Son still dwelled in *our* world; we had no such luxuries! So, we built our walls, our wards, to protect us. And when the others saw our city, our protection, they sent us their stones to protect as well. Now, in the year of the planetary conjunction, the stones must be brought together again. We pray for their swift retrieval."

She seems to look down each of the rows, scanning the room. My eyes water each time she lands on me and holds my gaze for a second longer than any other. With a downward motion of her hand, we sit. She bows her head to the stone likeness of First Mother, prompting every other head in the temple to do the same. "Forgive us, First Mother, for your children have grown wicked."

The entire congregation repeats it in unison, a collective harmonious voice. "Forgive us, First Mother."

CHAPTER TWO

I crank the handle of the tall, leaded glass windows with one hand, balancing a stack of leatherbound books tucked under my chin with the other. The Estate library's windows illuminate sharp beams that reveal little dust particles. The seal opens just a crack, enough to air out the stuffiness without rustling any papers.

The sound of laughter carries in on the dry breeze. I look down at the group of women from the Temple of Divine Mothers in the courtyard. Some lounge on chairs; others walk around holding their heavily pregnant bellies. Elder priestesses dote on them like they are living dolls. They wear white, airy dresses with deeply cut necklines that mimic most temple gowns. A woman with long hair stretches her arms up into the sky. The ones who have pilgrimaged to the temple are easily spotted with loose, flowing hair. They are not divine, but their chances of giving birth to a divine child increase when done in the temple. The few priestesses group together, veils giving away their divinity. They are guaranteed the honor of a divine child, furthering the ranks of the temple. Both ways are accepted by the priestess order.

Every time I see them, I picture my mother's pilgrimage. She would have worn her hair loosely. My sister Leema once told me it was dark and long like mine. Her labors in birth to me were blessed like she hoped, but she did not survive it.

I tiptoe around a tower of books cluttering the walkway to the private desks. The dark and secluded portion of the library feels more intimate, with the lower ceilings and little opaque stained-glass windows. The book-littered aisle is lined with wooden desks just like the pews in every temple in Cosima.

Mary hunches over her workspace, walled off on three sides by texts in need of translating. "Have I told you my last assistant threw herself from that window?" She holds a magnifying glass closer to the parchment.

"You have," I strain out, lifting my long black dress to step over another pile of books.

"Appeared as though you were about to do the same, but I was conflicted on telling my guardsmen to stop you," she says without looking up.

Her guard stands in the widely arched threshold between the main library and the private desks used by Estate scholars. Since being appointed as our representative, Mary has been accompanied by at least one guard at all times. He keeps his gaze straight forward unless called upon, so still and stoic, I walked by him like he was part of the architecture.

I slam down the load of books I've carried from my room across the Estate, my knuckles red from the sharp binding. "It is stuffy in here, smells of old woman." I scoot my small wooden chair next to her more ornate oak one.

She purses her lips to hide the smirk I've teased from her. "The outside air is bad for the parchment, Priestess Ferren."

The magnifying glass shakes in her weak grip as she pretends I am not next to her. I know it is painful for her to hold; her smallest finger trembles. The second knuckle crooks in an odd direction, showing the inflammation in her joints.

"How are your hands today?" I say, finally grasping her attention.

She turns toward me, head angled with a flat look, the crepey lines in her cheeks turning down in a scowl. I should not have asked. I can always tell when they are bothering her. She does everything she can do to use them more, to push herself the days they hurt the most.

"And you do not have permission to pluck the answer from my mind," she says, placing the glass down.

Our relationship is unique enough that I do not think I would need her permission like I do with others. Her translated words are spoken into my ear as I scribe them down—ancient books meticulously translated word for word. Her wisdom and my . . . penmanship. We have done hundreds together, making a connection whether she likes it or not. And a small connection is the only thing I need.

"I would not do that to you." I clear her desk and spread out the stack of journals she has given me to practice on: recipe books, a family tree, and a nauseatingly boring study of ferns from the planet Frith.

Mary gestures for me to open the translated work, with its original bound in emerald green. She runs a misshapen pointer finger down the lines of text, humming as she cross references. The fine tooth of her examination halts on page six.

"Here you have scribed *the fern recoils from the touch of metal*."

"Yes?" I dart my eyes from the original to my work but cannot find the error.

"Technically correct, but *draw back* would be better suited here. In the next line, you can see the fern does not coil back up to its natural position; it simply moves away from it. Dull, but whoever wrote it believed it to be important enough."

"I will rework this page."

"It may be best to go back to practicing on unbound pages for the journals. They tend to have a little more nuance."

I try not to groan at the thought of being demoted to lose parchment, but ruining an entire book on page six is wasteful.

"We will need field guides and journals that are straightforward. Secondhand accounts tend to skew the truth." She hands me a small, wrinkled paper from the ornate wooden box she keeps at the front of her desk. "You will need to study these before the journey. Go pull them so I can check the rest of your work without your hot breath on my neck."

I open the poorly folded paper, the words written in a slant with a shaky pen. One is barely legible, but I don't have the heart to ask her to clarify. I recognize a few we worked on together, but most are long before my time with Mary. I get a strange emptiness in my gut as I scan the titles. *Conjunction Traditions of Frith*, *Flora and Fauna of the Planet Frith*, and *The Sacred Stones of the Three Worlds*.

"Should I pull any on Viathan?" I say, staring down at the scratchy words.

"No, their representatives will tell us anything we need to know."

"Are you sure?"

"Ferren, you are a smart girl. That's why you are accompanying me to Frith and not . . . one of these." She waves a bent finger in her guard's direction. "We do not need any more brutes on the journey with a ship full of Viathans. We need intellect, a quick mind. But you are still thinking like a priestess, not a scholar's assistant. Our bags will be searched as we depart. What will it look like if we have books detailing our travel companions."

"Suspicious."

"Hmm, the same reason you cannot wear . . . this." She gestures up and down with a branchy hand to my priestess gown and veil.

"Viathans are wildly suspicious, strategic and violent. That is all the books will tell you."

Viathans have a long history with the temple. They want to protect the world with their weapons at the forefront and the temple behind it, believing we are too extreme. But standing against First Son with the gifts of First Mother is the only way. Mary has made sure that if I assist her on the journey to Frith, it will be as a citizen of Cosima and not a priestess of the order, backed up by Crixa and the emperor I have no room to argue with. But it does not stop me from voicing my opinion on a planet with such contempt toward my temple.

"They are indecisive too. Crixa says because they embrace the old world and the new. . ."

Her head snaps toward me, like I have said something awful. "If they believe there is any temple involvement, it will compromise the entire journey with Viathan and the elders of Frith. They are not fond of Crixa's methods, as I have told you. They will not so easily hand over their stone if they know you are a priestess. When I say we cannot bring those books, that you cannot wear your veil or reveal you are part of the order, I mean it, child." Mary grabs my hand in a firmer grip than I thought possible for her. "When we travel to Frith, Crixa will not be there to protect you. I will."

I smooth my hand over her freckled knuckles. When she speaks in this tone, reminding me I am going to a place that will not be welcoming, with cruel-natured Viathans, my stomach does a strange twist. Mary is not divine. She is no elder priestess, but she is respected like one. If she were to report me for bad behavior, I would be punished, regardless of the favor Crixa shows me.

I must act and dress like a scholar's assistant for the journey to Frith—a normal citizen from Cosima. Mary was chosen as representative for her wisdom. I know if she tells me I need to remove my temple veil, I should listen. But the thought of being without it while we are away makes my palms itch.

Mary pulls back, grabbing the magnifying glass to finish the critique of my work. My throat feels dry at the serious shift. Our normal teasing banter has turned more weighty since Mary received word she was chosen for the journey to Frith again, her second conjunction year in a row. Her condition and the fact that her assistant is a priestess, has her temper burning a little brighter.

I hide in the darkest corner of the library, taking extra time to search for the titles on my crumpled paper. The walls of bookshelves make little pockets of varying antique smells. The dark cases hold books only meant for scholars and the temple, creating a cozy fortress away from my responsibilities.

I hear a hushed giggle toward the archway where Mary's guard is stationed. Thea's sweet laughter permeates the space as she turns the corner with a vivid smile and stops when our eyes meet.

"There you are. Ben said you were back here," she says and leans against the end of a bookshelf, dusting off the ledge with a blow of air.

"Ben?"

"It's perfectly normal to know a guardsmen's name."

"Right." I huff and round to the next shelf. "Are you teaching today?" I run my finger down the spines to match a similar title with the illegible ones on my list.

Thea follows me, angling herself to see guardsmen Ben through the sparse row of books in this section. "The children are in silent reflection, so no need." She sighs.

"Silent reflection. I do not miss those days."

"Stop it, it's good for them. Teaches them self-soothing and to commune within themselves."

"Do you think Ben is communing with himself or with you in his *silent reflection*?" I wave a book at her with lifted brows.

Thea crosses her arms. "I will hit you with that, Ferren."

We both peer at him through a hole the books make and stifle our laughter. He's staring forward at nothing, like he excelled at silent reflection in his school days.

"Has another transmission come through the beacon?" she whispers, breathing so close, I can feel it on my cheek.

I turn to her hopeful expression, her eyes so genuine as she waits for my answer. I shake my head no, which does nothing to deter her optimism—the kind that smudges out any negative fact of reality. Thea is sweet and even wise, but I do not think she understands who we will be traveling with. She only sees the opportunity I have, completely blind to anything other than a positive outcome.

"I want to show you something." I pull her to the back corner of sacred books. I press a finger to my lips as we pass close to Mary's desk, only a bookcase separating us. The smell of deteriorating binding glue and old leather hangs in the air. I pluck a tall candle to illuminate where the sun does not filter in. On a short shelf at the bottom row, I see the book I am after. Thea takes the candle from me as I squat to draw it from the snug fit between two others.

"What is it?" Thea leans in cautiously.

I flip the thick paper instead of reading her the title. The book is larger than most, maybe double the size and more illustration than written word. I lay it flat on top of the short bookcase it came from, and there, in the middle, I find the page. I gesture, inviting her to look at it. I want her to understand.

Thea squints one eye at me in apprehension to move closer. The candle flicks an eerie glow on the book, making it seem more forbidden in the darkness. She leans over the open face of the pages with me. I have to clasp my hands together to stop from smoothing the old paper like I do when I'm about to inscribe on a new page for Mary.

Thea sucks in a sharp little breath. "What is this, Ferren?" Her voice sounds so small, I almost regret bringing her back here.

"Mary says one of them will likely be a commander."

"One of the representatives . . . from Viathan?"

I nod slowly.

She hovers the candle down the illustration of a commander. Her hand shakes as she moves it back up to the ominous, helmeted figure. I've seen depictions of them in battle during the war with First Son. But this one reminds me of a flora study, just a simple figure on the page with notes in the margins pointing to various parts of the enormous body armor—a still life of something so otherworldly, it is kept in the back of the sacred books.

"Is it a man?" she asks.

"It looks more machine than man. They still wear the armor they did during the war. Mary says the commanders never take it off."

The second page has an interior view of a commander's helmet, the visor that allows them to look out, glowing buttons on either side similar to the ones on the beacon.

Thea opens her mouth to say something but is cut short by the familiar sound of the ground rumbling. Her candle drips wax onto the page next to the inscription of the commander's mask. I hold up a hand to her as she tries to wipe it away. It will be easier to peel off in one piece when it dries.

"Sorry," she says, holding onto the wall as the tremor levels out.

As soon as it stops, a larger, more hammering one begins. We brace ourselves against the stone walls, book piles messily arranged swaying and knocking to the floor.

"Mother's womb!" Mary yells from her desk.

"We should move out into the common area!" I say over the sound of the whole world shaking.

We duck as books drop around us. The ground still shakes as we cross the large archway, seeming to jump up and down. We take messy steps into the common area of the library as a large burst of sound comes in from the window. This is the longest and loudest one I have ever felt, even in the last days of the prior conjunction.

The ground stabilizes after dizzying minutes, but the sound continues. Mary huffs her way into the communal area, holding onto Ben's arm for support. Their faces are just as confused and worried as Thea's.

A sound bellows so deep, yet so sharp, my ears instantly pop. It cuts into the air like it's sucking it away then blowing it back, all at once. The stone floor jolts to the side then back before starting its rolling vibration again. The four of us brace ourselves with the large oak tables in the middle of the room. I follow a hair-thin crack that travels up the floral painted plaster on the wall. As it meets a thick line, a plate size chunk falls in a dusty mess.

"It's still going. How is it still going!" Thea says as she closes her eyes tightly.

In a quick snap, the sound is gone, making my ears pop again. The tremor rolls to a finish as we stare at one another in shock. It's completely silent . . . then the sound of birds singing comes in from the window, letting us know it is over.

But it's not birds. Women are screaming below in the courtyard.

It's the Divine Mothers, their cries all blending together. Another roaring sound I have never heard before drowns them out.

Ben runs to the window, looking down on them. I see his head look upward like something caught his eye. "It's . . . There is a sky ship landing within the walls."

"Impossible!" Mary walks in a sway. Her chin lifts as a black sky ship crosses the window, blotting out the view for a slow moment, the strange sound growing louder and closer.

The bell tower begins a rhythmic toll in the beautiful pattern to call the faithful to the temple. Then the chimes become chaotic and urgent, like an alarm.

"First Mother save us," Ben whispers softly to himself.

"Will you shut up? It's a Viathan ship. They have arrived," Mary snaps at Ben like he is being irrational.

"Were they meant to land within the walls?" Thea whispers to me.

"I'm not sure," I say with a shaky voice. Viathan is here; I can feel my throat getting dry and lips cracking from my anxious panting. There is a landing dock that I can see in the lower part of the city from some of the Estate windows, small ships arriving and leaving but never within the walls.

Mary turns to look at me, her expression sending a chill down my spine. I can't help the backward step I take as she approaches.

"Go to your room and put on the items I sent you. Do not argue," she says in an uncomfortably serious tone.

I can't answer, so I give her a shaky nod.

"High Priestess, do you need an escort to return to your post?" Mary says to Thea.

Thea's eyes flick to Ben for just a moment before she shakes her head and submissively separates from our group.

"I want you to meet me in the emperor's wing. Do not let anyone from Viathan see you in a veil. From here on, you are not a priestess until we return. Do you hear me?" Mary painfully grabs my chin to make me look into her creased eyes. "If they do, they will be . . . unkind to you. It will complicate matters."

Over Mary's shoulder, Thea nods to me before exiting through the thick wooden door of the library—a single nod, completely deprived of a formal goodbye for the sake of urgency. I feel sick at the thought of not seeing her for First Mother knows how long while we are away.

"I understand," I lie to Mary, jaw fighting against her swollen grip. Would they truly hurt me if they know what I am? Do they hate the priestess order as much as Mary says they do?

A strange metallic sound bursts in like the sky ship has landed, an ominous declaration that Viathan is here for us. With it comes men wearing terrifying armor, concealing their faces with forbidden technology. I can no longer pretend this day will not come. Viathan has landed.

CHAPTER THREE

The atmosphere in the Estate is thick, a sense of urgency I cannot shake. I lift the hem of my scratchy linen dress as I climb the large staircase in the grand hall. I look the part but feel ridiculous in the inconspicuous dress Mary has chosen for me. The tan fabric looks monochromatic against my skin. I have not worn any color but black since I was a child. I notice every glance from guards and handmaids as I pass. Normally, they see a veil and part the way, even if their shoulders relax a bit once they realize I am not a high priestess. But now, they are completely unfazed, some even bumping into me in their rush.

The halls of the emperor's wing are large enough for three people to walk down comfortably, with room for ornate furniture and statues on either side. Candles cast illuminating orbs on the floor as I reach the heavy doors to the counsel rooms. Ben and another guardsmen stand at the entrance. I smile at him as I enter and he nods, barely breaking his frontward stare.

I slowly stride until I am planted in the middle of a tile mosaic in the center of the gathering room—an unintentional mark to view it from all sides. I scan it for familiar faces, feeling a little underdressed compared to the council members, who mumble to one another in small groups.

I almost reach out a hand in relief when I see Crixa approaching me in her stunning midnight-blue temple robe. I bow my head, keeping my eyes on my feet.

"Blessed evening, Ferren. I'd like to see you in the temple after, my dear." Her tone is hard to decipher. I cannot tell if I will be punished for showing Thea the Viathan book or if she wants to pray with me before our departure.

She gives me a flat smile that does not reach her hooded eyes when I look back up at her. The enormous, pale stained glass reflects onto the long sleeves of her gown as she floats away from me, giving my shoulder a final squeeze. With that touch, I realize, she is restraining her attention for me. To an outsider, she is the highest priestess talking to a woman dressed like someone who wouldn't be in a room this brilliant. My instructions to play the role of a scholar's assistant is already a shock to my system.

Mary catches my eye across the room with an uptick of her round chin. I take a large breath before stepping off the dark tile mark to cross the sea of unfamiliar people.

"Have you prepared your belongings to depart? The Viathan commander was angry when the guards asked them to wait in the table room until the emperor arrived," she says before I can even say hello.

"I did as you said. They are in the table room?" I glance over at the connecting door where the large oval table rests for matters of the most important kind. I've been inside a few times: when Mary needed a scribe and one occasion with Crixa on our way to the temple. The Viathans just arrived, already showing their domineering ways as they wait for our leaders in a room too beautiful for them. The thought of an armored Viathan commander just on the other side, already angry, makes me want to sprint away.

Mary purses her lips, making tiny little lines. "Hmmm, be a dear and fetch me a mug of something hot." She ignores my questions while flexing a hand at her side. Her knuckles must be stiff.

I scan the room again for a handmaid to ask but see a large table of food and kettles with small discs of fire underneath. I weave through the crowd of people until I reach it. The food is miniature and ornate, like the kitchen serves for special occasions. My stomach growls at the sight of tiny, knotted morsels of sugar bread.

"Blessed evening," Lord Hollis says with a creepy slide to my side.

I fake a smile in his direction, purposefully angling away as I pour Mary's tea. She won't drink it, only hold it to soothe her joints. I know she likes to smell the herbs so I stir in a small scoop. I can feel him watching me and glance over for proof. His clothes are a mix of temple member and guard. It makes him look . . . stupid.

"Pays to be the highest's pet, doesn't it," he whispers too close.

"Excuse me?"

"Most priestesses who haven't ascended at your age are sent to some place awful to serve." He flashes a slimy smile.

I stare at him with dead eyes, contemplating if it would be worth the punishment to talk back. I squeeze the fragile teacup so hard, I am surprised it has not shattered.

He huffs, satisfied with himself, then joins a group next to us like he never interacted with me at all. His favor with the emperor seems to give him a stilted sense of self, when normally he would be at a lower station than even me—a fact that is equally as frustrating as it is amusing. He purposefully tests those boundaries at every encounter, gaining some sort of power from it, and I can't help but hate him.

Mary is at my side before I can bring back her tea. "We are

entering. You are not to speak," she whispers.

Guards open the doors to the table room as council members shuffle in. Only a few elder priestesses accompany Crixa. The rest are ornately dressed people who live in the other part of the Estate with the emperor, the opposite side of the temple and priestess order.

Mary pulls back on my elbow before I can take a step forward to enter with them. She holds me in place until the threshold is clear and most have been seated.

The room is bursting with people murmuring while shifting in their seats. I keep my eyes on my feet as we crisscross through them. Mary drags me to the short side of the oval table.

"Put it down," she whispers through gritted teeth, looking at the cup in my hands.

I brought it in with us without thinking. I place it on the table in front of me as Mary climbs down into her seat. No one else has brought any of the food or drink into the meeting, the realization making me flush with embarrassment. I whisper an apology to her as I descend into my chair and shoo the mug farther away with my fingertips, hoping it will go unnoticed. I almost tip it over as I look up and see the person across from us.

There, sitting a half a pew's length away, is a Viathan commander.

I sink down into my seat, realizing the visor of his black helmet is pointed in my direction. It's completely opaque, but I still cast my eyes down in case he noticed my reaction to seeing him so close.

When I flick my eyes up again, he has turned his attention to the person at his side. His armor is dark, heavier in more vulnerable spots, like his chest and down the broad arms rested on the table. He makes the guards lining the wall behind him look like children's toys.

Emperor Matthias enters through a private door and sits at the top of the oval with Crixa and Lord Hollis at his sides. The commander stands to his full towering height, revealing more of the dark armor covering his body. The illustration I showed Thea does not do the sheer intimidating size of him justice. Every time he moves, I can hear the council members whisper to each other nervously. Two men stand with him, dressed in Viathan clothing. They look more diplomatic, fitting in with the nobleness of the room. The commander looks like he is going to war.

The pasty, bald Viathan next to him is older and eyeing the guards like he wants to fight anyone who moves too quickly. He reminds me of the weasel Crixa keeps as a pet. It sneaks out to the courtyard to eat the doves then puts itself back in its cage before she notices—cunning and slimy.

The third Viathan is a younger man with closely cut dark hair and handsome tan skin. He stands more casually than any other person in the room. His bright-green eyes and soft expression are a relief compared to the harshness of the other two, who look like they could kill us all.

"Welcome, 99th Commander," Emperor Matthias says. He gestures a hand for them to be seated while blinking slowly, like a pause for utter silence. The emperor is as striking as he is aloof, completely still at the head of the table like someone painted him into the setting. "You have brought the Estate to utter chaos, landing where you did," he says calmly.

"Your beacon is compromised." The Viathan commander's helmet bobs down as he speaks. The deep boom of his voice makes a few seated close to him jump in surprise. I can make out small holes where his mouth would be positioned, words muffled by the metal of his mask.

"Compromised," Crixa says with a condescending quality.

The commander tilts his head in a slow nod. "Yes, Highest

Priestess, as is Frith's. We have not made contact with them."

"Cosima's representative," Emperor Matthias announces, a summons for her to speak.

Mary clears her throat with a rasp. "Frith has been known to ignore their beacon or shut it off completely during a conjunction year."

I notice the Viathan signet on the commander's massive shoulder plate. Three planetary bodies are embossed on dark metal, Viathan's, Frith's, and ours in dancing conjunction. Viathan embraces nature and technology equally, believing they can be balanced. They use weapons of metal that spit light and sky ships that travel to the three worlds. Of course, this commander does not understand why Frith would not be receiving their messages. The people of Frith are even less tolerant of their lust for technology.

The commander waits for Mary to continue then turns his attention back to Emperor Matthias. "We believe First Son will attack this conjunction."

There is an audible gasp in the room, followed by the ringing of everyone speaking at once. I turn to Mary to gauge her reaction, and she only exhales, like the news has drained all her energy.

"And what makes you *believe* this?" Crixa says over the chatter of other council members.

I've never heard anyone calmer under pressure than Crixa until I heard this commander speak. "Viathan has received word that First Son plans to retrieve the sacred stones before we do."

The voices in the room lull to an eerie silence at the mention of the sacred stones.

"Are your people finally regretting housing your stone on Frith? Ours is safely within the temple wards, as they all should be—" Crixa stands, purposefully slanting her head down to the commander.

"First Son moves to steal the stones from Frith . . . and ours?" Emperor Matthias cuts in.

The commander nods slowly.

"This changes nothing!" Mary makes an exasperated sound and rises from her chair. I quickly stand to aid her shaky arm. "The threat of First Son is present on every conjunction year. We must uphold the proper traditions and merely invite Frith to house their stone on Cosima. If they deny us for this conjunction, we must not break their laws. Each world has a choice of where their stone rests, their decision entirely up to them regardless of an attack."

The room is a mix of annoyed groans and nods of agreement. Mary told me tensions would be high. The three worlds who normally leave each other alone having to agree for the greater good seems impossible. Every conjunction year, the stones are brought to Cosima for the final alignment, but placing stones next to each other on an altar is not enough to wake First Mother, just like my desperate and distracted prayers are not enough for me to ascend.

First Mother demands more from us, more sacrifice, a show of our collective devotion. The three worlds themselves have to come together. Each conjunction, it becomes clearer how separate we continue to be.

"Thank you, Mary. We will look to you in handling Frith's tradition. I'm sure their elders will remember you from the last retrieval," Emperor Matthias says with a down motion of his hand to calm the room.

Mary nods as I help her back into her seat. I feel a little awkward at the attention on us, even if she is the one they are focused on. I scoot my chair in and make the mistake of glancing over at the commander. I can feel the tops of my ears heat at the sight of his blasphemous helmet. I know for sure his eyes are on me as he tilts his head a fraction, holding my gaze. The dull shine of his mask voids any semblance of human features, somehow more terrifying than the ominous threat of an attack by First Son.

How can a tiny slant of his head be utterly paralyzing? The armor study from the Viathan book had notes in the margins about the capabilities of a commander's helmet. I wish I paid more attention to them now. Can he tell that I am a priestess? Has he known I am lying since I entered the room in this stupid linen dress?

I drop my eyes to my lap, hoping he ignores me for the rest of the council meeting. But every time there is a pause in the back and forth of the diplomatic conversation, I steal a glimpse. And every time I do, his helmet slowly turns toward me, letting me know he notices.

CHAPTER FOUR

I slip into the empty Estate temple, desperate for clarity after the council meeting. My feet echo as I walk up the aisle. The candles on the altar have burned down, dripping wax onto the prayer cloth. I stop in front of First Mother's statue, feeling naked in my simple dress. Carved stone looks down on me with extended arms—a mother reaching down to pick up a child, gentle and regal. This statue is my favorite. Most of the other temples have First Mother with her arms and chin lifted upward, but the Estate temple is fortunate to have one of the last original depictions of First Mother about to embrace one of her children.

"First Mother . . . keep us safe on our journey to Frith. I am afraid." My voice sounds lost in the open, empty air. I'm ashamed of the messiness of the words. I wish I could pray without rambling, but my thoughts jump from the journey to the threat of First Son and keep landing on the memory of the commander's scrutinizing stare.

I walk to the tall leaded glass behind the main altar. The sky is pink with a lovely blush now. I look down at the courtyard and the sight makes my stomach drop to the floor. A black, menacing shape blots out the view of the cobblestone below. The Viathan sky ship takes up the majority of the courtyard, the metal edges almost cutting into the light stone of the buildings on all sides. Guards make thick lines around it, seeming to put their bodies between it and the architecture.

I hold onto the sill of the window tightly. Standing in a temple and looking down on a sky ship does not feel right, but I cannot peel myself away. I notice a large, empty hole in the side, like a large door has been opened. It lays itself in an angle, up to the ship and into the sandy cobblestone. The opening is as massive as the double doors to the emperor's wing but dark and completely void of any color. Someone moves in the blackness of the opening, the shine of metal catching the pink light of the evening, a figure as tall as the opening itself. The Viathan commander steps out of the blackness, walking down the inclined path from his ship.

"Ferren?" Crixa's voice calls out behind me.

I suck in a startled breath so fast, I cough through my greeting back to her. She bows to First Mother then scoots into a pew a few rows back from the front. It creaks as she adjusts her gown on either side of her narrow hips, then she pats the empty, grainy wood next to her. I hesitate but she nods to reassure the invitation.

She stares forward, eyes on the statue of First Mother while I examine the side of her face, the detailed lines in her high cheek. "I almost did not recognize you," she says and looks over my linen dress. "I trust Mary in this decision. I am not worried you will forget your vows."

I adjust the fabric on either side of my lap—scratchy compared to my silken gowns. "I will find time to pray privately, I promise."

She hums in approval, staring forward again.

"Crixa . . . do you believe First Son will come to the Estate?"

"Perhaps, dear. But it would be better calculated for him to snatch two of the stones from Frith. We only have one stone and I have made our wards around the city strong, impenetrable. With all three stones together as they should be, I could guarantee the wards could withstand any force First Son brings."

"Why does Viathan house their stone on Frith and not their own planet?"

"A planet that embraces the old world and the new cannot be trusted to make sound decisions, my dear."

She has answered more things than I thought she would, but I still have so many questions. Pestering her is one of the very few things, however, that can make her lose her calm demeanor.

"You did well in the council meeting."

"Thank you, Crixa." I run my finger over the sore nail bed of my thumb, where I anxiously chewed on my walk to the meeting. Her praise feels short-lived, the guilt of my doubts giving it an awful aftertaste. "I begged First Mother for my ascension before they arrived, hoping if I did, I would not have to go. Forgive me, Highest," I say in a confessing exhale.

"Have those thoughts passed?" Crixa turns her torso toward me, giving me a narrow-eyed look.

I lie with a nod of my head.

"I need you to be good, Priestess Ferren. I need you to be devout and obedient. Can you do that?"

"Yes"

I'm suddenly aware of where I am seated, that I shouldn't be in a pew like this. Even if the highest priestess asked me to join her, it feels wrong. I fidget with the sleeve of my arm, trying not to look at her directly. I want to talk about anything other than the direction she is pivoting me to. The tone in her voice is soft but somehow more abrasive, like when she tells me to complete an awful task for breaking a rule or when her physical punishment won't do and she has to resort to other means.

But this doesn't feel like a punishment. This is something altogether different. I want to go back to talking about the danger the three worlds are about to face. That seems far away and distant, but her words are close and caging me in. With her breath so close to my shoulder, this feels more immediate. I try not to bounce my leg as the pressure in my gut constricts.

"I need you to make sure Frith allows us to house their stone. They must agree." She hunches a little to speak to my down-turned face. "You have my permission to use your gift of mind's eye to ensure their retrieval."

I have to close my mouth from gaping. I pull at the tight tendons in the side of my eyes to see her searching my face. I have no words in answer, at least no appropriate ones.

"Highest Priestess, I will do anything you ask, but I am not sure how I can do that. Mary said we must follow their laws if they disagree . . . ," I say meekly.

"Yes, well, Mary is wise but she does not always understand matters of the temple. If the three stones are not here for the conjunction, I will struggle to keep us safe. Traditions will not matter if First Son can breach the wards, my dear."

I want to get out of this pew, go back to the library, and dive into my work or lock myself in my room.

"You have an opportunity no other in your situation has had. First Mother could find you worthy by your assistance to the journey, of course. But if you ensure Frith will agree to housing their stone here, I can *guarantee* your ascension."

"How?" I swallow a clump of dry air.

"Do you trust your highest?"

"Yes, with all my heart. But First Mother—"

"You will go, you will succeed, and the day you ascend, I will send word to your sister, " she says flatly.

The mention of Leema is the only thing that awakens the muscles in my neck to lift my head finally. Crixa would not speak of her unless she was serious. A twist moves from my stomach to my heart, the familiar contortion of it breaking apart at the thoughts of my sister.

Crixa scoots closer to me, her breath a caress on my face. "You will have ascended. She will no longer have to feel shame. Do you not want that for her?" She pushes a long strand of hair over my shoulder.

Leema was five when our mother passed bringing me into this world. My birth was blessed with divinity because of her sacrifice, and if I ascend, it will not be in vain. Leema did not leave the city because she was ashamed of me. She left because it was too painful waiting for our mother's death to somehow make sense. I could erase the years of our disappointment and heartbreak. I could prove to her that it was all for a reason.

"Yes." I fight with the sob in my throat threatening to unhinge my jaw and outpour itself into the echoing temple. Would she come back to the Estate if she knew I ascended? I think of her face and the last time I saw her, how sad she looked when the pain of my station finally drove her out.

"I know you won't disappoint me, Ferren," Crixa says, standing and smoothing the front of her gown.

I watch Crixa's light tread in front of me, graceful but too fast. I struggle to keep up and hope that she slows down, that she remembers she forgot something and we turn back, anything to buy me more time. I want to reach out for Crixa's hand or to cling to her arm.

The wind whips up the sandy dirt, making it stick to my clothes.

A hot morning like today with an airy temple gown would be no problem, but black pants cling to me with purposefully placed leather patches on the outside of the legs. I run my hands down my hips where they hug the tightest. The thick boots on my feet feel hazardous on the uneven cobblestone, and on top I wear a loosely layered jacket perfect for hiding items I do not want confiscated within my breast binding.

I pull at the strap of my shoulder bag that crosses my chest. It pinches at the letter opener I have buried in my cleavage. After meeting with Crixa, I debated well into the night about bringing an actual weapon. I could have easily taken one of the small ritual knives from the temple credenzas. But having something that at least resembles a weapon makes me feel a little safer traveling with three Viathans, even if it has been done every conjunction year since the beginning.

As we get closer, my nerves shoot through me like I have made a mistake. But then I'm hit with an electric excitement that makes my stomach turn as the sky ship comes into view. It seems smaller when standing on the same level, not viewing it from the temple tower or watching it blot out the sky. The dull chrome looks like unpolished silverware with black details, the front pointy with three huge windows. The wings on either side and top make it look like a massive, deformed bird. It's oddly planted in the cobblestone courtyard, stained-glass windows on the tower behind it, an odd mix of our world and theirs.

Crixa slows to walk beside me out into the open dust as we cross the courtyard toward the group of council members. "Remember what I told you," she whispers.

A large group of elder and high priestesses stand at the edge closest to the Estate walls, their veils breezing in the wind, reminding me how different I must look.

Mary steps forward and silently wraps her arm around mine for support and lifts her proud chin. We shuffle the rest of the way to Emperor Matthias and Lord Hollis, who stand just before the sky ship with two of the Viathans.

They both greet Crixa then turn their heads toward Mary in expectation.

"I am called Mary; this is my assistant."

The less-frightening-looking Viathan without armor smiles.

"99th Commander, you have two citizens of Cosima in your care. We expect their safe return along with the stones." Emperor Matthias lies effortlessly to them about who I am. I doubt he even knew my name before Mary called a council meeting on concealing my priesthood just days before the Viathans arrived.

"I assure you we will complete the retrieval," the commander says in a low timber with a slight nod of his helmet.

I take note that he didn't quite assure them I would be protected, just that we would be successful. But everyone seems to be satisfied with his answer.

"Very well, blessed travels to you both. May First Mother bless your endeavors." Crixa places a cold, stiff hand on my shoulder. Any hint of softness in her face flashes away as Mary replies in her studious way of speaking.

We're saying goodbye. *No, not yet. Please.* I can feel my eyes watering, but all of them are watching, waiting for a natural reply.

"Thank you, Highest Priestess." My words are cold and unnatural.

Crixa furrows her brow, gripping her fingers into me. Maybe she would hug me if circumstances were different.

"Blessed travels," Emperor Matthias cuts in.

We bow our heads to him in return. When I look up, Lord Hollis is smirking, no intention of wishing us luck. Then, in unison, the three of them turn on their heels, walking back toward the group of council members. I stare at their backs, willing myself not to run after Crixa, to hug her and say goodbye properly. I survey the long line of gray veils, searching for Thea's face. But their heads are bowed now as Crixa joins them. I know Thea is out there; she would not miss seeing me off.

The commander and Mary travel up the ramp in her slow pace. The Viathan with green eyes waits at the bottom, giving me another polite smile.

"After you." He opens his hand in a waving motion toward the ramp.

I stare down at my boots in the dusty ground, the ramp a smooth step up. I've never walked on something like it before, so I carefully lift my foot, placing it on top to test. It's metal and steep, and I would for sure fall up something like this in my temple gown. My eyes follow the metal lines up to the top where Mary enters the large, dark opening. The commander stands perfectly still, his head tilted down like he is waiting for us—a guard to the enormous opening I have to pass through.

These are our travel companions. Mary assured me we would have privacy and our own space, but I doubt I will be able to hide away from them the entire trip. I will need to be cordial if I am going to pull off my deception. I'm a simple scribe to Cosima's representative, not a temple priestess with a disdain for Viathans and their unnatural predilections.

I smile flatly up at the commander, but my stomach does a flip when I see the confused slant of his helmet as if he has never seen a polite smile before. I can't see his eyes, but I know without a doubt he is watching me.

"You're not quite what I was expecting," the Viathan next to me says as he watches me hesitate then plant my right foot.

The casualness of his tone is more striking than his statement. I ignore it and manage to place both boots on the odd surface.

"I was told all the Estate scholars are ancient. Or frail old men. But you're neither." He smiles again.

"Oh. Well, I'm only an assistant," I say, trying not to panic that he thinks I already look out of place.

We walk up the steep incline of the metal ramp. It has a grated texture, which helps. The commander and Mary have gone deeper into the ship, out of sight, and my eyes flick around, trying to locate her. The bald Viathan lounges on a stack of metal boxes, cutting pieces of an apple with a small knife. I realize he was missing while Emperor Matthias and the highest addressed the others. I cannot believe he had the nerve to sit up here while she blessed our journey.

"How many languages do you speak?" the green-eyed Viathan asks.

"Um, some. Not very well. I can only understand written words in most. Books don't tend to speak back."

He huffs. "Well, this is the cargo hull. We enter and exit through here, mostly for supplies."

I stand at the top of the ramp where it hinges. One more step and I will enter it fully. It's illuminated by long, thin lights at the top of the metal walls. There are more handles, buttons, and knobs than I can count. The floor is stockpiled with black crates of all sizes and heights. There are some small chairs attached to the wall to the front and left. To the right, it opens up and continues into the larger portion of the ship.

"I'm August, by the way. That's Vickers," he says and points to the other man, who smacks on the fruit and watches me with his beady eyes.

"I'm Ferren. Does it have a name?"

August's handsome face contorts with confusion.

"The ship. You are the pilot, right?" I point to the signet of a winged planet on his shoulder. "I have read Viathans name their sky ships like children, or with silly phrases."

He smiles and leans against the metal wall. "Funny, I haven't quite figured out a silly phrase yet." He emphasizes the last part.

"I'm sorry," I say, realizing how rude that sounded.

"Ah, that's ok. I've considered *The Empty Flask* or . . . *The Little Brother.*"

"I can see why you haven't settled on one yet."

August stands up straighter, gawking at me, then throws his head back in a hollering laugh. I just nervously smile and wait for him to stop. He seems friendly enough, but I still feel like I really need to catch up with Mary.

"Alright, Ferren, let's show you to your room," he says while trying to stifle another chuckle with a dramatic sigh.

I follow him as he climbs a shiny ladder that runs straight up into the ship, steeper than the stairs to the bell tower. My boots make it a little easier, but I cling to the sides with white knuckles. The space immediately opens up to another room at the top, dimly lit with blue lights. There are closet-like compartments lining the walls, and the fronts are smooth and odd-looking. I follow cautiously into a brighter room with a large round table in the middle.

"This is the mess hall. We eat here. It's a space for everyone so you will find us gathered here most of the time."

It's not as tidy as the temple rooms for gathering, but it's not as messy as I pictured a Viathan sky ship would be. Large cubbies line the outer walls, some half open with blankets and pillows draping out.

I notice a boxed off area that looks like a water closet for bathing. By *gather* he must mean they eat and sleep here.

"Help yourself to any of the food stations. If there isn't something that you like, we may have it in storage," he points to some interesting-looking boxes across from us. "And your room and Mary's is right up here."

There is another small ladder to a half level that takes us to the front of the ship. The three windows I noticed from outside are now in front of us. There are more buttons in here than anywhere else, with metal chairs that face the front. I try not to look around; it seems wrong to be interested. I feel a wave of shame fall across me. No amount of preparation could have primed me for all this technology in one place. August is completely natural moving around the ship. He is sweet and has even made me forget he is from Viathan. But he is, this ship is, and it feels wrong to be on it.

"Right through here is the pilot suite, and yours is next to it. These are the only rooms with a private water closet. You do have to cross the room, but it's normally just me in the cockpit once we get going." He waves his hand over a panel of small blinking lights, compelling the door with the same signet on his shoulder to open. Then a small door next to it. "Suite is for Mary. This one's yours."

I nearly jump back as the door disappears into the wall. The light inside comes on by itself, revealing a small bed and a single metal furniture piece. I try to seem more pleasant than I'm feeling. I'm not doing anything wrong. First Mother will not punish me for being on a ship with a door that moves without pushing it.

"You hate it? It's not fancy, but we won't be on the ship for very long."

"No, no it's fine. This is fine. Thank you! Does it have a window?"

"It does not, just those up front. That's for the best anyway.

Windows can be disorienting when we are out there."

"Out there?" I say and lean to look out the large windows at the front.

"The space between the three worlds. It gets dark once we get above the clouds. Haven't been?"

"I have not. I've read about it many times, but not quite described like that."

"Ah, well, you are in for a treat then, Ferren. I will let you get settled. We will be heading out soon."

"Thank you, August."

He nods and points to a button on the wall, making sure I see him press it. The door slides closed and I am left in the strange room by myself. I sit on the thin mattress of the bed. The lighting is low and lines the trim of the floor and ceiling. The quick view I got of the pilot suite tells me it's about half the size of my already small room on the Estate. But this room is a trinket box with no window.

I unsling my bag and withdraw the letter opener from between my breasts carefully. I crane my arm to the back of my binding to free the small prayer book I've hidden without permission. The moonstone Thea gave me the second she heard I was making the journey is in a small pouch tied to it. There are no temples or statues to pray in here, so I will have to pray to the moon for First Mother to hear me like the priestesses of old. I'm glad she made me promise to bring it along. Now I can at least use it as a well-intended substitute. Hopefully First Mother understands.

The thick soles of my boots insulate the well-known vibration of the ground shaking. The tremor feels strange coming up through the ship instead of the stone floor of the Estate. But then I hear a horrible metal shriek and a loud slam. I wave my hand frantically over the door panel like August did. There is no knob for me to turn or pull so

I pound on the flat face of it. A whirling sound begins, like a strong wind. The whole ship jumps like it's alive.

What is happening? Why haven't I seen Mary since we boarded?

"Mary!" I pound on the door, then at a red button. It finally slides with a swish of air across my nose. The cockpit is strangely dim, the little screens and buttons casting the majority of the light in the room, and the windows have a strange, shaded film on them now.

"Mary!" I call out and orientate myself, heading toward the hall I entered through with August.

Instead, I slam into a solid black wall with a gasp. The metal of the ship I collided with sways ever so slightly, then it releases a deep huff of air. My elbow is encompassed by a strong hand, another on the dip of my waist, fingers digging in as I sway back unbalanced.

It's not a wall. It's the commander.

CHAPTER FIVE

I have to crane my neck up to see the commander's helmet hovering over me. His solid chest rises in another breath, expanding out until I'm pressed up against the cold plate of his armor.

"Easy." His voice sends a terrifying thrill through me.

I slink from his hold on my elbow, stepping out of his proximity. My back hits the other side of the narrow hallway. I press myself into it, sliding across to put distance between us. The black-glass material in the front of his helmet reflects my face, distorted and embarrassingly petrified. I keep inching around him while his mask moves at the same speed with me, following my halfhearted escape. He is letting me walk past, watching like I'm prey, but he isn't stopping me.

August stands at the end of the now cramped hallway. I'm caged in again. I can't get past either of them. I have the urge to put my hands on either side of these walls and push.

"Everything ok?" August flicks his eyes to me then over my shoulder.

"I heard loud noises."

"That might have been the ramp shutting. You will get used to all the ship sounds," August says.

The commander's deep voice cuts in over my head. "We are departing."

"We will need our bags brought to our rooms." Mary passes through as if the hallway isn't clogged up. I'm relieved to see her after my thoughts jumped to the worst but notice she rubs her knuckles. Climbing the ladder up from the hull must have caused her pain.

"There you are, child," she says in a tone that makes me a little less sympathetic.

"I was trying to find you."

"Oh, nonsense. The ship isn't that big, no offense." She throws a roll of her eyes to August.

"That's alright, ma'am. I will bring your possessions up after we refuel."

I turn to follow Mary's little bow-legged waddle and notice the commander is gone from the bridge end of the hallway, leaving it wide open without a sound.

"Aha, let me guess. You need to refuel at the landing docks, where you should have parked this thing to begin with," Mary says.

"Oh, but then you would have had a trek to board it. Saved you the trip," August calls out to her.

Mary huffs, a little amused by his innocent charm.

"There are seats in the front; we strap in during takeoff," he says to me, his voice a little softer. He must see the misplaced terror on my face. But as his words sink in that we are taking off, it's not misplaced at all.

"I will walk you through it." He gently ushers me back into the cockpit. It's alive with beeping and illuminated buttons now. There is a large chair at the front with a metal lever positioned on its armrest.

"You can sit here, next to me." August pats the second open chair at the front before plopping down on his own.

Mary sits nonchalantly directly behind him. I pass the wide aisle between her spot and mine, but she has her eyes closed and chin up like she's concentrating.

The commander sits on a side wall behind Mary with his legs stretched out, almost to the middle of the aisle. He hasn't done anything directly wrong, but his presence is unnerving. Unable to see his face, not knowing where he is looking is going to drive me to insanity. I avoid glancing over to that side of the cockpit. I know if I think about my clumsy run-in too deeply, my face will redden.

My chair is an off-matte leather material and stiff when I sit. August leans over, making me press into the firm backrest. He pulls a tight strap across my chest, fastening it with a click at my side. I lean forward once he has moved, but there isn't any give. A gasp slips out when he clicks another strap across my lap. I have to remember to be cordial, to not be offended by his casualness. Only a stuffy priestess would be put off by a relaxed demeanor.

"You're going to be just fine. I've done this before," he jokes with a big grin as he clicks the buckles at his side.

"Aw, August, you gave up my seat! Thought I was your main gal," Vickers says as he enters behind us.

August's soft expression turns serious. He breathes loudly, pressing buttons overhead, ignoring Vickers entirely.

I crane my head back to Mary, but she is still perfectly calm with her eyes closed. If she wasn't massaging her hand, I would assume she is asleep.

Vickers takes the seat behind me, and it clicks with a little ping of metal. Something about him makes my skin crawl. The straps across my chest are too tight, so I strain my eyes to gauge how close he is to me, only managing to angle my head enough to accidentally catch a direct view of the commander. He looks too large for the chair, the armor on his shoulders making them take up a large portion of the wall. It continues onto his chest, thighs, and even the front of his shins. He slowly turns his helmeted head toward me like he knows I'm staring again.

I quickly dart my eyes to the screens in front of me. August is pressing candlelight-colored buttons so I pretend to fixate on them. I look over briefly again to see if I can sneak another look out of the corner of my eye, but his helmet is still facing toward me. He could have his eyes closed with his head facing my direction and I would never know.

August taps a button that makes the gauzy film on the windows less opaque with just his finger. Then he lifts a handle slowly, and the ship seems to come off the ground like someone is picking it up.

I hold on to the armrest, digging my nails into the softer top. I can feel us getting higher. The peaks of the buildings come into parallel view, then there is nothing but blue, open sky.

"Doing ok?" August looks down at my white knuckles.

"Yes," I say through a clenched jaw. Breathing loudly helps with the strange feeling of floating, but he keeps glancing over at me with a concerned look.

"It will be a little bumpy until we get to the dock, but after that, when we get up to, well . . . When we are higher and on our way, it will be much smoother. You will even be able to walk around."

August continues to distract me, talking about some of the buttons on the control panel as we travel sideways across the world. I mostly nod, too afraid of revealing how terrified I am of the rough ride.

The edge of the city is so odd-looking from inside the cockpit, with the shadows of the buildings engulfing us in their shade as we slowly descend. It only took moments to arrive, a walk that would have taken me all day if permitted this far from the Estate. My stomach feels like it's higher than it should be. The fluttering stops when the ship lurches down, leveling out like we are firmly planted.

"Not too bad, right?" August asks in my direction. He undoes one of my restrictions, waiting for me to unfasten the other, then smiles when I unclick it on my own. His little way of teaching me the buttons on the panel of my door and how to unbuckle is cuter than it should be.

"This shouldn't take long. Feel free to get some fresh air before departure, won't have it again for a while," he says.

Mary takes much longer to unclick her straps, I contemplate offering help. I wait until the pound of their boots drift to the other end of the ship before squatting in front of her. She looks a little spacey, using the pad of her thumb on the buckle over and over. I smooth my hand over hers, unclicking it with ease.

"Mary, are you . . . Can I get you anything?" I fumble over words, careful not to draw attention to her hands.

"Thirteen years younger during the last conjunction, and I was considered an old woman even then."

"I'm here to help you, please let me. You think Crixa would do her own buckles? No." My attempt to raise her spirits fails when I see her serious expression. I withdraw from my position at her knees to stand with my head bowed. "I'm sorry," I whisper.

"You are not to speak like that," she says, standing slowly then leaning into me with gritted teeth.

I assume it's because I have acknowledged her limited abilities while her joints are swollen, but then I realize I said Crixa and not the highest priestess. Such familiarity would be noticed; no one uses her given name. Only a handful of people in her inner circle have been given permission to use it. The embarrassment of being so careless makes me a little dizzy.

"Do not bow your head," she whispers.

I snap my head up, meeting her eyes. I have to be more careful. A simple mention of my everyday life or bow of my head leaves a trail that could lead them to suspicion.

"I will take tea in my room. Awful lot of hastiness for not even being ready to leave." Her voice drifts as she walks into her suite, elbowing the panel a little too aggressively. The door whooshes shut, cutting off more of her agitated mumbling.

A bell tower begins its rhythmic tolling, the sound soft and muffled through the ship. It pulls me to the large windows, now clear of the strange film they were shaded with while we were traveling. Sky ships line up in front of the massive building we face. Some are ushered into the ship-size openings by people with waving arms. The altitude of the cockpit feels like standing on the second story of the grand hall's balcony. The workers seem so small at this angle.

I see the Viathans with metal boxes of cargo below. Vickers and August carry a black crate together, holding it on either end. The commander takes one all by himself, carrying it like it's empty from the loading dock to the underside of our ship, out of view.

※

I stare at the shiny silver boxes on the back wall of the mess hall. August waved his hand this way when he mentioned eating, so they must store food inside somehow. I press a button on top that looks like a water symbol but nothing happens. If I do not get Mary hot tea soon, her mood will continue to decline.

The temple bell is even more faint in the mess hall. My chest flutters, a feeling normally reserved for my stomach. We are only just beginning to leave, but it's like we are worlds away already. Somewhere close, a bell tower is calling in the faithful for a ceremony, and I am in here with strange silver food boxes. I give the square an undignified smack on the side. Maybe there is a control panel somewhere like the doors. Maybe it's a lid. I pick it up, but it feels like it's part of the ship itself.

"What are you doing?" The commander's voice behind me compels my fist to unclench.

I was hoping to slip in and out of the mess hall unnoticed, but thank First Mother he didn't see me punch this thing like I was planning to do next.

"I . . . need to make tea," I say, unwilling to turn and face him.

He is beside me before I can hear his steps approaching. With a black-gloved finger, he presses a sequence of buttons at the top. It comes to life with a whirling sound from within, and I can hear liquid being poured inside. Time moves a little slower with him next to me so I shift my weight back and forth between feet, taking a tiny inconspicuous step to the side, his close proximity making me a little flustered. They must be used to being in each other's space on this ship with tiny hallways and a cramped living area.

I gasp as a compartment opens at the front with a single chime. He carefully withdraws a metal mug, placing it on the matching flat surface more gently than expected. There is a pause that hangs a little too long as I stare at the steaming tea. He is waiting for me to say something.

"Oh! Just the one, thank you," I say nervously.

His stature mixed with the darkness of his armor blots out the ship's lights. The enormous shadow he casts is relit as he opens his shoulder to face me.

I wrap my hand around the circumference and snap it back from the boiling heat of the mug's body. "Really hot," I say awkwardly, shaking out my hand.

He nods.

I carefully balance the liquid by its handle. He is still watching me as I round the metal table in the center of the room. I've said thank you and that I didn't need anything else, so I don't know why he is still waiting for something.

"The other one said you are her assistant." His voice stops me. It rumbles into the coldness of the room, making my body jolt slightly, and I almost spill the piping tea over the side. I nod, mimicking his gestures.

"She did not give your name."

I've heard his words clear as day, but I am still confused by them somehow. *He wants to know my name?* It's not an unusual question, just completely unexpected. *Be cordial and casual.*

"I'm Ferren."

The table between us adds a comfortable buffer, but it's not enough as he stares me down. It's impossible to read him. Even his voice seems to conceal just as much as the helmet does. I glance down at the steam rolling up from the mug. I need to get this to Mary. I wait out the tense pause for as long as I can stand before turning my back to him to return to the cockpit.

I hear his strong voice again. "I'm sorry I frightened you earlier."

I look over my shoulder to see him exiting the mess hall, shoulders almost taking up the entire walkway. I would have not known what to say if I turned back and he was still standing there. I'm not sure what is more odd: a Viathan commander politely asking for my name or apologizing for scaring me to death after I walked face-first into him.

CHAPTER SIX

A soft knock shoots me up from my prayer pose on the cold metal floor.

I snatch the moonstone and prayer book from the metal nightstand, shoving it under the thin pillow on my bed.

"It's August," the muffled voice says.

"J-just a moment!" I call out, wishing I knew how to lock the door. I pat the crown of my head, reassuring myself that I am not wearing a veil and I am still in the clothes given to me. My finger thuds on the control panel, guessing which button is correct.

"It's the red one," August says flatly, most likely hearing my struggle.

I glance one last time at the space around me, making sure nothing screams *priestess* before pressing the correct spot.

August sets down my large canvas bag in front of me, stuffed with more strange clothing for the journey. He flashes a boyish grin. He's sweet and charming, but not in a confrontational kind of way that most Estate guards tend to be.

"Thank you for being so kind." I instinctively push my hair back from my shoulder then pull it forward again, realizing it's not a veil.

"Of course." His eyes do not flick down as I adjust my locks to sit naturally on the side of my chest; they stay firmly on mine. "We eat a meal in the hull before takeoff, a sort of tradition. 99 made stew if you and Mary would like to join."

"99?"

"99th Commander," he says like I should have put that together myself.

I stumble over a reply, but he smiles with a nod. My stomach growls at the thought of filling it with stew, but having another run-in with the commander drives that hunger away.

"Will you tell Mary? She scares me," he confesses with a passive furrow of his thick brows.

I cover my mouth, trying to smother a laugh. With a nod and a cupped hand, I whisper, "Me too."

August's eyes widen as he looks at Mary's smooth door next to us. He throws up surrendering hands, taking a few exaggerated steps back. I wait to step out into the cockpit until he exits with a parting grin, ever so light on his feet. He is tall and has broad shoulders but has a softer way to his mannerisms than the other Viathans.

I wait for Mary to answer my knock, twisting my hair into a long braid then pulling it to the side. I want to wear it loose, but I'm afraid it will get caught in the ever-whooshing doors.

"There it is. Bring it in. Bring it in!" Mary says with a frantic beckoning sign at her trunk placed at the foot of her door.

I push it to the middle of her suite. It's heavy and cuts into the flat of my palms. "The pilot came up to let us know they are serving dinner," I say with a final shove.

"Open it, dear." Mary closes the door, leaning against the seamless wall it creates.

I crouch next to it, unhinging the workings that hold it tightly together but are not fully locked. "He said it was tradition to eat in the bottom of the ship, where all the supplies are."

The inside of the trunk is full to the brim with clothing and books, journals and accounts Mary mentioned bringing for us to review on the journey.

"Under those, a red pouch." She points to a stack of folded jackets, ignoring my words completely.

I rifle under the clothing, careful not to unfold the crisp edges. I feel soft velvet and pull it from its nestled spot. "Can I stay in my room? I brought some sugar bread in my bag. I am fine eating that."

Mary looks at me strangely then holds out a hand for the little pouch. I drop it by its string, dangling it between us, waiting for an answer.

"I can study one of the field guides," I say.

But she only snatches it and sits on the bed to begin working at the lacing of its tie.

"You can have some of my sugar bread. I just don't want to eat with the Viathans!" I spit out.

Mary shakes her head at my outburst but smiles on one side as she opens the scrunched top of the velvet sack, withdrawing a long green finger-like leaf from it. It's dull and cracked like a tea leaf before it is milled.

"What is it?" I ask, getting a better look.

"The physician sent them for pain."

I step back at the mention of a word she normally avoids at all costs. "Are you in pain?"

She sets her hand down on her lap, weakly holding the leaf, a mix of anger and exasperation on her face. "It is bad luck to start a journey by skipping a tradition."

I let out a rumbling groan, a habit Crixa has teased she would punish me for in the past, then I sit on the trunk across from Mary, plotting a way out.

"I need you to bring back hot water for this when you are finished."

"When I am finished? You aren't coming?"

"I *am* in pain, Ferren. I cannot grip the ladder into the hull again today."

Any fight that was building in my defense dies. Mary is in pain, and the ship's interior demands more than she may be used to. I'm almost embarrassed how rattled I am by the Viathans. I am here to assist her, to make sure she can do her responsibilities as Cosima's representative, and right now, that means attending a dinner and retrieving hot water for her medicine.

First Mother, forgive me. I will do better.

The last step of my descent down the hull ladder is undignified. I enter the cargo area where I can hear the Viathans talking, but to my surprise, none of them greet me despite my loud last step. The commander sits on a large metal crate that has been pulled around a box used as a makeshift table. August ladles stew into bowls from a silver steamy pot. More totes line the walls now than when I entered through here this morning. I pass one with the lid askew, nonchalantly peeking at the contents.

Weapons.

Guns of a few different sizes and levels of terror. There are ones I have never seen before, but others I recognize from accounts and illustrations of weaponry used in the war with First Son. A chill runs down my spine. *Are all these crates full of guns? Why would they be bringing weapons?* This is a peaceful retrieval. It's another harsh reminder of who we are traveling with.

An echoing steel sound fills the hull, then a strange humming begins. I recognize it from earlier when we departed. Vickers stands in the opening of the ship as the ramp moves on its own, sucking in a breeze as it shuts. He joins the strange dinner party of pulled together boxes and totes.

"Mary is resting before we leave. She won't be attending. I apologize," I say.

"Ah, that's too bad," Vickers says sarcastically as he brings a wet spoonful to his thin mouth. He watches me with his prying stare. I recognize that look now; he doesn't trust me. It's like he knows I'm hiding something.

"Have a seat." August holds out a bowl of the oddly colored stew.

I smile as a thank you until I see the only open spot left is on the same crate as the commander. I contemplate if it would be terribly rude to sit on one of the little seats bolted to the surrounding walls.

Vickers and August slurp with abandon, hunched over their own stew. The commander's bowl is strangely placed on the floor between his boots, untouched and full to the brim. I line myself up and slowly descend onto the hard seat next to him. My side brushes down his as I do. I hear a deep exhale as he makes more room for me. I have the urge to apologize, sitting stiff as a board, too nervous to adjust and possibly brush against him again. But the uncomfortably hard surface immediately makes me shift, which throws my spoon from my bowl somehow. I clamber for it while balancing and curse as it lands on the dirty ship floor.

The commander bends with another exhale, his large arm hitting mine lightly as he retrieves it. When he rises again, my dirty spoon is dunked into his broth with debris still attached. Then he withdraws a spotless version, offering it to me in a trade.

"This one is clean," he says.

"Oh . . . thank you," I try to hide the tremble in my hand as I take the spoon that was just his. The thick broth creates peaks as I slowly stir it, a little confused.

"Bread?" August asks, already handing a hunk across the pot.

I thank him and take a satisfying bite. It's stale but the taste of it is nice.

The commander shifts again. I almost choke when I see his helmet on his knee in the corner of my vision. Mary said Viathan commanders never remove their armor; they are never seen without it. But one is sitting a paper's thickness away from me with his helmet removed. He leans forward to collect his bowl from the floor. I do my best to keep my eyes fixed on my food. There is a reason he waited to remove it and start eating until I couldn't see him fully, and I have no intention of finding out what that reason was.

I accidentally see a blurry view of his hair on the back of his head in the corner of my eye. It's dark but not as dark as mine. More of a brown to my pitch black. It's a little longer than expected and has a bit of a wave to it on the ends. I turn my head as he straightens with a clearing of his throat.

"August, you mentioned it was tradition to eat in the hull. May I ask how it started?" I say, wanting to chase away the crippling silence, but I forget my mouth is full of bread and chew over my words.

"Uh, something we have always done, I guess. Way to bless the cargo, come together before departing and things get unpredictable."

I smile pleasantly but glance over at the tote I saw with guns inside. *Bless the cargo?* Such an odd phrasing, yet not very surprising.

"Problem?" Vickers cuts in.

I meet his eyes for too long, questioning if he was truly speaking to me. "Excuse me?"

"You just keep looking at the crates like they have done something to offend you. Is there a problem?"

I finish chewing the last bite of my bread, looking between him and August. He swallows hard, quickly flicking green eyes to the commander, which doesn't go unnoticed.

Vickers lifts his brows impatiently, never removing his beady eyes from mine. I promised Mary I would watch my mouth, that I would behave, but I'm confident I can answer him without exposing myself.

"I saw a crate that had some weapons inside."

August furrows his brow then glances over at the commander again, like they are communicating without the need for words.

"Don't like guns, huh?" Vickers asks.

"It doesn't matter what I like. Modern weaponry is not permitted on Frith."

Vickers huffs, dipping his bread sloppily.

"The people believe it disrespects First Mother to handle the tools of First Son. Perhaps a sky ship with crates full of them may be a problem," I say right to him.

"Are you serious? *The tools of First Son,*" he mocks, waving a piece of soggy bread around.

August holds up a hand, patting the air down to pacify Vickers's rising voice.

"I'm afraid *I am* serious. It is something that is mentioned many times in the books about their history."

"There is no way I am stepping foot unarmed on a planet with a bunch of spear happy Frithians."

"Then you will likely die by said spear."

His expression changes, a subtle thread snapping like I have threatened to kill him myself. He gawks at me like he did the guards in the council meeting. More than suspicion or disdain, a living breathing hatred blooms in front of me. I hold his jet-black stare. I want him to know mine blooms too.

His face and tone change abruptly, like he is trying to hide how mad I've truly made him. "Are you hearing this, Commander? I mean, come on! Seriously, no weapons?" he says with a condescending laugh.

"We assess the situation when we arrive," the commander answers plainly.

His voice next to me is deep and crystal clear, unmuffled by the metal of his helmet. I can almost feel the vibrations in the finality of his tone. I'm too nervous to say anymore now that he is weighing in, even if the urge to drive my point scratches at the surface. It's clear the commander has the final say, and even someone like Vickers respects it because he doesn't say another word.

The rest of the dinner is silent, only featuring the slurping sounds of Vickers and August finishing their food. I'm treated to more Viathan etiquette as they leave the moment they take their last bite—a gesture that would get me severely punished in the Estate.

The realization that I've been left alone, sitting with the commander, hangs awkwardly in the thick air. August's seat is empty across from us, and I contemplate moving to it for just a moment, but that would mean I would have a clear view of his face unencumbered. As ominous as it may be, I prefer his helmet on. I hope he keeps it on for the rest of the trip. The anticipation of possibly seeing him without it is too intimate, which is just silly.

I glance without thinking out of the corner of my eye. His bowl is empty in his lap. I'm not sure why he's still sitting next to me. I stop mid chew, realizing I may be eating really loud.

Please just be rude and leave before I'm finished like the others.

He isn't saying anything, just sitting next to me in silence, our sides not quite touching, in too close proximity again. The tendons in my eyes tug painfully to the side as I stare. His head is turned away slightly, and he's looking off like he is deep in thought. The strings in my sockets almost rip following the side of his jaw enough to make out a blurry shadow of short facial hair. I take in long slow breaths, mimicking his without realizing. Slowly, the awkwardness in the room calms into an almost strange, serene feeling. His presence is not unnerving like I thought; it's admittedly intriguing.

"Will you excuse me?" I say. Suddenly my stomach is full, and I'm panicked by my own thoughts.

I have to rehearse standing in my head a few times before I can actually make my body do it. I place my dirty bowl next to the other ones left on a tall box. I can hear the commander stand up from our seat behind me like the men in the Estate do during fancy dinners. Is he being polite, waiting until I began to eat and not leaving until I'm finished? Do Viathans do that? I run my teeth over my bottom lip and debate turning to look at his face so I can stop fixating on the mystery.

"Ferren!" Mary yells, irate tone shooting down the opening of the ladder.

We must have been taking longer than she was patient for. I practically bolt for the ladder to escape the unexpected situation the dinner has turned into. I climb it, glancing over my shoulder. The commander is picking up the small area we dined in. I'm almost grateful his helmet is firmly in place again.

This time, I buckle Mary's straps without asking. The long-leaf tea has relieved her pain, but I do not want the overuse of her knuckles causing more damage.

The Viathans are eerily calm and somber in their seats. August makes sure I strap into mine correctly then smiles with approval. He flips a switch, bringing the sky ship to rumbling life once more. The switch seems to work on his personality as well, changing it from sweet charm to a deadly seriousness. The contrast is like a slap in the face to watch. His voice is monotone as he spouts off phrases I do not understand with the press of each button. Vickers repeats them back in confirmation as the ship roars with a low vibration.

"Ferren!" August's finger hovers over a flashing red button, and he makes an enticing flick of his brow toward it, like an invitation to press.

"No, that's ok!" I shout over the loud engine sounds.

He shrugs, showing a little crack in his serious mannerisms, then presses the button himself.

The familiar feeling of being picked up from the ground begins again. This time, it doesn't stop; we do not level out. My weight is tugged from the top of my head and dragged through my body to stay on the ground below. We angle in a slight upward tilt to the clouds then pass them so quickly, the sides of my face are pulled back.

Everything out of the large windows is dark blue then pitch black. The light in the cockpit slowly turns on to compensate for the darkness around us. The heaviness in my body levels out and I feel light, buoyant even, like I'm sitting in a deep bath. Looking back at Mary to check on her swishes my head in a dizzy spell. My vision now a little cloudy in the corners, I blink rapidly, trying to focus.

"You doing ok?" August asks as he works on the control panels below the disorienting windows.

"No . . . I think I'm dizzy."

"That will wear off soon!"

I close my eyes, pressing into the headrest to wait for it to drift away. I feel . . . strange, drunk almost.

August speaks again but when I open my eyes, I can't focus on his face. Something feels wrong. When my vision does finally focus, Thea is in the pilot's chair. She looks so petite and strange in the cockpit. Her hair is pulled back, her face furrowed as she works on pressing buttons and moving the silver levers with purpose.

"Thea? What are you doing here?"

"Shit! No, it's August." August's voice comes from somewhere in the distance.

My head bobs like the fermented berries the Estate kitchen places in wine for special occasions.

"Be so brave, Ferren. You can be scared when you get back home," she says with a sweet smile.

I pry at my buckles with weak fingers. I feel confined, strapped in like this. The windows need to be cracked to air out the hot fog in the cockpit. I turn my head to Mary. Will she tell Crixa that Thea has snuck in. Will I be punished?

Someone is standing in the middle of the space.

Leema? My beautiful sister looks strange in this metal room. Her skin is glowing but her eyes are reddened from crying.

"I'm sorry," she whispers around the nail she bites, pacing on the loud floor.

"Please don't go," I beg over my shoulder.

I hear her footsteps as she turns away from me. She's leaving again—I have driven her away. I want to scream for her to come back, beg her to hug me and tell her how sorry I am, how much I need her. We both lost a mother, but I feel like I have taken hers away. I have only seen her through Leema's eyes, heard her through my sister's sweet voice, my heart almost blending the two people into one just to comprehend those emotions.

I catch my bobbing head, steadying it like I've fallen asleep during a temple ceremony. An insidious shadow watches me in the darkest corner. The blurred outline of a figure becomes defined as I blink.

The more I focus, the more pleased it becomes, like I'm calling it into existence from nothing.

There is a thudding at the front of the ship, a rhythmic flapping, then a pound. I sloppily pull myself from the thing calling to me. A gray bird frantically flies into the windows at the front of the ship. Feathers and blood smear the glass as it continues to throw itself forward, trying to escape over and over. It falls into a brass bowl of moon water on the control panels, its unrelenting wings spraying flecks in every direction.

The moment I close my lids, my body surrenders, sinking into a weightless sleep.

CHAPTER SEVEN

My stomach is empty but heavy, sour water sloshing around as I sit up in bed. The blue lights remind me I am on the sky ship and not in the modest comfort of my own room on the Estate. Illuminating the trim, where the floor meets the wall, they are dim but still make my eye sockets ache. I press the pounding spot on my head, eliciting an automatic groan. My mouth tastes like I've thrown up the strange stew I ate with the Viathans. The floor wobbles as I stand, like the red jelly desserts Crixa orders from the kitchen.

I smack the panel of the door and it opens with luck in a swoosh of air. I inhale the briskness of the cockpit, and it instantly cools my flushed face. I can almost see my breath, illuminated by some of the buttons at the front. The smell is like nothing I have ever experienced, chilling as it enters my nose. The water closet is an outline of thin light, a guidepost as I stumble to it. The unsteady trudge prickles my skin, exposed to the open air. An eerie feeling of being monitored by an unknown source compels me to walk faster.

I stare at my sickly reflection in the crisp mirror with blinding lights as a frame. I splash warm water, drinking some from my cupped hands, hoping to settle my stomach. I saw Thea, Leema . . . other things. But I know they were not truly here, a delusion of nausea and altitude. I rub at my eyes until they are bloodshot. What did I say about what I saw manifested in front of the Viathans?

First Mother, I beg you. I can withstand embarrassment, but please . . . if I have endangered myself and Mary for saying something damning . . . If I have exposed . . .

Concentrating on prayer makes my head drum with my pulse. With one last splash of water, I press the less complicated door panel. The light from inside illuminates the darkness of the cockpit for a brief moment. It takes my foggy brain too long to realize what I see before I press the light button to extinguish it: a figure sitting in one of the chairs bolted to the walls.

I freeze, trying to catch up with the image. A split second of crisp clarity or another hallucination? I saw armor and the side of a man's jaw. Now, there's only a blurry face blotted out by shadows. It's not another manifestation, the ones I saw before did not look right in the environment of the ship, but the commander looks like he could be part of it, almost blending in entirely.

"How are you feeling?" His voice is a low baritone from the shadows.

"Fine," I say, not able to take a step over the threshold.

The contrast of stark brightness from the harsh lights has blinded me to the little buttons that blinked so brightly before I entered the water closet.

"Have you been here long? Were you in here—" I stop myself. I sound too frazzled.

It's very clear he has been in here for a while. The exposed feeling I had crossing the cockpit were his eyes on me as I stumbled past him. The outline of his form slowly becomes defined, the reflection of the colored lights on his armor chasing more of the shadows away. He says nothing, not even shifting in his seat as I squint.

"How long was I asleep?" I try with a steadier voice.

"You were not sleeping. You were unconscious—couple hours."

The flashing buttons finally cut into the darkness as my eyes adjust, casting a dim glow all around me. The commander stands to his impressive height. For another tiny moment, I can see the side of his strong jawline with the short beard I saw before. In the faint glow, half blind, I cannot tell if he is handsome. I can only assume he is because his voice is so . . . appealing.

"Are we . . . in the space between?" I ask, trying to drive my thoughts away, but I am feeding them by making him speak again.

"Yes."

Mary said it would feel like nothing at all, like standing as still as we do within the Estate. But the ship is not still. It's traveling between worlds. The thought of its movement twists the sour sensation in my stomach.

He raises his bulky arms over his head, placing his helmet back in position. Then he steps toward me, a single, slow and deliberate step, his massive form outlined by the blinking lights behind him. Another step . . . and another, until I feel like I should move out of his way, but I can't.

"Mess hall . . . when you are ready," he says, almost brushing past me. I watch him enter the hallway then disappear around the corner into a blue-lit room.

August is leaning back in his chair, boots resting on the shiny table. "There she is," he says, sitting up from his casual recline.

I smile flatly, trying to hide my embarrassment.

Mary palms a mug of steamy tea, the long green fingertips of her medicine sticking up over the top.

"I need to speak with you," I whisper and pull my chair close to her and sit with a ducked head.

Something happened to me during takeoff. I felt sick like I never have before. I saw things I know for certain were not there. I need to make sure I did not speak of the temple. Mary will not look at me, only furrows her brow and glances down at her mug.

"Hey, don't worry about uh—ya know. My first time in between worlds, I saw my dead brother. Thought he came back to kill me. Then I puked on my boots." Vickers perches on a stack of metal totes like a buzzard. He leans in with pointy shoulders, watching, waiting for my reaction.

Hallucinations must be common then, like some of the medicine used in the Estate's apothecary. No one takes them seriously, like a babbling drunk, but I am still concerned.

"You spoke nonsense, nothing of importance," Mary assures me under her breath, like she knew the reason for the worry in my voice.

"Why didn't you warn me?"

"The first time I traveled between worlds was a lifetime ago. I simply forgot, child." She finally raises her face to mine with an ambushed expression.

"It shouldn't happen again, now that you have adjusted. I apologize. It's been years since I have traveled with someone who is not seasoned." August sounds so sincere, but I cannot bring myself to look at him.

I watch Mary, study her face, her posture. It is unlike her to miss any detail at all. She has made me restart an inscription for writing a period too largely.

The commander reaches through the space between our chairs,

setting a metal cup on the table in front of me. I clamp my mouth shut and stay perfectly still as he brings his arm back through. I didn't notice him moving around the room, and now he's looming behind me.

"It's tea . . . Settles travel sickness," he says, answering the awkward pause in the air.

He is fast and alarmingly silent for how large he is. His armor doesn't clunk around as he moves or make his footsteps loud like it does the Estate guards. I watch him round the table to the open spot across from me. I try to keep my eyes on the steam coming from the dark liquid, but as I glance up again, the visor of his helmet is directed right at me. There is something about being in the same room as him that makes me want to open the hatch and breathe in until I pass out.

I sip the edge and smile at him thinly. "Thanks," I say, almost muffled as I sip again. It's bitter but I feel it settle the acid in my gut, warmth coating my insides.

"Anything?" August asks the commander.

He finally turns his helmet away from me to answer a conversation that seems to have started before I entered the mess hall.

"Sent two more, no response from their beacon," he says.

"If they do not respond before we land, then that does pose complications," Mary says.

August holds a flat square. It looks as if he has pulled one of the control panels off the wall. A glowing green circle illuminates the middle of the table as he presses buttons, seeming to call it forth. An orb emerges, taking shape, rising into a small sphere. It grows in size, floating over the surface, lit and suspended by nothing at all. I'm mesmerized, like one of the flying insects that get consumed by the torches in the courtyards.

"Hello, old friend," Mary mutters to herself.

"It's Frith, well, a map of it. We will use it to plan our descent," August says, noticing my dazed expression at the sight.

He taps at the black pad, compelling the orb to expand, zooming in closer to its details. He moves to a mountain with flat plateaus toward the top. There are forests all around it, with grassy plains on its border. I recognize the mountain immediately. It's where the majority of Frithians settled, protected by the forest. The sacred mountain.

"The field below should get us in closer range to send another transmission," Mary says with her familiar authoritative tone.

"Here?" August asks Mary.

I sit up straight to view the spot his finger points to.

"A secondary plan. Their beacon gives off no signal." The commander speaks in short sentences jam-packed with meaning, no filler words or description, getting straight to his point.

"I have no intention of hiking up the sacred mountain. It's been done in previous conjunctions, but there are easier ways to die," Mary says.

She has spoken of the things that dwell in the forest around their mountain. We have copied chilling accounts of travel expeditions returning with half of their parties missing.

Vickers slams a jagged finger down on a flat part of the mountain. "Here. Avoid the forest entirely," he says.

"On one of the plateaus? We don't know which ones are inhabited, have crops on them. The one with the beacon looks to be overgrown by the forest," August says.

"We hover until we find the right spot. You've done more intricate maneuvers."

August squints at the map, looking back and forth between the flat plain and the spot Vickers suggested.

Our landing place is a topic Mary has discussed many times; it's in every journal. All successful journeys to Frith have landed in the same fashion and warned against any other way: land below the mountain, call to their beacon, and wait for an invitation to land on the top to be granted an audience with their elders.

"No," is all Mary says to the stupid suggestion, a single definitive punch.

"Cuts the mission in half, more time to celebrate." Vickers winks at me.

I scowl in return. Mary has given her answer. She is more experienced and intelligent than all of us combined. She is cold and abrasive, but I trust her like no one else.

"You want to hover over their sacred mountain until you find a good spot? Uninvited?" The words come out before I can stop them, anger boiling over at the smug look on Vickers's face.

Mary places her hand on my forearm, a pacifying measure. She could punish me, scold me in front of them for speaking out of turn. I bow my head, a subconscious habit.

"There are laws to uphold, Viathan. Do I need to remind you of their importance?" The venerable tone in her voice cuts across the table, making Vickers slouch in his seated position.

"We land in the field," the commander cuts in.

"Yes, and I have found that often, talking through possibilities can be a waste of time, Commander. We send another transmission when we arrive. All our worries could wash away with a simple invitation once in range."

August gapes at the commander like he has never heard anyone speak to him in such a way. I have witnessed Mary's effect on Crixa and the emperor. Whether it's her age or confidence in her knowledge, she is always taken deadly seriously.

The commander nods, ordering August to turn off the floating map without hesitation. The entrancing light is gone, leaving the table ordinary and flat again.

"With that, we will take our leave for the night," Mary announces, stiffly standing from her chair.

The sudden shift from planning to Mary cutting the Viathans off has my head spinning. I glance at each of them, a little confused. She holds out her arm, beckoning me to join her in leaving the mess hall.

"Blessed night then." I hesitate and then stand. August smiles at me in return, but Vickers leans around him, narrowing his little eyes in my direction.

Mary waits for me in the threshold and pats my shoulder as I pass. I can hear the shuffle of her steps behind me as we walk down the hallway.

"It is hard to distinguish time in here, but it is very late, Ferren."

I wait until we are in the cockpit, far enough away from the others to turn to her, looking for some sort of indication of where we stand and if that odd meeting was less combative than it sounded.

"I apologize for my outburst. He just sounded so . . ."

"Disrespectful? Yes, well, they are Viathans, child. It is ridiculous to expect them not to try and pull at the strings of the old world to make things easier," she says, inching her way across the bridge toward her suite.

Mary is diplomatic. It is not often I hear her opinion on the beliefs of other worlds outside of written facts. Crixa would have leveled Vickers for speaking the way he did, even if she isn't as committed to upholding Frithian laws and traditions as Mary.

"And do not apologize. That man is a little shit," Mary says with a smirk.

I smother a laugh with my hand and open the door to her suite, now much quicker after some practice.

"Good night," she says.

"Mary?" It's unlikely but I have to try. I don't think I can handle being alone in my room. She didn't scold me for talking out of turn and seems to be in better spirits. "I am not tired. Would you like to pray with me?"

"I would not," she says, not waiting for me to move from the threshold as her door whooshes past me. I stare at the dark metal of it, too close to my face.

Mary is right. Being on the ship is disorienting. I stay in my room for longer than I can stand, waiting to hear anyone moving around. I no longer feel the strange sickness from last night. I'm not sure how long I slept for—a priestess ringing a handbell through the priestess wing is normally my indication of morning. But in this windowless box, I can't tell if it's morning, midday, or if I've only slept for a very restful hour.

The sounds from down the hallway call to me as I peek my head out. August's laugh is inviting and friendly enough to allow me to leave the comfort of my little room. I follow the trail of the deep male voices into the mess hall. Everyone is sitting in the exact same spot as they did the night before, and for a brief moment, I think I could be dreaming. But Mary sleeps in her chair, taking the midmorning nap she always sneaks when we get started on inscriptions too early.

I greet the Viathans and take the cold cup of tea from Mary's placemat. When she wakes, I know she will want to warm her hands.

The commander is standing by the shiny metal squares that dispense food. With a deep inhale, I summon enough courage to try my hand at making tea again. He turns his head slightly as I approach his side.

"Blessed morning, 99th Commander," I say more softly than I intend.

His response is a single nod to me in return.

I follow the lines of the metal cube he used to make Mary's tea before, hoping I can do it myself this time. He must sense my struggle because he raises a gloved hand and presses the same sequence on top, eliciting the internal liquid sound.

"Thank you," I huff nervously.

When it's done, I gently carry it to Mary's spot. The other Viathans are not making any effort to lower their voices, but she's still sleeping.

"Mary, I have some hot tea for you." I squat down next to her and gently run my arm up her forearm. Normally, a hushed tone and touch startles her awake.

"How long has she been sleeping?" I ask August over my shoulder.

"Not sure, she was when we came in."

The tea from the physician likely makes her lethargic, like many of the Estate's pain remedies.

"Mary?" I say in my best version of a pleasant tone.

I shake her shoulder but brush against her exposed hand with my arm. I can feel cold skin even through the long sleeves of my blouse. I stare down at the frozen, misshapen hand on her lap; the color is strange. My hand trembles as I brush my fingers over her knuckles, the cold from them feeling like a strike across my skin.

I stand in a dazed calm.

August's voice asks a question in that strange serious tone he uses when he is seated in his pilot's chair. I turn to look at him, to ask what he said, but his expression terrifies me.

Vickers pushes past me like he is trying to somehow help. He touches the side of Mary's neck then pauses. He announces something to the room like reading a message aloud, one that may pertain to everyone, but it doesn't register.

He nods to August and says it again. This time, I hear it as plain and crisp as a temple bell.

"She's dead."

CHAPTER EIGHT

The Viathans have made themselves scarce since this morning's horror, giving me almost too much space to be alone and grieve. I'm not grieving though. I'm . . . afraid. Knowing there is death present and so close does something peculiar to my nerves. I attempt to suppress the feeling of being in danger with prayer in the privacy of my room, but Mary's body is somewhere on this ship, alone and waiting for ceremony.

I follow a shrieking metal sound down into the cargo hull. August and the commander drill into an opened panel in the wall. The terrible sound their machine makes allows me to enter without notice. I watch as great flashes of light hit the metal, seeming to melt it in distorted circles.

"99th Commander, may I speak with you?" I yell between the loud bursts of sound as they work.

He nods and approaches me, standing with hands behind his back. He is more receptive than I assumed, and I have to almost shake my head to begin speaking.

"How long until we return? Mary needs to be buried in ceremony."

He stares at me in utter silence, like I have stunned him.

"How many days until we arrive back on Cosima?" I continue.

His stance becomes more human than I've seen so far. He takes a step toward me, as if expecting me to flee, before he answers. "We are not turning back."

"We have to! Mary . . . She was Cosima's representative. They will need to appoint another," I snap over the sound August continues to make with his machine.

The commander flicks his helmet over his shoulder to August, a silent request to step in and go over the details he cannot be bothered with. August rests his handheld machine on a metal crate then stands at the commander's side to relieve him of the task.

"Ferren, I am very sorry about Mary but we cannot turn back. It would cost us days." His gentle tone puts my sense of raising panic on hold. I almost understand why the commander preferred I hear it from August instead.

"Then I would like you to send a message to Cosima, please. They need to know what has happened."

"Cosima's beacon is compromised," the commander now decides to chime in, but I ignore him. If he can't speak to me plainly, then neither can I to him.

"Frith will be expecting a representative from both worlds. I doubt they will relinquish their stone any other way," I say only to August.

"And Mary spoke highly of your knowledge on Frithian traditions. We will be fine."

The delayed compliment from Mary lingers for just a moment, until the rest of his words sink in. They want me to take over as representative. The Estate would never allow this, especially Crixa.

"August, I don't think you understand what you're asking." My voice is almost a whisper. I bite at my nail, hoping the line of water at the bottom of my eyes dries before they notice. I can't focus on what he is saying. I need to get to Mary. I have already wasted hours trying to come out of shock.

"I'm sorry." August's face drops as he realizes he has overstepped, asking too much of me too soon after her death.

"Take me to her, please." I do my best to steady my voice, but it comes out watery.

The commander's restrained stance wavers a little. I can tell he is about to deny the request. I know it is up to him even though August is holding most of the conversation now. I step into the commander's space, hoping to jar him into sympathy.

"There are things I need to speak over her body. Traditions. Please."

He tilts his head down, watching and contemplating. "I will take you," he finally says and then looks to August, another silent update.

August acknowledges and carries on with the terrible handheld machine. The bursts of light continue as the commander guides me to a door behind the ladder of the hull's entrance. I wonder how many rooms I have missed on this ship. Each one looks like a solid wall panel, completely hidden. The swoosh of this door blows out frigid air in flumes around the frame. My steps echo on the grated floor. The lighting is intense, like the bright frame around the water closet mirror.

The commander stops in the middle of the aisle, angling his body toward a strange metal frame on the wall with a smaller glass square. It's blue and bright inside, more of the fog rolling past the pane window.

"Is she . . . in there?"

He confirms her resting place with a single downward nod.

An empty sensation in my gut churns at the grim space in the wall where Mary's body rests. I hold my own hand to steady its trembling, brushing a thumb over the knuckles, playing the role of both comforter and terrified onlooker.

"My home has death traditions as well. I'm sorry Mary's are interrupted."

He repeats the apology a second time when I refuse an answer, tilting his helmet down like he is trying to meet my eyes in a show of forced compassion.

I press my hand flat against the freezing wall and close my eyes, not caring if he sees me sink deep into my own thoughts. Each inhale is labored, fighting against me as I blow it out. Mary's slumped form flashes in my head, and I quickly open my lids to chase it away.

The commander watches me, still and patient. His gloved hand moves slightly to reach out in an attempt at comfort, but then he balls the fist instead, showing the same stoic sympathy I witnessed when the other Viathans moved Mary's body out of the mess hall, purposefully angling himself in front of me to block my grizzly view with his form. The visor of his helmet reflected my stunned expression when I saw a glimpse of her ashen hand hanging off the side of the metal plank they carried her on.

"Had she been ill?" His voice scatters the grim image in my head.

"No."

"You spoke of her needing to rest. She did not eat with us."

"She has inflammation in her joints. She was just in pain and wanted to lie down," I say in an exasperated breath.

He nods, stance straightening like he is unsatisfied with my answer and intends to continue.

"Shall we call for August to finish any other questions you have, or is that all?" I say before he can.

"August is more articulate with delicate matters." He speaks with gritted teeth, even through his mask.

I see the slow rise of his chest taking in an enormous breath as he watches me. My eyes flick to the armor as the exhale falls silently within his helmet.

"I'm sorry for your grief," he says.

My grief. I do not think I feel that yet, or . . . anything. Not sadness or loss. The closest thing I can reach for is the feeling of being utterly alone on this ship. That realization brings in a wave of guilt, and only then do I break away from his intense stare.

Forgive me, First Mother.

"I will give you privacy," he says as he turns to exit. His boots on this floor make a rhythmic pattern unlike the other parts of the ship where he moves around nearly silent.

I press my fingers to the glass window, quickly withdrawing them at the cold bite. If Mary had died in the Estate, the bells would be singing for her, every temple member in attendance at her ceremony. The Estate would cease its daily work and mourn for the loss of her, her contribution to our history. But we are not on Cosima. They do not know she is dead, that her body is laid in a hole in the wall.

I can count the number of times I pressed into Mary's mind's eye to view her thoughts. The first time was an accident, a hazard of the close nature of my responsibilities in the library, and I exited as quickly as I entered in a panic. The second time was a calculated deep dive, but her mind was so focused, so honed into the text she was reading, I couldn't push past those parameters. This time feels like nothing at all, like staring intently at a solid wall in utter darkness. I can touch it, feel that it is there, but there is nothing to latch onto. No call or crack in the bricks to invite me inside.

As I peer into the small window of the cubby, the fog bellows across her body, exposing the outline of her brittle arms crossed in a death ceremony pose. Seeing her does not gain me entry into her mind's eye.

Mary is gone; her body is dead. She deserves better than this, not lying in the bowels of a Viathan ship and a lesser priestess praying over her, but I know First Mother is waiting.

"Dearest Mary, we thank your second mother for bringing you to us. We ask First Mother to keep you now. May she see fit that your body returns to the soil and your spirit may be by her side forever and ever. May you not have to endure another cycle of this life. Be at peace with First Mother. Blessed Mary—"

"Heart failure," a slimy, grating voice chimes behind me.

I snap my eyes open to see Vickers standing in the threshold. His smile is menacing and almost satisfied as I wipe away the moisture from my eyes.

"Excuse me?" My voice breaks with the pain of reciting a death prayer and the rage of being interrupted.

"She died of heart failure. The cold storage scanned her, took a reading of the cause of death," he says, pushing off the doorframe to walk closer.

"You used a machine on her body?" I say through gritted teeth.

The thought of a Viathan machine defiling Mary's body just so we can know how she died disgusts me. Mary was not a temple member, so technology was not as forbidden to her, but I know how she felt about it. She would not have wanted this.

"What were you whispering, huh?" His tone is suspicious, his neck ducking down like a vulture that's seen something rotten to eat.

I open my shoulder, trying to look bigger, take up more space, and let him know he cannot intimidate me.

"Sounded like praying," he says, shining the side of his teeth.

"I was unaware prayer was not permitted on the ship," I say sarcastically.

"Just odd."

"Every family on Cosima prays for their dead. I am not doing anything wrong."

"No need to pray. She's not coming back. Here, I'll show you." He presses a smaller panel over her, and it illuminates with a flicker. This is the machine he used on her, and now he wants to do it again.

"Don't you dare!" I spit out, putting myself between him and Mary. "You won't touch her again, Viathan!"

He is not afraid of me, instead looking amused from my sudden aggression. He narrows his vacant eyes, satisfied with his work. I have given him what he wants. I let him rattle me and showed a crack in my defenses.

A massive, gloved hand grips on Vickers's shoulder in a hard slap, making him wince. Vickers jumps ever so slightly, then a sick delight washes over his face like he's excited to be caught. The commander pulls him away, pushing him to the wall across from me.

"Woah, Commander, I didn't mean—" His voice is cut off in a painful breath.

The material of the commander's gloves creaks as his grip tightens.

"I'm sorry, ok? I apologize, alright!" Vickers tries to throw his hands up in surrender.

The commander's helmet whips over his shoulder, and he looks right at me. Waiting for my reply, both peer to me to either accept or deny the apology. The commander squeezes again the moment my eyes leave his mask to see Vickers's yielding expression, knees buckling in pain.

"It's fine," I say, holding up my hand in a plea. I hate Vickers and he has disrespected someone I care for, but I do not want to watch this, not so soon after praying over Mary anyway.

The commander does not release him gently, instead guiding him by the collarbone out of the cold storage room, shoving him out into the cargo hull, then turning back to me.

"When you are finished, you will join us in the mess hall," he almost demands with left over grit as he exits the room.

"I am finished."

I'm not but I am too rattled to continue with Mary's prayer, not suited to hold this type of ceremony in the first place. I have started it, but it will need to be completed when we return to Cosima.

"Alright then." He holds out a huge, armored forearm to invite me to pass him.

Vickers and August crowd around the mess hall's table with large parchment rolled out, bowls of more strange stew used as paper weights. The chair Mary sat in has been removed, and instead the spot is open, making it more apparent that someone is missing.

August's smile is almost relieved when he sees us enter, and he quickly rolls up the large papers to make room. He pulls out the strange panel he used previously to elicit the planetary orb. I anxiously take a seat and wait as he thumps away with his fingertip.

"We need to go over the secondary plan. We will send another message on arrival but it's not hopeful. We need to be prepared for an alternative," he says.

The lush green planet appears in a floating sphere over the table. Stars twinkle around it before the landscape is zoomed and the view of the sacred mountain is in focus.

"Ferren, are you well enough to step in?" August says softly.

"First Son will make a move this conjunction. We know this for certain," the commander adds behind me.

August's eyes widen toward him then narrow in silent frustration as if he thinks the commander is undoing his own careful approach.

"We will need your help on Frith." The commander recovers in a tone that I'm guessing is as close to polite as a Viathan can be.

I remember Mary's strong reaction when they spoke of a First Son attack, how she didn't take it seriously. But Crixa said it's possible, wanting to prepare her wards for it. The only way to do that is to have all three of the stones together for her to protect us. I gave her my word I would ensure their retrieval at all costs in exchange for my ascension. If we do turn back and another representative is chosen, would they even need me? Would my final chance at ascension be stolen?

"Yes." The word comes out on its own, not waiting for my fear to stuff it away.

August's shoulders relax. I almost feel foolish for not putting up more of a fight, but I know in my bones if I can do this, I will ascend. First Mother's plan can be mystifying but I know this is the right path. The pressure of taking Mary's place may crush me, but I have to try.

"We land here, in the field," the commander cuts in with a point of his glove.

"Under the assumption their beacon is unreachable, we will need another way," August says.

They both wait for my reply, holding space for my answer. Being asked to weigh in on strategy is not common for me. Mary mentioned walking through the mountain as a last resort, but I can't see any other way around it. Landing on a plateau will ensure a hostile situation. We would be lucky to leave with Viathan's stone, let alone granted permission to take Frith's.

"We could enter into their lands on foot, with as little disruption as possible. We need to abide by their rules as much as we can," I say.

Vickers groans in disapproval.

"She's right. Up the sacred mountain may be the only way," the commander says as he examines the floating map.

I feel the hairs on my arms pin upright and try to brush off a chill at his praise. "It could take days. The forest is dense, full of poisonous plants, creatures, and even old gods, but it's been done before. I've read the journals of past expeditions."

"Old gods," Vickers says, sitting back down in a huff.

"Enough!" the commander orders in Vickers direction. "Continue, anything relevant," he says softer to me.

I feel a flush in my cheeks. I was divulging information without noticing. They want more, but I'm not sure what is relevant. It feels all tucked away in my mind, things I read a long time ago. I start to panic that they will see I don't really belong here, that I don't add any value to their retrieval party. Then a memory shoots to the front of my mind from back deep in my archive of information.

"A gift of peace!" I blurt. "We should bring them an offering of peace as we step into their lands."

"What kind?" August asks.

"There was an old memoir, ancient. It spoke of a tradition of peace offerings on Frith. It's a flower, but not the actual flower. The bulb. It grows on the faces of boulders."

"Do you believe this is something we can find on the journey up?" the commander asks.

"Yes, I think so, yes. I know what it looks like, so I would be able to point it out."

"What of the forest? Anything we need to beware of or avoid?" August asks, placing his forearms on the table to lean in. I notice it blocks my view of Vickers, which immediately makes me feel more comfortable speaking.

"Everything really. It's all poisonous or can kill you. I know of a few edible plants, but there are also just as many mimicking plants that change shape to fool you into eating them."

August's eyes go wide, and I see his throat bob. "Why would the plant want you to eat it?"

"From what I know, everything in the forest has a purpose, all working together to protect the people at the top of the mountain. It's had thousands of years of practice and creative tweaking. It will know we are not supposed to be there, it will know we are unwelcome."

"*It* will know?' August asks nervously.

"Yes. We will need to be the least invasive as possible," I say.

"And you want us to go *through* it," Vickers mutters under his breath.

"Thank you, Ferren. This has been really helpful," August says louder over Vickers's negativity.

"We will reconvene tomorrow before we arrive," the commander says.

August turns off the map as if it were a command.

"We land on Frith tomorrow?" I ask, a little stunned.

They both nod.

"Eat and rest. Let me know if you think of anything else relevant," the commander says.

August scoops a portion of stew and serves it to me. I cup the bowl in my palms. My brief moment of certainty on the knowledge I have acquired slips away. I need to compose myself with prayer to First Mother. Right now, I feel like I am being tossed around in different directions. I need to pull back on any tiny string of control that I can.

"I am eating this in my room, blessed night," I say abruptly.

"I will walk you," the commander says in an aggravating response.

I don't need some Viathan helping me off to sleep like I'm a hunched over elder. I make my steps faster, trying to put space between us. He moves close to silently when I'm not paying attention, but now that my guard is up, I know what to listen for, and he is getting closer. I shake out my hand in a flash of anxiety. Relief washes over me as I make it into my room, like I have evaded capture.

The light beaming in from the cockpit is blotted out by the commander standing in the doorway, taking up the entire opening. I step back on reflex, farther into my room, but he does not follow.

"Lock yourself in. It's safer." He points to a button, indicating how to lock the door.

It doesn't feel like a threat or that he is saying I am in any direct danger. It's more of a protective reminder. I shuffle over to press the panel to shut the door, and it whooshes past his shoulders that reach either side of the frame. I wait by the closed door, not hearing his careful footfalls when I press my ear to it. I know he is just on the other side. I wait as long as I can stand it and then tap a red button that has a key symbol for it to lock. It's a strange combination of old-world symbolism and new-world application, one I was afraid to test before explicitly told its use. The panel makes a clicking sound—locked.

The commander's footsteps slowly move away, like he needed to hear the lock for himself to know I was safely inside.

CHAPTER NINE

I am already sitting in my assigned chair, memorizing a field journal, as August tells me to strap in. A pleasant but mechanical sound chimes through the entire ship, echoing off every metal surface.

"Might be a little bumpy when we first break in, but after that, it will be nice and smooth, promise," August says as he plops down into his station.

I snap my buckles into place, giving myself a little breathing room. My chest bone still aches from the tightness of them from the days prior.

The commander walks slowly next to my seat. He looms over me, blocking the blinking lights above.

"Tighter," he says.

I stare up at him, confused and almost offended that he can't use more than one word to speak to me. He demonstrates with a gloved finger, pointing in a floating line across my chest, gently jabbing the air to mimic the clicking buckle. "Straps, they need to be tighter."

I reluctantly obey but stop just before it's painful across my breastbone, keeping my head forward as I hear him and Vickers settle into their spots. The film on the windows slowly undims, like peeling back a layer with each touch of August's finger on the control panel.

The lush green world displays across the entire front of the ship. Frith is right in front of us, more dense and detailed than the glowing orb on the mess hall's table. We zoomed into almost every part of it this morning, studying it for our arrival. But that does not compare to this colossus before us. Life radiates from it, like the entire planet breathes together all at once.

The ship angles down, top pointed on a fixed spot. The weightless sensation begins in my stomach again. August recites numbers aloud, and Vickers echoes them behind me. The ship bobs rapidly, then they turn into long rolling shakes that remind me of the tremors in the Estate. I just have to close my eyes and hold on. They always stop and the world will be stable again.

But I can't close my eyes this time. The blanket of green starts to become more detailed as we get closer, and I can see giant boulders and denser forests. We cut into puffy wisps of clouds, and they brush over the windows, making it hard to see. The air in the cabin smells different, like I'm breathing in the mist we disrupted.

Then the ship levels out, dropping at a slower pace, the horizon in front, parallel with us as the ship lowers. Just moments ago, we were up in the space between worlds, and now I can hear the ship's feet planting onto the ground. We are here. We have landed on the planet Frith.

From the top of the cargo ramp, I can see far into the field where it touches the tree line. On the map, the distances were distorted. The forest seemed so small, the mountain taller. Looking at it now, this close, the mountain looks like a giant hill spreading out into the edges of this world.

August and the commander stick tall rods into the ground with blinking lights on top. I watch as another is driven into the tall grass, making a half circle around the side of the ship. August mentioned the first thing they would need to do after sending another message to Frith's beacon was to set up a security perimeter. A Viathan version of a protection ward is how I understand it.

The breeze is so soft, it rolls over the grass, making it dance in textured waves. The commander all but forbade me from even stepping foot on it until they made sure it was safe with their strange miniature beacons. I decide to retrieve some of the Frithian books to study while I am waiting. I can set up a spot on top of the ramp and enjoy the vastness of the open field.

Vickers glares at me as I pass him to climb the ladder. He hunches over a metal tote filled with boxes with symbols of food on them. We decided to pack enough on us for the days up the mountain and then rely on the people to give us food for the way down. It's easier than trying to figure out the edible plants, though there are a couple poisonous ones I wouldn't mind telling Vickers to eat.

I change into the clothes that were provided to me for this terrain: more form-fitting pants, an airy undershirt, and a drapey long-sleeve hooded jacket—all black to match the dark forest. One of the more terror-filled field guides I stayed up to read last night strongly recommended dark clothing. The account mentioned the travel party noticing only the people in light colors were being picked off at night.

I fill my little cross-body bag with study material and rest it on my shoulder, wanting to free myself of any restriction across my chest. I wrap up a piece of my sugar bread stash to enjoy while I read. The tiny bit of joy that brings me is traded for guilt with the memory of telling Mary about my stash our first evening on the ship and the way she finally confessed to me she was in pain.

First Mother, please expedite our journey so that we may lay Mary to rest in ceremony on Cosima.

I cut off my steps as I enter the mess hall, noticing Vickers standing in the exit, blocking it. He crosses his arms in a casual stance, watching me, smiling in a sinister, uneven grin.

"I'm headed out that way, if you will excuse me," I say, making sure to keep the large table between us.

"Oh, yeah, sure," he says, stepping to the side easily.

I want out of this space more than anything. It's one of the largest areas in the ship but right now, it feels too small to be alone with him. I clutch the strap on my bag, holding the main pouch close to my hip. His eyes flick to it for just a moment, like an idea has dawned on him.

I need to get outside. My skin is crawling. Another step and I will be in the doorway, but he slides back to block me.

"What's your deal, huh? I can't seem to wrap my head around how you are here," he says.

"I'm . . . Mary's assistant."

"Yeah, but you talk different. *Blessed night*, really?" he says, getting even closer.

My heart pounds. He is creepy, obnoxious, but he is not stupid. He has been putting pieces together, watching me with those little analyzing eyes. I'm afraid if I step back, he will follow into the deeper, more secluded part of the ship. My only way to safety is through this exit.

"I guess I'm just polite."

He laughs, pasty face creasing on the sides of his cheeks.

Stay calm. If I'm calm, it may allude to innocence.

His expression abruptly turns serious, then he uncrosses his arms, darting out to reach for my bag in a quick snap.

I step back right as he lunges for it again, but he grabs my arm instead, his hand digging into the soft skin of my bicep.

"Let me go," I say, trying to sound commanding.

He squeezes, shaking me by the grip, and reaches with his free hand for my bag, holding me in place.

"You should let me go, Vickers," I warn.

I have dealt with men like him before, and I have also seen men like him hang for touching a priestess. If this stops now, we can come back from this, move on. It's not too late. I stare at him deeply, trying to convey that I'm not afraid. I'm uncomfortable around him but not afraid.

"See, I knew you weren't the meek type like you lead on, dropping your eyes, bowing your head. Knew you had a mouth on you. You Cosima bitches all carry yourself the same way . . . uppity," he says, not breaking my stare.

I need to do something drastic. Will a scream carry through these walls, or could it trigger Vickers to cause more harm? I'm alone in here. I need to do something and fast to get away, to rattle him.

So I push into his mind's eye. Permission be damned, he is bruising my arm with his hard grip, and that violence is a strong enough connection to sink in. It's like traveling with heavy, drenched clothing weighing me down as I sift through his memories. I see a person who looks like him through Vickers's eyes. We walk up to a man with the same face. He smiles, but then his expression is contorted. I see flashes of Vickers stabbing him in jumping sequential order, chilling and garbled. The man's voice is sad and confused. *No! Please, brother—*

I pull myself out. It only took a second to find what I need. I lift my chin to him, pushing in closer to his greasy face instead of pulling away.

"No brother, please," I whisper. "Shame on you."

His shoulders go slack, and he drops his painful grip, eyes widening in horror. I take my chance and bolt out of the mess hall toward the cargo hull, but he grabs me again as I reach it. This time, he gets a hold of my bag as I try to pry myself away from the arms he has encased me in. I fall back into a metal tote and watch as he rummages through it quickly.

I know what he has the moment the smirk crosses his face: my prayer book. I left it inside, forgetting to stash it away again. He withdraws it, inspecting it like it's a lost, ancient text. When he looks at me again, I know for sure he knows what I am.

"Give the bag back to me now."

He laughs and shakes his head slowly. "Or what, high priestess, you will read my thoughts again? Go on, see what I'm going to do to you," he says.

The thoughts are so invasive, permission so direct, it's impossible not to catch a single image of him hurting me and the sound of my own scream, but I push it away. He knows I'm divine. I've given myself up, provided enough evidence in my desperation. But he is the only one who knows, and it's his word against mine. I just have to get rid of the prayer book.

My possessions are dropped in a thump, revealing a small silver blade from his cuff.

He lunges.

Without thinking, I raise my hand, trying to stop him, hoping it's enough. But it's not. He has me pressed against the back wall in the cargo bay with the small knife to my throat.

"Why are you really here? Why did that highest priestess bitch deliver you herself? See, I knew that was weird at the time. But now, I'm thinking it makes sense."

August's voice cracks into the tension. "Vickers! Let Ferren go."

He has a gun pointed at the back of Vickers's head, looking deadly, nothing like the sweetness I've seen the last few days.

"Can't do that," Vickers says. He presses his forearm into my chest, making it hard to breathe. I wince and draw back, hoping to gain more space.

"Put the knife down. Ferren, are you ok?" August asks.

I shake my head but then feel the blade's edge press into my skin just a little more. August's eyes flick to me for just a moment then right back to his target.

"She's a spy. She's dangerous! She has a prayer book," Vickers says.

He sounds unhinged and crazy, so maybe there is some hope after all. Maybe August won't believe him.

"She got in my head, could see my thoughts, August! One of those religious fanatics. She's divine!" he says, more agitated.

August's expression looks less confident than before, but he recenters his aim with a furrowed brow.

"Wait until boss hears what you really are. You are in for it," Vickers says low and just to me. "He *hates* your kind. Hates. You're disgusting."

"Ok, just take the knife away. Let's talk about this. She's not going to hurt us, right, Ferren?" August says.

I peer right into Vickers's eyes, as intently as I did when I sank into his dull mind. I don't need to do it again, I saw enough, but I do need him to seem more unhinged if I have a chance of keeping my secret.

"Get out of my head, you temple bitch!" Vickers says with a hint of terror in his voice, the whites of his eyes strobing with red veins.

I stand my ground to make sure he sees me looking at each one, taking my time like I've found something else.

"Ferren! Tell him you aren't going to hurt us! Ferren!" August shouts.

We all hear it at once. The low bass of the commander's voice calls out to Vickers. He stands at the opening of the ship, broad and authoritative visor locked on the knife Vickers holds to my throat.

CHAPTER TEN

Vickers's eyes are wild, his hand shaking enough for the weapon to drop on the floor with a clang. He pivots his encasing shoulders toward the ramp opening, hands held up in a halfhearted plea at his sides.

"Listen, Commander, you're gonna wanna hear this, ok. She's a liar," Vickers quickly says.

The commander's helmet tilts up and down, scanning me as Vickers moves away. He steps into the hull, slowly approaching us silently, as if no explanation will change his mind. As he comes up to a now trembling Vickers, he extends an arm straight out, wrapping his hand around Vickers's throat.

August moves in front of me to block the slow violence, but I peer over his shoulder. A terrible gurgling sound comes from Vickers as the commander lifts him off the floor. He clutches at his neck, beating the hand that chokes him as the toes of his boots barely touch the floor. I want to run back to my room and lock the doors to get away from the sounds.

The commander carries Vickers with his outstretched arm like he weighs nothing, feet dangling just above the floor, suspended by the single grip. They stop at the edge of the cargo bay. Then, the commander releases his hold, letting Vickers's body thump down the ramp, out of view.

August shields me, gun still in hand but no longer fixed on a target. I can feel his anxious tension as the commander walks back to us with the same calm stride he did when he was carrying a full-grown man and disposing of him like it was nothing.

"Explain," he says.

"He said she's divine. I don't know. I only saw some of it. Ferren, what happened?" August says, turning around to face me.

The sound of a throat crushing wiped away any confidence I had in the situation. I stammer my words, unsure of what to divulge and what will keep me safe.

Vickers catches my eye before I can speak, he stumbles up the ramp with a long piece of metal, then raises it, drawing back like he intends to swing.

I gasp.

The commander turns, catching him by the forearm as he brings it down in a strike. They stay in the struggling pose for just a second, the veins in Vickers's forehead bulging with his deranged hysteria, face swollen and red. He buries his shoulder into the commander's stomach, attempting to tackle him out of balance. But he only steps back a few paces, absorbing the blow into his armor. An ear-piercing snap is followed by Vickers's agonizing scream.

August's back is against me, guarding me and blocking my view, but I raise to my toes to look over his shoulder again.

Vickers stumbles, holding his twisted, limp arm. "You're fucking idiots, both of you. She's a spy! She read my mind. She could be sending information. We need to smother the fanatic cunt! You—"

His demented shouting mixes with another scuffle, then it is cut off abruptly, leaving a strange emptiness in the room. The commander palms either side of Vickers's head, turning it at a weird angle. He lets go, the body folding unnaturally on the floor.

Then, he turns his attention to August and me.

My heart is beating so fast that I can feel my pulse in my teeth. I'm gulping for air but my chest can't heave fast enough.

August seems terrified too, his thoughts colliding with mine. Our contact and mutual fear creates a thin connection with a life of its own. He thinks he is going to die. I won't let that happen. August was helping me; he's sweet. I'm the one who lied, not him.

This murderous Viathan is going to kill us all.

I step around August as the commander strides toward us. I throw out my hand to stop him just as my vision goes black in the corners for a moment, then the entire room is lit up.

"No!"

A pale beam sucks in the surrounding light, bouncing off my palm straight into the commander's chest plate. On contact, his body flies out of the open door of the cargo bay. The light bounces from him, spreading out into the hull like water rings in a glass. It flashes so brightly, bursting outward and disappearing, stealing my breath with it.

I peel myself off the cold metal floor. My face feels bruised from my collapse. My head is foggy and drained, a similar feeling to when I have looked into someone's mind's eye for too long.

I crawl to August and cup his scrunched face. He seems ok. I think he only fell back from the final burst of light, but the commander was directly hit by it. I smooth a hand over my face, utterly confused at what I saw. I walk to the opening of the hull, peeking over the side.

The commander is lying in the tall grass, motionless. Whatever it was, I think it may have killed him. I've never heard or seen anything like it. I've read about all the divine gifts there have been and currently are. Whatever it was, it was an accident, an unexplained thing that came to my aid.

I carefully stride down the ramp, my hands clutched to my chest. I don't think I wanted to kill him, just stop whatever was about to happen. If he could just hear me out, listen to reason, maybe he wouldn't resort to violence again.

He stirs a little, groaning as he rolls onto his back.

"Um, 99th Commander?"

He is on me before I can say another word, pushing my shoulders back until I am against the ship's side, completely boxed in by him in a single motion.

"Who are you?" he asks.

"I—"

"Explain now."

"I am a priestess, a *lesser* priestess. I work in the Estate library with Mary as her assistant." I sound more terror stricken than I want to.

August stumbles to the opening of the ship, resting his hands on his knees like he is out of breath.

The commander shakes me, wanting more answers.

"I was instructed by Mary and Emperor Matthias to keep that part to myself for my own safety! And with just cause, it seems."

"I've never seen a lesser priestess do that."

"Well, I am, and I have never done that before. I don't know what that was. We don't even know that was me! I'm just a priestess; I assure you. I was promised ascension if I helped Cosima's representative."

He says nothing, just holds me hard against the ship, helmet tilted down to me in inspection.

"I was following instructions, Commander. I am trying to win the favor of First Mother so that I may ascend. I am not sure what you know of high priestesses, but I am not one."

I can see my angry reflection in the visor of his helmet. I've done nothing but try to protect myself from someone who was charging at me, who very recently murdered someone. I shake my shoulders, trying to get free.

"I am sick of being manhandled!"

The commander drops his hands instantly, almost making me lose balance. He crosses his hands behind his back then takes a large step away, giving me space. I'm not thankful though. He wouldn't do that if he wasn't sure he could grab me again if needed.

"I'm sorry Vickers . . . touched you."

"Did you know what he was? What he has done?" I ask.

He slants his helmet in a question.

"Murder, but I guess that doesn't shock you. And he wanted to hurt me. I saw it."

"You saw it? Is this what provoked him to attack you?"

"Provoke! Really?" I step into his space.

"Do you think that is why he attacked you?" he repeats with a sigh.

"I have the gift of mind's eye. When I saw something I wasn't supposed to, he grabbed me. I am only a priestess; this is the only gift I have."

I keep my gaze up at him towering over me, intent on not lowering my eyes at his interrogation. I am not sorry for answering his questions in truth. I was the one provoked, so I did what I needed to.

"August, get the cuffs from the armory," he says abruptly.

"What?" I try to leave from my spot but he throws up an arm to block me.

"Is that really necessary?" August stands at the top of the ramp, looking down at us.

"Regardless of what happened with Vickers, she still lied to us. Cuffs," he says.

"The highest will hear about this."

"I'm sure she will, Priestess," he says flatly.

I stare daggers into that stupid visor. I want to rip it off his head. I hate that I thought his jawline was handsome, a trick of low light and travel delirium.

August throws the metal cuffs down to the commander—two thick circles attached to each other, cold and barbaric.

"One of us has to touch you to put these on, pick," he says.

I look up at August, extending my wrists. An obvious choice. I cannot be mad at him for following orders.

"I'm sorry about this, Ferren," he whispers as he spins me, gently grabbing my wrists from the front.

I glare at the commander as the metal cuffs click into place behind my back. I can't wait to tell Crixa what he did to me.

I pull at the tight cuffs on my wrists, my skin already feeling raw. No Viathan can keep me from following through with this task. I will ascend and show First Mother I am worthy. She will see what I have endured, my sacrifices. But Crixa will likely punish me when she hears that I let my sharp tongue reveal who I really was. I will have to wait and confess until after the stones have been returned and I've ascended. Then she will hear of this mistreatment.

August is quiet now, glancing over at me with a regretful look. I do feel bad for lying to him, but I was just following instructions. It seems like a pilot and a commander could understand such things.

The metal on my wrists sticks on a panel near the edge of the mess hall, where the commander instructed me to sit. I rattle my restraints, pulling at the cuffs that have become part of the wall.

"Can I take these off now? The cargo door is shut. I'm not going anywhere."

The commander doesn't say anything, not even an annoying slow tilt of his helmet. I can't even look at August. He will give me a sad boy look if I put him in another position to have to be cruel. They stand over the illuminated map of Frith, zoomed in on the forest coating the sacred mountain in a dense layer. The beacon must have been unresponsive because I can hear them whispering about our secondary plan. My stomach churns at the sight of the dark forest. If I was not afraid of traveling through it before my previous night of studying, the reality of it in front of me is paralyzing now.

"Commander, can you please remove these." My voice is bordering on panic. We will travel through the forest, up the sacred mountain. I will need to go over the field guides again with them, what I found in the texts Mary brought.

"Hello, I'm speaking to *you*, Commander!"

"No," he says.

"Don't you think if I knew how to do that light thing again, I would have blasted these off by now? We need to go over the map of the mountain."

They ignore me, muttering to themselves and pointing to portions of the forest.

"Can I at least take them off to sleep?"

"No."

"Well, if you do not need me to go over the map, then I'm going to bed. Blessed night, August. I am sorry if I somehow hurt you and only you earlier," I say as I stand in a hunch with my wrists still stuck to the wall panel.

"Sit down," the commander says.

"I don't think so," I say, pulling on my wrists with all my body weight.

"You're sleeping in here with us, sit down."

"You can't be serious." I turn to August, hoping he will be on my side.

"Ferren, you've been real nice to have around, but I'm sorry. I've never seen anything like that. You . . . I've never seen that before," he says, dipping his head low. It's clear he isn't enjoying this. I feel awful for breaking his trust.

"I, at least, need privacy so I can pray then, either outside or by the cockpit windows," I say.

I could pray on my own given my unique circumstances, but I'm compelled to inconvenience the commander. I notice them looking at each other, August in particular seeming worried at the mention of prayer.

"Mother's womb, I've prayed many times on this ship. Nothing's happened to you yet."

The commander straightens to his full height, squaring his shoulders. I theatrically roll my eyes and groan, so he knows I am not intimidated. But then he fixes a hand-size gun in his waistband, and I regret insisting on being difficult.

I'm escorted to the cockpit, the commander a tight shadow behind me on our way up. He taps the button for the window film to fade away. I walk over to them to see the freckling of stars above.

"I don't see the moon," I say.

"It's up there," he answers.

"I need privacy."

"No. Make it quick."

"No." I smirk back at him.

I position myself close to the front aisle and close my eyes, trying to calm myself and find my center. I'm still fuming, so it may be impossible.

"First Mother, in our hour of need—"

Strong hands gently grasp onto the balls of both my shoulders as the commander turns me to face the far window.

"Moon is that way," he says flatly.

He is not getting a thank you. I center myself again with a deep breath.

"First Mother, come to us in our hour of need. Your children suffer at the hands of a mad man. Your poor, sweet servant August is terrified."

"He's not. August doesn't need your prayers, Priestess."

I open one eye to glare at him. "He *is*. I saw it in his mind's eye when you charged at us."

"I've known August for a long time. If he was afraid, it was of you," he says, stepping into the hall doorway, leaning against it with crossed arms.

I shut my eyes and face forward again.

"A most grim foe, a deranged wolf with a tin chamber pot for a face," I say louder.

He huffs behind me.

"Should I pray for the man you killed, Commander?" I say, trying to get under his skin.

"Do you think he deserves your prayers?"

I stare at him over my shoulder for a long time. "Are you planning on killing me too?" I say, a little more serious.

He shakes his head no in a slow, agonizing answer.

I shouldn't be using prayer to make him mad. I should be using this time to commune with First Mother. As satisfying as that was, I need to be praying to her now more than ever. I feel lost, like everything is falling away from me. I use the pilot's chair to brace my cuffed hands as I get down to my knees. I don't have privacy, but he can't stop me from praying within myself. I lean forward and press my hands to the floor, getting my face as low as I can.

First Mother, forgive me, for your children have grown wicked. I have let distraction take hold of me when I need to stay true the most. I have let my sharp tongue get in the way of my purpose and compromised it and my safety. I beg your forgiveness. I will retrieve your stones cuffed and beaten if I have to, but I will show my devotion.

The sound of August clearing his throat breaks the utter silence created by the inward prayer and the commander's refusal to say more than a word at a time. I turn my head to the side to see them both looking at me in my downward position.

August looks embarrassed, averting his eyes and holding up a set of keys. "The pilot's suite locks from the outside. I'll let whatever this is finish," he says and promptly leaves.

I stand ungracefully, clinging on the chair for balance. I am done praying, for now at least. Yes, I could have done that in my room like I have since we left, but I wanted him to see. I wanted him to know that no matter how shackled I am, he can't keep me from First Mother.

"I am finished."

The commander passes me, tapping the panel to cover the windows in an opaque shade again.

"If we are journeying through the forest, then I need to go over the rest of the books Mary brought," I say, gesturing to the door of her room where her trunk sits.

"No, we have enough information."

"I don't think you understand what we will be walking through,

Commander. I need to review them. There could be something in there we may need. Please, they're just books." I stifle the satisfying amusement I get from saying the last part.

To my surprise, he slams a hand on the panel to Mary's room, disappearing into it. He returns a few moments later with a stack of books that looks dwarfed in his arms. He saunters by me, opening the door to my suite and placing them on my bed.

I watch him from the threshold of my doorway as he rests each one on the blanket. He faces me, slowly walking through the exit as if I am not standing in it at all. I shift to the side, letting him brush by me. His movements are slow and intentional.

"I know what you think of me," I say right into his visor.

He holds a long pause then towers over me, stepping into my space. His helmet tilts to the side as if he is studying my expression.

"You've no idea what I think of you, Priestess." His voice almost a whisper, muffled by the thick metal, the soft rasp pulling me in. He brushes by me as he passes, the door whooshing closed where he stood. This time, I hear him lock the door from the outside, encasing me in and leaving me dumbfounded by the meaning of his words.

CHAPTER ELEVEN

66 **T**he creatures that live in the forest don't follow the same rules we do. Guns will only serve to agitate, not protect us," I say.

The commander continues to attach Viathan weaponry to his body armor. He latches one to his calf then opens another metal tote full of guns of all sizes.

I turn away as August withdraws something as long as my arm, leaning on the stack of crates I first noticed in the cargo hull.

"Commander, you said these would be left on the ship. We need to make sure we keep the peace."

"Things have changed," he says harshly, snapping something metal to the bottom of a gun with a clicking sound.

"If we run into an old god and you use a Viathan weapon on it, what do you think will happen?" I say in a challenging tone.

He walks up on me, opening the crate next to my shoulder. "I am more worried about running into First Son followers, Priestess."

Even though he has a fetish for weapons, I was not allowed to bring the letter opener I stowed away for my own protection. The commander watched as I packed my small bag this morning then rifled through it, rudely throwing anything he didn't like back on my bed. I adjust the strap awkwardly draped across my chest. My cuffed hands keep me from wearing it securely.

August packs their bags full of supplies, clothes, and strange Viathan food from the panel lockers along the walls, more compartments I didn't notice until opened. He has kept a sad distance from me as they prepped the ship to sit idle while we are gone and packed up the necessities for the journey. I want to speak with him, but the commander won't let me out of his sight unless I am locked in my suite.

"I can't travel with my hands like this. It's not safe," I say to the commander softly.

"Until I have more information, you will stay like that," he answers directly, mask inches away from my face.

I'm so stunned, I don't protest as he grabs my arm, ushering me toward the opening of the ramp. I almost stumble as we walk down the steep incline, his grip seeming more intentional as he keeps my balance. I jerk away from it the moment my boots step into the tall grass of the field.

August holds up a forearm covered in a metal cuff similar to the commander's. He taps at it like the buttons on his handheld panel, and the ramp begins a metallic hum, rising from the ground. The moment it shuts, I'm overcome with a sense of exposure, vulnerable out from the safe nest of the ship.

We trudge through the tall grass of the field. Both Viathans have their guns raised in opposite directions. I walk between them, taking large leaping steps to keep up in the thick grassland.

The tree line is dark even as we get closer. The grass right up to its border is a bright lime green, then there's an abrupt darker shift at the first tree's base, like it's a shadowy entrance.

The commander is the first to step into the forest's dark gateway. The moment his boot touches the underbrush, every leaf, branch, and plant stills itself from the breezy sway. He raises his weapon—a more focused and threatening posture as he scans the area in front of us. He folds his fingers in my direction, calling me to enter the forest.

I go slowly, the breeze that whipped my hair and stifled my hearing cutting out with my first step. I turn to look at August and his back is to me as he scans the field. It's like looking at him behind glass, on the opposite side of a window. The thigh-high grass dances around him, wind moving the fabric of his pack strapped to him.

"It's a protection ward," I whisper the moment I realize.

"What?" the commander says, hushed, over his shoulder.

"Like the beacons you placed around the ship. Look at the leaves, they are perfectly still."

August crosses over it, and with his last step, the stillness in the forest ceases. It's calm and gently alive again, like it held its breath as we walked in, observing us.

"The ones on the ship's perimeter alert us when something crosses it," the commander says.

"Yes, well, I think the forest knows we are here," I say, pulling at my sore wrists.

"Comforting." August slowly steps in front as the commander covers him, visor affixed to his weapon in concentration.

We begin a slow-paced walk deeper into the dense forest. It's morning, but the canopy above is so thick, it smudges out the sun. The ground shakes in a conjunction tremor, a strange reminder leading me to a homesick feeling. Instead of clambering windows, the ground rolls, making the trees sway and the leaves above shimmer in a strange-sounding hiss.

Hours into our walk, it becomes more inclined and rocky, making sweat bead on my forehead. The Estate is large and requires a lot of walking, but it's all flat. This trek would be challenging on a good day with broken in shoes and free hands. I trip over stones and large sticks even though August warns in a hushed voice of obstacles on the path ahead. They both move through the brush with little effort, maneuvering while holding their giant guns pointed outward, leaving me some privacy to struggle and keep solely focused on the semi path.

"99, maybe you should take her cuffs off. She is going to fall on her face," August says as I toss myself over a fallen tree.

"She's fine," he answers.

I stand from an uncoordinated roll over a tree trunk, panting for air.

August swings his gun down on its strap to remove his canteen. He lifts it to my mouth, not quite touching my lips, and pours, completely missing and spilling ribbons of water out the sides and down my chin.

Then the commander grabs it out of August's hand roughly, like he has done something gravely wrong. He cups my chin with his massive, gloved hand, lifting it up and holding it in place. He pours water into my opened lips, squeezing for me to open wider. It's aggressive yet oddly intimate at the same time. His movements are slow, methodical, and even slightly confusing, as if he forgot for just a moment how much he hates me. But I wouldn't care if he made me drink it from his cupped hands; it's cold and clean.

I know he is watching the water fill my mouth because he adjusts the angle of the canteen when I sway a little. I swallow the pool of water, but he keeps filling, holding my jaw in place. I swallow again, furrowing my brow at him, trying to squirm away from a slow drowning. He pulls the metal canteen away from my lips long before he removes his gloved fingers gripping my chin, holding me there for just a moment, enough so I can watch him take a single chest-lifting breath.

The slightest movement of his thumb brushes against my skin like he is stopping himself from wiping the water off my skin. I tug away from his hold, freeing myself.

Then, he seemingly snaps out of whatever that was and slams the canteen back into August's stomach.

We continue for an exhausting distance up the gradual incline of the mountain, forest getting dense and even more shrouded in darkness. The sun shines pinholes through the bushy leaves above to the soft forest floor. The trees are at least three times bigger than the one in the courtyard of the Estate, richly brown and more lush. They sway ominously at the top ever so often, the leaves whispering to each other.

I'm completely out of breath again as the path levels out to perfectly even ground. We walk across the flat plateau that seems carved into the mountain, skirting the tree line. Tiny flying insects dance in swarms in the middle of the grassy field where the sun beats down on it. The only greenery is the same hairlike grass we walked through to enter.

"We need to find the bulb soon, before we get any farther up," I say, trying to hide my panting.

The commander nods his helmet once but pushes me along to keep walking. I want to cry. My legs are on fire and the boots that were provided to me for this terrain are surprisingly not that great after all.

August points to a rock formation as the trees consume our path again—an open-air cave, unnatural and most likely placed intentionally there for shelter. The largest boulder is taller than the statue of First Mother in the Estate temple and just as wide. They decrease in size, creating an almost full circle. The smallest is no more than the size of an apple.

The commander circles the structure in a strange defensive posture, holding his gun more deliberately. August stays next to me, going into a similar stance.

I stand, cuffed and sweaty, watching them like an idiot.

The commander waves a hand, inviting us to come closer, determining it to be safe. "We camp here," he says.

August slings his gun over his shoulder, picking up small twigs as we walk into the odd semicircle.

I can feel my knees buckling in relief as I sit down and try to catch my breath, my cuffed wrists preventing me from bracing my back against a boulder to fully rest.

August arranges the twigs he collected into a peaked shape in the middle of the rock formation. There are pieces of charred wood and ashes, like someone has used the same area for a fire as well.

"These ok to burn?" he asks.

I nod. "We probably shouldn't have a fire past dark though. All of the texts warn against it. And when we get farther in, where the ground is covered in moss, we cannot have a fire at all."

The commander places logs next to August. "The temperature will drop tonight. Place some of the small rocks by the fire. We can use them for warmth after it goes out," he says.

August withdraws a tiny metal weapon from his bag, aiming it at the underbrush he has stuffed beneath the snapped twigs. He pulls his finger back and with a click, a blazing torch ignites with a flame almost as long as a candle stick. I watch as the fire catches, drawing my legs closer, away from it. It engulfs the twigs August feeds it, eventually needing the larger branches from the pile they collected.

The commander squats next to me and points to my back in a wordless order. As I lean to the side, he unlatches one of my hands, letting me bring both to the front only to be cuffed again. I huff at the short-lived hope of them being taken off entirely. Then he digs through his bag, pulling out a brown square with flecks of similar shades. He shoves the square in my palm, and I realize in horror it's intended to be eaten.

"No, thank you. I have sugar bread," I say, trying to pass it back as he stands, ignoring me.

August slinks down, leaning his back on a smooth rock next to me.

"Ferren, you have sweets and you're holding out on me?" he says with narrow eyes.

I smile and dig through my bag, pulling out three options with different fillings. He covers his mouth, trying to hide his grin, but I can see it all the way up to his green eyes. Charming premature lines are around the corners from smiling frequently like he does.

"How many did you bring!" he says, pointing to his choice.

I pass him the custard-filled morsel, my cuffed hand pulling at the other. His eyes flick down and for a second, I think we both forgot what happened yesterday, that I was cuffed at all. We spoke like friends again, and seeing him smile tugs at the muscles in my heart. The commander said he was afraid of me. The fear I saw in his mind was directed at me, at what I am.

"I'm sorry, August, truly," I whisper, afraid to meet his eyes. I want to say more, assure him that I won't hurt him.

He doesn't answer, just scoots closer to me to share the treats I stashed away. He finishes it fast, savors it at times but mostly tears into it with large bites, then he opens a map, spreading it across our laps.

"Where do you think the flowers . . . or bulbs are? We are here," he says while drawing lines on the map with his finger.

"They grow on cliffs or anywhere there are a lot of rocks. They attach themselves to the side and the roots hang down in strings. The bulb is exposed so it should be easy to pull off . . . in theory," I say.

The commander squats down in front of us, interrupting our peaceful strategy session with his invasive presence and widely spread thighs. He holds out a piece of old charcoal from the fire.

"Draw."

I snatch it and draw the flower and bulb in the margins of the map. "The center of the flower is an irritant so just don't touch it with bare skin. We only need the round bulb. Cut it right off along with any long stringy roots." I draw a line indicating where he should cut the plant.

The commander stands, walking to the other side of our little camp.

"This is important, Commander. There are some plants that mimic it that are poisonous. What will we do when we encounter them? Will you shoot the leaves for us? Snap the flower's neck?"

He stares down at me for a long time, shoulders rising and falling in frustrated breaths.

"We aren't going, just August." He puts his gloved hands on his hips, belt tight and fitted with weaponry. "You're the best suited for climbing if they grow on cliffs" he says to only August, as if I'm not there.

"We should all go," I say.

"It's dangerous, no."

"Who will complete the retrieval if all three of us are dead?" August says, agreeing with the commander.

"No, he shouldn't go alone!" I say as I struggle to get up from the ground with my restraints. August helps me and brushes the dirt off my arms.

"99 is right. I'm the best suited for it." He grabs the map and folds it. "Rocks are that way, I will start there. If it gets late, I will make camp for the night and continue in the morning."

I scan the lines around his eyes, flattened but still vaguely outlined. It's not my choice, and I realize I have little say when the commander digs his heels in.

"No fire."

"No fire," he agrees.

"Don't touch anything. Don't eat anything," I say, surrendering to the idea of him leaving into the poisonous forest alone.

I want to hug him. I never thought I would get close to one of the Viathans, but I almost consider August a friend now. He follows orders reluctantly from his commander, which I cannot fault him for. We are alike in that way, following instructions from someone who cannot be reasoned with, not agreeing entirely but understanding.

The commander pats him on the shoulder, and they whisper to each other on the other side of our camp. August nods then heads out into the dark forest alone.

I stand by the fire, feeling the temperature already starting to plummet and warming my hands until the flames turn into glowing coals.

The commander leans against a tree just outside the formation. I can feel the weight of his glare on me, like I'm going to sprint away into the forest now that there is only one person guarding.

"You are staring at me; it's unnerving."

"You could ask me to stop."

"Like you would listen. In the short time I've known you, I don't think you would."

He walks right up on me, his steps encroaching, forcing me to back away. "Do you ever just shut up for more than a minute?" he says, lifting a hand like he wants to place it on my collarbone.

"How dare you! Men have been hanged for talking to a priestess in that way!"

He huffs a laugh, kicking dirt on the remaining embers. Then he disappears behind the rock formation, only to reappear at the top of the largest in the center.

"I can still yell at you when you're up there, Commander, trust me."

"It will be dark soon, shouldn't risk it."

I make an exasperated sound loud enough for him to hear, then move down to my knees, taking in large breaths to center myself. I make the mistake of opening my eyes just a sliver to see the commander watching me again, arm resting on his bent knee like he owns the boulder he sits on. He points upward in the direction opposite me, indicating again where the moon is. I exhale painfully and scoot that way.

I don't pray for long. I'm exhausted and my knees hurt more than after the long hours of prayer in the temple. The rock I placed next to the fire is burning hot. It's much smaller than the others, but I thought I could place it in my shirt to warm me.

The sounds in the forest are strange. I can hear things high up in the distance that sound like they are calling to each other, but there is nothing directly around us making much noise thankfully. The commander doesn't seem to be distressed so I try to relax and not think of the creatures I've read about or August out there alone with them.

CHAPTER TWELVE

August isn't back. It's dawn and he's still out there.

The commander hasn't moved from his post at the top of the largest rock, watching out over our little camp. He doesn't seem worried, but I know it's more likely something went terribly wrong than the odds of August finding that bulb alone.

Did I draw it correctly? Did he cut the wrong kind and is dying somewhere from its poison?

I gnaw down on the now slightly stale sugar bread, watching the commander for any context clues of August's arrival. I stumble to my feet, trying to stretch out the soreness of sleeping on the ground with only a coat as a mattress.

"Should we look for him?" I strain my voice to carry up to him but stay hushed at the same time. The forest is eerily silent. Any noise too loud could carry farther without the constant rustle of trees to drown it out.

Not surprisingly, he does not answer.

"I'm worried," I confess.

"Are you?" The tone of his voice is husky and monotone, almost sarcastic.

"Yes, of course."

"August can handle himself."

I have seen very startling glimpses of that, a stark difference from his sweet personality to the serious and intimidating demeanor when he is in the pilot's chair or holding someone at gunpoint. However, any act of violence or hostility from the commander makes sense, fits in the universe like it should. I doubt he has any complexity inside that thick helmet of his. My disdain for him is starting to turn to something more solid, evolving each time he speaks to me.

I twist the terrible Viathan restraints, my skin red underneath. "I want these removed. I have done nothing wrong. We both want to retrieve First Mother's stones. We want the same thing."

"No, we do not," he says, tilting his mask down to me.

"Oh, how could I forget—Viathan. You agree with us but won't pick a side."

"I am on no one's side but my own, Priestess. I want the gods to leave us. If retrieving old stones maintains order, then so be it."

His response is perfectly Viathan and more selfish than I imagined from a commander bound by duty.

"Order is maintained by picking a side and defending it," I say.

Insects float past me as I fume, thinking about his words. With my hands bound, my only defense is to lean away, to avoid contact. The forest has started to come to life again, the sun letting in dim beams to chase away the night predators. A thud captures my attention from behind the rock the commander is on, and when I look, he has jumped down, out of sight.

I round the smooth corner and see August with his dazzling smile, the two of them grabbing onto each other's forearms in a strange greeting. The commander whispers to August, rudely indicating to keep my distance as I try to join—a reminder that I am not only an outsider, but not part of whatever this started to be. For a single day, I was brought into their inner circle and asked to weigh in on decisions, to say my thoughts on important matters and not just take notes for someone else.

August approaches me with a small, wrapped bundle in his hands. He smiles and lifts the side to reveal the pale bulb.

"Got it despite your awful drawing," he teases.

"That's amazing. It will make the first meeting much easier," I say, smiling flatly, not able to bring myself fully out of the reminder of who I am to them.

It's not long after we begin hiking again that I notice the moss layer—another gateway to pass through on the sacred mountain. The ground is spongy, like walking on a soft mattress. It's harder to stay balanced on than the under layer of leaves and twigs we walked through yesterday.

The commander is at the front today, making us keep a brisk pace. The incline is subtle and much more gradual, but I notice August is lagging behind and even *I* am walking faster than him. I look back when I hear some rustling and see him leaning against a tree, panting.

"You ok back there?" I ask.

August pants, sweat pouring down the sides of his neck. I notice his tan skin has gone pale, a grayish cast that sends alarm bells off in the pit of my stomach.

"August, what is it? What's wrong?" I say, walking back to the spot he is resting in.

Something isn't right. He looks unwell. I lift one of his closed eyelids, checking if they appear normal, knowing that some flora poisons first present in the eyes.

The commander backtracks to us and looks him over while keeping a watchful eye out into the distance.

"Look at his coloring," I say up to him.

August stammers.

I try to stay calm but inside I am panicking, watching him struggling to speak. I press into his mind's eye and hear him say my name and then something about his hand.

"My hand . . . numb," he manages.

I grab at his arm, lift the sleeve, and see a small dot with a red veiny ring webbing out in a circle. I lift the fabric more, hoping it isn't what I suspect.

But it is. There's a long red trail headed up his arm.

"Shit!"

"What is that?" the commander asks me.

"He's been stung. I can't remember the name but it's not good."

August's breath becomes erratic, like I've scared him.

"My arm is getting numb now," he says, labored.

"I need these off. Now!" I say to the commander, shaking my wrists.

He hesitates then finally relents, releasing me.

I rip the fabric of August's sleeve, exposing his bicep. I need to see how far the red trail goes, following it up to where it stops at the pit of his elbow.

"Listen, Ferren, you're gorgeous, but you're not my type," August manages with a weak grin.

"I need rope or a belt. Something to tie this off."

The commander hands me a piece of cloth, and I tie it tightly around August's bicep. He looks down at the red line with shocked, wide eyes.

"This is going to hurt but we have to do it, ok?" I say softly to him, trying to pacify.

"I need a sharp knife, Commander."

His silhouette blocks out a trickle of light that has made its way through the canopy. He hesitates again, but there is no time.

"I need your fucking knife!"

He smacks it into my palm.

"Be still," I say softly to August.

I line it up to the stinger and press it into August's skin, the entire forest silent for that moment.

"Hurry up, Ferren. Cut it off if you need to. I see something coming," he says drowsily.

"Oh no, there must be venom. He's hallucinating now." I press the blade a little deeper, blindly fishing for the stinger.

I hear the now familiar sound of the commander raising his weapon with a click of metal.

His voice is low and gritted as he says. "He's not hallucinating. I see it too."

CHAPTER THIRTEEN

A chill runs up my spine.

I can't look. I have to keep my eyes on the knife in August's arm.

I feel a small bump at the top of the red trail. I flick under it with the blade, and August winces as he watches me. It should be incredibly painful; I'm almost grateful his arm is numb. I think I have it, but then the line becomes visible above the pool of blood I've made in August's elbow crease.

"Where is it going?" he asks.

"Up."

It's going to travel up his arm until it gets to the very top of his head. The stingers from this insect travels into the brain. Anywhere they sting, it is lethal.

"It's getting closer." August's eyes are glassy as he looks out over my shoulder.

I follow the slow trail up with my blade. I need to cut it out before it gets any higher.

"What does it look like, Commander?" I ask with a tremble in my voice I cannot hide.

"Large, looks like one of the trees and an old man," he calls back.

An old tree god, completely harmless if not provoked.

"Shoot it, 99!" August's eyes look wild.

"No, don't! If it's what I think it is, then we are safe. It won't hurt us. Take your helmet off, so it knows you are human!"

I find the bump right above the ever-growing red line.

"Don't shoot. You won't kill it. It's as old as First Mother. You will only agitate it. It could kill all of us. Just take off your helmet, please Commander!"

I plunge the knife into the bump, missing again. The ruby thread in his skin continues its climb.

August leans his head back against the tree in surrender; his lips are so pale.

I hear the rustle of the commander's armor and a thud like he has placed the giant gun on the forest floor. Thank First Mother, he must be taking off his helmet.

The stinger disappears under the cloth I tied around his bicep. I have to remove it before it gets lost, turning into his shoulder then his chest. I yank at the knot. The stinger may speed up, but this could be my last chance.

I hear the sounds of deep footsteps and branches snapping. The old god is behind us, right by the commander.

Please don't shoot it.

I cut a morbid slice down from his shoulder to the bump and wait. I place the blade at the back of the wound, hoping when the stinger passes up over it, I can flick it out.

I hold still, waiting for it.

I blot at the blood inside the pink, cut flesh.

The ferns next to me turn to the right just as I hear a snapping branch.

126

August sways his head to look, and I can see the tree god's reflection in his watery eyes as it passes by. I want to look so bad, to see an old god. But more than that, I want this thing out of my friend's arm.

Twigs snap as it travels farther away from us, ferns falling back to their natural placement.

The bump is right below the opening. I cannot take my eyes off it for even a second.

I brace and blot the blood away to get a good look; I have to time it just right.

Then it breaks into the open wound.

With a twist of my sore wrist, I flick my blade fast out to the side.

The stinger flies out.

I blot the wound, waiting to see if there is anything else. Nothing emerges and the red trail has halted.

August looks down and smiles at the large cut.

The long needle-like stinger landed on a log next to us, inching up a rotten branch, still trying to get to the top of . . . wherever. I cut it in half with my knife so it can't inflict any more damage. I am finally able to look upon the old god that passed us so calmly, but it is nowhere in sight, either blending into the thick trees or disappearing altogether.

August keeps his eyes closed as I clean the wounds. I feel awful for the cuts I made, his arm butchered, but he's alive. I use the rest of his canteen water on cleaning them and making him take sips. All the books I read to prepare with Mary, the ones I studied on the ship, and none of them covered basic wound mending.

The commander scans the forest around us, his helmet securely back on, when I glance over my shoulder to steal a peek. I'm surprised he listened, and it probably saved our lives. If the old god thought he was a First Son creation and not an annoying man under all that armor, who knows how it would have turned out.

When I finish wrapping August's arm, I sit on a moss-covered rock next to the commander, looking out into the trees. What little light comes through is being chased away as night gets closer. This part of the forest is the most dangerous. It's the worst place for us to have someone injured.

"I've never seen him like that," the commander says, looking out in the completely green bed of spongy moss coating everything from knee height down. His tone is different, soft or worried maybe.

I glance over at August. He still looks pale but not as gray and lethargic as before.

"I don't have a string and needle to close him up, and the bleeding won't stop on its own," I say to the commander in a hushed voice.

"We can cauterize them, burn them shut. That will stop the bleeding until we get to a Frithian village." His helmet turns toward me, waiting for my reply.

"No, we can't risk a fire. We are too deep."

"We will have to if we want him to continue with us—with the torch quickly and then move on."

The thought of using the little torch for fire starting on skin is too gruesome.

"No, I don't like it. It's a bad idea. We shouldn't have fire here."

"We will have to, Priestess, or risk infection." He stands, making me crane to look up at him. His armor is so dark, he almost blends right into the growing blackness of the forest.

"Do you have any idea of the things, the night creatures, we have attracted from shouting at each other? Now you want to wave a torch around to call First Mother knows what toward us?"

"We need to keep a fast pace, which will be impossible if he gets an infection. I've seen smaller wounds kill men larger than him," he says, squaring his shoulders toward me.

Guilt punches at my insides, a pounding synced with August's heavy breathing behind us.

"Fine, but not right here. We should move a bit. We will need to shield the flame no matter how small. Then we move again," I say.

He slants his head down, studying me in the way that I've grown used to. I'm sure he is annoyed by my demands. Normally, he is the one telling us all what to do.

"Fine," he says without protest.

We both stare at August for a long time, watching his chest rise and fall. I'm stalling but I'm not sure what the commander is waiting for. I don't want to hurt August more, cause his body more distress. I wring my trembling hands, willing them to steady.

The commander's visor flicks to them as if the sound of my finger bones shaking has called his attention.

"Thank you for helping August," he says plainly.

"Did you think I wouldn't?"

He takes a long pause, convincing me more and more what he truly thinks of me.

"I wasn't sure," he confesses.

"Oh." My tone comes out sad.

"It's my duty to ensure the retrieval at all costs. I hope you understand."

"I do not, but nothing you say or do to me will stop me from ensuring I retrieve the stones as well. I would have helped you, too, even after you accused me of being a spy and a liar," I say, stepping into him, trading the sad feeling at his judgment for anger.

"I did what had to be done," he says with finality in his voice.

But I'm not done. I will never stop. I will scream at the top of my lungs that this Viathan commander cuffed me unlawfully.

"I liked you better before, Commander, when you ignored me."

We walk until it's completely pitch black, something I advised against since they first asked me about the forest. Every book and journal warns against traveling by night, and fire is also noted as a death sentence.

I awkwardly walk with August's good arm draped on my shoulders for support. Even when I can tell he is feeling better, standing a little straighter, he still leans most of his weight on me. We trudge through the trees agonizingly slowly. The canopy farther up is less dense, letting in bright moonbeams. The commander signals back to us with a raised fist. The armor on his forearm catches the milky light, a silent gesture letting us know to stop here.

I lay August against a tree, propping him up.

The commander takes a knee next to us, pulling out the torch they used to make a fire.

"It made a strong smell," I whisper.

"The wounds will make a smell too. There is no other way," he says, pulling the trigger.

We both hover around it to block the orange glow. The commander scoots close to my side, the feel of his hard armor against me making my inhale a little too sharp and obvious.

"It needs to be a little bigger to get the knife hot enough," he says, turning the flame on in a longer spike, changing it to a bright blue.

I feel him press in tightly, making a wall around it. I try to ignore the warmth that covers my skin where we touch. When he moves, a small twig snaps under his knee, then it echoes in the forest.

I place the knife right next to the flame and wait, just enough to make the blade discolor. I never gave the knife back to him after I finished cutting the stinger from August. I see the realization dawn on him as he slowly looks up at me from my hand holding it. He's going to have to trust me. He can have it back after we are done if he needs to feel better.

"This shouldn't hurt, August. I think you're still numb from earlier," I say to him softly.

There is a whispering breeze weaving through the giant trees around us.

"Should be good now," the commander says, placing the torch on the ground and twisting to put his back to us. Gun raised out into the forest, he leaves me to work on poor August alone.

I push the flat part of the knife on the smallest cut by his elbow crease. August looks away as the skin sizzles.

"You really did a number on me, Ferren," he whispers.

"I know. I'm sorry."

A faint echo floats on the breeze, repeating my words. *"I know. I'm sorry."*

August blanches, like he's been stung all over again. He heard it too. The forest whispered, echoing back my voice.

I feel myself go rigid with a terrible sense of urgency filling me.

The commander lifts his gun, pushing into my side, confirming that we all heard it.

With a shaky hand, I pull the trigger of the torch and place the knife next to the flame again.

"Commander," I say.

"Commander." The voice in the darkness is breathy and softer, but just like mine.

"Hurry, we need to move," he says at a normal volume, no reason to whisper. Whatever is out there knows we are here.

I quickly scan the area as the knife slowly glows like an ember.

Another crack sound goes off to our other side, and the commander swings his gun in that direction, pushing into me in a rough sort of protection.

"Do it," he says.

"Almost ready," I whisper, but the knife isn't getting hot enough to close his large wound.

"Almost ready." The whisper comes from the forest at our front.

I look at August with the red-hot knife. His eyes are wild again, and he sighs deeply. To our horror, it is mimicked in another part of the forest.

"Did you hear that?" he says.

"Did you hear that?" the ghostly voice mimics.

I nod, too afraid to say anything that a disembodied voice will copy.

The knife cools as soon as I remove it from the pointed flame, only leaving a small orange glow in the center. I know it's not enough to close the wound.

I grab him, bringing the torch directly down on the cut without warning. His skin sizzles, and the smell is terrible. It smokes as I hold the wound together and draw a gruesome line.

"I can feel it!" August squirms, gritting his teeth and clenching his fists. The numbness has worn off at the top of his arm.

"I can feel it." The whisper is closer now.

I frantically tap the commander's shoulder, letting him know I am done, that the wound is burned closed.

We help August stand and lean him on me again. The commander puts a hand up to leave the still blazing torch. I realize he is trying to buy us time, that maybe whatever is mimicking us in the forest is only drawn to the fire.

We take off, away from the tiny flame, in between giant trees. I ask August if he's ok and hear it echo behind us, his answer echoing as well. I can't help but glance back as I help August over a fallen branch.

I can't quite process what I am seeing. Two blue orbs reach the fire and manifest as August and me just as we were moments ago: him lying against the tree and me holding a knife to the flame. We are blue and translucent but distinctly us. The *things* act out the cauterizing process and repeat the words we said. When August gets over the log and leans on me again, I jump.

I keep my eyes fused to the back of the commander's armor where the moonlight hits it. We need to get as far away as we can from the living, echoing proof of the dangers of Frith's moss layer.

CHAPTER FOURTEEN

The commander fights me to stop and make camp for the night. He is adamant that we traveled far enough away and should be safe. But I want to keep going, to get as far away from what I saw as possible. I don't care if night travel is dangerous. I won't feel safe unless I'm moving. Every time I blink, I can see the blue orbs in the darkness in the shapes of August and me. What would they have done if they reached us? Those things weren't in any of the Frithian books or firsthand accounts.

The commander holds out a piece of food for me to take, the weird brown squares he eats.

"No, thank you," I say.

He shakes it gently in front of me, urging me to take it.

"I don't want it. I'm not hungry."

He crouches down to where I have nestled myself against a rock. "What is it?"

"Nothing, I'm just not hungry."

"You're lying," he says after a long pause.

"I've given you an answer, Commander."

"I know you are lying. Your heart rate and breathing are erratic."

I gape my mouth in shock. Thank First Mother it's too dark to see my reflection in his visor. "What an intrusion! How dare you!"

I suspected his helmet could do such things, but now I know for sure. That's why he's always staring at me when I speak like he is inspecting me, because he is.

"It's my duty as commander."

I whip off the jacket I'm using as a blanket and stand, bending down over him where he still squats.

"Where was your duty when I was telling you I wasn't a spy, when you didn't believe me, when you could have checked if I was lying then, when I told you I had no idea what that was in the cargo hull!" My tone is a mix of a whisper and a shout.

"I am not familiar with divine powers and how they can manipulate."

"Where was this duty when you cuffed me . . . like a criminal." My voice cracks, pain showing through. "Oh, but now you can tell if I'm lying or not when I don't want to eat your disgusting square food!"

The commander rises chillingly slowly, towering up. He watches me, probably reading whatever he wants with that stupid mask.

"And I swear, if you even try to put those cuffs on me—"

"I am not."

I cross my arms in suspicion and to hide my wrists from him.

"I'm not going to cuff you again, Priestess. You could have let August and me die, but you didn't. I needed some proof to trust you."

"Proof? Fuck your proof and that ridiculous helmet, this forest, and whatever the fuck those were back there!" I say with a wildly pointing finger.

He is silent, unphased by my outburst.

"You saw them too?" he says softly, ignoring every other word I said. "I saw you look back. Did you see them?"

"Yes." The question snaps me out of my rage. I wring my wrists, trying to hide my shaky hands.

"I only saw one. It was mimicking your voice, then it was your face, your . . . body, but a little different," he says.

For some reason, his phrasing has me squirming a little.

"I only saw as we left. The other one was August," I say.

He grunts then places his hands on his hips to look out in the tree line. He looks powerful and broad . . . stupid but very broad.

"You should try the squares, Priestess. They are only a little disgusting."

I'm too surprised at his attempt at a joke to laugh at it. His helmet slants down slightly, like he is watching me press my lips together to hide a smile. Or maybe he can read my heart rate, can see that it has evened out from talking about what happened.

"I'm taking first watch tonight. I can't hold us up anymore. I'm starting to feel like a burden." August brushes up against the commander's shoulder to interject.

"No one thinks that," the commander says in a shockingly compassionate tone.

"Such a flirt, this one." August smiles and puts his good elbow on the commander's shoulder, a tall reach even for him. "Save some of that for Ferren." He smiles wickedly.

The commander visibly stiffens at the words.

August's eyes flash back and forth at us, his expression a mix of finding himself funny and realizing he overstepped.

Yes, the commander has stared at me, but now I know it is because he's trying to read me, make sure I am not working against them. But what about before the cargo incident, when I could tell his eyes would linger on me even though they are obscured? Or the way he almost reached out twice to comfort me but stopped himself. He's a Viathan.

It doesn't matter how he was before. He cuffed me at the first sign of divinity.

"I need some space," I say in an awkwardly rigid tone, putting my back to them both.

I find a bush within earshot but with enough privacy to relieve my bladder. It's not safe to venture too far no matter how much I want to get away from the commander right now. He said he isn't putting the cuffs back on, but I don't forgive him. I refuse to be grateful. They shouldn't have been on me in the first place. What August said was a product of feeling better and coming close to death, nothing to read into. What would flirting from the commander even look like? Letting me hold his favorite gun?

I notice a metallic shine a couple trees over. It looks similar to the way the moon reflects off of the commander's armor. I creep toward it slowly. It looks so unnatural, a completely different color and material than anything else around it.

I stop as my vision adjusts to the object. It's a First Son creation, a metal human, but it doesn't look like a human at all. It has the same number of limbs, the same general shape, but the head and where its face should be is just a smooth oval. I've never seen anything like it, only drawings in some books when I first started my post with Mary. I creep closer and see it's sitting at the base of a tree, looking out off the flat plateau of the mountain. Spears stick out of its stomach with vines covering most of its arms and legs—cold and lifeless.

I hear a whooshing similar to the mechanical sound of the large levers in the ship. The sound comes from within the metal human, concentrated in its smooth, featureless head. I take a shaky step back, realizing my mistake.

A beam of red light shoots out at me, scanning. I feel no pain as it cascades down my face then crisscrosses down my body. It's not dead, just dormant, waiting for someone to come upon it, unable to move but still able to send out whatever this streak of light is.

The commander pulls my shoulder back as the red beam draws up again. I stumble, falling to the ground but out of the range of the terrifying light.

I watch him bludgeon the oval face of the metal human-thing. I crawl backward on my elbows, trying to escape from the sparks and pieces coming off it. Its light cuts out with the whooshing sound, but the commander continues then turns his gun barrel side right at it, aiming to fire, wanting it dead so badly for scanning me, that he is willing to alert any creature in the forest.

"Wait! I need to see inside," August says and pries the commander away from it, and he reluctantly lowers his gun.

The commander checks on me with a long look over his shoulder to my position on the forest floor. He scans down and back up my body in a slow, obvious movement of his head, shoulders still heaving in large breaths.

August pulls the misshapen face down to access something on the back. "It's pretty deteriorated back here, not suited for this climate. What a piece of junk," he says, slamming the head back into the tree.

"Why is it here?" the commander asks.

"I don't know for sure, collecting information maybe. There is no signet or identification. Looks like the information doesn't store, just gets pinged back instantly to whoever . . . or whatever. But it's old and been here a long time. Whoever sent it probably knows the signal has gone cold and moved on," August says as he inspects its body.

"First Son?" the commander asks.

"Maybe, or at least one of his followers, but again, not recently."

The commander glances down at me on the ground again, looking me over like he didn't just push me. I know I look ridiculous.

I crawled backwards to get away from the violence and then froze in that position when August started opening that thing's head. He slings his weapon over his shoulder then reaches out to me. I take his hand with a slap, and he pulls me up in one swoop to my feet. I press hard against his solid chest for a moment too long, staring at him and waiting for some kind of acknowledgement that I was thrown.

"Well?" I say, stepping back from his proximity and throwing my palms up with wide, expectant eyes for an apology.

"You're safe. It won't hurt you," he tries to reassure.

"Commander . . ." I give him a confused, knitted brow.

"I will not apologize for keeping you safe," he says like an announcement.

Then August audibly laughs and smacks the commander's chest, like he finds the hardheaded way the commander interacts with me amusing.

I lay my jacket on the ground and hold my bag close to me for some warmth. It's freezing now that we have stopped moving. I wish I had a heated rock to sleep next to again.

I feel movement behind me, hear shuffling, like someone is getting comfortable, and see armor out of the corner of my vision.

"What are you doing!" I say, looking over my shoulder.

"The temperature will continue to drop. It's safer if we conserve heat." He adjusts his massive shoulders to relax on his back.

"I think I will be fine, find another spot."

"You could be dead by morning."

Then he flings a scratchy blanket over himself, extending it to my side. It's admittedly warmer the moment he does but hard to enjoy when the person providing the heat is so enraging. I exhale dramatically and adjust the blanket, pulling it a little to reach down my stomach.

"Did you need to go pray? Is that why you left?" His voice is muffled and hesitant.

"I left because you were being insufferable . . . again."

He stills completely behind me, close but not quite touching, and the blanket tugs slightly at my side with each large breath he takes.

August leans against a trunk a few trees in front of us—too far to hear our hushed voices, so I can't risk raising mine to ask how he is feeling. He seems better but keeps touching his arm, like the numbness has fully left it and he can feel what I did.

"Did I harm you?" the commander says low and breathy.

"No."

"I apologize."

"For what exactly?"

"Again, I won't apologize for keeping you—anyone in our party—safe. But I am sorry I was . . . rough with you."

Rough with me? Why does the way he phrases that make me suddenly aware of how close we are? But I can tell it was a painful and unmeaning apology. He can keep it. If he wasn't so warm, I would be far away from him.

I take a long, dramatic breath to calm myself down. If I grow too angry, I will say something awful, he will leave, and I will freeze to death. I look out at the spot where the metal human sits, and I can still see a sliver of it. It's such an odd place for it to be, as if it chose to rest there when it knew it was about to die.

"Why do you think it rested against that tree like that? It looks so human."

"I'm more worried about the spears in it. Means we are close. And not welcome," he answers, knowing exactly what I'm referring to.

"Yeah, you should leave your beloved guns—"

"Do you want to talk to August?" he asks abruptly.

"No. Why? Am I bothering you?" I duck my chin into the warm blanket.

"You just seem comfortable with him. I can ask him to trade off with me."

"August is easy to get along with. But no, it's too cold to be switching around."

I feel him scoot closer to me as soon as I say it. His side presses against my back, his hip against the back of my thighs. I go rigid until he settles again. My eyes must be wide because August silently laughs a little as he glances at us, shaking his head. It's awkward and not ideal, but I can't deny the heat radiating off him.

Mother's womb, I need to stop thinking about how warm he is under the blanket with me. My skin prickles and I realize I can't blame it on the brisk night anymore now that the commander has made a heated cocoon for us to snuggle in.

"He calls you 99. That's his nickname for you? Or does everyone call you by that?" I ask, trying to distract myself from the way my body is responding to his.

It's clear they are close. He has mentioned knowing August for a long time. For all that he is terrible to me, it does seem like he has a soft spot for August. I noticed him calling the commander *99* when he was scared, and before when the conversation was more casual on the ship, something that made their closeness more evident. The first break I got from the commander's disdain was when he thanked me for saving August. What he said after was rude, but I could tell he was sincere by his tone of voice. He couldn't hide the affection for his friend even behind the thick helmet.

"I suppose he calls me that because I'm our world's 99th

Commander. My predecessor was the 98th."

"Hm, just shy of 100. Commander 100 . . . legendary. Commander 99 . . . not as memorable," I tease.

The small laugh I can hear has me wondering if he smiled with it and what that would look like without his mask on.

"Do you have a real name?"

"Yes, but it is not used anymore," he says in a sleepy sigh.

"Well, can I call you something else? 99th Commander is a mouthful," I ask and stop short, realizing what I've said. "You know what I mean. Shouting at you becomes exhausting with such a long name."

"You may shorten my name if it helps with your shouting." His tone has a hint of amusement that has me relaxing back into him.

I grit my teeth at the casual conversation. He has given me permission to use a shortened version of his title, but I don't know what that means. I'm convinced he purposefully leaves an air of mystery in his answers to watch me squirm. Even if I do use his nickname, it won't be the same way August does. It will be to get under his skin at the perfect moment. To really piss him off when he is being insufferable again. Asking him questions is merely a curiosity, like opening a forbidden book. Like I'm waiting to report it to an elder priestess once I've flipped through the blasphemous illustrations and notes, had the thrill of peeking inside.

"How long have you been a commander?"

I expect him to get frustrated and speak in his deep, serious voice, but he replies naturally, like it's no trouble answering my odd questions.

"A very long time," he says, the tone a little brighter. "How long have you been a priestess?"

I let out a large exhale. "Also a very long time."

"Do you truly not know what the green light was?"

I stare out into the black forest, only a few tree outlines visible from the moonlight. I feel a stab of defensiveness that I can't push away. The redirection back to this makes me almost regret opening up. I am sick of repeating and defending who I am, of trying to explain something I'm not sure how or why it happened. The thought makes me want to pretend it didn't at all, similar to the feeling I get when I've accidentally used my gift and heard something I'm not supposed to.

"I only have the gift of mind's eye. I was just following instructions. Mary believed it would complicate our journey." I crane my neck over my shoulder. "How many times should I tell you? I agreed to come here to win the favor of First Mother . . . by assisting Mary. Do you need to check if I am lying? Your helmet seems to be working better tonight."

He turns his head toward me, letting out a long exhale, and I feel a little kiss of satisfaction that I've annoyed him. But it does seem like he is coming around to the idea that I am not a threat, that I am telling the truth. As agonizingly slow as is to gain his trust, I think I have chipped away a small crack.

⚶

A strange dragging sound pulls me from my anxious sleep. The forest has gone utterly silent except for the slow commotion out in the darkness.

The commander is fully pressed against me, lying on his side. The dropping temperature must have made him migrate closer in his sleep. It's not terribly uncomfortable, but it's strictly for survival. I can hear his steady breaths behind me, muffled through his helmet. My nose is freezing but my back, butt, and legs are engulfed by his warmth. I inch closer to get more slack on the blanket, hoping to move enough up to cover my nose.

I scoot a hip toward him.

The moment my butt rubs against his lower half, his breathing hitches. Then he lets out a throaty exhale, which makes me halt any movement, staying perfectly still from embarrassment. I am not sure what part of him I am touching but it's rock solid against me so I can only guess the reason for his reaction. The thought of him becoming aroused in his sleep from my touch has me suddenly overheating.

But then I hear the rustling sound again out in the forest. It's not August. He is still in the same spot at the base of a trunk, alert but not moving. He's looking off at something too. When I follow his eye line, I see a light dimly in the distance just as the rustling starts again. A dragging, almost pulling sound across the moss and seems like it's getting closer.

I move my hand back behind me to shake the commander awake.

"I see it. Stay still," he whispers.

Oh, he is already awake. Which means the breathy groan that came out on his exhale wasn't quite a subconscious response to my body against him like I thought. I have to fight the urge to try and elicit that sound again.

August slowly draws his gun up, then he looks over at us like he is waiting for orders.

The commander takes his arm out of the blanket behind me and makes a downward motion right over my hip.

August lowers his weapon in response.

A light dances in slow loops as the dragging sound starts again. For a moment, I think it's the mimicking orbs, but then I can see the light is attached to the outline of a large creature. Then a hairy animal that looks like a pig walks into the circle of illuminated light, oblivious to what it is attached to.

The commander rests his hand on my hip, waiting to give August more instruction. It's heavy on me, the feel of it weighing me down strangely grounding as I watch the ghostly light in the forest. I never knew I could be petrified and utterly turn on at the same time.

The hairy animal licks its teeth and follows the orb as it cascades back and forth. When the animal almost loses interest for a moment, the light dances in front of its face. It's teasing it, enticing it to follow. The light shines slowly on the larger creature's long, pointy teeth. It's getting the hairy pig to come right to its mouth, using the darkness to hide the true size, but I can tell it's big enough that its mouth could swallow me whole.

My terrified breathing must be too loud because I can feel the commander grip the soft layer of my hip, reminding me to be silent.

The animal is fixated on the orb, not noticing the perfectly still needle-toothed thing it's attached to. The giant black pupils the size of dinner plates roll back, and with a high-pitched yelp, the prey is consumed entirely. I jump but the commander's strong hand presses me down, steadying me. The monster turns and drags itself deeper into the forest, the glowing hue around it fading.

The commander releases his grip and adjusts himself under the blanket again. I pull it up over my nose and I'm hit with the smell of him. The scent is like sandalwood but earthier, with just a hint of smoke from our previous camp. Without thinking, I breathe it in again, remembering it from the day I ran into his chest in the dark hallway of the ship. I smelled it then and liked it but was too afraid to fully acknowledge that.

I feel him scoot away to give me space, but it's too cold not to be pressed up against each other. I must be delirious from waking up so abruptly because the only part of my body not freezing is currently throbbing between my legs. I can't stop thinking about the way his breath hitched when I brushed against his pelvis. I wonder if that is why he has decided to suddenly respect my space. He did warn me I could be dead by morning, so I lean back needing to feel his body heat . . . for survival.

His body tenses. "It is almost dawn, Priestess. It will be warmer soon," he whispers.

"Yes, but it is currently still freezing."

"It is." He relaxes and leans his body into mine again.

I feel warm and safe with him close to me like this. I pull the blanket up one last time and breathe in his scent and press back farther, making sure every part of me is touching him.

CHAPTER FIFTEEN

I've never seen illustrations or read anything about the creatures we saw last night, any of them. I'm completely unprepared. It's unlikely we will survive another night in the moss layer. I chew on the last of my sugar bread, glancing over at the metal human. How stupid I was to approach it. I freaked out when August showed me how to use the washroom buttons. Why did I think it was ok to investigate something I know is against First Mother? I can't even bear to think how disappointed she must be in me right now—intrigued by a First Son creation and snuggling up to a Viathan. I told myself before I fell asleep last night that I was too distracted by outside things to pray, but really, I didn't even try. Instead, I chose to chat with a commander who comes into my space anytime he gets the chance. Even he noticed I needed to pray, which thinking about even now enrages me.

I press my back hard against the tree, seeking out the same sensation of his chest against me. I shake my head to dispel the thought. He's a Viathan; he killed someone in front of me. I rub the spot where he gripped my hip, thinking of how grounding and safe it felt.

It's been silent for too long, so I stand and dust the crumbs from my lap. Even the trees aren't rustling anymore. I look around and see both August and the commander looking into the denser part of the forest.

"August, we need to clean your wounds before we leave."

Neither of them turns to face me, or even move out of their alert stances.

Something is . . . off.

The commander clicks a metal-sounding button on his gun and in unison, they both square to whatever it is they see in the forest, guns raised and ready.

"What is it?" I whisper.

"It's them," August says.

Them? We have seen so many horrors in our trip up the mountain, I have almost forgotten the inevitable hostile meeting with the Frithian people if they found us first.

"Put your guns down, both of you," I say, starting to panic.

"They have spears and knives," the commander explains.

"Of course they do. We are in their forest with guns. So put them down . . . please!"

I strain to look around the Viathans. Nothing is visible, no sound comes out of the trees, but they are both fixed in a specific area just past where the tree line meets the plateau, where the forest grows dense and haunting.

"They will never trust us if we do not show good faith first. It has to be us who submits. We are the unwelcome ones. Please, both of you! Put them down," I say with gritted teeth.

Their stances build in intensity as they aim for the forest. I can feel the tension rising as each moment ticks by.

"Please, please trust me."

The commander is the first to withdraw the defensive posture, then he slowly places the large gun on the ground. He opens his arms in a peaceful gesture and August follows.

People seem to come out of thin air, springing into action from behind trees: men and women dressed in dark, similar colors, their clothes an eclectic mix. Some even look like they were made on Cosima. They all look different too, a blend of all regions of the three worlds, varying in complexion and hair color. I notice an older man so pale, with milky eyes that seem translucent. I make sure to hold my hands up in submission and slowly walk to the sides of my travel companions. The line of people in the front slowly steps forward, spears and knives in hand, solely focused on the Viathans.

"Where is the bulb?" I whisper discreetly to them.

"In my pack," August answers with the side of his mouth.

I slowly move to unlatch the bag, digging through it.

"Hurry up," the commander grits out.

A tall woman flicks her gaze to me and then to the commander. She moves up on him, her spear inches from his throat, and is followed by a red-haired man. He slides closer and points the blade of his large knife at August.

"Wait! Ok, just wait, please!" I say, withdrawing the bulb.

I duck under the spear aimed at the commander's neck, presenting the bulb to them while throwing my free arm across August's stomach. I attempt the greeting in their language, but they look at me like I'm a mad woman as it comes out with a stammer and all out of order.

"Please, put these down, just wait!"

I speak right to the red-haired man. He is closer, the others a long spear distance away. I use their word for *injured* and point to August's arm, hoping he won't seem as much of a threat. But they do not give in; they do not back off.

The woman won't take her eyes off the commander while I speak.

I wish I had another arm to cover the spot she could so easily plunge into. He is close enough that I can lean my body over him slightly, a poor excuse for a shield.

"Priestess, please get behind me." His whisper is strained.

I ignore his almost pleading request. The Frithians aren't looking at me with the same angry expressions. I have the urge to pull August and the commander close behind me and drag my body over them in protection.

The commander is so calm and steady as I bang into him, shielding them in a desperate panic for peace. We all know it is escalating with every passing second no matter how docile the Viathans are trying to be with their raised palms. I'm panting and begging for them to just pause a moment, but no one is even acknowledging me.

Then, a tall, slim man emerges from the forest, and the others part for him.

He must be the leader of this group. He is the one I need to talk to, the one who should accept the bulb. I duck back under the spear in front of the commander, none of them moving theirs to point at me as I approach the tall man. I take a deep breath and recite the speech I have practiced to greet them and tell them we mean them no harm.

With a shaky voice, I butcher it and get down on my knees, bowing my head, raising the bulb up to present it to him. A symbol of peace and humility. I feel him take it from my hands and the other people shift a little closer in the direction of the commander, like he moved.

Their leader examines the bulb and smiles.

"You know our language." He doesn't speak it back to me. His accent is thick when he uses the common tongue instead.

"I do," I say as I stand.

He looks me over. "You are from Cosima, but your friends are not."

"They are not, but they *are* friends."

He does not look at me with the same agitation in his eyes as he does for the Viathans behind me. It's a small sliver of hope that I am able to communicate with him, that he is willing to listen to one of us.

"They bring modern weapons into our forest."

"Only for protection against those who wish to harm us."

"If you are respectful, her creatures will not harm you," he says with a smile.

He assumes I mean the animals in the forest, but the commander said the guns were mostly for protection against First Son. They do not know he is after the stones yet, which means we are not too late.

I hear August scoff, and when I look behind me, the commander tilts his helmet slowly toward August in disapproval.

The leader walks over to August, looking him up and down, lingering on his wounded arm. "You took something that does not belong to you. I'm sure she wants *you* dead," he says and rolls the bulb around in his hands.

"It was meant to be a gift. We only took it with that intention. We meant no disrespect," I say now, facing my companions still being held in place by the others.

"A gift, no, a tradition, yes. A willingness to anger the forest in order to show peace with the people. How do you know of such traditions?" He circles me.

"Books . . . from Cosima's library. I'm a translator of old books."

"Can you write better than you speak?"

I can feel the commander's eyes on me as the tall man who looks like a warrior circles me again. The intensity coming from him is so thick. Another person comes to stand next to the commander with a spear, like they believe he will lash out at any second.

"I have never had the chance to speak it until now, only translate the written words, so I apologize for my . . . mispronunciation. I could much easily write you a letter," I say, trying to break some of the tension as he circles me closer.

He stops at my shoulder, examining the side of my face, then chuckles. Some of the others smirk but keep their weapons pointed.

I notice more Frithians have moved to guard the commander, like they are afraid he is more of a threat as the tall man closes in on me. I give him a pleading look with a small shake of my head, hoping it conveys for him to not do anything crazy.

"And why have you come, translator of words?"

"We need to speak to your elders. Will you grant us safe passage? It is a matter of the great conjunction."

He holds up his hand for me to stop speaking. "Only speak it if it is a matter of the hunt. I am no elder. I accept your offering for passage. That is all," he says more seriously than he has before.

Two Frithians retrieve the guns from the mossy ground, holding them awkwardly. The commander and August are then searched for more.

The tall man invades my space again, patting the pockets of my jacket, and I let out a startled gasp at the quick contact.

"I have no weapons," I tell him.

He nods then pats the pockets at my hips, and my eyes flick up to the Viathans. My face must look horrified because the commander's calm, frozen form finally falters. He grabs a spear from the person closest and snaps it over his knee like a twig. The cracking sound makes every Frithian with a knife engage in his direction. I feel my body lunge slightly toward them. This entire deal might be off now, but thankfully, the tall man holds up a hand. His people stop and even take a few steps back.

The commander makes no other move, just raises his hands in

submission again as if to say he could take them all but won't.

The tall man slowly runs a hand over my back pockets. "Is he going to be a problem?" he says over my shoulder.

"No," I say firmly.

He calls out to the others, phrases I've never heard before. I'm not even sure it's a known language. They finally take their weapons off of the Viathans. The three of us are herded into a group, pushed along by the warriors on all sides. We follow the party into the forest, weaving through giant trees, directed by the weapons at our backs.

The incline of the mountain levels out as we hike. The mossy ground is less dense, more grass growing between patches. Eventually, we are on regular ground like when we first entered the forest—ferns, twigs, and leafy debris.

August leans in close to whisper. "Are we to assume the gift didn't go as planned? It seems we have been granted passage as their prisoners."

"There's a kill being carried. They stumbled upon us in their hunting grounds. You did well," the commander says, looking down at me.

"I think the bulb stopped them from at least killing us right away," I whisper through my teeth and ignore the little flutter in my stomach in response to his words.

The plateaus are smaller and more frequent the higher we walk. The hunting party slows then spreads out in different directions as we reach a clearing with little trails of smoke climbing into the air. This must be their village. We breach the tree line right into a full community of families and children. It looks very normal compared to the interaction we had with them in the forest.

People stand in their doorways to watch us walk past. There are dozens of small houses, some made of stones with thatched roofs.

Others seem more temporary, made of cloth for a single person. The structures are clustered in groups, angled to face a fire in the center. Everyone looks different, like they were scattered across the three worlds and ended up here, on top of this mountain. I notice more people wearing clothing similar to Cosima's fashion, but older styles than ones worn currently, like they left long ago. We are marched to the center of the village where larger homes cut into the blue sky with their roofs.

The tall man and a few left over Frithians still guarding push us to enter into a building with a flap for a door. They point for us to sit around a fire, a floor hearth with rocks surrounding it, then slam the commander down by his shoulders into a chair. He groans and exhales all the air in his lungs, and I can tell it is taking every ounce of him to keep holding back. By size alone, he could easily overpower them.

The room is open, like a large courtyard, and the space above has a hole in the center for smoke to drift up. There are wooden seats all around the fire, like people gather here. The doors in the back appear to lead to private quarters or other rooms similar to the Estate's temple.

A woman with long white hair catches my eye as she tinkers toward the back in what looks like a small kitchen. The tall man hands the older woman the bulb then scowls at the commander as he exits with his hunting companions.

"Someone has made the forest very angry," the white-haired woman says, examining the bulb in her hands. She smiles then drops it in the boiling pot over the fire in front of us.

"Yeah, you didn't tell me a whole forest would be angry at me for taking it," August whispers, leaning in from the seat next to me.

"I did not know. It didn't say that in the journal," I whisper back.

"Well, maybe make a note in the margins," he spits out through his teeth.

The old woman stirs the bobbing bulb and looks up at us through the steam. "We will help you apologize to the forest later. Give her some time to cool down," she says.

I notice her robe. It's clearly a temple gown a high priestess would wear, but it's been modified and well worn. This woman is not an elder of Frith, so why were we brought to her instead?

"I am Selene," she says, adding tiny leaves to the boiling water.

I introduce myself first, then August, but the commander stays silent.

"They tell me you travel through with modern weaponry. Hmmm, to risk offense on a year of the great conjunction and with such a medley of a group—"

The commander straightens in his seat on the other side of me, inhaling to speak, but is cut off.

"Must we speak through plated glass and metal?" Selene says, waving a hand up at his helmet.

"I am Viathan's 99th Commander. We believe First Son is planning—"

"First Son . . . and you've come for your stone? But not *just* yours," she says, stirring lazily.

Selene's eyes are on me now, examining my face, my expression. "I am Mother blessed, or divine as you call it on Cosima. I have the gift of intention sight. I knew each of your intentions the moment you took your first step on the grass. The roots are connected in a network, branches reaching out as you brush by, reading your motivations miles away. The leaves whisper to me of your true intentions."

I hear the commander take an exasperated exhale. Selene speaks in long flowery words, and it must be killing him. It's almost too much even for me.

He tries to speak again but is cut off once more.

"One goal. But each with a very different reason to achieve it. All valid, all strong. Should I tell you what I know of yours, 99th Commander?" she asks.

He sits back in his chair. She is pushing his buttons, pulling rank like the high priestesses do when they think I have spoken out of turn. It's fascinating to watch.

"You have come for your stone, but I'm afraid it is not in our direct possession. It was protecting our stone so well that we put Viathan's stone with it to guard," she says.

"It . . . as in the forest?" August says, his voice panicked.

"It . . . as in the Albright."

What book have I read that word in? Is it a place on Frith?

No.

I suddenly remember and feel a deep terror-stricken pit in my gut. The Albright isn't in any book on Frith, no field guide, no terrain study. It's in the ancient text about the war—an old god, one of First Mother's earliest children. A creature that lived on her moon with her, called down to help with the war.

"The Albright has the stones?" I whisper.

Selene nods with an odd smile.

I can feel August staring at the side of my face, trying to gauge the tone of my voice, itching to ask what the Albright is. All of them seem to be looking at me now, waiting for me. But all I can think of is the oil painting in the Estate's grand hall of the war with First Son. I've passed it a million times, even admired it. Never did I think I would see one of the creatures depicted in it. The haunting portion of the giant painting with the Albright is almost too shocking, so the surrounding curtains are always fluffed by handmaids to cover the section it is painted in.

"We believe the stones will be safer guarded in the Estate," the commander says, snapping me out of my horror-stricken thoughts.

They are waiting for me to step in as Cosima's representative, but I can't find any official words. I haven't put in any thought or planning past getting through the forest alive. The commander can see me drowning and is filling in where I should, but I am Mary's substitute, not him.

Selene ladles some of the simmering liquid into bowls. "On this, we agree. The Estate's protection wards are very effective against First Son . . . so far."

I clear my throat, letting it be known I will speak. What words I will use, I'm not sure. "Forgive me, Cosima's original representative Mary has perished in our journey," I say without thinking, my words exposed and tone more vulnerable than an official representative should be.

"I knew Mary well. Our elders were fond of her. I am sorry to hear such news."

"Thank you. If Mary were here, her words would be more articulate than mine. She was dedicated to upholding Frith's traditions on the journey. Her intention was to ask permission from your elders to bring *both* stones to the Estate."

Selene smiles like I have said something clever then hands me and August full bowls, and then she holds out another one to the commander, making him lean forward to take it.

"You are free to retrieve your stone from the Albright, just like you can try to eat my soup through that helmet, 99th Commander."

Selene walks to the back of the room where the small kitchen is.

"Take it off, don't be rude," I whisper to him, taking my frustration out for speaking of the Estate before I got a chance.

"Yea, drink the dirty bulb water like the rest of us," August says as he forces another spoonful.

"What is an Albright," the commander whispers to me.

"It's . . . not good."

Selene returns and ladles herself a portion. We sit and eat in silence. Well, three of us do. The soup is earthy and bland at the same time. If Mary were here, she would be commanding this entire interaction, not having to dance around Selene's ever weaving words. Then again, if Mary were here, we may have been taken right to the Frithian elders.

"Will we have Frith's blessing to retrieve both stones from the Albright?" I say, trying to break the silence.

"Many have tried to take the stones, but you are the first in a long time to ask permission."

The commander leans in. "Many?"

"With increasing frequency," she says.

"Who?"

I shove another spoonful in my mouth to cover a huff. Both parties are throwing the conversation everywhere but the direction I am meant to take it.

"I know not of who, only of intentions. Some I cannot even read at all. They have no human motivation, only programmed goals. It's like trying to read a familiar book in the dark—you know of the story, but what does it mean today?"

Mother's womb, please save me from this woman's ramblings.

Selene smiles at me then sips at her soup. She is slow and graceful, in no hurry to give us information. I can feel the tension building, a slower, more painful escalation than the hunting party but just as suffocating.

"As for a blessing to take Frith's stone, I will ask the elders on your behalf. They will be saddened to hear of Mary."

"You're not an elder?" August says with a confused, knitted brow. They do not know she is from the Estate. Only another temple member would notice the repurposed priestess robe.

"I am no Frithian. I am from Cosima, something Ferren noticed of me right away," she says with another slow smile.

I suddenly feel exposed.

"You will join us for dinner tonight. I will have Rouke show you to your tent," she says with a wave of her hand for us to stand with her.

"Oh, and Priestess? If you need to pray tonight, the far side of the village is the most private, just take an escort. Some of the villagers are funny about your religion."

I whip my head back when she calls out to me, feeling myself going pale. She knows what I am. Is she warning me or was that a threat?

We are escorted to the door by the same men who brought us in. I can't help but notice Selene said *your religion* not *ours*. She is from the Estate and admitted it, so what is a high priestess doing on Frith? And why does she hold enough weight with their elders that she can speak to them on our behalf?

CHAPTER SIXTEEN

T he building they take us to is made of canvas and close to Selene's. It's spacious with a fire pit in the middle. Cots line the outer walls, able to house at least eight people comfortably, with some curtained off areas in the back. It looks like a temporary structure, every home around it made of brick.

I claim a bed off to the left by lying flat on the stiff mattress and letting out an exaggerated sigh. It's not great but it's better than the forest ground. I prop myself up on my elbows, watching August pick a cot a few down from me, one closer to the entrance. The commander's selection is directly across the fire from me.

Rouke stands in the doorway, watching us like he is memorizing, as he gestures to some of his men to bring our items they confiscated in our camp. They place them in a pile in the middle of the open room. I notice Rouke's eyes go from my breasts to my face in an obvious scan.

The commander rises from his cot with a creak, squaring his much larger body to Rouke as he walks toward him. Maybe he noticed, too, from the way they face each other for just a moment, but then the commander pulls the tied back flap of the door, shutting it in Rouke's face. He picks up my bag first then sets it on the foot of my cot.

"Thank you."

He nods and returns to his bed across from me.

August sits on the foot of my mattress and leans in. "How did she know you're a priestess?"

"I'm not sure," I say, checking the contents of my bag.

"Do you know each other from the Estate?" he asks.

"What? No, of course not. I've never heard of a Selene. I didn't even know people from Cosima lived here to be honest. But I noticed a lot of them when we walked into the village. Maybe that's a new thing. My books are somewhat dated," I say.

"Somewhat dated! That also would have been nice to know," he says, standing.

I don't blame him for being upset about the implications about taking the bulb. I should have known.

August is pacing next to me, but I can only focus my eyes across the fire. The commander removes his gloves slowly, revealing his strong hands. I watch him flex them and crack his knuckles. His posture is relaxed and comfortable. I try to disguise my staring with fixing my braid. It's loose and needs to be redone.

The commander tugs on the collar of his shirt, moving the armor placed there to the side. I almost pull a strand of my own hair out when I figure out what he is doing, why he is moving so slowly. He is about to remove his helmet.

August says something else in a frazzled tone but I miss it completely. I watch him pace from my bed to his, pointing his fingers in the air like he is trying to calculate something.

When I look back at the commander across the glowing fire between us, my heart palpitates out of sync. He runs a hand through his hair, looking right at me with dark-blue piercing eyes entirely unobscured by his mask. I have to force myself to close my gaping jaw.

His eyes flick to me again and then away, like I've made him uncomfortable. I know I am staring but I can't peel myself away from examining his face. I was only able to see pieces of it before, the side of his jaw or the hint of his features blotted out by darkness. I haven't seen any part of his face without a helmet in days. I forgot how handsome those pieces might be, but altogether sitting across a fire, he is gorgeous. I knew he had a short beard and his hair was dark brown and somewhat long. But now, I can see his furrowed brow creased in the middle from all the scowling he probably does, his strong nose, and haunting eyes. He runs his fingers through his wavy hair then places his elbows on his knees. He is almost glaring at me, staring through hooded lids.

Mother's womb, what am I thinking? Stop looking at a fucking Viathan like that.

I stand up in a huff.

"Maybe if you two didn't cuff me like a prisoner and parade me around the forest talking about what a liar I am, she would have no clue!" I lash out, needing to release my flustered thoughts somehow.

August shoots me a shocked look as I cross my arms.

"This may complicate things with their elders," the commander says. His voice is clear and crisp, the base and breathiness of it still there, but it's not cloaked in a layer of metal.

"And how dare you blame me!" August ignores the commander, pointing right at me.

"Well, it wasn't him! It's near impossible to get him to speak most times and you—you can't seem to stop! Whispering and huffing ever since we came in contact with the people of Frith."

"I am being attacked at all fronts by an *entire* forest, Ferren! I am allowed to huff!"

"Well, you must have slipped."

"When would I have the time? Between being held at spear point and then made to drink weird soup water, I haven't had a chance to let Selene know you are secretly a priestess. Nope, sorry!"

"She reads intentions," the commander says, making us both look over at him in unison. "She said the moment we stepped onto the grass, she knew and figured it out based on that."

August pushes off one of the beams holding up the center of the ceiling, turning his back to me. He looks so upset and . . . hurt. How could I blame him for that, lash out at him like he hasn't been the closest thing to an ally since I stepped on his ship? Of course it was Selene. She told us upfront she knew our intentions. Her flowery language wasn't direct but that part was. Her gifts gave her the answer, not August.

There is a soft knock at the front, making the three of us straighten, on high alert looking at each other like one of us somehow knows who it is. The commander is at the door with his helmet back on within seconds, opening the flap roughly.

A young woman greets him with a smile. She has beautiful golden skin, almost glimmering on her high cheekbones. Her hair is dark and tightly curled, pulled back at the base of her head, but small wispy coils frame her face. She looks at me with a bright, friendly smile, and I can't help but smile back.

"Hello, I am Calliape."

"What is it?" the commander says, the only one seeming to be unphased by her ethereal presents.

"Hello!" August says, perking up from his sulk.

"You must be August and the 99th Commander. It's really nice to meet you, and you too, Ferren. My aunt . . . Selene asked me to show you the watering hole to wash your clothes if you like. There is a washroom in the back, but you have to haul water in buckets to be heated up."

I step next to the commander, drawn by the welcoming tone of her voice and the halo that radiates around her from the bright sun.

"That would be wonderful, Calliape. Thank you," I say, smiling a little too hard.

The path to the watering hole is mostly dirt, like it's been used too many times for the grass to grow, which is high and almost hip height on either side. The flora changed the moment we stepped out of the moss layer with Rouke's hunting party. The poisonous ferns and haunted trees have been traded for lush peaceful ones and grass like the field we first landed on.

Calliape offered to carry my bucket and clothes but I refused. She is much kinder than the others we have met so far and even seems excited to see us. Her clothes are similar to mine: tight, dark canvas leggings with layers as a top. Some of the other women and Selene wear long dresses or flowy gauze pants. I struggle to keep up with her long strides. She is tall and slim like one of the beautiful statues in the Estate.

The watering hole comes into view, down a small hill on the next plateau. The giant trees all around make it hard to see how high we are up the mountain.

"You are a priestess from the Estate," Calliape says.

"Oh . . . I am, yes." I say nervously.

"I would be too if I lived on Cosima."

"Are you divine?" I ask, glancing back at August and the commander behind us, both pretending not to listen to our conversation.

"Mother blessed."

"Oh, then yes, you would be a priestess too," I say. I want to talk more about familiar things with her, but I'm still cautious. Mary said the people here are not fond of the current highest priestess and refused to go into detail when I asked. Calliape is gracious but she is still a stranger.

"Do you live in a temple?" she asks.

"No, not *in* it."

"I would love to see one. We don't have any. The forest is our temple, the way First Mother intended."

I press my lips together tightly and cast my eyes to my feet. Calliape is really nice and so welcoming, but I'm afraid if she asks too many questions about me and the temple, she will realize she doesn't want to be welcoming after all.

"I'm sorry. I didn't mean—" Calliape says.

"No, no, it's fine. And you're right. I've read some very old book testaments about that actually: the way the original people worshiped before. I guess we have just become much more formal in the Estate."

"To be honest, I used to dream about visiting Cosima when I was a child—still do. Formal is good sometimes," she says, putting any worry of judgment out of my mind.

Small groups of families wring out laundry and watch children play in the water as we reach it. There are large rocks and sandy areas that open up to the pond. Tiny micro waterfalls run into it from giant boulders on the far side.

Calliape lets us know we are welcome here and to use the path back when we are finished. She hugs me goodbye to my pleasant surprise and I notice the deep blush in her cheeks when August makes sure to address her directly as she leaves.

I pull out my extra clothes and the jacket I've been sleeping on. It's going to be awful carrying a full bucket and waterlogged clothes back up the dirt path no matter how small of an incline it is. I've had enough walking to last me a lifetime.

August strips off his shirt, revealing his lean frame, as he walks closer to the shallow water.

"You shouldn't swim, not until their healer looks at your wounds," I call out.

He gives me a scowl and turns his back to me again. He's still mad. Of course he is. I blamed him for something that couldn't have been prevented.

"August, can I speak with you?" I say, slowly walking up to his side.

He lifts his chin and looks off to the treetops below the flat plateau that make a faux horizon.

"I'm really sorry—" I start.

He turns toward me quickly, making me step back, eyes a little glossy. "I fucked up with Vickers. Me and 99, we both did. And we owe you an apology for how that was handled afterward. I am sorry. I want you to know I would never purposefully put you in danger here. Do you think of me so poorly?"

I stammer, trying to form my thoughts. I was not expecting him to say sorry to me, at least not right now. Something between us has broken, the easy friendship we started now messy and complicated with outside events. He watches me, waiting for an answer, and then looks out onto the landscape again in disappointment when I can't find words. August doesn't deserve my accusations. His heart is so big, even mad he is apologizing for his part in cuffing me.

I shoot a pleading look to the commander, who sits on a large rock that meets the water as he wrings out a dark tunic that matches the one he wears under his armor plates. I open my palms in a plea for advice.

"I would never do something to put you at risk, Ferren. I thought we were friends. Leave putting the mission in jeopardy aside. I thought we were . . ." His voice cracks.

The commander is at August's side without any noise of his approach. He grips his shoulder in an unexpected comfort, while my heart breaks in my chest across from them.

"She does not think poorly of you. You were following *my* orders."

Helpful.

I let out a frustrated huff, but August's expression is less harsh, his posture relaxed at the commander's bluntly honest words—a reminder that he is to blame, not August. That if anyone fucked up, its him. That if anyone should think poorly of someone, it should be him. It's not an apology from the commander, but the acknowledgment does make me a little less bitter.

I catch just a glimpse into August's mind's eye and see flashing images of him fighting with all his sisters and then embracing them. There's such love and deep, bottomless emotions, no walls of status between their friendship, nothing holding their love at arm's length.

"I'm so sorry. I wanted it to be for any other reason than—" My eyes flick to the commander. The apology is for August alone, but I have both of their attention. I chew on my lip, the vulnerability making me want to bite it off. "Any other reason than I failed again, but that wasn't fair."

His expression softens with a large breath, like he is coming to terms.

"I messed up, August. I haven't had a lot of practice . . . with friendships," I say, a little embarrassed, and bow my head. "But that's not an excuse. I am just so sorry."

After a moment that seems to go on for eternity, I am jolted by a smack on my shoulder. "Priestess, did you ever think you would have a Viathan pilot for a friend?" August says, gripping me with affection that same way I have noticed he does with the commander.

I can't stop beaming with watery lined eyes at his forgiveness. "I'm also sorry that you can't get your wounds wet."

"More bad news." August sniffles a little and pulls at his bandages. "Guess you will have to wash these for me, huh? You said it yourself; I am wounded." He kicks his loosely stuffed canvas bag with his boot.

The commander wordlessly snatches the bag of clothing and heads back to his washing station like he intends to do it himself even though August asked me.

"I bet your sisters did all your washing for you, didn't they?" I tease.

"Quite the opposite," he says with a laugh.

I empty my bag of clothes in the water and swoosh them around aimlessly. I look over at the commander's more vigorous method, one that looks like he should wash mine too. He has removed the armor plates that normally adorn his forearms and rolled up his sleeves. He wrings a piece of clothing out, twisting it hard, the cords in his arms flexing. His large hands wrap around August's shirts like they are for a child. He tilts his head up and notices me staring.

"Don't ask, I'm not doing yours too," he says.

"You look . . . ridiculous. You can take your helmet off. Calliape said we were welcome."

He slaps a shirt down on a rock next to me, spreading it out to dry.

"Why aren't these things bothering you guys?" August lounges in the sun behind us, swatting dramatically at a swarm of tiny gnats flying around only him.

The two children swimming in the water paddle themselves over to us. I say a greeting I have memorized and giggles are the only responses I get back. I must have butchered it. They swim to the shallows in front of us and stand. The water reaches their stomachs,

THE VIRIDIAN PRIESTESS

but I can see one is holding something.

"What do you have there?" I point at the girl's cupped hands.

She opens one, revealing a greenish-brown slimy-looking creature. She moves closer for the commander to see as well.

"Ferren, what is that? Tell them to take it away," August says, trying to sound calm.

"It's fine. It's like a frog-fish thing," I say over my shoulder.

"That changes nothing for me," he says with panic in his voice.

She holds it up in the air for August to see but it jumps out of her hands. She moves quickly, flicking water around to catch it again, making a large splash hit the commander in the visor of his helmet.

The children and I slowly look at each other in surprise, slack-jawed. I can't hold back my laughter when they start high-pitched giggling at him. I cover my mouth, trying to smother my laugh but it comes through fingers in a spit of air.

He runs his hand over the wet metal, trying to clear it, then turns toward me with a dirty water-speckled mask and I almost fall over laughing harder. Even the children, who looked a little nervous of him at first, can't contain themselves.

Their parents call out to them and they start swimming in that direction still giggling. The girl with the creature struggles to swim with one hand, still holding onto it.

The commander uses a dry tunic to wipe the visor clean.

I glance over at him, pressing my lips together to hide the last few snickers I have left.

He watches me, not seeming annoyed or angry like he normally does. It throws me a little off balance when I realize I know what he looks like behind his mask now. When he stares like this, I can picture his piercing eyes.

"Are they keeping it as a pet?" August says, snapping me out of my

169

memory of the commander across the fire with his helmet off.

"No, I think they will eat it," I say and dunk the next piece of clothing.

"Well, if that's what they are serving for dinner, I'll be heading back down the mountain tonight."

CHAPTER SEVENTEEN

The washroom is more of a curtained off area in the back with a brick floor than it is a room. It's awkward to undress when I can hear people walking by outside, just a thin wall away from unfamiliar voices of the villagers, the living quarters next to us just a narrow walkway distance. I hang the thin bathing robe I found on my cot, along with a beautiful long dress to wear to dinner and a sweet note with it.

For my new friend from a different world. -Calliape

I wish I had something to give her, something special from Cosima. August and I polished off even the crumbs of the sugar bread, and I don't think I can part with the stone Thea gave me. I touch the metal clip in my hair as I release it to fall down my sides. It's a plain, hammered metal piece and I know I have the matching one somewhere in my bag: a gift for her when we leave, maybe.

I lift the steaming bucket on the wooden bench in the corner and cringe at the cup used for scooping the water out. At least the soap is new, thank First Mother. The hot water feels amazing as I wet the crown of my head, but I would give anything to be completely submerged in the bath house in the Estate.

I hear someone enter our tent, recognizing the flapping noise of the door, and cover my chest as if I am not behind layers of canvas.

"It's me," the commander says.

"Ok . . . well, I'm not done yet. You will have to come back later!" I say, panicking.

"Take your time, I will wait here."

I can hear the creak of his cot like he is lying down in it. I clutch at my body, not having enough arms to cover it. I know he can't see me—there are several layers of cloth to walk through, hanging at different angles for privacy—but even moving water around brings attention to the fact that I'm bathing in the same room as him.

"I'm all the way on the other side of the tent. I can't be out there anymore. People were talking to me."

"First Mother forbid." I try to keep my splashing to a minimum and pour warm water down my front to chase away the prickle of my skin from hearing his voice.

"Where is August? Did you find him a healer?" I say loudly to drown out the sound of washing my hair.

"Yes, now he is talking with the red-haired man who pulled a knife on him."

"Oh, not Calliape?" I'm surprised. He's seemed all but consumed by her since she knocked on our tent to introduce herself.

"I'm sure she is next."

I use the bar of soap on my long hair. It's going to be impossible to rinse out at this rate, with just a small wooden cup to pour on the lather.

The commander exhales loudly into the silence.

"What?" I say without thinking, like I am inquiring about the troubles of a friend and not someone who is more guarded than anyone I've met.

"We are wasting a lot of time. I was hoping to retrieve the stones tonight and be on our way."

I've stopped moving again, a little in shock that he is talking to me so openly, almost like he does with August. I dump some of the warm water over my head, scrub at my hair, and do it again.

"This . . . is no waste of time. After the forest, I would make First Mother herself wait for me."

"I do not believe you," he says with a tiny hint of teasing in his tone.

I press my lips together to hide a smile even from myself. "Do you think their elders will give us permission to bring their stone back?"

"Can't say."

I feel a pull to mention our interaction with Selene. I would have done much better if I wasn't so distracted by her priestess robe or knowing she is from the Estate and not being able to figure out why she is here instead. I didn't prepare but I could have done much better, been more formal.

"Selene was difficult to speak to. I wasn't expecting . . . I will need to prepare to speak with their elders. I—" I say with multiple false starts, trying to articulate.

"You did fine, Priestess. We have asked a lot from you."

"Oh."

The small sliver of praise is a little too much while I am standing naked a few feet away from him. I quickly finish and wring out my hair and wrap the soft robe around me, then I stop short, right at the curtain. I am going to have to walk out in my robe where the commander is. I didn't think this through, but then again, I thought they would be gone for longer.

I listen at the curtain to hear where he is. His cot creaked a few moments ago but then it went silent. I peek out from my ridiculous hiding spot and see his armor, boots, and helmet neatly laid out on his bed.

A shadow obstructs my view. The commander stands in front of me, blotting out the light. I slowly step out of the curtain and grip the neckline of my robe to my throat, dirty clothes in my other hand protecting my chest. Even if I'm covered completely except my hands, feet, and face, it's still brisk in here and the robe is a little too thin.

"Where did you get that?" he says too close to me.

"It was on my bed from Calliape," I say, keeping my eyes on his chest. I can't look at him this close, not when I am like this.

But he doesn't hide the roaming of his gaze on me. While he does, I take in his face, rugged in a softly handsome way. I drift to his devastating jawline, to the strong muscles of his neck. Then his intense eyes climb back up my body and I know he can see my peaked nipples against the robe when his pupils dilate. My heart is thumping on my forearms where I'm clinging to my robe when his eyes reach mine.

The look he gives me sends a hot static over my skin. But I don't want him to just look at me, I want him to touch me, devour me with his large rough hands and feel how wet he makes me when he shamelessly gazes at my body. I'm suddenly struck with the thought that maybe this is how intently he has been staring at me behind his mask from the beginning. All those times his gaze was so intense and lingering that I had to look away. Now I know why.

He brushes past me, entering the curtain just behind. "Excuse me . . . Priestess." His voice whispers low and breathy into my ear, sending a pulse of heat right through me and concentrating between my thighs.

I turn and see he is barefoot and wearing his dark tunic and pants. It's the first time I've seen him without all the armor, and it adds no bulk like I thought it would. His back and shoulders are just as broad without it. The tunic around his biceps is a little tighter, and I can see the cords of muscles bulging through.

First Mother, give me strength.

I dash across the tent, trying to shake off whatever I just felt between us. I throw my clothes down and rip all the blankets and linens off the cots to either side of me, tying them together and flinging them over a support rope above. I finesse them around my bed until I've made a wall of blankets all around it. I demand privacy after the few nights in the forest, and I do not want to accidentally see anything while sharing a room with these two men. I'm not shy, the temple bathhouse is one giant pool, but I will have my privacy here.

With the linens making a small, walled-off cocoon around me, I feel a little more secure. I hold up the lovely dress with long sleeves Calliape left me. The silhouette is close to a temple gown, the lines simple and fabric more durable. I've seen some of the Frithian women wear similar styles in all colors. This one is a dove shade and wraps around with a string at the waist, creating a beautiful *V* shape.

I brush out my hair as August saunters into the tent with a dreamy hum.

"Ferren, love what you did to the place, hanging blankets . . . very homey. Oh, and 99, you put my bucket on the fire for me! I could kiss you both," he says.

I hear the commander walk out of the washroom, his footsteps right outside my blanket wall. I see the shadow outline of him, the fire illuminating his form from behind. He stands there for a while, inspecting my work. I think he might say something, but his shadow gets smaller, then I hear his cot creak as he sits on it without a word.

Dinner is in fact the frog-fish we saw at the watering hole. I see them being prepped as we walk over but refrain from saying anything to August.

We sit on logs around a huge fire pit, dozens of people and families nesting in little circles and talking to each other. This is obviously where they commune, and the conversations seem familiar and effortless. They are free to mingle and speak with whom they wish to without watchful eyes. I can feel the envy from seeing how they interact with each other forming deep within me. Not envy, that is too hateful. It's more of a longing, a pained sadness at never experiencing something similar or knowing others lived like this. No book or journal could capture the way they look at each other or the comfortable nature of just eating with their families.

I bow my head when some of the villagers notice me staring in awe of them and adjust the neckline of my dress. It's a little snug on my breasts, but August reassured me several times on our short walk over that I looked nice. He seems to be in full spirits after receiving herbs from their healer. I watch him take a bite of the food, waiting for his reaction, hoping he doesn't notice what the fishy meat came from. But he just takes another bite and smiles at me.

There is a small group of Frithian elders sitting across the large fire. Selene is chatting with them and occasionally gestures in our direction. The lazy glances from each elder make me uneasy.

The commander watches them closely, not paying attention to anything else. "I do not like this," he says almost to himself.

I lean in a little to hear him over the cheerful sound of the people around us.

August seems unfazed by the commander's words, and as he whispers something to Calliape, she rolls her eyes and widens them at me like she wants to be saved.

Rouke and two of his companions come to sit with our tiny group, and I can feel the commander straighten on the log we share.

"We must know, Priestess—the bulb. What do your books say?" His tone is slightly combative, like he does not like that we have that kind of information. He also called me priestess, so it is clear that most of them have either heard or know what I am now. I try to ignore the smug look he is giving me. I know he wants to see me react by revealing this knowledge in such a casual way. From the outside, it's a neutral question, but I know better. I've dealt with manipulating words like this from people much better at it than him. In the Estate, words are hidden jabs used as polite weapons. Rouke will have to do better than that.

"It was archived in a field journal originally," I say, completely calm, giving him nothing to work with.

He looks confused but then translates to his friends.

"It is an account of travelers, time spent here, what worked and didn't. The journal was put into the library then was referenced in some books later on. Each time information is copied, tiny fragments are missed, and overtime, chunks get lost. But I believe maybe the journal entry was something the writer heard and not the original because sadly, it did not include the consequences of the tradition."

He looks at me with a blank stare and he doesn't bother translating to his friends, confirming my suspicion of his true goal.

I catch myself smiling and look over to see if the commander noticed it too. His helmet tilts toward me and even sitting, I have to crane my neck to see where his visor is. I give him wide eyes to convey how ridiculous Rouke is. He presses his side into mine for a brief moment to answer, a little bump of acknowledgment. He is observant. I knew he noticed it too. I feel a small chill pass over me, knowing we shared the same thought about something that maybe no one else realized. The memory of his eyes shamelessly roaming over me and his broad back stepping into the washroom shoots to the front of my mind and I have to clear my throat, looking back into the fire.

Rouke is poking it with a stick, making red-hot embers float up into the air unnecessarily. "Are all the priestesses as beautiful as you?" he says in his language.

I nervously laugh, only picking up some of what he said.

"What did he say?" August whispers to Calliape.

Everyone around us in our group is quiet now as Rouke stares at me, waiting for a reply after purposefully making me uncomfortable. Calliape translates loud enough for the commander to hear because I notice him slowly turn his helmet toward Rouke, finally acknowledging him. Rouke looks over at him, realizing the scrutiny he is suddenly under. Then, the commander leans in ever so slightly, like he has locked his sights across the fire, as if it were not a compliment and instead something terrible. But it *was*. It felt awful to hear him say. I wonder if the commander assumes he is being offensive or can feel my disgust radiating.

"You should eat, my friend!" Rouke says to him, trying to get another rise.

The commander says nothing, just a blank visor pointed in Rouke's direction. I've been on the other end of that, and it's admittedly scary, but this seems different. Even his posture has changed.

Rouke looks away and focuses back on me. "A translator of books and a priestess. Very busy," he says, making sure I know he knows.

"Yes," I say between bites.

"Wow, a real virgin temple priestess in our very own village," he says with outreaching arms, faking amazement.

I lean forward and narrow my eyes. I've had enough of this odd conversation, of Rouke, of his friends staring at me with judgment.

Yes, the rest of the villagers have stared at us, but this is different. It's as if they want a fight, want us to be offended, to cause a scene in front of their elders. The last time Rouke did something the commander didn't like, he snapped a spear: that something was touching me.

I can feel the commander breathing hard, his side unapologetically pressed up against me now, which can't be a good sign. He is still affixed on the Frithians across from us. I am a little nervous of this going sour so I decide to change things up. A joke perhaps.

"That's not quite what I said. I am a priestess, a scribe, and a translator. A vow of celibacy *isn't* a requirement," I say with a grin.

Rouke throws his head back in a bellowing laugh and wags a finger at me like I've said something scandalous. The corner of my eye catches the commander's gloved hands on his knees. I can hear the suede crinkle as he flexes them into tight fists.

I just want the hunter to see we are not willing to play whatever game he was trying to start. Why I chose that topic to joke about, I am not sure. I didn't need to correct him, but it wasn't true, so I did.

The commander makes a fist again. For some reason, there is something satisfying in knowing that he is so clearly annoyed at them too, or maybe he is angry at Rouke's subject choice?

"Forgive me, Priestess. I'm unfamiliar with your vows," Rouke says.

I nod and take a few more bites of my frog-fish dinner, trying to figure out what just happened. No one has lost their temper and ruined things, so I guess that is all that matters.

Selene walks toward our group from the elders across the fire with clasped hands like Crixa does. They look to be about the same age. I wonder if they knew each other.

"The elders have given their blessing," she says as she reaches our spot near the fire.

"When do we speak to them?" the commander asks.

"There is no need. Their decision has been relayed to you, 99th Commander. You are free to take Viathan's stone of course. As for Frith's, the elders have said they leave it to the Albright to decide."

"What does that mean . . . the Albright will decide?" I ask.

She nods, refusing to go into detail.

"Rouke's hunting party will take you to the Albright's cave at first light," Selene says.

Rouke looks over at me, bowing his head with an almost satisfied smile. "With pleasure."

Selene walks back to the elders without another word.

A long, frustrated silence covers me, one of shock and not knowing if the commander will follow Selene to speak with the elders himself. The reality of having to retrieve the Viathan's stone and the cryptic permission that we can try to take theirs sends me deep into my own thoughts. I close my eyes, trying to picture the portion of the oil painting covered by curtains to hide its horror.

August interrupts my downward spiral, holding up a cup to toast. "To the Albright, whatever the fuck that is!"

"I would save your celebration, my friend," Rouke says, his two friends snickering.

August searches each person's face for an answer, but everyone takes a drink, giggling to themselves. I don't have the heart to tell him it's bad news or the stomach to tell him what the Albright is yet.

The commander stands abruptly and reaches his hand down to me. "Let's go."

I stare at his gloved hand, outstretched for mine, waiting for me to take it. I scan the group around us who have gone back to their food and murmurings.

"Priestess," he whispers, snapping my attention back to him.

Without commanding my body to do so, I take his hand.

The commander guides me to the farthest point of the village. I come to the conclusion he is taking me to the spot Selene mentioned so that I can safely pray. There is a tree line with a small clearing enough to see the sky.

With the fire and voices still within reach, the commander stops and leans against a tree. He points to the obvious full and bright moon as if I wouldn't see it hanging in the black sky on my own. But then I realize he is teasing me about the times I had no idea where it was and press my lips tightly together to hide my smile.

I walk to the middle of the field and drop to my knees. I touch the grass with my palms and then lean forward to brush the grass against my cheek. Can Selene hear my prayers through the grass and ferns by my hands whispering to her? What was she in the Estate, and would Crixa know her name if I mention it when we return?

When I am done, the commander walks me back to the tent in silence. I sit on my bed, leaving one panel of my blanket wall open, letting in the warmth.

The commander is sitting on the foot of his bed with his helmet off, rubbing his brow. We lock eyes but neither of us feel like talking, it seems. I can't help but wonder what would have happened if the commander wasn't there escorting me while I prayed in the woods, knowing that Selene mentioned that some would be unwelcoming to me.

He throws more logs on the fire, making me remember how cold it was the night before without one. How he had to press against me for warmth. How we eventually inched closer the colder it became, and the way his breath hitched when I moved my hips back into him.

August bursts into the tent, stumbling a little, his eyes semi closed like he's been drinking. He lifts his shirt over the commander's cot and shakes it out, making bread rolls fall onto the blanket. He grabs a flask from his belt, handing it to the commander, then stumbles to his own cot, flopping down face-first.

"Calliape, beautiful Calliape," August says, voice muffled.

It's sweet and makes me forget about the bad news we got. I can't help but cover my mouth to stop from laughing at his little performance. He starts breathing deeply, like he has already passed out.

The commander chuckles a little too, then he takes a long swig from the flask. I see him sauntering over, bringing a roll of bread to my makeshift room. He holds out the roll, almost breaching the boundary into the little private area I've made.

"You didn't eat much, too busy talking to Rouke," he says, a smile hinting on the side of his face.

I stand and grin. "Are you jealous, Commander?" I wrap my hand around the roll, but he does not let go when I tug.

I look up at him towering over me.

Fiery frustration, impatience, and something else swirl in his face, concentrated in his intense eyes.

I look down, breaking the exhilarating tether just as he releases the bread to me. I stand in place, a little dumbstruck, while I hear him put another log on the fire and the creak of his bed again. I can't get distracted by trying to figure out what he is thinking. It's not my responsibility to decipher what is in his head. I stare up at the ceiling, watching the shadow the commander's body makes as he climbs into bed. I hold my hands together, trying to imitate the feeling of his as he helped me stand to go pray, of the grasp on mine, of it lingering just a little too long to be casual.

CHAPTER EIGHTEEN

The hike to the Albright's cave is mostly uphill, with a path for some of the journey. My hiking clothes are uncomfortable but allow me to move more freely on our ascent farther up the mountain. I bring my small bag of supplies slinged across my front with some of the dinner rolls from last night.

Rouke and his hunting party speak loudly to one another, which makes me feel like we are safe. The creatures in the forest know we mean no harm now that we travel with the Frithians.

I glance over my shoulder often at my travel companions. The commander stays close behind me like a watchful dog of sorts. I know he is staying close to August, who looks a little winded, his wounds still slowing him down.

Rouke keeps a light conversation while walking beside me, asking questions about what I know from books on Frith. I know better than to reveal everything, only enough boring information for him to move on. I can tell he is trying to hide how much it bothers him that the other worlds know anything about Frith at all. He tells me about their world's only library, built into the side of the mountain, columns of books going stories up into it. I can't even imagine what that must look like, the ancient texts it contains. But he abruptly changes the subject when I try to ask more information about it, turning it back toward the Albright.

I listen as he rambles like he is desperately trying to cover the tracks of our previous topic. I notice some of the things he's saying as fact about the Albright are not true. My skin crawls as I listen to false information he tells me, ways to retrieve the stones that would get us killed. I decide it's best to act like I know nothing of the Albright, to just listen and observe him. *Why is he lying to me?*

When he tells me it can be killed, it becomes very clear: Rouke doesn't want me to retrieve the stones—maybe none of the party we are with do. He wants to give us a false sense of confidence as we go into the cave of an old god, thinking we can defeat it.

They don't want us to come out at all.

As the terrain becomes littered with giant rocks, Rouke calls to the front of the party. It's returned with some rhythmic whistling from ahead, pacing everyone to a stop. The Frithians drape themselves on fallen logs and boulders like they are making camp.

I stand with August and the commander awkwardly in the middle of the semi path, watching the others unwrap food and make themselves comfortable on the forest floor. It's casual and odd, only adding to my uneasy feeling. The air is thinner now, and I can hear August breathing heavily as he goes to lean against a tree, chewing a root the healer gave him.

As soon as his back touches the bark, Rouke walks aggressively toward him, wielding a machete. I gasp and grab at the commander's forearm to get his attention.

Rouke lifts his knife high into the air before August has a chance to even see him coming. He hacks straight down without hesitation. The blade is inches from August's head, his eyes shocked and wide.

The color from his face drains like it did when he was stung. Then a brightly colored snake, split in two, falls dead next to his feet. Rouke withdraws his weapon from where it is lodged into the trunk. August jumps back, making a disgusted sound. What looked like a random attack was really a quick measure of protection against the animal's venomous bite, but it felt more aggressive and showy than necessary.

I realize my hand is still tightly squeezing the commander's forearm when I feel him move closer to my side, like he thinks my shock is a plea for protection.

"The forest is very angry with you." Rouke grabs August's arm, holding up a smaller blade. "You need to atone to her."

August furrows but does not pull back.

The commander moves toward the pair in the same second I let go of him. He pushes into Rouke, breaking his hold on August.

"It's fine," August says, trying to pacify.

Selene mentioned August needed to apologize to the forest for taking something from it. I realize what Rouke is doing and put myself in between Rouke and the commander before the aggressive posturing becomes violent. I can already see a few of the other Frithians standing to come to Rouke's aid.

"Commander, I think he was trying to help," I say.

"He needs to atone to the forest. She will not stop until he does," Rouke explains.

"Selene said he needed to do something to apologize," I whisper to the commander.

He takes a large inhale then walks away, bumping into Rouke's shoulder.

The blade is pressed into August's lifted hand. When blood beads to the surface, Rouke touches the wound into the ground.

"Thank you," August says genuinely.

"You were putting us all at risk," Rouke says then closes his eyes, speaking a mumbled prayer over August's hand in the dirt.

The commander pulls me off to the side by my elbow, placing his back to them in a private shield. The others are too busy watching August and Rouke to notice us. I need to tell him what Rouke said, but I feel my stomach turning with anxiety, like I'm going to be caught whispering during a temple ceremony.

"He can't be trusted, Priestess." He squeezes my arm gently before letting go, making sure I am listening.

"I'm starting to realize that. He told me the opposite of what I know is written of the Albright. At first, I thought maybe he was telling me ghost stories, ones that had been passed down, knowing that they aren't completely true. But he was insistent. So I told him I had not read anything of the Albright before. Then he told me something I know is false," I say.

"And what is that?" He leans down, closing into my space, intently listening.

"He said the Albright can die, that we can kill it. That's when I knew he was lying to me. He doesn't want us to have the stones," I whisper

"You laid a trap. Good girl." His hushed tone is smooth with just a hint of amusement.

I stare at him, a little dumbstruck by his words, blinking in surprise for a little too long. "I'm afraid Rouke is the least of our worries," I say, crossing my arms, trying to refocus and ignore the blood rushing to my cheeks.

"How much farther?" August asks Rouke as he wraps his hand.

Rouke points to a large rock formation, almost completely hidden by dense trees. We are here. That must be the Albright's cave. They aren't resting just to eat; they are setting up a camp while we go inside.

Rouke hands August and the commander knives. I hold my hand out, but he only smiles at me like I am a child asking for a second treat. Back in the village, the Viathans argued to bring their guns but were refused by the elders. It was never directly but always through Selene, which was enough to put the commander in a foul mood as we packed up.

"Where is the mouth of the cave?" the commander asks.

"It is not known. There is no opening," Rouke answers then joins the others, who are building a small fire and leaving us with no direction or plan, as if we know what to do.

We rest on our own, closest to the cave. None of them settle anywhere near the rock formation. The Albright has been here since the war with First Son, so they were likely raised fearing it, warned to not go close. I notice every time I look up, a Frithian is watching me. I can't imagine what they are thinking, but some do not look happy.

There is no opening, no clear way in. I rack my mind of the facts I know about the Albright, ones we went over together in our tent this morning and ones I've remembered since. It felt good to strategize with them again, to feel like my contributions are internalized and understood. It will do anything to get its way. It could kill us, but it would rather drive us crazy, and it's clever and likes to play games with humans. That, at least, gives me somewhere to start.

The commander sits with wide legs on a large fallen tree next to me. August unwraps some food, holding it out to us, but we both shake our heads in unison. I can't eat with my nerves, and the commander has refused to remove his helmet anywhere but our tent, which is for the best if I want to concentrate on the task.

I make sure to meet the eyes of every Frithian who glances over at us and stare hard until they avert their gaze. They are following the orders of their elders, bringing us here and hopefully taking us back with the stones, but I know they would not be bothered at all if we never came out alive.

"How are you feeling, August," I say without looking at him in case I miss another judgmental glance.

"The root helps. The cut on my palm is a distraction from the ones on my arm," he jokes.

"I'm sorry," I say, offering a quick sympathetic look.

"What else do we need to know, Priestess?" the commander asks.

The question slaps me in the face. He has no problem not knowing every aspect of everything, secure in what he does know and doesn't. I'm not sure when I will get used to being asked my opinion on such important things, asked to speak up when I am normally scolded for such.

"It's one of First Mother's children from the beginning. It was brought and left here by the priestesses of old, forgotten after the war was over—"

I cut off my sentence when the others glance over at my whispering. I leave out that it will do anything to get home, that it is likely still angry. All the secondhand accounts of the Albright don't compare to the ominous feeling of being next to the giant cave it dwells in. I knew I would likely face creatures and monsters trying to kill us in the forest, but if I knew the Albright was protecting the stones, I would never have left Cosima. I want to confess to them that I'm overwhelmed, but I know they are looking to me for answers. Just because I know a little about the Albright does not mean I know enough to convince it to give us something so precious.

"Commander, can you watch over me while I pray?"

He nods and follows me closer to the cave. When we get just out of speaking distance, I turn to look at him, seeing my terrified expression staring back. I want him to take off his helmet. I want to say he has to take me home, that I cannot do it.

His hand lifts a little like he wants to reach for mine. He must know I'm distraught. I always forget what his helmet can do.

"I am fine. I will . . . just be a minute," I say, crossing my arms out of his floating reach.

I decide not to get down on my knees into my prayer pose. There are too many who can still see me even if they cannot hear. I turn my back and try to center myself, to reach out to First Mother the way I do in the temple, which is difficult even on a good day with no distractions. My hands tremble, and I can't shake the feeling I should run back the way we came.

The commander presses into my proximity. "I can tell you are not praying," he says over my shoulder from behind.

"Do you mind? I am trying to."

"You said it's an old god. Anything like the tree man we saw in the forest?"

"No, not at all. It was called from its home and not able to go back. We will have to convince it, tell it what is happening," I say.

"We're going to talk to it. That's your plan."

"Yes. Maybe . . . I don't know."

"Did Mary know they were with the Albright?" he asks.

"No, she was convinced the elders would bring the stones to the field like the last conjunction. I do not know what I'm doing, not sure why you think I do. I agreed to help navigate the forest, to help make peace with the people, not this! I had no idea the stones were going to be guarded by the Albright."

"What did you think was going to happen?" His tone is a little too pompous than I have patience for right now.

"Will you shut up? You're much more tolerable when you're silent and brooding in a corner."

I give up on my prayer and sit on a large rock next to the cave and instead whisper to myself for First Mother to give me wisdom.

The commander squares himself to look at me with his hands on his hips like he does when he disapproves. "So what happens if we speak to it and that doesn't work," he says in a more receptive tone.

"We die . . . probably."

I see his head lift over mine to something behind me, and he holds it there. Good, he's taking my advice. But he has gone into his weird defensive posture, like when something is off. I turn to look at what he is staring at. The rock formation has changed, an opening there that wasn't present when we walked over.

"It's open." I take a step forward. Just a few more and I will be inside.

The commander lunges, trying to keep me from going in.

I walk into the open area without thinking of the danger we just spoke about, drawn to it like it's calling me inside.

"Come out slowly. We need to let the others know."

When I look back, he is standing halfway in, keeping a boot just outside the cave archway.

"No, August isn't coming in. He just atoned to the forest and we don't know if it's worked yet. The Frithian people look like they don't want to come anywhere near it. Only me and you are going in," I say, taking another step farther into the tunnel.

He matches it.

"Come on, Commander, before I come to my senses."

His shoulders relax like he knows I am right, and he leans down to pick up what looks like an old discarded torch from people who have explored the cave before us. Then he takes out his fire sparker and ignites it. I find another one and touch it to his.

The moment the entrance is illuminated, I can see drawings on the walls of the great conjunction, the three worlds breaking apart and the planetary bodies around the sun and moon. They're sketches in red and browns from thousands of years ago, perfectly untouched by the outside world.

We hold the torches up and explore the walls in the open mouth of the entrance. As our backs are turned, we hear a grinding sound. A large rock rolls in front of the exit, shining the last sliver of light as it closes, entombing us inside.

He runs his gloved fingers on the seam in the rocks, wedging them in to push it open. I wanted a way into the Albright's cave, but there is something unnerving about the choice to leave being taken away.

"It probably knows we are here. It's very clever," I say, defeated.

The commander gets really close and says, "Well, you're going to need to be more clever, Priestess."

We travel down the tunnel, knowing that we can't exit the way we came, our only choice to push forward. It's surprisingly not like most caves I've read about. The air is dry, and it almost hurts to breathe it in. Everything is crumbly, dry, and dusty.

I shuffle forward through the tunnel-like passage at the front. I see drawings on the walls, more depictions of First Mother breaking our world into three, of banishing First Son to dwell on Cosima. The drawings are messier, violent even on this wall. I brush my fingertips over them and realize they aren't drawn on like the ones in the front of the cave. These are etched in the stone in frantic scratches. I hold my torch closer and run my hand over the sharp grooves of our history.

As soon as I am out of arm's reach from the commander, I hear another rock rolling noisily behind me. I twist rapidly, the air making my torch choppy until I still. There's a solid rock wall where he was standing.

I am alone.

The Albright knows we are here, already beginning a game. I beat on the wall and I hear the commander punching it on the other side, grunting like he is trying to move it.

"Commander!"

"Priestess, listen to me," he says, finishing his struggle.

"I don't know what to do! Keep pushing on it!"

"Ferren, stop!" he says.

The sound of my name on his lips stops my panic. Not priestess, not her, not you . . . Ferren.

There's a small opening in the rock wall, and I see his torch light on the other side.

"Listen to me, Ferren."

My breath is ragged. I can feel the cold chill of panic overtaking reason again. But the way he says my name, in a soft voice I haven't heard from him before, is the only thing keeping me from spiraling.

"You have to keep going," he says.

"No."

"You have to. I'll try to find another way around."

"Please. No. I-I can't move." I feel paralyzed. I'm stuck with my face pressed against the stone, looking through the tiny opening, trying to see him, wishing he were next to me.

"You can. You have to," he whispers into the small hole in the cave wall.

"99 . . . I'm scared."

There's a long pause, like he's almost unsure if I am speaking to him. "That's okay. It's okay to be scared. I was . . . in the forest when those things echoed back to us, when one had your face, but we have to do this anyway."

"I can't." An overwhelming feeling crashes into me, tugging

downward on my throat. I want to be home safe, praying in my stone temple or protected in my stuffy library with Mary.

"You are brave, Ferren. I've seen it. Would you do anything to get those stones? You told me you were doing it for First Mother, right? Answer me!"

"Yes, to win favor, to ascend."

"That's right. You said that to me with no hesitation. This is the thing you have to do to get them . . . that *anything*. Now go get them."

I stare through the opening in the rock for a long time. I don't feel any braver or any less scared of seeing the Albright, of it possibly killing me, but my body feels like it will move now. My feet turn on their own and walk down the tunnel, my flickering torch leading the way. I can hear the commander behind me, his banging on the rock growing more distant.

The firelight pulls me forward into a narrower tunnel. There are carvings on the stone walls of the First Children and of First Mother in the beginning.

The tunnel gets so narrow, I have to turn to the side to pass through it. My body tugs between closely wedged rocks, jutting out at different angles. Whispers echo off the cave, and I turn quickly, making my torch almost flicker out.

I can smell something now.

It's dry, like a burning similar to the smell of August's skin when I cauterized his wounds.

I press into the encroaching channel, dragging myself through a slender opening. My hips get lodged in between two rocks, but with my torso free, I push down, wiggling myself with one hand, but my bottom half won't budge. I'm trapped. My breathing becomes so erratic, I get light-headed and drop my torch to the floor, pushing down, desperately trying to shimmy out.

With a painful thrust, I fall loose to the cave floor in a thump next to my torch. I stand, illuminating the large, open cave chamber, the fire dancing on the high ceiling above. My eyes adjust to structures I can see lining the edges of the wall.

Bones.

But not randomly discarded bones like a wild animal would leave. These bones are . . . categorized. Long thin bones that look like they could be from legs are together. Maybe the Albright eats animals from the forest, bringing them in here.

I move my torch to brighten the other wall and see rib cages, stacked and distinctly human. There are dozens of four-foot-high towers made of skulls of people who came into this cave and did not leave.

My torch extinguishes in a phantom breeze the moment I realize.

I spin, trying to find the rock that I entered from, but it's pitch black as I run my hands across the wall, painfully digging in with my fingernails.

A small light shines on the wall like there is a lit candle behind me. It brightens the space for just a split second, a flame with no warmth, a cold and empty flicker.

It twinkles again, longer and brighter, illuminating the room for a second stutter, then there's blackness again. With it, there is movement behind me. I spin quickly, almost relieved, thinking it must be the commander, that he found the chamber as well. But he's not there, nothing is, and it's completely black between bursts of sharp light.

I can see how large the cave chamber really is with each illumination. There is a huge hole at the top of the ceiling about a story and a half up. Maybe I can climb my way out; there could be an exit out the top.

THE VIRIDIAN PRIESTESS

Pebbles crunch under my boots but when I look down, the next flicker of light reveals bone fragments too small and broken to stack. The entire floor is littered with human bones.

Then I hear a voice speak, and it's terrible and torturing down my spine—human sounding, but just off enough to know it's not coming from one.

"Who is it that makes the air taste so sweet with breath?"

CHAPTER NINETEEN

The Albright.

The glow of light stutters with each word it speaks. I can make out its form on the other side of the cave, up toward the ceiling where the wall meets it. I swallow a scream, trying to hold my breath, but I don't think I could scream if I tried. My jaw is locked, sewn shut. I try to inhale quietly and shallowly, but my lungs lurch for more air.

The light shines again, longer in rhythm. As it does, I can see a long spindly arm reaching down the wall, crawling downward slowly with each flicker. I realize the light is coming from the creature, from its pale blue skin, rippling outward like circle vibrations in a puddle, slow and billowing. I realize if I don't do or say something soon, I will be ripped apart and stacked in pieces like the victims around me. I need to entice it, appeal to its wants and desires, and play a game to calm it.

"I am Priestess Ferren from Cosima," I announce.

It finishes its long-limbed descent down the wall with the next flicker of light. I can see it sitting like a perched cat just under the view of the hole in the ceiling. It's a pale moon-like blue, its skin almost transparent, which fades to a pale flesh tone on its face.

"I know of such a place, Priestess," it says with flashing lights.

Speaking like it's tasting the last word on the air with a long serpent tongue, it almost seems pleased to see me. The light flickers and I get a glimpse of what is in front of it.

An altar. The stones.

The flicker pulsates longer and larger, allowing me to see its face: human-like from the nose up but bony, rigid, and monstrous. The tips of its muscular shoulders come to a point from long collarbones. Its torso and biceps are ribbed with muscle like a human man's.

It looks at me, tilting its head in examination, long tail flicking and then curling around the four feet it perches on.

"Do they pray for me, Priestess? Do they pray for me in Cosima, like the ones before you promised?"

I contemplate saying yes, flattering it, getting on its good side. But it's clever. We don't pray for the Albright. Its name is tucked away, I've never heard it spoken aloud until yesterday.

"We do not pray for you. Most have never heard your name. I'm sorry."

The Albright looks up at the hole in the ceiling with sadness on its face. I raise my eyes to see what it peers so painfully at, but it's just a black hole.

I look down at the stones and the moment I do, the light in the room flickers and becomes more constant, an ambient hue, then a brighter flicker occasionally when the Albright moves.

"You have come to admire my mother's stones?"

It said *my mother* and not First Mother. That's right. First Mother didn't make this creature; she birthed it like all of her First Children.

"Not to admire, no."

"To take!" it grits out, and light ripples off of it.

"I come to protect Mother's stones."

"Why you?"

The question kicks open the cracks I've been holding together. Why me? Why is a lesser priestess in a cave with an old god? Because Mary cannot be and it is my duty to retrieve the stones now. I gave my highest priestess my word.

"First Son threatens to destroy her stones. We need to keep them safe."

"Safe," it says with strange humor in its tone.

"First Son plans to come for them this conjunction year. He will take them, destroy them so that Mother can never wake. They're safer in Cosima behind our protective wards," I say.

"You speak to Mother? When you speak to her, does she answer? When I do, my words float up to the ceiling in puffs of smoke. They make little stains on the rocks above me."

"Not with words," I answer meekly.

The Albright slumps.

"With signs, with a feeling," I continue.

Then I feel the Albright wrap its tail around my back, pulling me in, bringing me closer to its large face. Just the altar separates me from its feral expression.

"No, when you speak to Mother, nothing answers. You speak, you pray, and there is nothing but air rippling out of your lungs. You are like me, Priestess, and you will stay with me. We will wait for Mother here, together. Wait for her return," it says, holding me closer, smiling with dozens of sharp little teeth.

I grapple at its tail and push down on it, twisting to get away, but it's useless. It restricts me more. I remember how clever it is, how the commander said I need to be more clever, so I will be. It caught me in a lie and the second it did, it took advantage.

"Mother does not answer me. Not yet," I say with a purposeful air of mystery, baiting it to inquire.

The Albright stops tightening its tail, its face interested.

"Do you remember the priestesses of old?"

The creature tenses, clearly remembering what happened, what they did.

"I'm sorry they forgot you. But do you remember their power and how they received it?"

"From Mother."

"Yes, from Mother. I haven't received mine. She hasn't given me my gifts yet."

"No riddles!" it says and starts to pull me closer again.

"Which means I will see her soon!"

I have to play a clever game of trading, a game I know the Albright won't pass on. I have something I can bargain with, a means to give it the thing it wants more than anything in the three worlds.

"When Mother comes to me, when she shows herself, I will ask her to take you home in exchange for one of the gifts she was going to give me."

The moment I blurt it out, I regret it. What if First Mother only has one gift to give me and I've just traded it away. But it's the only thing of value that the Albright would understand.

The room shifts. Its tail's grip loosens, the creature's expression becoming less intimidating, more sad. It looks . . . lost.

"Home?" it says, looking up at the ceiling again.

Now that I'm closer, I'm able to see the ceiling hole directly above. It's decorated with little trinkets hanging from the rocks, a drawing of the moon on its cave, and scribbles of little people.

"Yes, home. The Highest Priestess of Cosima assured me that if I successfully protect the stones, that I will ascend. I can speak to First

Mother when I do."

I know the old god understands ascension, what it meant even in times of old. It knows this promise can be fulfilled.

"First Mother? I have forgotten humans have a second. You have a second mother, don't you, Priestess? But she is not with you," it says like it found a secret.

"No . . . she passed in childbirth."

I'm terrified to lie. I almost have the trade, so I try to just stay calm. I know the Albright is tricky. Even in the war, it liked to trade and play games with humans, so I need to steer the conversation back.

"It was your birth, wasn't it? A divine birth for a second mother's sacrifice. What beautiful balance. But I see another before you." It turns off to the side like it's listening to a whisper in its tall, pointed ear. A grin slashes across its face in satisfaction. "A sister. She seeks balance too. She will have it. Oh, and I hope to see it. To taste it. What will you trade me for this?" it says with a pointy-toothed smile.

It's talking about Leema, her birth before mine, I think. It's hard to tell when its words seem like living, shape-shifting things. The Albright is old as time and magic itself. The longer I stay in here, the more it will know about me and the more secrets it will pluck. Even now, it's watching me like it's going to pounce, swaying slightly, waiting.

"One trade at a time, Albright! We have not agreed on terms for the first."

It gives me a larger, more satisfied smile, like it's enjoying its game fully now. "You believe this highest priestess?" it says again, tasting the air with a tongue that looks like a sharp pale blade of grass.

"I do."

"And you would give up a gift from Mother to send me home?"

"Yes. In exchange for the stones. Both of them!" I realize I need to say exactly the words that I mean, specifying the terms of our deal.

"All I have to do is let you take them?"

I nod.

The Albright lifts its chin and closes its lids. "Take them."

I keep my eyes on the creature as I collect the stones from the large flat rock they sit on, my hands shaking as I move closer. They are both pale and palm sized and distinctly different, just like the three worlds even though they were once joined together.

"And now you have them," the Albright says, black eyes on me.

I pause at the Albright's pleased expression, hearing the eerie tone in its voice. I look back where the exit should be but it's still closed up. My lungs remind me how dry the air is, a dusty kind of dry that leaves a taste in my mouth as I inhale. As careful as I was with the words I chose, I have been bested.

My stomach turns. I need to get creative and fast before I'm trapped here forever. I have to stay calm and play its game. I put the stones in my bag and brush against the moonstone Thea gave me. I suck in another gritty breath, realizing I can trade it for my freedom.

First Mother bless you, Thea.

"Thank you, Albright. These fit nicely next to my moonstone. Should be easy to travel with them all," I call out.

Light crashes into the surrounding walls and ripples upward.

My trap worked.

"Priestess, have you a stone from my home?"

I reach in and pull it out nonchalantly. "It's just a moonstone. It mimics your home," I say, holding it up, turning it in examination.

"Tricks, deception?"

"Perhaps, but isn't it beautiful?" I ask.

The Albright moves closer. It's much taller, but it ducks down underneath to examine the stone from below. "It must be mine."

I snatch it away and hold it tightly in my palm, smiling politely. "In exchange, you will let me leave the cave."

"Yes! I accept these terms." The Albright swishes its tail in frustration.

I place the stone in its outreached spindly hand then hear rocks moving behind me. It made an exit for me to leave.

"Thank you."

"I hope you ascend soon. Your friend will be waiting with me until you do," it says as I turn to exit.

The commander. I've been bested again. Every move I make, the Albright is one step ahead of me in perfect strategy. My stomach turns again. The commander is trapped. I've retrieved the stones but failed him.

He would gladly stay if it meant the stones would be taken back and protected against First Son, if the mission was completed, but no one is staying behind. No one is going to die in this cave. We all go back together; we complete it together.

An odd calm overcomes me, replaced almost immediately by a thick rage dripping off in sheets. As I turn to the Albright, a ripple of green cascades outward from the cave ceiling.

I've had enough games.

The Albright's attention is on me as it straightens taller, palming the stone to its chest.

"You will let me go," I say.

The creature's brow lifts as I speak.

"No more trading. Me and my friend leave this cave. Together."

"You will leave alone. As for your friend, he will wait with me, and then he will become . . . decoration," it says, wafting a hand to the stacks of bones.

I square my shoulders, sick of the conversation, the twisting of words. Sick of trying to be more clever. My body screams to take the stones, to leave while I can.

"Leave, Priestess!" the Albright shouts, its face turning deranged and angry, aura flashing with bright strobes of light. The rest of the room is dark around us, a black vignette between outbursts.

"Leave now or I will decorate my walls with you as well."

We stare at each other and with each threat, my rage grows.

"No."

The room strobes green.

The Albright is crawling low toward me now.

The commander is stuck somewhere trying to get to me. I feel my body tense then focus suddenly, like the second before boiling water cusps a pot then spills over. Dark green smoke rings flume outward, dancing on top of the Albright's strobes of light.

It stops its crawl toward me, watching the green ripples with large human-like eyes and when they meet mine again, its face looks . . . terrified.

Another trick? I gain just enough courage to take a step forward, shaky but forward, and to my surprise, it steps back.

"You will let us both leave. No trades, no more tricks, Albright."

The phantom green smoke rolls up the sides of the walls, gathering at the top. The Albright glances upward and ducks at the sight. The confusion at the spectacle in front of us threatens to break my focus. But I'm too determined on my goal to think of what it could be and too angry to care.

"Fine. Just leave. Leave this place!" Its words come out in a strange plea.

The green smoke retreats and a soft glow fills the room again. The fog tendrils dissipate as I slowly back out. The Albright crawls backward up the wall, neither of us wanting to take our eyes off the other.

"Soon, you will see you were all wrong, all worlds in all of time—except the beginning. When you ascend, Priestess . . . whatever old god you see, do not even utter my name," it says in a whisper that echoes off the walls.

"I will never speak your name. That is a deal."

CHAPTER TWENTY

I shuffle through the pitch black, stumbling over what I am hoping are rocks and not more bones. I feel my way through by touching the sides of the crumbly walls. I know I have my eyes open, but it's so dark, it's as if my lids are closed tightly. Panic threatens to spill over the longer I am in here, thinking that maybe this was all a game. That the Albright looked petrified and said that I could leave as part of a clever way of tricking me again. Maybe it was emitting the green light, not me. All of this could be a big ruse to play an elaborate game with me.

I'm getting lost in the cave. I can't tell if I'm getting deeper or closer to the exit. My hands are trembling as I feel down the walls, their roughness scraping at my fingertips, making them raw.

I hear something close to me, rocks clicking.

It's the Albright! I know it is.

It tracked me down into a tunnel, hunting me. Or maybe there's something else in the cave, another creature from the forest.

It's getting closer. My heart starts racing as I shuffle as fast as I can in the dark, but I'm afraid I'm going to touch something awful or fall through the cave floor into a never-ending chamber.

It knows I'm here. I'm on the verge of screaming. I want to curl up on the stone floor and give up, but terror drives me stumbling forward.

Then it has me, its arms reaching out, grabbing, enclosing me. I kick and punch, gasping like I'm drowning.

"Priestess, it's me. It's me."

The commander. I can smell him. It's not a trick, not the Albright pretending to be him. I know it's him. I would bet the stones on it. I would know his smell anywhere. I feel him pressed against me, his cold armor. I feel his helmet but I continue to thrash. My mind knows it's him, but my body is still catching up. He holds me tighter, absorbing my petrified fit.

"Ferren, it's me. It's okay. It's me!" he says, letting me go with one arm then pressing me against the cave wall with the other.

A solid forearm across my chest holds me still as I shamelessly hit him. Then something touches the crown of my head. I feel it brush downward, like a loose band encircling my face. It encases my whole head, almost down to my collarbone.

His helmet.

"It's me. It's ok. Look at me."

My eyes focus, looking out the visor. It's blurry from the contrast of being in the dark for so long, but then I see his face, so close to mine, his arms bracing on either side of me, caging me in. I can see him but the color is wrong; his eyes look strange. A tendril of panic comes to the forefront of my mind that this isn't him, but then I breathe in through my nose.

I'm hit with an overwhelming smell again, his smell. It's all around me with the helmet on and strangely comforting, even through my panic. I can see things the way he can, and breathing in the air inside, it almost feels like I am in his mind's eye. My chest heaves as I steady my breath, eyes fixed on him. I can see the black tunnel and my hands shaking even as I hold onto his arms for support.

"Please, tell me you are alright," he says.

I nod feverishly.

"Use words. I cannot see you."

"Yes. I'm fine. I'm alright," I croak.

"What happened?"

"I . . . got them. The stones." I drop a hand from him to lift my bag.

"Well done, Priestess." He smiles on one side, eyes creasing slightly.

"Surprised?" I say breathlessly.

He slowly shakes his head no.

"Keep those close. Don't take them out until we get back to the village. We need to get going. I'll need that back. Okay?" he says.

He tenderly rubs on my shoulder, waiting for me to answer. When I don't, he moves his arm up to lift the helmet but stops as I tighten my grip. I don't want to be in the darkness again. Through his visor, I can see. I can't be in the pitch blackness again.

He rests a hand back on my shoulder, dragging it across my collarbone like he is feeling for my racing heartbeat.

"I will get you out. I will get *us* out," he says in the most sincere tone I've ever heard.

I release my grip as he gently pulls the helmet off. I hear his armor and clothes rustling as he places it back on. Then I feel the touch of his gloved hand on me, gently brushing back the hair that fell messily forward in my face. I find it with mine and run my trembling palm down it onto his forearm, bicep, and then over to his chest. I feel the rise and fall of it under my hand, his heartbeat so strong, it thumps against the metal of his armor. The air hitches in my lungs as I feel the fabric of his glove encompass my hand and press harder into it, like he wants my touch closer to him and not just over his chest plates.

He is here, solid and real in front of me. Without him, I would have still been kicking and screaming on the enclosed cave tunnel, trying to turn back and flee. He had no doubt I could get the stones, knew exactly what I needed to hear to drive me forward and to calm me down after. In the darkness, I step forward and push into him, wanting to feel him closer and pressed against me. To feel shrouded in his warmth and protection. I tuck my arms between us as his wrap around me in a wordless embrace.

"I have you," he says, so close to my ear, his voice muffled and breathy in his helmet.

I feel his hand slip into mine as I pull back, overwhelmed with the sensation his words carry. Then he flexes his grip on my hand twice, a sweet intentional squeeze like he wants to stay like this but he has to get us out.

We walk briskly through the narrow passageways of the cave. He guides me with a strong hold on my hand. Every couple steps, he flexes it twice, letting me know he has me, and every time he does, the panic subsides a little. His instructions are calm and even, letting me know what is ahead and when to watch my step. I still stumble but he holds me steady.

I see a light from the outside and know we have made it to the mouth of the cave. I want to let go and run for it, but he holds my hand firmly, keeping the same pace as before. He's calming and reassuring me not to panic, that we are free. We just have to walk out.

I see August's face first. He looks so scared, and then relief washes over him and he opens his arms at the sight of us exiting. He hugs me tightly, pinning my arms against my sides in a vice. In the same moment, I feel the commander let go of my hand, squeezing it twice a final time, hard enough to let me know it was again intentional and just for me.

Then August tries the same greeting on the commander, which is shrugged off and traded for a smack on the shoulder before he goes to speak to Rouke.

"Are you okay? You look . . . dazed," August says, looking me up and down.

"It was very dark in there," I whisper.

August's eyes are burning a hole into my bag where the stones are safely kept. He looks afraid, almost worried, with a question at the tip of his tongue, one I know he is too smart to say aloud in front of the Frithian party who don't seem happy to see us again.

"They were about to leave," August whispers to me.

"The Frithians? All of them?" I whisper as close to him as I can, using him as a shield from their scrutiny.

He nods with a troubled crinkle in his brow.

The commander checks on us with a flick of his helmet from his conversation with Rouke and the two other men who are always by his side. I realize the atmosphere outside the cave is tense as I look around at the packed-up camp. I know Rouke was certain we would not come out, let alone with the stones in hand.

When they are finished, we take off down the mountain just as we came, back toward the village. Our journey is veiled in an odd silence, only broken by heated whispers the Frithians mumble to each other. I know some of them must have strong feelings about their stone going back to Cosima. They respect their elders' decisions but that doesn't stop them from glaring at me even now. I clutch my bag, bringing it closer in protection, and keep my side glued to the commander's arm. I can feel the back of his hand bumping into mine as we walk, like a lifeline to reach out to if I need it.

Selene and the Frithian elders sit across the fire from us in her gathering room. The commander speaks to them and Selene translates.

I grasp my bag tightly in my lap as they stare at me. I'm uneasy, still unable to come down from the adrenaline of being in the cave, and I'm afraid of breaking the deal I voluntarily made with the Albright.

I won't utter your name.

The deal was on my terms, but I intend to keep it. The Albright's expression and what it said runs through my mind on a loop. We have the stones, but something else happened in that cave with the Albright and in the tunnels after with the commander.

Selene throws a log on the fire, making it spark in front of me and August. I look over my shoulder to the commander in the rows of chairs behind us and give him a tight smile. His legs are spread casually, like he does in the cockpit, elbow on the chair back next to him. His helmet tilts in response to my forced smile. As he slowly examines me, I know he can tell something is off.

Then August leans in, pressing his shoulder to mine. "You ok?" he whispers, almost too low to hear.

I rub my lips together and nod, hoping that they drop it. Both have inquired in their own ways—August's sweet and direct, the commander's silent and annoying but somehow still comforting. He gave a small head tilt, but I knew with that tiny gesture, he realized something was wrong.

Selene speaks with the elders much longer than anything the commander said to her, and my head is too foggy to pick up a single word to translate for myself.

"Priestess Ferren, the stones," she says.

I withdraw them from my bag, placing them side by side on the low table that separates us. She runs her hands over the top in adoration then scoops up the Frithian stone to take to the elders, holding it out to each of them as they press fingers to it.

"The Albright found your cause important enough to part with them?" she says, returning the stone.

I nod, hoping she does not ask for more details.

"With that, well, I'm afraid I have bad news. The trees whisper of something in the forest—something human but not, something here but . . . not," Selene says.

I hear the commander lean forward slowly, coming closer to my back. I can't pay attention to her words, just the proximity of him.

"Something here but not?" he repeats, deep voice so close to my ear.

"That's right. Like an echo with no point of origin," she says.

"We leave tonight," the commander says abruptly.

"The elders have asked that you leave before our ceremony. It is a holy night for us, 99th Commander."

Calliape enters through the door out of the corner of my eye, and Selene pats the seat next to her. Calliape puts her hands on the stones and smiles softly. I'm happy to see her but my attention is on the holiday and which it could be.

"We would appreciate you departing before that commencement," she says.

"We will leave immediately," the commander answers.

This could be my chance to pray to First Mother for clarity in a way that is formal and familiar. My last days of praying have been filled with distraction. It's a long shot, but I have to try.

"May I join the ceremony?" I ask.

Selene fingers the hem of her dress. "I don't think that would be appropriate, Priestess Ferren."

I can feel everyone's eyes on me and almost hear all their individual thoughts.

"Not appropriate? We are all praying to First Mother, are we not?" Calliape interjects.

"Yes. However, Ferren's prayers are . . . different, being a priestess from the Estate," Selene says.

"Like you," I say and want to immediately take it back.

She snaps her head to me, cocking it to the side with a narrow look. "Yes, that is no secret, but don't be mistaken. Just because you walk the same halls I once did does not make *us* the same."

Calliape sits back on the cushion, clearly uncomfortable, but I stare dead ahead at Selene. She only turns her attention to the whole group, dismissing me.

"Be sure to double wrap the stones. They tend to chip away at each other when left exposed," she says, emphasizing the last words, then stands.

Everyone joins and I wrap the stones up in my bag.

"The elders extend their appreciation of your service to the safety of the stones. They will protect you on your way back down. No creature of the forest will harm you when they are in your care. But do remember I heard an echo of something here and not here," Selene says.

She gestures a dismissal that seems much less friendly than before. I feel like starting back up with her; it's killing me that she has the last word. Then, there is a solid hand on my lower back pushing softly toward the door. I'm so dazed by it, I'm completely snapped out of my rage for Selene. Now, all I feel is the warmth of a Viathan commander's touch, guiding me, leading me back to our tent.

The commander leaves his hand on my back the entire way. I try to convince myself it's only because I have the stones in my bag and he is protecting them, not just me, but that feels like a bigger lie than telling them nothing is wrong.

The moment we are alone, both of them ask if I am alright. August also flat out asks me what the Albright looks like and how I got the stones. I tell them both I don't want to talk about it, but really, I can't, even if I want to. I made a deal, and the rest of what happened in that cave with the commander has my head spinning: the way he hugged me, said he had me as we traveled through the tunnels. I can't stop thinking of the way he soothed me when I thought I couldn't go on alone. I didn't think he was capable of such softness. Watching him across the fire makes my body feel flush, and I keep dipping my stare to his hands, hoping they will reach out again and hold mine the same way he did in the cave.

CHAPTER TWENTY ONE

I pack up my small number of things. I don't realize how tense I am until my teeth start throbbing from clenching them. I take a deep, intentional breath. I have the stones, I should be celebrating, but the commander keeps complicating things for me. I need to focus on getting the stones back now, and that is the only thing that matters.

I hear a small knock on the posts that support the tent, near the flap door. I peek through the crack in the fabric and see Calliape's smile. As soon as I open the canvas, she hugs me unapologetically.

"I didn't get to say goodbye," she whispers.

"First Mother forbid, I would have been devastated if I didn't see you before we left," I say.

She looks past me at August and the commander, where they strategize our exit in the back of the tent, running their fingers down the map.

"I was hoping you could stay for the holy night."

I look down, feeling ashamed for being so harsh, for putting Calliape in an awkward spot with me and her aunt.

"I'm sorry for the way I spoke," I say, bowing my head.

"Don't be. If it were up to me, we would be praying together."

Calliape's expression is soft, then a light hits her eyes as she looks around. "You can watch . . . witness us, pray with us from afar. No one but me would know. I would die for a chance to see a temple ritual on Cosima. I won't deny you this," she says.

"I don't know . . ."

"I'm on my way to the opening ceremony now. You stay in the tree line, no one will see you!"

It's a terrible idea. Selene specifically said it wasn't ok if I joined. I'm not invited. I open my mouth to object.

"Please, Ferren. I can tell you need to pray. And I would really love to pray *with* you even if you aren't next to me. Please, a parting gift?"

I think of the metal hair clip I intended to give her, but this is more substantial. I breathe out loudly and look back to see the others still bickering over the map then stuff my bag under my bed.

"I'm saying goodbye to Calliape," I call out to them.

August's attention snaps my way then past me at Calliape in the threshold. He can barely peel his eyes off her as the commander taps a portion of the map for him to focus on.

"No, you're not," the commander says without looking over at me.

"Yes, I am. We will be quick. We will probably be done before you both are."

"Don't be long," he says, finally drawing his head up to meet my eyes. His words are more of a request than a demand like they have been before.

"That's *exactly* what I just said, Commander," I say and feign a smile for him.

🌿

215

We walk through a grouping of trees just outside the edge of the village. Calliape stops me at the tree line before the forest opens up again, and she points to the next plateau down where they will be, farther away than I thought. But I will be hidden here within the darkness of the trees. It's dusk now, the torches lining the plateau below offering more light, but my position is veiled in heavy brush.

Calliape hugs me tightly. It's all-consuming and long enough to relax into. The other Frithians may judge me, see something awful in me, but I am lucky to have met Calliape. She is warm and caring. If she lived in the Estate, no punishment could keep me from seeking out her friendship.

"Blessed holy night, Ferren. Know that you will be in my prayers."

"Blessed holy night, my new friend, and . . . thank you."

She walks out of the trees, heading down to the torch lit ring. Others emerge from the trees across the clearing, all wearing long dresses and moving in synchronicity to their spots in the field. I watch as the last of them take a seat on the grass then position themselves to pray. The moon is above them, watching from the dark blush sky, as they raise their palms in devotion. It's more beautiful than any Estate painting or illustration I've ever seen—ceremony out in the open field, free and uninhibited.

I wish I could compel my body to pray with them, but my mind is racing, and I know if I even try, I won't do it justice. I want to commune with First Mother so desperately that it tugs on my heart, but I just need some time to process and breathe. Everything's happening so fast. I have the stones, but it still feels like they're in danger. I get a terrible slice of guilt in my stomach for leaving them back in the tent, but I know the others won't let anyone touch them. I don't think I will be able to rest my mind until I know they're back in the Estate.

"Forgive me, First Mother," I say on an exhale.

The people on the plateau rise in unison and begin to dance in a ritual formation, their movements telling a story. I recognize the imagery in the dance. It tells the story of First Mother's creation, how her children treated the world. How we forgot our magic and created weapons and spoiled her soil.

The Frithians draw their hands up to the moon and slowly bring them down into their wombs. They act out the times when First Mother was called back to help her children by the priestesses of old during the war with First Son.

I lean my shoulder against a large tree next to me, watching their dreamy movements, but I hear footsteps coming from behind. I know it's the commander—I can tell his footfalls now. In the beginning, he could sneak up on me so easily, but I've trained my ears to his movements.

"Can you wait until it's over to yell at me?" I say.

"I can make them let you join."

"I don't know what that means, but no. Selene said no."

"Selene says a lot."

"Yes, but this one she was right about. Forcing my way in will just prove their thoughts about me, us."

"Watching in secret . . . completely fine?" he teases.

I feel my eyes roll in my head, tendons straining in the sockets. "It is different."

We watch as the women continue their ritualistic dance. A feeling of homesickness washes over me as I realize I'll never see anything like this again, unbound and fluid. It makes me yearn for the rituals of the Estate. As stern and stoic as they are compared to this, they are familiar.

"What are they doing?" the commander asks.

"When First Mother beheld us, she saw our division, so she broke us into three. They tell the story of the three worlds."

The women come together and then separate, spinning in large circles. The commander comes closer to watch, pressing against me. I feel every nerve ending of my arm where he touches it with his, leaning in to listen, letting me know he wants me to continue.

"First Mother grew tired and fell into her slumber, leaving a stone for each people, for each of the three new worlds: maiden, mother, and crone. If we can come together, we may call her back again," I whisper.

I can't help the tears that fill my eyes at seeing the spectacle before us—beautiful and ancient, utterly tearing me apart. We watch the conclusion of the dance. I try to narrate the rest, but my voice betrays me and cracks with emotion.

"You have not been yourself since . . . Will you tell me what is wrong?" the commander asks.

There is no use pretending I'm ok. He knows and won't let up until I tell him, and for some reason, that doesn't annoy me. This time, I'm happy to have someone to tell.

"In the cave, I had to make a deal, bargain in exchange for the stones. The way the creature looked at me, it seemed frightened. I thought it was a trick at first because it didn't make sense. The way the people here look at me is the same way you and August did when you found out what I really was. Like you all know something about me that I don't. Like you all know I'm . . . evil. Like I have offended you when you watch me pray, communing with First Mother the only way I know how."

I glance over at him, and he says nothing, just holds space for me to continue.

"It was nice at first—you and August listening to me, taking me seriously. I'd like to go somewhere where I'm not pitied for my station or looked at with judgment. Frith is no different from Cosima in that way." I stop myself, feeling pathetic for being so vulnerable.

"Why do you care what I think?" It comes out with harder edges than I know he meant, the words uncareful but his tone soft.

"I don't," I say with a sniffle.

"Seems you do."

The women trail into the forest, taking the torches with them. I watch as the last woman disappears into the trees, leaving the field in darkness. We are all alone in the woods now, making the feel of the commander's gaze on the side of my face a little too intense.

"Where is August?" I say too suddenly, like I've lost him.

"Guarding the stones you left. After all that work too." I can almost hear a half smile in his voice.

"I knew they'd be safe."

The commander scoffs. "I would not worry what the people of Frith think about you. It's not your fault the three worlds are divided or that the division is still at the forefront of their minds. It's the way things are."

I can feel my pulse beating on my chest like my heart wants to jump out onto the forest floor. He didn't even say anything *that* nice, but the sincerity in his voice smoothed any jagged lines of his words.

"We should get back," he says, cutting off my own thoughts.

"Oh, okay. Well, I never thanked you for helping me in the cave, for getting us out and for what you said."

"Surprised?" he says, mimicking my tone from when I said it to him.

I nod. "Well, not that you got us out. Not that part."

The commander leans closer, one deliberate step. I push my back against a tree, giving him space, but he towers over, making me stare up into his visor.

"What part then?" he says low and baritone.

I squirm a little under his intensity, stumbling on my words. "You made me feel."

"Made you feel what, Priestess?"

"Don't call me that. It sounds like before when you didn't trust me."

His forearm reaches to the tree over my head, encasing me in. The moon reflects off his metal armor in a dangerous halo. I am alone in the forest of Frith with a Viathan commander. The thought alone sends a sinful chill over the exposed skin on my arms and neck.

"Commander . . . ," I say in a sigh.

He shakes his head. "No, Ferren. Then you do not call me Commander either."

"99," I whisper.

He pushes closer, his body just inches from pinning mine.

I feel like prey, my heartbeat quickening, my breath moving to my chest, the rise and fall not fast enough.

His mask moves down to my collarbone, and I know he is watching the labored pant as my breasts squeeze against my neckline for air. His alluring scent unwinds my tense muscles into a warm puddle.

"If you're so concerned with my thoughts of you . . . then take a look," he says, gesturing to his head, inviting me to look into his mind's eye—something I've been too afraid to do until now.

I see my own reflection in the metal. I close my eyes and try to push through. The door is open but it's so hard to muck into. I reach out to touch his chest, cold with armor but still an electric connection. He opens for me instantly.

I cross the opening of his thoughts, and it's like coming out of muddy waters. There is amber light and memories floating around: images of me, my smile, of me helping August when he was stung, the sound of my yelling at them to put their weapons away, me standing between them with spears pointed at their necks, then flashing images of my lips as I speak to him, stolen glances. Then I'm in the cave, my eyes closed in the dark, and I'm feeling my hand in his as he says he has me. I see what he is seeing now. Not in his mind's eye anymore, but through his eyes.

My lips.

He's watching me as I look into his thoughts. I open my eyes, dazed by the influx of images, staring up at the large helmet that blots out the light from the moon.

99 reaches up with a gloved hand to brush a strand of my hair from my cheek. I exhale shakily, the amber light of his mind still lingering between us. I feel a rough knuckle trace down my cheek, then he slides his thumb across my bottom lip slowly, like he is savoring it.

My body tenses, reminding me just how close together we are. With every exhale, he draws closer, leaving less space between us. Then his pelvis presses into me, pinning me against the tree. My body responds instantly, heat flooding my core. There is a low rumble in his chest at the feel of my hips rolling toward him. His hand tightens on my jaw, drawing my head back to expose my neck. I pant, staring into his visor, savoring the pressure of him against the front of my pussy. I want to wrap my legs around him and rock myself against the hardness of his length that's digging into my stomach.

But the caress of his hand going down my collarbone halts suddenly.

Then his posture changes as he looks out into the woods, as if checking if we are still alone. I start to speak but he cuts me off with a rude shush.

"Excuse me!" I say, snapping out of my daze.

He covers my mouth with the hand that just touched my skin so softly, now holding my words hostage. I wiggle underneath him, the familiar annoyance at his mysteriousness coming back.

"I heard something. Stay here," he whispers, leaning in closer.

He leaves, just leaves.

Sometimes his mysteriousness is intriguing, but most of the time, it's enraging. I watch 99 trail off into the woods, leaving me alone after what just happened and what I just saw in his head. I run my hands down my face, feeling the flushness of my cheeks at what was building between us.

I knew something changed in that cave, but now I know for sure 99 felt it too. Something has . . . shifted. The thought of him coming back is exciting and terrifying. I picture him sauntering out of the darkness toward me, the way he does with his undeniably muscular form under all that armor.

Should I just leave and go back to the tent? If he comes back, I don't think I will be able to stop myself, and that could be dangerous.

This is someone who has made me miserable, cuffed me, and also killed someone in front of me. *But,* he also defended me, offered to escort me while I prayed, asked if I needed to go pray when I had forgotten, and kept me safe. I bite at the spot on my lip he touched.

I should go back with August, my sweet chaperone. This is too much to get my head around after today and the long journey through the forest. I can't add another thing that I need to sift through. I've already let what others think of me cloud my thoughts and affect me communing with First Mother.

I just want . . . to go home, back to my routine. I mimic the soft gesture of his thumb over my bottom lip and almost fall back into the rough bark.

With a huff, I take a single step toward the village, and as soon as I do, I hear rustling as he walks back toward me. I get overwhelmed with nerves, but he doesn't say anything—so mystifying again. I press into his mind playfully, but I cannot enter it. There is no amber light; there's no light at all.

I'm frozen, the sensation of something dark slinking up behind me, not the warm, safe light I got from 99. I turn to look, knowing how different it feels now, and it's not 99 at all. The figure is completely dark and smokey. It's a ghost of a man coming toward me from the dark forest, one who is here but also who is not, just as Selene said.

CHAPTER TWENTY TWO

Everything in me screams to run.

There's a ringing in my ears so loud, it's hot and icy all at once. My palms are on the forest floor. I feel a pull on my back, a tug like I'm connected to something—a children's puppet plucked upward. I claw at the ground, grabbing onto anything to get away. Dirt and debris wedge under my nails as I skid across roots with no purchase.

The shadowy figure has me.

Then a thunderbolt plunges deep into my skin. It pushes me facedown into the leafy ground. I cough and gasp, discarded bark scraping my cheek.

Then it releases with a searing pinch that takes my breath from me.

I roll over to my side, touching the red-hot spot that went through my back and out my chest.

Time passes languidly.

I feel my chest tightening with every labored breath.

99 is on top of the person who attacked me, his movements brutal, blowing downward with vicious strikes that are savage and unhinged.

The sounds of 99 killing him must be horrific, but I hear nothing but my body screaming its pain.

I move to my back, looking up at the dark freckled sky, blacked out leaves dancing for me in the canopy. I am drifting, like I'm falling asleep, but I know it's not going to be the same. I will not wake up. I will not be here when the stones are returned or when First Mother comes.

I gasp for air, unable to take in a satisfying breath. I'm going home to my First Mother and to see my second, to finally meet them both.

I hear 99's voice calling out to me.

My body is suspended.

I'm traveling somewhere, cradled. Amber light warms me like the sun. I hear voices, 99 shouting. Why is he shouting? Where is First Mother, my second mother? Why don't I see them?

My body is released onto a hard surface, eliciting searing hot pain that shoots through me. Snapping my eyes back to reality, I scream, letting out too much air. But it doesn't feel like I'm the one screaming; I'm separate. My body cramps in pain, I can feel it, but I'm just an observer. My chest is restricted, the pressure unbearable. I try to take a breath but it stops short, like something won't let it in. I thrash wildly, my wound raw and sharp. I'm lying in something wet, fabric sticking. I can't smell 99 anymore, only the metallic smell of blood, so much blood.

"Get her on her stomach!" Selene says.

99's strong hands turn me roughly and I fight him, screaming out in agony. His helmet is off, hair messy, with so much blood on him. His expression is . . . unfamiliar.

I'm on my stomach now, letting me take in air a little better.

"Calliape, go get Ruth!"

I panic as my breath gets more labored and shallow. I watch 99's face, trying to get any clue of what is happening.

"Hold her!" Selene says.

99 pushes down on my shoulders, making me cry out. Any extra touch is torture. I watch as Calliape leaves the tent.

August is standing in view now, his face half covered by his hand, eyes giving away how scared he is, how much he is crying. I watch him for the answers I can't get from 99's expression.

I'm dying. My friend is watching me die.

"August, you need to go get the stones. Go now!" 99 says.

August exits, leaving a hollow spot.

A woman rushes in with Calliape, carrying a large bag. They walk past my view and behind me.

I can feel myself fading, going back into a green billowy room of light. I can't tell if time is passing but the pain keeps shooting me into the present, back on the hard surface. I feel another set of hands on me, and they are cutting my top, exposing my back.

"It just missed her lung. Something is wedged in there. Hold her very still. Calliape, help hold her!" a woman's voice says.

"What is that?" 99 sounds concerned.

"It's a piece of metal. I need to get it out. Hold her still," she says.

"99," I say, throaty and broken.

He crouches down next to me, expression changing from scared to something else. I reach for his hand that's holding my shoulder and without hesitation, he grabs it, bringing his face closer to mine.

"I have you," he says.

I turn as much as I can tolerate to see a long needle and giant tweezers sitting on a table next to me. She said she had to get something out with those gruesome tools. A panic flushes over my skin, making it harder to breathe. I can barely take in any air again.

"Keep your eyes on me, Ferren." 99 holds me still as I gasp and gulp on nothing.

I squeeze his hand twice like he did to mine in the cave, then I notice just a hint of water on his lower lids. My breath makes pink speckles on the pillow as I heave, watching his beautiful face.

"We need to do this now!" the woman says.

99 gets so close to my face, a bloody mist kisses his lips as I exhale.

"Squeeze my hand as hard as you need. I'm right here."

I feel the healer press a clamp into the opening in my skin, just under my shoulder blade. I feel a tiny point press into the surface, the intensity suffocating. I brace down onto 99's hand as she fishes in my wound, opening and ripping it apart over and over.

"Shit, it's stuck in there! Hold her!"

I hear the sound before I feel it: the squelching flesh then a splatter of liquid. I feel a pinch and then a dull punch to the back. Gripping fingers dig into my body, hooking and exploring. With my next breath, my whole chest explodes, ballooning outward in a scream.

"Got it!"

I exhale more dense red speckles onto 99's face and cling to the table with one hand, grasping at him with the other. His expression is so unfamiliar, but it's enough to distract me, as if he's in as much pain as I am.

I can feel myself slipping away again. I squeeze on 99's hand twice. Then squeeze again.

And again.

The pain is just too hard to process, and the edges of my vision ripple. I close my eyes, there is a flutter sound like wings, and then it's black. All black.

I wake up on my side, facing the wall, sunlight dancing on it.

When I roll to my back, a shooting pain elicits a shocked gasp.

A gauzy nightgown clings to my skin in cold sweat, and I am tucked into a bed like someone put me here. I adjust myself, groaning in pain, but I can tell the edge of it has been dulled from the strange taste in my mouth. They're familiar herbs used for surgery in the Estate, minty and distinguishable. Excellent for pain management but terrible for keeping your wits.

"Hey, hey, easy," August says.

He is sitting in a chair next to my bed, hands out like he's afraid to touch me.

"August," I say, a mixture of bubbling tears and confusion.

"I'm so happy you're okay." He brushes my hair back, getting on his knees next to my bed.

"What happened?"

"You were attacked. We believe it was on orders from First Son."

"The stones?"

"Here, safe still. The metal human we saw in the forest, we think— well, it may have sent some information back after all," August says and drops his eyes.

He thinks this is his fault? I should be the one feeling guilty for touching it, for being so stupid to approach.

"99?" I ask.

A small grin teases one corner of his mouth at hearing me say the nickname. "He stayed with you for as long as he could. All night. They are out scouting, and it took a lot for me to convince him to leave you with me," he says.

"Is there water?"

He shoots up. "I'll go get you some. And I'll let Selene and Ruth know you're awake," he says.

I sit up slowly, making terrible groans as I do. I look around, wondering whose little room I'm in, trying not to picture 99 in here with me all night, watching over me. It's too intimate and makes my heart hurt, thinking of his expression when I was in pain.

I hear August back in the doorway, but he doesn't say anything or enter with water. I look over my shoulder at the silence. Instead, it's 99, armored and helmeted, taking up the whole entrance. My eyes track him as he slowly enters, pulling the chair from next to my headboard and placing it beside me, sitting down without a word. I feel strangely vulnerable, tucked in bed with just a sweated through nightgown on. It contrasts against his formal armor, hard and cold. I feel his gaze on me even though I can't see his eyes again. He must be mad at me, must think this is my fault.

"Did you find anything?" I say meekly.

He shakes his head.

"Can you take that off?" I say, wanting to see his face desperately.

He shakes his head again slowly.

Frustration boils inside me. He's just sitting there, not speaking, staring and hiding behind that stupid helmet. After what happened in the forest between us, the cave, after I saw glimpses of real emotion last night when I was on the table bleeding out, now he is silent. *Now* he chooses to be stoic again. I want him to wrap his arms around me and say he has me and that he's so happy I'm alright.

"I'm serious. Take it off," I say and cringe in pain.

No response.

"Take the fucking thing off, 99!" I plead.

"I can't."

His voice is different, softer, almost pained. It's enough to ease my building frustration. He raises his hand, placing it on the bed next to my thigh palm up, like he wants me to place mine on his. "We know it was First Son. We have to scan farther out, August, some of the village members, and me. Selene has agreed to let you stay—to care for you."

"Wait, you're leaving? Without me?" The pain in my chest grows, my heart starting to pound, pulse ringing in my ears.

"There could be others," he says with a big breath.

"Ok, but you're not leaving me here."

"You have to stay. It's dangerous—you're injured."

"I don't want you to leave me." I look down at his hand then slide mine into it. His fingers engulf mine at the small contact, thumb dragging over the top.

"99, please," I whisper my plea.

"It's not safe." His voice is as desperate as mine.

"It's never been safe."

"I will come back for you," he says.

I stare down at his large hand in mine, the light, comforting touch urging me to understand. And I do. I know I am too weak to leave as I am, but it still hurts and I am terrified of being left behind. I feel him lean closer, the top of his helmet resting on my forehead. He is refusing to take it off, but he doesn't need to. I know he thinks this is his fault, that he failed to protect me so now he has to fix that.

I draw back from him, holding a hand to the side of his mask, wishing I were looking into his eyes. I know they are affixed on mine, burrowing into me with his regret and guilt. I want to say so many things to him. I want him to talk to me, really talk, but we are both frozen in place.

August and Selene come into the room. 99 rises from his chair, erasing any remaining bit of connection between us. August burrows a hole into the side of my turned-away face, probably realizing that 99 has broken the news to me.

"I need to help her up. Ruth is on her way. You both have to leave,"

Selene says.

I sit up straighter painfully, using my forearms as a weak brace.

I wait until I know 99's back is to me to look over. He pauses for a moment, as if contemplating saying goodbye or turning back, but then he exits as if he couldn't bear seeing me looking back at him as he leaves. Like it would stop him from leaving entirely. August gives me a half smile and a sincere apology.

Selene helps me undo my nightgown and pull it down my body to my abdomen. My breasts are bound by the bandage that wraps around my ribs. She helps me drink from a cup, green pieces floating in it—more strong minty leaves—but I don't care. I'm so thirsty.

A woman I recognize from last night walks in, setting her large bag down on the chair. Selene touches her shoulder on the way out without a word.

I watch the healer hunch over her bag of supplies, glancing down at the cup to see my progress. "You will want to drink all of that. Nasty, but helps with the healing," she says.

I crinkle my face as I down the rest.

"Your body has been through a lot. It will take some time to recover. But healing can also be very taxing on the mind. We need to tend to that as well," she says.

"You are Ruth?"

She nods and holds up her palms, asking permission to address my bandages. I lift my arms slightly for her to wrap around me. Her touch is gentle and motherly as she peels off the last painful strip. I can't see the wound but can feel exactly where it is.

Ruth lays the bandage next to me, and I catch a glimpse of it: red, yellow, and, to my surprise, green.

"Is it infected?"

"Oh no, that's an herb paste to ward off infection. It's very deep so we have to be careful," Ruth says.

Hearing that makes me start coughing uncontrollably. She holds on to me as the panicked cough makes my eyes water.

"That's okay, Priestess Ferren."

My lungs scream and my chest constricts. I can taste blood in my mouth, see it on my palms as I cough into them. Ruth braces me as I mist blood onto her linen sleeve. She comforts me and encourages me to cough more.

"It's good to get that out. It's not supposed to be in there. Your body knows it," she says.

"There is blood in my lungs?" I wipe my mouth and see more blood on my hand.

"A little from the trauma. The metal piece was right next to your lung, so coughing is the only way to get rid of it. Lean into it."

By the time she's done cleaning and changing my bandages, my head is swirling from the effects of the green leaves. I thank her lazily as she tucks me back in bed.

I face away from the doorway and stare at the wood grain pattern on the wall. Maybe I should pray, but I'm too weak to form any formal words or to string something beautiful together.

I close my eyes tightly but see flashes of 99 in the woods, of the man—the thing—that stabbed me. 99 is holding me and yelling for help. August's face is teary. 99's beautiful, pained eyes are on me, his amber light. He's touching me, holding my hand in the cave. I brush my lips where he touched them in the forest. More amber light.

I'm overwhelmed and dizzy from the medicine. The images and the thoughts keep ticking by, making the pillowcase under me damp with tears. I just need to sleep, to stop thinking.

Please, just sleep.

CHAPTER TWENTY THREE

I can feel someone in the room with me, hear a soft and calm breathing. I reach out into the space with my mind's eye, trying to find theirs, a hook waiting for them to unknowingly latch on. I'm too weak to turn my head, but whoever it is, their presence is pleasant and familiar. I press forward into their thoughts, slithering in and seeing the forest, grass, and moss streaming past me, like I'm running.

Calliape's voice breaks the mystery.

"Okay, well, now I know you're awake. I felt that," she says, amused.

I smile and slowly turn to look at her, seeking some comfort. "That's impressive. I am pretty sloppy when I don't get permission first."

"I don't know about sloppy. Annoying for sure. Like a tiny gnat in my ear."

Even laughing a little makes me cough. Calliape helps me sit up, holding on to me as I finish. My cough stops but I stay there in Calliape's embrace, not wanting to let go.

"You scared me, Ferren, scared us all."

Selene barges in before I can answer and lets out a deep exhale at the sight of us. I let go of Calliape and lie back, wincing as I adjust myself. She hands me another cup with green floating things.

"Drink. We need to get you up and walking."

"Walking? She can barely breathe. She needs to rest," Calliape says.

"Ruth said she needs to walk. To get whatever is left in her lungs out. Ferren, you've been coughing nonstop all night."

"It does feel like something is rattling around in there," I say, clutching to my chest.

"Moving will help."

She draws my blankets down, almost clawing at me to sit up more. Her touch is much different than the calm motherly way Ruth has about her, gentle and patient, always asking if she can first.

"Selene, really?" Calliape says.

"I'm fine," I say and clear my throat.

"Just to the gathering room."

They help me to the edge of the bed as I struggle to hold onto them, body screaming to be put back. I have to stop and cough every few steps, making my head spin as we shuffle forward. I'm hunched over like a sickly elder priestess. The sight of them always made Thea sad. I find it fascinating seeing their frail forms still housing so much power, their gifts at their peak. It seems like a privilege to grow so powerful and old.

"That's enough," Calliape says.

"No! I'm okay." Sweat beads on my brow, and my chest restricts like a clenching hand.

In the next few steps, we get to the gathering room and I drop to my knees, coughing.

"Alright, that's good. Let's have you rest here," Selene says.

"That was too much for her," Calliape says as she helps me rest back against an ottoman on the floor, grabbing blankets and putting a pillow behind my back, propping me up.

I squeeze Calliape's forearm as a weak thank you. I'm completely out of breath from a small trip and I'm afraid if I speak, I'll start coughing all over again.

Calliape smiles at me and whispers, "Rest, friend. I will go let Ruth know you're awake."

Selene roughly hands me a bowl of plain broth. I sip it and watch her clang things around, giving off a very unwelcome air. The passive aggressiveness is something I am very familiar with. It's almost a second language for high priestesses and elders. It doesn't faze me at all. Completely unsurprising, Selene is predictable at best.

"I can move to the other tent. The one I was in before."

"No . . . because then I would have to make trips every time I need to care for you."

"I'm sorry to burden you," I say, not meaning it.

Selene slams a kettle down then takes a deep breath, holding on to the table. "I told you and the Viathans to go, to leave."

I knew she didn't like me, but now I'm starting to realize how cruel she really is. I can barely breathe and my allies have left me here until First Mother knows when.

"You've had a . . . problem with me long before that," I say, gulping down air.

Selene walks over and grabs the bowl of food that I haven't finished.

"No need to argue, you're too weak."

I stare daggers at her. "Trust me, your odds are better now more than ever."

I lean back to stare at the ceiling, not caring enough to see or hear her response. The medicinal herbs I've been drinking make me feel like I'm floating while also taking away the sharp, pinching pain. Nothing she says can hurt me, and no amount of shaming me can make me feel any lower than I do.

I drift in a groggy wave from the tea, my body wanting to sleep but my mind clinging to consciousness.

Time passes differently in my stupor. Seemingly in the very next moment, I can hear the breathy mumbles of Calliape returning with Ruth, careful not to wake me, then heated whispers all around me. I fight against the fever dreams, forcing myself to wake fully again. It takes me a moment to realize where I am, that August and 99 are gone, the whispers not from them.

I look around, trying to adjust my vision and scoot myself back up against the ottoman. It's soft and covered in a white pillowy animal pelt like most of the blankets in my room.

Selene and Calliape whisper to each other in the kitchen, hushed and tense. I know they are speaking about me when they both gaze over their shoulders. Selene washes the large ceramic pot she cooks with, scrubbing hard as if she's using it as a way to get out frustration. Even though they don't seem happy with each other, it looks peaceful . . . homey even. Like the families who live close to the Estate, ones I can see living their lives from the stained-glass windows in the grand room. Happy, frustrated, or just concentrated on cleaning, they are together, sharing those feelings freely, not pushing them down in fear of speaking out of turn or angering a temple member.

"How are you feeling?" Ruth's question snaps my attention to her, sending my head into a dizzy spell.

She sits down in the layered blankets next to me. Already, her presence is calm and thoughtful, a welcome buffer from the hostility emanating off Selene.

"I'm . . . just so tired, dizzy." I pause, holding my head until it settles again. "The tea makes me feel strange."

She cups a bigger bowl full of green mossy liquid, drawing it back as if she knows I will protest more of her remedies. Steam from it hits my nose, the scent sending me straight back to the moss layer of the forest. I breathe in greedily, squeezing my eyes shut to savor the memory: the aroma of dew on the spongy ground, the feeling of lying next to 99 for warmth, and the three of us walking through the moss, kicking up the smell.

"Well, this one is only to breathe in. You don't have to drink it," Ruth says, wafting a hand over the rising mist. She acts out breathing in deeply with a smile.

I gladly lean in and inhale the hot vapor through my nose, denser and more pungent than the hint I got before. I draw in large, slow drags of it, filling myself until my troubled lung aches. Ruth smiles with encouragement, humming and praising my deep breaths.

With another intake, a prickling sensation spreads through my throat, like a sharp soreness that comes with a fever. I clear it with a huff but it bites at the walls of my neck, now tingling in my chest. I cough with no relief at the new sense of restriction in my throat.

Ruth holds the bowl higher to me wordlessly, instructing me to breathe in more of the steam that chokes me. I clutch at my chest, no longer able to politely smother my hacking. I push the bowl out of my way, pulling my torso from the fur covers then planting my palms in an animalistic hunch.

Ruth moves closer and places a smoothing hand on my back that turns to a strong thrumming pat. Something is stuck inside me, I realize now. She is trying to draw it out, and eliciting a cough to force it from my body. With one deep, labored hack, the thing stuck is gruesomely unplugged, leaving an empty feeling. A mucusy red clot expels from my throat onto the blanket. As soon as it's out, I take in a satisfying gasp. It burns but I can finally fill my lungs freely. I sit up, gasping greedily for more, falling back to open my chest.

She scoots over, picking up the cloth I just evacuated on, nods to me proudly, and puts it in the fire.

"Your wound is healing beautifully, but the fluid in your lung was worrisome. You did well, Priestess Ferren," she says.

The air I can take in is colder and more refreshing now, the large gulps of it making me feel more alert.

Ruth runs a cold wet rag over my sweaty forehead, pushing back the hair that sticks to it. "I'm sorry I didn't tell you. Sometimes our mind puts limits on what the body can do. Yours did so well," she says, taking a full cup of water from Calliape and handing it to me, making sure my hands grasp it before letting go.

I suck it down in long gulps, finishing it with a gasp. My actions are undignified and messy, manifesting in ways I never would behave even with the healer in the Estate. Ruth is right. I would have held back if I knew what she wanted me to do. I would have restricted myself from bursting in front of these women in favor of an unproductive poised cough. But it felt . . . good, something my body and mind needed to expel. I look up at the women who held space for me to do so, encouraging me even.

"Do you think whatever was in there is out now?" I say, clearing the last of the dryness in my throat.

"Yes, I do. But I won't be surprised if you cough for a while longer. Do not fight it," Ruth says, pressing the spot over the wound on my back like she is feeling for obstructions as I breathe in again. "I want you to keep drinking the tea for the pain. There is no reason to be clearheaded while you're resting. Rest and sleep."

After another full day of sleeping, brain-fogging tea, and Ruth fussing over my bandages, I start to feel like myself again. Hunger drives me from the bed, so I press my ear to the seam of my door, but the crackling fire is the only noise. My hosts must have gone to bed. I steal some bread from the pantry and decide I am in desperate need of fresh air. I feel somehow closer to August and 99 out in the open air, waiting for them to return. I cross the threshold of Selene's front door, lightly treading on the wooden landing of her porch.

"Blessed night, Priestess Ferren."

The phrase sends a homesick chill down my spine, prickling my skin in the already brisk night. Selene sits in the pitch dark. My eyes are not quite adjusting after the glow of the fire inside, so I'm only able to make out her calm outline. The bound up feeling she gives me is not quite as intense as before. She sits with no light, no torch, perfectly still. I inch closer to her in the corner of the small, covered platform. The lattice roof above lets in moonbeams between the vines that snake through it. At her feet, there is a bowl of water nestled in the grass, the moon above reflected in it.

She's making moon water.

"I assumed you abandoned all our rituals," I say, sitting down with a wince.

"No, of course not."

There is a long, blank pause from her, like she is listening to someone else speak and waiting for her turn. I can hear the rustle of the trees around us, small saplings between the houses and larger mature giants toward the forest line.

"Mary must have cared for you. I do not see her tolerating any priestess as an assistant unless that were true."

"I cared for her as well . . . as much as she would allow," I say, a little dumbstruck that she has brought her up.

"I can hear it in your voice when you have to speak on things she would have. You have not grieved her, have you?" she says, looking out into the darkness of the night.

"No, of course not. I couldn't hold a death ceremony for her on the Viathan ship." My tone is defensive. Mary deserves better, and if that means she has to wait, then so be it. Her death will be respected, and I cannot fulfill that task as I am now.

"That is not the grief I mean, and Mary would not have held such standards and restrictions even in death. But I think you know that."

Selene may have considered Mary a friend, reminiscing on her prickly nature but still insulting me in the same breath. Mary spoke of the Frithian elders, how we would speak to them, what traditions we would uphold. Was she waiting to tell me about the people who live here, who wear Cosima clothing, ones who now call Frith home for reasons I can't begin to understand?

"Mary helped me leave Cosima, me and Calliape's mother."

"Oh?" I say, realizing they have not mentioned the rest of Calliape's family until now.

"We were both high priestesses in the Estate. She died years ago; the trees around her burial site still whisper to me from time to time, sending me memories they absorbed from her essence."

"I am sorry."

"No need. It is a nice thought that I could have the same endless connection with my dear friend Mary, but she will be buried on Cosima where she belongs."

The sadness in her voice creates an empathetic cushion to my harsh criticism of her, of why Selene left in the first place. I can spare a morsel of compassion, temporarily at least.

"Mary never mentioned you in all my years as her assistant, or any other person from Cosima living here. Never once did she tell me."

"To this, I have no doubt. Mary was very good at keeping secrets. We simply wanted something . . . different, Calliape's mother, the people you see here, and me. I hope you will do the same in honor of her."

Small insects sing in a buzzing hum, seeming to take in a breath between notes all at the same time then resuming the melody. In the next moment, I realize what Selene is asking of me: to keep the same secret of her and the people living here. That includes Calliape, daughter of a high priestess. If the Estate heard of her existence, I have no doubt they would all but order her to come to Cosima—a fact that would get complicated fast. Between my respect for Mary and not wanting to cloud my own return, the answer is clear.

"I will keep your secret."

We both listen to the musical inhale and exhale of the chirping insects. I realize I am breathing in synchronicity to their sound, trying to pacify the dull ache in my wound. It takes every bit of concentration to keep my thoughts present and focused. I internally recite every object I look at to ground myself. My thoughts drift to the grass, the moon water, then somehow to 99.

"Your Viathans will return soon, Priestess Ferren. They left the stones with the elders."

I scowl, trying to sift through mistrust and anger toward her. They left the stones here, which is safer than carrying them to find any other First Son followers. Any doubt of their return, I fought with in my weak herb-induced moments would have been washed away if I knew that.

She touches a leaf from the vine climbing the porch pole next to her, a tiny whimsical movement. She is flexing her gift right in front of my eyes. She said she can read intention from miles away, through the forest and the roots network.

"Even in this very moment, the leaves whisper of the 99th Commander's desire to return . . . for you."

Somewhere out there, in the forest of Frith, 99 is scouting, trying to find the followers of First Son who did this to me.

Selene smiles at me with tight, lined lips, brushing her puffy white hair back with an expectant look toward me. "The trees also gossip of your ever evolving gifts."

"What?" I tense my body all over again, knowing exactly what she is referring to.

"I was not able to speak to them before I arrived on Frith. I had minor gifts, just enough to ascend, some I don't even remember anymore. But the moment I stepped into the grass, the entire world seemed to welcome me." She pauses, looking out into the tree line then moving the bowl of moon water with her feet. "The trees talk to each other below the surface here. They know when one is sick, needs more light, or has to be sacrificed, the roots holding each other perfectly in place. Anyone can tap into the veins of the trees, talk to them, but they select very few to link to their sacred language."

There are so few trees in the Estate. The one growing in the courtyard looks so sad compared to the ones here. I've never sat on grass or pressed my palms to it while I prayed like I did the first night. It felt different, like I wasn't quite alone, like someone was truly listening. When I press my palms to pray in the temple, the stone is cold and empty.

"Stones can speak as well, but when a stone has been cut into pieces and rearranged, its answers get mixed up. The stones become confused. They're porous and start to absorb the words and ideas spoken in rooms they adorn. They start to take on the morals of the ones speaking the loudest, the ones who speak most often. I believe your highest priestess was one for speeches, if I am remembering correctly," she says, seeming to answer my thoughts about praying in the temple.

I tug on my own tether, making sure we have not accidentally made a link, giving her too much insight into my train of thought. I stare at her suspiciously, but she ignores me. I have to stop myself from lashing out at hearing the name on her lips, but I know Crixa would not even entertain these almost mad babblings. Selene can have her opinions; they mean very little hidden away on this mountain.

"I am not surprised more of yours manifested here either, exactly when your body needed to protect itself," she says as if she didn't just say something offensive moments ago.

I looked down at my flat palms, fully taking in the lines and creases like I have never observed them in such detail before.

"I was not sure if it was mine."

"Whose else would it be, Priestess Ferren?"

Calliape stands over me as Ruth works on my bandages. Her eyebrows flick up to check if I have finished the smaller dose of medicinal herbs, just enough to dull the pain and hopefully keep me from a spinning mind.

"Ferren, this looks almost healed. What have you been doing?" Ruth asks, applying more of the cold green paste to my back.

"Just . . . whatever you tell me too." I am a little confused that she is surprised her own remedies are working.

"I'm not letting you out of my sight today. You will have to deal with that," Calliape says as if it's a punishment.

We spend the rest of the day planted in the gathering room by the fire. Calliape's cheeks are red on her golden skin from sitting too close. We survive off large hunks of bread, biting right into the loaf. She asks me more about the temple, the Estate. I tell her about my small room in the lesser priestess wing, the guards that blend into the walls. She whispers gossip about some of the Frithian villagers, some with gifts from First Mother. I do not know their names but easily become invested in each story, most of which are racy and leave us laughing into a puddle.

She asks me about my gifts, what it's like to see into someone's mind's eye. I give her examples of some extreme experiences, leaving out what it was like to be in 99's. That one is just for me.

"Selene told me about your other one, the green light you can elicit," Calliape says in a hushed voice.

"Elicit? No. How do you keep anything a secret with her? It was impossible to block her out last night."

"We have an understanding," she says, nodding with big eyes, letting me know it was possibly a problem that needed resolving for her too. I can only assume Calliape has a ward up against it by her tone.

"You should lean into it, Ferren. Try to control it, harness it," she continues, rising to her knees as if it's too important to sit.

"And what about *your* gifts? I've wanted to ask since you said you were . . . Mother blessed but wasn't sure if it was rude."

"You could have asked. I have a couple of small gifts. And one I've mastered with some practice. I can fold distances while I travel."

I try to figure out what she means, and she can read it on my face. She has me hold out my hands flat. She stands her two fingers on the ledge of one, and with her other hand, she indicates I should close my hands together and then walks her two fingers across.

"Are you serious?"

"Yes, even if I don't know exactly what the destination looks like. The ground knows and it folds for me. I just take one step."

"That's amazing. I have to see it."

"Doesn't look like much from the outside, but a real priestess from the Estate beholding my gifts, swoon," she jokes.

I double over, feeling floaty from the wine we have stolen from the kitchen. Sipping it doesn't take away the ache in my chest but rather makes me feel too giddy to care.

"Calliape." Selene's voice is strained. She carries a bundle of wood in her arms for the fire, glaring at our little camp around it.

Calliape presses her lips together so tightly, trying to smother a laugh that when it does come out, the sound is a watery hiss.

"Coming!" she calls out and runs over to unburden Selene's arms.

I stare into the warm glowing coals of our fire, feeling a little more comfortable taking up space here after my day with Calliape. Even Selene appears to be tolerating me more. Though, that was before Calliape retrieved the wine from a locked cupboard and drank most of it with me.

I sit up from my reclined position to see why neither of them has made their way farther into the room. I can hear their voices, but I can't make out what they are saying. They lean in to hush whispers, still standing in the doorway.

"What is it?" I ask.

The two of them stare at me, frozen like statues who were almost caught moving. Calliape glances at Selene, who returns the look with a small, almost imperceptible nod. But I notice it. Days in the forest with 99 have taught me to be more observant, that every hand flex, every tilt of the head means something, gives something away. Selene looks at me and forces her expression to be unnaturally pleasant.

"I've received word about the scouting party," Selene says.

I widen my eyes for her to continue, preparing for the worst.

"They ran into some *trouble*, but they are on their way back. Expected tomorrow."

There is a fluttering deep in my stomach at the thought of the Viathans coming back for me.

They are returning.

CHAPTER TWENTY FOUR

I am finally leaving this village to finish what we started. I feel another nervous flip in my stomach at seeing 99 again. An image of embracing him makes my mind drift to feeling his armor pressed against me. I try to remember what I saw in his mind's eye the night I was attacked. It feels so far away, as if the entire ordeal was a fever dream.

It must be close to dawn. I can see light coming in through the slats in my window shutters. I anxiously dress and sit on the dew-covered porch, already feeling better breathing in the cold morning air.

I extend my bare feet, touching the chill in the grass.

Where are you, 99?

It's a long shot to push into his mind at any distance other than right next to me, but it was so distinct from any other I've been in. To my surprise, I feel myself sink into the ground through my feet, traveling through the blackness in the soil. My vision shoots up into the forest, a thrilling warmth embracing me as I find him. He's on guard while the rest of the scouting party still sleeps around him. Their small fire has gone out, just smoke trailing out of it. He sits with a bent leg, looking out into the morning light stoic and deadly, as if any creature that the forest sends is no match.

I press forward, straight into his thoughts. When I enter, I pass through an amber lit veil, seeing what he thinks in real time. His body is completely still but his mind is a frenzy of anxious emotions, ones that are constant and frantic, ones he fights to suppress. The amber warmth responds to my presence inside with him. It embraces me, flushing over my skin, making my physical body respond. It slows his thoughts, sending images of kissing my lips, touching my bare skin. He presses against me, running a tongue down the column of my neck as he plunges himself inside me.

Shocked, I pull from his mind, snapping our tether. My breath is labored, like I ran the distance back. Green, flashing orbs dance in the morning fog around me then fade out, the rush of adrenaline sending the still unfamiliar light from me. I'm alone but feel like I have been caught spying. I cover my mouth to stifle a secret breathy laugh.

If you want to know what I think of you, then look.

He made me a willing link to look into his mind's eyes, permission freely given that night in the forest, but I wasn't prepared for what I saw this time. I feel another flip in my stomach, nervousness now mixed with anticipation. Knowing that he is thinking of me in that way is a deafening reminder that what we started that night in the forest can not go unresolved.

"Concentrate, what did it feel like each time you manifested your light?" Calliape asks, crossed-legged in front of me with her eyes shut.

"Like overwhelming fear, but this morning it was . . . because of something else," I say coyly, not fully understanding what she is trying to do.

"Close your eyes!"

"Ok, sorry!"

The gentle breeze makes the tall grass we sit in tickle my sides. I feel as jumpy as August thinking it's a bug and pull away.

"Take my hand. Do you feel anything?"

I open one eye to cup her palm, and she yanks it lightly as if she knows I'm not concentrating again. But then I feel her reaching out—the calm, pleasant hook to her mind's eye. I snag it with an undignified swing, slithering in like a snake.

Her thoughts prompt me to stand alone in an open plateau, the sun blotted out by ominous clouds. I hear her whisper my name from the forest behind me and follow the sound of her fearful voice. For a moment, it feels so real, so vivid.

"Calliape, what is this?" I call out to her, not understanding what she is showing me and why.

The trees part for my path as I enter their border. Calliape stands fear-stricken, with a shadowy creature stalking her, a moss layer predator crouching down to attack.

Then, a green fog rolls along the forest ground, glowing from within. It morphs into spiky tendrils that jut upright like giant thorny vines. I scream in my mind and the thorns strike like a spear into the animal just as it leaps. It feels like a dream I am only partially in control of.

I open my eyes, staring right into Calliape's. They reflect a green light in her pupils. Her eyes fall to my palm and I'm cradling a green flame that flickers like a candle. I pull my hand away and the green glow dances like a firefly floating between us. I move my hand over it, and the orb bobs around my finger, leaving a long lazy tail like a falling star. I look at Calliape in disbelief and the green is reflected in the white of her toothy smile.

"Wow. Now, that's something," she says.

I'm panting from the rush of anxiety she forced from me to recreate the same circumstances, but it's thrilling, and even though the danger seemed so real, I know we are safe.

"Again," she says.

We practice until I can call it forth without fear, then without closing my eyes at all. My temples are sore from flicking the switch in my thoughts, but evoking it is easier each time.

As the sun gets higher in the sky and sweat forms on our skin, we decide to wade out into the cold watering hole. There is no one here now, but we keep our thin undergown layers on to swim because the water is so crystal clear, we decide to play it safe.

Calliape dunks her head into the brisk water, washing her hair. I only go up to my stomach, afraid of getting my wound wet even though the few people who have seen it say it's almost completely healed miraculously.

I watch my friend swim around like a forest nymph, waiting for her to come close to me. She gives me a tight smile, dragging her arms just below the surface gracefully.

"I'm sure Selene has told you about the Estate, maybe even some of the unflattering things. But what you said before . . . You want to visit?"

Calliape shrugs. "Of course, to see for myself. Get answers about my mother, who she was. Not everything she has told me is awful. I imagine all three worlds are terrible and beautiful at the same time . . . even Frith."

"I suppose you are right. Is it selfish that I want you to come home with me?"

"It is a beautiful thought." Calliape smiles and watches her own fingers drag across the surface of the water.

I soak until I can't stand the cold any longer. I call out to Calliape, letting her know I'm going to lie in the sun. I walk to an open field, next to the body of water, covered in a layer of bright, inviting ferns. I lay my back to the ground, pressing my shoulder into the soil, making contact instinctively.

The sun gets higher, drying my pale slip enough to put my dress back on without drenching it. The bugs sing in rhythm the hotter the day gets. Their song calms my nerves every time I think of 99 and August returning to the village. Today, we will make our way back home, leaving this place behind. I will have to resume the strict atmosphere of the temple, my rigid schedule. Still, there are days of journey home, down the mountain and in the ship. I have time to prepare myself to get back to normal. For now, I can lie here in a sense of unencumbered freedom, resting, watching my sweet friend swim.

I hold my hands up to the sky, blocking out the sun. For the first time with minimal effort, I can elicit green light from my fingertips, growing tendrils out and around my arm playfully. I twist my forearm, wrapping my lips over my teeth, trying to suppress a laugh. The light glides just over the tiny hairs on my skin, sending tingly pinpoints through me.

But then I notice a slight change in the wind, like the air has shifted.

The bugs fall silent, as if a predator is near. I dissipate my light but nothing changes.

Then I feel it, a flip in my stomach. I sit up on my elbows. My skin is prickling as if I'm back in the cold water. Something is watching me; I'm being hunted. I've gone too close to the forest alone, offering myself up to its creatures unknowingly.

I stand up, flexing my hands. I'm not sure what I will do, how my light could protect me, but it's the only weapon I have. I am ready this time. I won't be taken off guard again by a shadow. I am ready to defend myself and know how to call it forth now. Everything feels dizzy but also hyperfocused as my eyes dart around.

I search for anything that seems off in the tree line.

Then I see it.

A dark figure stands in a break of the trees, a predator watching its prey. I'm frozen; I can't will myself to turn and run. But I don't want to this time. I want to stand my ground.

As my eyes try to process what I see, the figure takes a step forward. A shine hits metal, a towering, intimidating silhouette. Weapons, armor, and a familiar helmet are locked onto me.

It's him. 99 is back.

He takes another slow step toward me, summoning mine like an automatic reply. I take another through the high ferns toward him, my eyes glued to his helmet, where I know his beautiful eyes are fixed on me. He breaches the tree line, making me pick up my pace. As I'm pulled in a sense of urgency, I forget any harsh thoughts of him leaving or nervous anticipation of this moment.

His pace is slow, steady, ferns brushing against his strong armored thighs, parting for him, drawing back at the touch of metal.

I'm almost running now, not sure what to do when I get to him. But then he reaches for me, lifting his gloved hands out with purpose. I slam my body into his in an embrace and hear my name as a whisper on his lips.

CHAPTER TWENTY FIVE

I feel his strong hand on the back of my head, cradling it against him as I rest my cheek on his solid armored chest. His other hand wraps around my waist, pulling me in tighter. I lose count of how many breaths we share holding onto one another. The insects resume their chirping, a high-pitched melody, as he brushes a hand down my hair gently.

"I am so mad at you for taking so long," I whisper.

"I know."

I close my eyes, taking in his smell, pressing myself harder against the rise and fall of his chest. It feels like he will let me hold on to him as long as I desire. We touch as if we always have, like it's the most natural thing in the three worlds. It's overwhelming.

I nervously break the embrace, his arms lingering a little longer around me like it's hard to let go.

"You should not be so far from the village," he says, still towering over me, refusing to give me any space.

"I'm not alone. Calliape is just over there. Where is August?" I say, realizing he hasn't popped out from a bush yet.

99 takes too long to answer, which makes me worry. He reaches

out for me again slightly, still seeking out more of our embrace, almost dazed from it.

"He's . . ."

"Where is he? What happened!"

"He is fine. I ordered him to guard the ship . . . He's waiting for us there."

I step back a little, giving myself room. We are still so close, I can't crane my head up enough to look at him fully. His hesitation wasn't just because he knew I wouldn't be happy about the fact that August isn't with him; it was something else too. It was as if he didn't want the moment we were sharing to end and our reality to begin again.

"Back on the ship," I confirm.

He nods.

"You've been gone for days."

"First Son sent a retrieval party of his own. The one that . . ." He tilts his head down like he is looking at the spot on my chest where I was stabbed from behind. "That was one of them," he says, flexing a strong fist by his side at the memory.

"Do they know we have the stones?"

"That was not clear. The thing that was in the woods. It scanned your face. You were targeted—not me or August."

"But, they are gone now, right?" I say expectantly.

There is a long pause. I can tell he is trying to string something less terrifying together for me. But he gives up and says, "I did not think you would be walking around yet."

I touch my chest. "Ruth, she . . . Well, I don't know what she did honestly."

I hear the sound of approaching footsteps behind me. Turning, I see Calliape with wet, dripping curls.

"Hello, 99th Commander," she says.

He nods a greeting.

"Is the rest of your party in the village?" she asks, trying to hide the searching in her eyes.

She is looking for August. Anytime I would speak of him, she would feign disinterest in the conversation, giving herself away each time with a fake apathetic shift. I watch her face fall a little as she realizes I am about to tell her the bad news.

Selene's gathering hall is full of people—some returning from the scouting party, some elders and anyone else who can pack in—to hear what was found.

Instead of joining the others at the front, 99 sits with me in the sea of other villagers. I feel his glances every time I shift, as if he's silently checking if I am in pain. I know he is surprised at how fast I have healed. I am too.

Rouke spots me in the rows of chairs as he enters by our side and casts me a smile and nod, but 99 leans forward, intentionally blocking my view. I guess nothing has changed during their scouting adventure together.

"You are very rude," I say with a smile.

His shoulders go up slightly, like they do when I know he finds something funny but will only allow a small huff.

People scoot forward as Rouke recounts the events of their journey, the findings and threats they may face. Some of the Frithians seated next to us move closer, sitting on the floor in the front of the room. In the crowded space, with all that is going on, my attention is only on 99, and I can tell he isn't listening to a word they say either.

Our thighs connect just slightly as we test boundaries in silence.

My breath travels from my stomach to my chest, head slanted slightly in his direction to breathe in the smell of him I've missed so much. My eyes cascade up from his gloved hand to his spread legs. I have to close my eyes to pry them away from looking between for any sort of . . . outline.

I have no idea if he is staring straight forward or looking me over too. I angle my head a bit more to look at his helmet from the side of my eyes. The armor that seemed so menacing is now fascinating and even seductive with its cold, hard lines. I am too afraid to push into his mind's eye, not after what I saw in there this morning. That would be too much to handle in a crowded room. My breath catches a little just thinking about it.

He leans forward slightly, and I quickly avert my gaze, staring forward. I feel him brush against my arm, leaning in.

"It is even more rude to stare," he whispers.

He knew I was looking at him, probably watching the whole time, so annoyingly observant. I straighten forward, crossing my arms and making sure to move my leg away from his. I've been caught.

I hear Rouke say he plans to escort us out of the moss layer and then circle around one more time. Selene and the Frithian elders seem satisfied with the rundown, only worried when they spoke of how far the First Son followers had breached the mountain.

I missed most of the information as I stared at 99, but he gave me the main bits on our walk back to the village, straight to the point with every question I asked—no speculation, no fluff, which I much prefer over the flowery language of Selene. Slow and beautiful as it is, the way 99 speaks is more comforting. It doesn't leave much room for my own fears to creep in.

People trail out of the room, leaving only a few left who chat with the elders as they help them out the door. We have not moved from our silent spot, almost like an excuse to stay close to each other without the others suspecting. I feel 99's arm brush against mine as he removes his helmet. I did not expect that he would here, the thought instantly making me feel foolish. Selene and Calliape have seen his face before, the night of the attack when I was spread out on a table in this room. I know the reason I think it's too intimate to remove in front of them is only because of the effects it's having on my own body. I take a steady inhale, trying to calm my racing pulse.

I pretend to stretch my neck, using the opportunity to angle my head in his direction to steal a glance. But when I notice his deep blue eyes watching me, I can't help but connect with them for a brief moment. I feel a little silly at the nervous coil my stomach twists into. I've seen him without his helmet before, but he is so close to me now, making all the points of contact between our bodies catch fire.

Selene scoops sloppy morsels of stew into clay pottery then hands him a bowl, and he nods a thank you. She serves me while examining 99 with a satisfied smile. He clears his throat, taking a large spoonful to his mouth, and only then does she break away from us.

Calliape lingers by the fire, waiting for me to notice her. She looks over at 99's face and then back at me with wide, insinuating eyes. I take a mouthful of broth to keep from giggling at her approving expression. I can tell she wants to speak but is afraid to interrupt the strange, silent reunion.

"I will be right back," I lean in to say softly to 99.

The closer I walk to Calliape, the sadder her expression becomes.

"I was just thinking of you leaving . . ."

I don't know what to say. I'm hit with the same sadness. Calliape is one of the few things I will truly miss leaving Frith. It breaks my heart that I've found someone who understands me so well, an equal friend, and now I have to leave her.

I hug her tightly, wrapping my arms around her taller form, and she bends down for me to place my chin on her shoulder. 99 watches us from across the room, leaned forward, hooded eyes locked. The whites under his pupils are so clear and haunting, and the erotic anticipation of his heated stare takes my breath away.

I pull away from Calliape, trying to focus on her, holding her arms to shield my view of 99.

"I'm so glad I met you. I wish I could take you home with me."

She smiles brightly and rolls her eyes at the ridiculous thought.

Ruth enters the tent, a little out of breath, with her big kit of supplies. She smiles and nods at me, then 99.

"Priestess Ferren, I hear you are leaving us tonight. Better get those stitches out."

99 rises, placing his bowl by the fire. "Tomorrow. We leave tomorrow."

"Why tomorrow? I say, surprised.

"It is not safe to move at night." The look he gives me is as if he is waiting for more of a fight and welcomes it.

I just exhale, frustrated.

"Ah, well, either way, let's get you all set up for your journey," Ruth says.

99 picks up his helmet and walks past her toward the door to exit.

"Oh, no, 99th Commander, you will have to stay. The main wound is healed but the stitches will leave superficial ones that still need care. You will have to learn how," Ruth says.

99 looks a little thrown off. I've never seen him look so close to being frazzled. I press my lips together tightly but then realize she's talking about him dressing my wounds the way she has the past few days. My cheeks feel flush at the thought.

Ruth stands in the opening of my room, holding the door

expectantly. Calliape whispers a goodnight to me and pats me on the shoulder for good luck. I just want to get this over with and walk straight inside with my head down so I don't see 99's face.

Ruth helps me on the bed, positioning me to work. She unties the back of my dress, and I hold the front tightly to my chest with my forearms, tucking my fists under my chin, locking them in place.

I hear 99 enter the room, the slow foot falls on the floor. I hear the wooden chair pulled just behind me, the creak of his large form sitting in it sending a chill up my spine, my bare back in full view. I hope he did not notice the cold prickles on my skin once he entered.

"She no longer needs the full wrap, just this," Ruth says as I feel her pull the smaller bandage off my back.

"I am going to begin now, large breaths for me."

I feel a sharp coldness zip through me as she pats a cloth that smells like alcohol across the stitches.

"Everything looks good, Priestess Ferren. I'm going to pull these out now," she says.

She tugs on one that feels stuck, then with another pull, a sharp needle slides through my skin, surprising me.

"Big breaths," she whispers.

Another sting pulls at my back. I try to focus on inhaling and exhaling deeply but I know I'm grimacing enough to catch 99's attention.

"Are you alright?" He leans forward a little, in an alert posture like he will make Ruth stop if I ask.

I nod. "It's like a really sharp pinch."

"Just a couple more," Ruth says. I can hear the concentration in her voice.

I keep my eyes down on the blanket, feeling a little exposed and vulnerable. 99 saw me like this before when it first happened, when they had to expose my back to stop the bleeding, but it was messier, more urgent then. Something about this is more elegant. Removing the tiny stitches quietly in my room with intention, with a choice of who is here now that it's not an emergency and is no threat of death feels more private, which makes me surprisingly shy even with Ruth as the unknowing chaperone.

She pulls out the last stitch a little faster, sending a zip of pain through my back. She pats me as a small comforting gesture, like she always does after a painful session.

"We are all done here," she says.

I can feel her gaze as she stands, looking back and forth at me and 99 and our awkward silence. We got into the routine of chatting and laughing with Calliape while she worked on my wounds. Now I'm probably exposing myself, not acting normal around her. She smiles to herself as she packs her bag.

"I changed Priestess Ferren's bandages every day, but Calliape stayed with her well into the night when you left, comforting her cries. Thought you should know, you owe a great deal to Calliape's tender heart," Ruth says.

I can't tell if she is on my side, angry that he left me here, or if she is trying to break some kind of tension in the room, but I can't believe *this* is how she chose to cut the silence.

99 snaps his head to her and then to me, looking for answers with a guilty expression.

"The herbs she gave me, they made me . . . delirious." I stumble over a somewhat fake explanation.

Ruth lets out a tiny chuckle, exposing how ridiculous I sound. Calliape did sit with me when I let doubts control my thoughts, when I was convinced they had left me here forever. But *I* am the one who owes a great deal to Calliape's heart.

99's eyes on me feel overwhelming. I can only meet them in fast flicks then take long breaks, staring down at the hem of my blanket. I wish his helmet were back on so I could only speculate where he is looking.

"Ok, so now you just pour some of this on a cloth to clean the little wounds from the stitches. It will keep any festering away," Ruth says.

Festering, yes, focus on festering to distract from 99's intense gaze.

"The adhesive cloth is placed right on top, and the herbs can be left in the bandage. They will help with healing."

"Thank you," 99 says, and they both stand.

"Of course, be sure that it gets cleaned once a day until you get back, just in case. It was such a large wound. I've never seen one close that fast. It's miraculous," Ruth says as she ties my dress up in the back and I'm finally able to free my arms from my chest.

"Thank you for taking care of me, Ruth, truly."

I enjoyed my time with Ruth. She tended to pry and gossip which is probably what fueled her comment to 99, but she was very comforting. Ruth made sure I could breathe again, treated me like I was one of her Frithian patients in need, not an outsider.

She exits my room with one last shoulder squeeze, leaving open air between me and 99. He pulls the chair to face me then places a hand on my blanket-covered knee, sending electricity through it. I stare at his thick, rugged fingers, wanting to put my hand on top of his.

"Ferren."

I look up at him, gazing into his dark-blue eyes, waiting for him to say something, anything. But he just grips my knee harder, like he has lost the words he carefully prepared the moment our eyes meet again.

Selene walks into the room, smudging out any soft expression, interrupting what he was going to say.

"The tent you stayed in before is still available, 99th Commander," she says, a little too upbeat for the current tone in the room.

His hand gone from my knee leaves a sad cold spot. He stands, brushing hair back before placing his helmet on.

"Goodnight to you both," Selene says.

I look up at him from my bed, towering above me, still waiting to hear what he has to say.

"Blessed night, Ferren," he whispers instead.

"Blessed night . . . 99."

I pace on the soft fur rug of my room, sick of waiting, of being stuck on this world. I want to go home, to leave tonight. I retrieved the stones days ago, and I'm anxious to finish what we started. I don't want to wait until tomorrow. It seems more dangerous with First Son already sending followers here.

99 has barely said a word to me since we got to Selene's home. He doesn't just get to leave me here and then decide we aren't leaving right away. I'm just as much of a part of this as he is. I feel bad for daydreaming about how the forest could kill him the first few days I knew him. Now, I only wish the tree man would have roughed him up a little, let him know he should really listen to me.

I pull a robe on over my gauzy nightgown and listen at my door to hear for anyone still awake—not because I'm sneaking or doing anything wrong, for courtesy, of course. Everything is quiet but the fire cracking so I burst out, pass the gathering room, and am out Selene's front door with quick, determined steps.

I storm through the dark, knowing my way around much better now. I realize I'm barefoot, feeling the cold, dewy grass on my feet, but trudge forward, barging into 99's tent. I suddenly realize I should have knocked but it's too late, and I've already made my point by angrily flinging the door open.

But he's not inside. I look around, getting more impatient. His helmet is lying on the cot he used when we shared this tent not so long ago. The blankets I used to create my walls around my bed have been removed, like someone came in and cleaned. His armor is set down and organized too, which means he hasn't left without me but is walking around somewhere without it. I think of what that looked like the night we took turns using the curtained off water room, how broad his shoulders and arms were without the armor.

This was a rash decision, coming over here like this. I should put myself back into bed. Leaving tomorrow sounds like a levelheaded idea. Before I have a chance to turn and leave the tent, 99 steps out of the curtained off area, his hair wet and disheveled. I follow a water droplet as it traces over the contours of his bare chest, the muscles on his stomach, down to the unfastened laces of his pants, then disappears into a shadow of dark hair. He eyes me with a sultry yet unsurprised look, then a smile teases the corner of his mouth.

CHAPTER TWENTY SIX

Darkened pupils channel into me as he slowly paces forward, biceps covered in a glistening layer. His corded forearms bulge as he flexes his hands into fists, somehow much more intimidating like this, without the helmet, when I know where he is looking and his expression gives away little hints of his thoughts as his eyes roam over my body. They flick around the room as if he is confirming we are alone.

And we are *very* alone.

Since he returned earlier today, we have been surrounded by others even if our focus has been inward or on each other. This is the first time we have been truly alone since that night in the forest, since he allowed me into his mind's eye. As if he is reading my own thoughts, he takes a step toward me.

"I want to leave tonight, now!" I blurt out.

His shoulders relax slightly as he passes by me, thoughts shifting in another direction. I wait for a response as he sits on the bed, moving his armor to the floor next to it.

"It is not safe at night," he says on an exhale.

"Yes, you have said that, in fact that is about the only thing you have said to me directly," I say, putting my hands on my hips.

He flicks his eyes to them, studying me like he's trying to weed through a hidden meaning, so I roll my eyes dramatically for him to see how frustrating he truly is.

"How are you after the stitches were removed?" he pivots.

"Commander, please, can we leave."

"I do not like when you call me that. And you have not spoken to me very much either . . . *Priestess*."

He sits forward, bracing elbows on his knees, looking upward at me across the room, ready to listen with that simple hint. But his hooded stare makes my knees weak.

"I am just anxious to get home. I am sick of waiting around."

Rough fingers run over the grown out scruff on his chin. My eyes follow his hand as it moves over his strong jaw then settles on his lips. I need to stay on topic and ignore the way he absently swipes at his lower lip while staring right at me.

"It is not easy waiting in a place you have practically been abandoned in, so forgive me if I am not as mouthy as I normally am."

I had almost forgotten how deeply it hurt when they had to leave me here, the happiness of seeing him again and the reality of going home washing it away, and now that we can speak freely, it's all coming to the forefront.

His expression changes and I almost think I have stepped over a line trying to prove my point.

"I told you I would be back," he says, standing expectantly for my reply, holding space for my frustration. Waiting for the next blow.

"I know. It was just really hard after everything that we went through. All three of us . . ." It's not as hard hitting as I intended, too honest to be hurtful. I sound fragile but I don't care. It's the truth.

"I want you to know that I do not take leaving a member of my team behind lightly." He nods understandingly, taking a step forward to line himself up to me.

His response is colder than normal, like he is briefing someone on a loss of a crew member during battle. But then he reaches for my arm, tracing his knuckles down it. "That decision was impossible, but you were . . . I thought you were dying, Ferren."

Flashes of that night flick into my mind, as if they are out of his own memories. I realize he is unknowingly sending them to me, so willing to be open that he has made a link.

"Where I had to go—what I had to do—I could not take you with me, could not risk you. I will beg for your forgiveness, even if it was the right decision." He grips my arms, and then, as if realizing how hard and intense he is holding me, he lets go altogether.

What he had to do?

I remember the sight of him on top of the shadowy figure who attacked me, blood and grunting as he unleashed violence onto him.

He waits patiently, searching my face. "It was difficult leaving. You made it very difficult while I was away. You . . . haunted me, Priestess," he says low and throaty.

A very small smile teases at the corner of his mouth. I'm almost not upset at him anymore. I do trust him; I just needed to hear him say it out loud.

The air in the room shifts a little. I can feel a pressure building, pulling my thoughts to . . . other things with him this close, the same way I did the night in the forest. I freeze under the intensity of his eyes and let out an awkward, nervous laugh.

"Well, I should go. Thank you for the explanation. I forgive you, 99."

He is suddenly even closer to me, closing in on me without any notice of steps in my direction. I watch the up and down of his breathing, how his chest looks so hard even without the armor. I said I was leaving but I can't break free so I angle my shoulders, hoping I can will my body out the door.

"But if something like that ever happens again, you can't just leave me behind and disappear," I say flippantly.

He places a heavy hand on my shoulder, gently pulling back. His face is angry, tone deadly. "If something like that happens to you again . . . I will tear the three fucking worlds apart."

I look up at him, held in place and surprised by his intensity toward whatever threat there is or could be to me, to whatever hypothetical attack.

"If you want to come with me to do that, then fine." His voice warm, husky.

"Don't you think that is a little extreme?" I say, trying to lighten the mood, the still pressure building. But 99's intense look does not waver.

His reply is unhurried, and he shakes his head slowly in disagreement. He peers around my face, neck, and breasts, finally landing on my eyes again. I pull back a little, testing the grip, but he pulls me closer, daring me to try again.

"And if you don't believe me, what I would do to anyone who hurt you, all you need to do is have a look. Feel free to sneak in again," he teases.

I fight the urge to slap his beautiful face. Instead, I pull at my arm, jerking it away. Does he know I secretly looked in his mind's eye while he was away? Did he somehow feel me in there? I'm not in the mood to bicker with him and I won't be made to feel bad for looking into his thoughts when permission was given to enter.

But then he presses his body against mine, squeezing my breasts between the strong hand on my back and solid chest on my front.

My muscles feel languid against his body heat. It engulfs me and any reason to stop him. He holds me, unwavering, like the three worlds depend on it.

Fingers lock on the back of my head, tilting me up to meet him. His devastating eyes dance across my face, landing on my lips. I pant, opening them slightly in response to the intensity emanating between us. The moment I do, his crash into mine. It's a sweet, measured kiss, broken away just on the cusp of us losing control. He hovers over me, breathing in each of my exhales, waiting.

I feel breathless, then the *something* that was building in the room boils over as I press forward to meet his mouth again. I grip his jaw then slide my hands to the back of his neck to hold on. The kiss is feral, deep and hungry as I melt into him, legs weak, but he holds me in place. His hot tongue plunges in, searching mine out. I feel a hand roam wildly down my back, and the other fists my hair at the nape of my neck.

This is what I felt in the forest that night, what we were building to when he first held my hand in the cave and said, *I have you.* He kisses me like he is almost relieved that I want it as badly as he does, unsure I would want someone like him at all.

A temple priestess and a Viathan commander.

The forbidden realization has me gasping, my skin almost too sensitive as he grabs me. My small whimper of pleasure flips a noticeable switch in him, a feral turning point.

He pulls the tie on my robe, making it slink to the ground at our bare feet. His warm lips travel down the column of my neck, nipping at my skin. Then, without warning, he cups my breast through the thin layer of my nightgown, eliciting a sharp inhale. The sound makes him grip harder, like he is on the verge of losing control. The sensation of soft kisses and rough hands sends sparks down my skin, settling between my thighs.

"I have no pretty words for you, Priestess. If you need them, need to know what I'm thinking, you have my permission to look . . . always," he rasps between contact with my skin, bringing my hand up to his temple.

Amber light collides all around us, seemingly filling up the space in the tent, not just contained to his mind. His always tousled hair is soft and damp sliding through my fingers. I run them from his temple to the back of his head, surrendering to another long devouring kiss on my neck.

"Your words are not what I want, Commander," I say, savoring the feel of teeth grazing my windpipe.

He pauses, hovering his lips over mine then pulling my head back, my hair fisted softly. I can feel his hard length pressed up against my hip. Holding his wild gaze, I run my hand down his chest, my fingers spreading over the width of his impressive bulge, and I rub my hand over the straining fabric. A surprised smile teases the corner of his mouth before it falls open with an inhale as I trace the outline of him harder. His brow twists like the sensation of my hand on his cock is exactly how he pictured it.

His groan is deep and rumbling, an animalistic growl from within, the bass of it sending vibrations from his chest against my peaked nipples.

In one swoop, I'm picked up off the floor, his large hands grabbing fistfuls of my ass as he carries me the two steps to the cot. My back gently settles into the stiff mattress just as he moves over me, hips pinning me down in an electric press.

Intrusive thoughts slither from his mind through our now open-ended tether: worrying about my chest and back, reminding himself to be careful with that side where I was wounded. It's achingly sweet, but my body wants all of him, his roughness, the wild feral strength of him I have only seen glimpses of him unleashing.

"There is no need to be gentle. I'm fine," I whisper in his ear, biting at the lobe.

He smiles and feverishly kisses me while I run my fingers up the muscles of the arms that block me in. I part my thighs to let him sink between, to feel his hard cock pressing against his pants. The heat of him through my nightgown has me arching my back in response. Without hesitation, he reaches down, pulling it up, and I see him smile lightly when he realizes there is nothing underneath it. I bite my bottom lip at seeing his pupils blow out at the sight of my bare thighs, flesh slick from my even wetter pussy.

To my pleasant surprise, his fingers glide up my folds as he nuzzles into my neck. I sink into the feeling of him touching me this way. Then, he brings two glistening fingers up to his lips, making sure my eyes are locked on his. I watch him open his mouth then taste me, plunging them inside, savoring the flavor of my wetness. His tongue slides between the thick fingers, and he watches my reaction, licking every surface that touched me.

The explicit display makes me pant. He's completely unapologetic, as if the first thing he wanted to do was relish the taste of my cunt, like he had been wondering. My clit throbs seeing him like this. I have to press my thighs together, seeking out a temporary relief from the ache.

Then he is moving down my belly, pushing the hem of my nightgown up farther to kiss at my prickled skin. I part my legs more to accommodate his body between them. His trail stops at my thigh with a bite at the inside of my knee as he stares ravenously between my legs. I press my lips together, feeling a small bit of shyness at being so freely naked and spread, so exposed to him. Without any pause, he notices the small timid thought. Fleeting as it is, he still sends me warm amber light, reassuring me. Pure emotion lets me know how he feels, how much he likes seeing my body bare like this.

"You are beautiful, Ferren." He kisses my inner thigh to brand the words into my skin.

My hips roll up in response, a soft plea. I watch as his lips trail closer, tongue tasting and sucking, and I can't help but fist his messy hair, pulling him to the ache I feel deep in my core. The reply is a low, approving rumble.

I can feel the scruff on his jaw, a stark contrast to his soft lips. His breath is on my entrance now and I close my eyes. With the first lick of his tongue, my other hand shoots to my side, clutching the cot's blanket. Lightening ripples through me as he encases his lips around my core, kissing my pussy with the same enthusiasm he did my mouth.

I hear him make another pleased sound in his throat, over the sound of my own pleasure.

My breath is labored. He slowly licks long trails and then dips his tongue inside me. He takes his time, eliciting whimpers from me. Then, my right leg is lifted over his shoulder and he braces my hips, holding me still like he's getting ready to make me writhe.

A hot, slow caress of his tongue ascends up my folds to my throbbing clit. I inhale in a gasp when his lips wrap around it, and he flicks his tongue rhythmically. My bucking hips are held still as I writhe in pleasure just like 99 planned.

He moans low and throaty as I look down, dazed by the sinful feeling of his mouth. His sultry eyes watch me as I run my fingers through his hair, pushing back pieces that have fallen, mesmerized by the way his strong jaw flexes with the fluttering of his tongue.

"99 . . . yes . . ." I gasp and moan, praising the way he works my most sensitive spot.

My free hand skims over the back of his that holds my hip. Without hesitating, he grabs it, holding it tightly, threading our fingers together like he is as overwhelmed with the feeling of being together as I am. I thrust my hips again as another shock wave ripples through me, another moan breaking free like a sob.

He squeezes my palm twice.

I have you.

His other hand moves off my hip, and in the next moment, I feel a thick finger slide inside me, his tongue keeping rhythm as he now moves a second one inside. The sound is almost vulgar as he pumps them into my wet core.

I cry out, pulling on his hair tightly. I hear a small but deep chuckle in his throat, like he is satisfied with his work. His fingers curl up, catching an impossibly sensitive spot at the top of my entrance. I moan and plead for him not to stop. He groans in approval of my cries, thrusting fingers inside of me in tandem with the circle of his tongue. I move my hips, seeking out more friction, so he presses harder, flattening his tongue against me to add the exact pressure I need. He knows the subtle cues of my body without falling out of sync.

But then I hear people just outside the tent, walking by. We both tense a little but 99 doesn't lift his head or even stop his attentions, only opening his frustrated eyes like he has been woken from a pleasant dream, wanting to go back.

The voices get louder, the women chatting as they pass us on the other side of the canvas wall. But he is still pumping his fingers into me, making it impossible not to moan as more people walk by. I can feel the familiar pressure building as my walls clench down.

He flicks his eyes up at me again, feeling the new tightness around his fingers, knowing exactly what he is doing to my body. I hold the back of my hand to my mouth, trying to muffle my sounds as the orgasm gets closer.

I practically sob when he takes his mouth off me, hips lifting automatically, seeking out his touch again. He gives my clit one last, long lick then comes up to my side, leaving his fingers, bracing himself on his elbow next to my head. He kisses me quickly then wraps a palm over my mouth as I moan more freely into it.

The rhythm of the deep, penetrating thrusts do not waver for even a moment, thumb circling in tandem, replacing his tongue. I fist the sheets next to me, holding onto the arm that muffles my cries.

"Bite down if you need to. I am sick of interruption," he whispers into my ear.

He holds his hand over my mouth firmly but tender, flicking his eyes to mine then to where his fingers plunge into me. He watches as I squirm under the building pressure again, smothering my cries, circling and thrusting with his fingers that make a slick sound as they move.

I caress the strong palm over my mouth, letting him know to keep it there as more people walk by. He pumps into me like not even First Son himself could stop us. He sweetly rests his forehead against mine, listening to me, enjoying the sounds he withdraws.

"I have wanted to make you come since the moment I saw you bend over to pray."

The whisper sends sparks through my body. It's sinful and forbidden and completely shatters me. My moan breaches my covered mouth as I ride out the release of my orgasm, walls baring down so hard, they almost force his fingers from my entrance. I am just about to reach the top of the rolling waves of pleasure when 99 slides his hand from my mouth to the back of my neck, pulling me into a deep kiss. I groan into him, tasting myself on his tongue.

He continues to kiss me as I come down from it. My breath slowly becomes more steady as he pulls his fingers from me, sliding them up my stomach, cupping my pebbled breasts as they heave for more air. His lips press into me slowly and dreamily, winding me down from the intense high.

His cock is rock hard next to my hip, bulging against the unlaced pants. I can't help but slide my hand over it, trying to find the full length without any luck. He groans into my mouth, leaning into my touch. But the kiss gets slower, sweeter, like its concluding. The wild franticness subsides, and now he kisses me sweetly, in a way I didn't think someone so harsh and rough around the edges could.

"If we do that, the whole village will hear you . . . Trust me," he whispers as I continue to massage the outside of his pants.

The threat only makes my pulse quicken again. He looks into my eyes, holding my face just under my chin, now propped up next to me, and shakes his head with a sexy, almost regretful smile.

"Then I could . . . for you," I say coyly, licking my lips at the thought of him in my mouth, pleasuring him like he did me.

His eyes darken again and flick to my slicked lips, making him let out a long frustrated breath. "You need to rest for tomorrow."

Just when I think he isn't going to be as annoying anymore, he has started again. I let out a huff and sink into the bed.

He laughs, actually laughs. Not a small exhale like he does when I'm bickering with him, a real one. The sound snaps me out of my frustration. It's deep and heartbreaking, like he rarely allows himself the indulgence.

But then he grabs me and I can't help the squeak that escapes. He picks me up and pulls the blanket out from under us, placing me back down gently next to him then pulling the coverings over our bodies.

I sink into the crook of his arm, snuggled against his expansive chest in a stretch.

He laces his fingers with mine so naturally, it almost feels like a routine we have always done. I glance up at him a little dumbstruck and pleasantly overwhelmed and notice he is smiling at me on one side. It makes me feel so . . . warm. The comfort of his amber light is addictive and even inescapable now.

With his free hand, he brushes gently over my forehead, pushing back my wild, stray hair. His touch is soft and more tender, so different from the man I saw looking down at me boarding the ship, vicious and deadly.

No, that was the 99th Commander of Viathan. This is 99, caring and gentle but with just a hint of the broody mysteriousness that first drew me to him.

I can feel him opening his mind to me again, emotion pouring out. I can tell he wants to say something, but he plainly explained he could not find the words for me. Feeling what is inside his thoughts is better than anything that could be said or any strung-together sentiment over what we just shared. I deep dive into his mind's eye, surrounded by warm, happy light as he holds me against him, staring up at the glowing orange shadows from the fire on the ceiling.

CHAPTER TWENTY SEVEN

66 "This is worse than the first time we said goodbye," Calliape says as I exit my room, only spending enough time in it this morning to pack after sneaking in at dawn.

"I don't think I can say it." My eyes finally give way to the tide of tears that has been gently building.

"Then maybe we shouldn't." I face her, and her eyes are pained but a little stronger.

"My dear friend from another world," she says.

"Thank you for showing me yours. I will be forever grateful for meeting you. I will miss you the most."

"Get home safe and take care of the stones, of yourself. Keep your eyes up and open," she says, hugging me.

The last few words seem pointed, like she is trying to send me a message but doesn't want to ruin a sweet moment. I hug her back tightly for as long as she will let me, then I hear the door open behind me and Calliape tenses a little.

"99th Commander has arrived to take you from me," she whispers into my hair.

THE VIRIDIAN PRIESTESS

I woke to the sight of him getting dressed just before dawn, followed by him handing me tea and telling me he had some loose ends to tie up, to wait for him at Selene's. He stopped in the doorway, this time looking back at me lying in his cot. He stared for a long pause which made my stomach flip in a way that has had my nerves on edge since.

I keep my back to him even when Calliape ends our embrace, trying to hide my tears, quickly wiping them away. I know he can probably tell, but I still want to keep them between Calliape and me.

He stands beside me, rough knuckles brushing lightly over the hand at my side like a secret, comforting gesture. The nerves of seeing him again creep back even more as he steps forward decked out in his full armor, all vulnerability from the night before gone, hidden away under layers of metal and a Viathan helmet.

Selene appears from a dark hall, holding a wrapped bundle tenderly.

"Safe and sound," she says, handing it to 99.

He flips a side of the linen up, revealing the stones, as if to confirm they are both there. Then, he saunters over to me, picking up my small bag, stuffing the bundle inside, and saying, "Do not even think it." He runs a knuckle down my arm. "No, they are not why I made sure to come back, so do not even think it," he clarifies.

I'm almost tickled that he wants to make sure I wasn't thinking something horrible about his intentions. It didn't even cross my mind. I believe him when he says he came back for me.

"I know," I say

I can almost see his shoulders relax, as if he's relieved that I believe him. I wonder if it was something he was worried about with how fast he explained. He slings the bag over my shoulder, adjusting it with the extra weight of the stones in there. I feel him subtly run a hand down

277

my hair out of view of others.

"Good," he says, confirming that he is in fact relieved.

There is a long pause in the room, one that makes me feel like saying goodbye to Calliape all over again, wanting that to be the last thing I do here. But Selene walks us to the door, clasping my arm to guide me.

"Remember our conversation the other night, what I told you," she whispers as we step out onto the porch.

I have to fight the urge to snap at her for sullying my final goodbye with a secret I already promised to keep. I have no intention of telling anyone about Selene, the Cosima citizens who live here, but especially my friend. The fact that she thinks I would put Calliape in a complicated situation with the Estate is insulting.

I step out onto the thick grass that grows between houses, walking with 99 toward the large group of Frithians who will escort us down the mountain. I can't stop myself from looking back to see Calliape one last time. Selene has a comforting arm wrapped around her.

Calliape smiles and waves from their doorway, her sweet presence radiating outward even from this distance. I hold up a hand and wave back, quickly turning away to hide the ache I already feel leaving the most genuinely deep friendship I have ever made.

The hike down the mountain is just as hard surprisingly. 99 stays close to me, keeping a distance between the others and me. The Frithians watch me, stealing glances when I am not paying attention, and I hold my bag tightly to my body when I notice Rouke staring at it. The only sounds around us are the breaking of twigs and leaves as we travel. The forest is eerie and silent, animals and bugs seeming to part for us, making way for the stones. I try not to think about saying goodbye to Calliape, of not seeing her again, trying not to picture her waving to me.

Instead, in the hours of silence, I consider the many other things that have occurred here that I will keep from Crixa, especially my new light. In the past, when she had found out I used my gift indulgently, I was punished. This would set her off for sure, so I won't mention it until after my ascension. She just wants me to be safe, I know that, but she won't understand that I can control it now. I am nervous about the probing questions she will ask me. I need to rehearse them so they seem natural. There is no doubt in my mind she will ask me about how I got the stones, who I spoke to, how much and how little I prayed. I need to tell her just enough to sound like it was challenging, exciting, but that I was blessed and grateful to get through it. I need to keep it as close to the truth as possible without exposing myself or anyone I care for on Frith.

Just get home, return the stones, show First Mother and everyone your devotion, and then you will ascend.

"You alright?" 99 whispers.

He extends a hand to help me over a large fallen tree. It's easier with him carrying the bulk of my stuff, but I take his palm anyway, just to feel the little squeeze every time he's about to let go again. I hop off the log and look him over, trying to hide my smile and the thought that comes to mind now every time he touches me.

"If you like, I can carry you!" Rouke calls back.

99 leans down to whisper, "If you say yes, I will have to kill him."

I snort a laugh and pat his chest, urging him to stand down.

We make camp just after we enter the moss layer of the mountain. I watch as the Frithians and single, very commanding Viathan argue about stopping for the night. 99's posture is stiff and defensive as they speak in hushed tones about First Son and his followers. Hearing where they saw the enemy last and how many they had to kill puts me on edge. I hate the way Rouke and the others look at me, but right now, I am almost happy there are more people to defend the stones with us.

Rouke and his men group together, making a small fire as the sun goes down. Some of the men stand guard against trees on the outskirts of our camp.

99 guides me away from them, and I don't protest after their heated bickering. I sit on a fallen tree in a huff while 99 stands behind me, glancing around like he can't trust they will guard the perimeter on their own.

I try to make myself comfortable on the squishy moss and hear my stomach grumbling, thinking of the food I packed. I dig through my bag but find something better than I expected wrapped up next to the bread and dried meat Selene sent us with. I unwrap it and find a damaged berry tart.

Sweet Calliape. She would always give me hers at dinner, saying they hurt her teeth. The tarts aren't nearly as sugary as the desserts I like in the Estate, but it makes my heart swell thinking that Calliape thought to send some with me.

I bite into it quickly, trying to curb the tears I know are building. I hold a piece up to 99, who is looking off into the woods. I have to wave it around dramatically to get his attention. His helmet shakes after seeing it's a sweet.

"You eat it all. Go on," he says.

Why does his voice make everything sound so . . . sexy?

I'm too hungry to savor it. With the last bite, I stretch my arms and legs out, watching him survey our surroundings. He walks out in front of me then descends to the base of a tree, picking the side of the mossy trunk that faces away from the others, then sits, spreading his legs out.

"I need to check your bandages," he says and slowly pats his thigh.

I can feel my eyes saucer at the sight of his muscular thighs waiting for me to sit on them. He takes my hand and helps me climb down into his lap. Shyness washes over me as I think of the others seeing us like this, but it's quickly gone once I settle in and feel his hard body against me, smell his addictive scent. I look over my shoulder, wondering if they can see me. My wound is so high on my back, I will have to be exposed.

I feel 99 shift his body under me, making sure I am hidden behind his large shoulders and chest.

"They would not dare," he whispers.

I lean forward a little, pulling up the back of my tunic. He holds it at my shoulder blade, tapping his fingers for me to replace his grip with mine. I can feel his rough gloves slide down my bare skin, and when they leave for a moment and his trailing continues, I know that he has removed it, seeking touch without the thick barrier of fabric. I lean into the caress, the heat of his fingertips. He lifts one side of my bandage, making me suck in a breath at the adhesive pulling.

"Sore?"

I shake my head, hoping to hide what his touch is making me think of. My tone of voice seems to always be a giveaway to him. He finishes tenderly dressing it like Ruth instructed him, smoothing a palm over the new bandage then running a knuckle down my spine to let me know he is finished.

"You should rest," he says as I hear him putting his gloves back on behind me. I wiggle to get off his lap, but he pulls my back into his chest then raises a knee slightly, boxing me in.

He wants me to stay and rest . . . on top of him. The thought makes me melt back into the hard armor of his chest. I'm so cradled and warm, completely protected. Our breaths sync, but I notice his is longer, more drawn out. I wiggle a little to get comfortable and feel his body heat against my lower back where his armor stops. I wonder if he is thinking about what happened between us the last time we were this close. I roll my hips a little on him then press my thighs together at the building heat between them.

"When are the others leaving us?" I ask.

"If you do not stop moving your hips around on my lap, it will stop mattering," he says low and husky in my ear.

I inhale deeply, his devious threat making it harder for me to think of anything else.

"Ground is too cold for you. You will have to sleep here." He wraps a blanket around me, tucking the sides in around himself.

I chuckle to myself; the ground is not that cold. But this is better, being this close to him, his arms around me, so I nestle into him.

"I'm excited to see August," I say, attempting to change the subject.

"Me too."

"What do you think he is doing?"

"He doesn't like being alone so probably pacing and fixing things on the ship."

"Flirting with himself in the mirror," I tease.

I can feel 99's chest tense and then shake a little like he is silently laughing. "Maybe we should knock before entering the ship," he says.

I laugh hard, probably enough for the others to hear me. 99 isn't a funny person but once in a while, his seriousness mixes just right and I cannot help but laugh, making me bounce against him. I hear him grunt low in his throat and then adjust me between his legs. I lean back, realizing any movement in this pose is probably dangerous, no matter the subject. I can feel the chin of his helmet on my temple when I lean back, looking up at the treetops. My head rests on his armored shoulder as I try to make out the shapes in the darkness.

I'm tempted to move a little more when I realize he is hard, his length jutting into my back. I listen for the others behind us, hoping they are settling to sleep. With the fires now low enough, the camp will be pitch black soon. I decide to grind my ass down into him, pretending it's an absent movement just to hear him grunt again. I move my hips in a circle, thinking of what will happen once the others are gone and I'm left alone in the forest with 99.

I feel a firm hand grab my hip, stopping my tease. "When the others leave, I will make you cry out so loud, every creature on Frith will hear you. Till then . . . stop squirming around, Priestess."

I let out an exasperated huff and sink into him fully. Once again, he has stopped me from taking things further. I try not to be frustrated. It's probably not the best idea to do anything right now anyway, but he can't blame me for trying. It's almost cute that he wants to wait until we are utterly alone, and clearly, he has been thinking about it too.

"Blessed night then."

He may not have pretty words, but the ones he does have are fiercely confident and full of lust, telling me exactly what he is thinking. I kiss the side of his helmet and settle back in.

"Blessed night, Ferren," he says, sounding a little amused.

CHAPTER TWENTY EIGHT

We hike in silence for hours, trying to make good time, but I know 99 is walking slower than he can, purposefully pacing himself for my sake. Rouke and his men were gone before dawn. I woke to see their tiny fires leaving small smoke trails from the memory of their camp. I would not have been able to keep my calm today if we had to deal with Rouke's abrasive presence. Not after waking every hour to vivid nightmares which continued until morning when 99 gently rustled me awake.

I dreamed of being exactly where I was, in 99's arms, but the forest was alive around us, creatures walking in and out of our camp. They killed and ate each other out in the darkness. The sounds were terrible and raw as they hunted, and insects screamed as plants reached out to grab them. As if we were cloaked in an invisible veil having the stones, the brutal moss layer continued on without knowing we were there. As if I could see into the mind's eye of the forest itself as I slept.

I follow 99 from the back. Letting him lead the way gives me space to will my head to cease spinning. He glances back often to check on me, subtly looking over his armored shoulder. It's sweet and a little amusing. Even though my mood is sour, I oddly feel comfortable being alone with 99. I thought that I would be nervous and anxious, but it feels natural. I don't have to put on a brave face or explain myself or feel like I'm being too unrefined. I don't have to be poised. I can just . . . be.

I keep catching shadows out of the corner of my eye as we walk, but each time I look, nothing is there. So, I keep my head down to my feet as I weed through my thoughts, but something keeps drawing my attention to the sides. I'm not sure if it's paranoia, so I stop in my tracks and stare off into the forest, waiting. Maybe something is hiding, only moving when I look away but there is still nothing.

I can't shake the feeling that someone, some creature or energy is reaching out to me. I can see tendrils of green light in my peripherals, then I hear a distant scream, snapping my head in that direction. I watch 99 from behind to gauge any panic, but he seems unphased, his steps strong and unwavering through the ferns as if he heard nothing. I rub my ear, thinking it must just be a ringing, but I can't ignore the sounds and dark movements in the corners of my eyes.

99 turns back to check on me, and my face must give away the horror that's bubbling around inside because he strides back quickly, closing the distance between us.

"Are you alright?"

I nod frantically.

I didn't notice his grip on the sides of my arms until it relaxes and his hands slide down with worry. He gestures for me to sit, gently handing me a canteen. I chug the tepid water, using a massive hollowed-out log as a back brace.

99 walks a few yards to a slow little stream, squatting over it and waiting for the water to fill his empty container. As I watch him, I can't help but feel a sense of dread, a strange sinking feeling in my stomach. Even though everything is peaceful and serene, I hear the

screams echo again. I look to him for any indication that he heard it too, but he doesn't even flinch or look up from kissing the canteen to the water.

They are so loud but only in my head, calling out to me from different directions in the forest. I can feel sweat run down my tightly closed lids. I cover my ears, praying the screams stop.

A strong hand wraps around my ankle, making my eyes shoot open.

"What is it?" 99 says, shaking my leg a little, trying to get me to focus. The screaming has stopped, but it was so loud just a second ago.

"I can hear someone," I whisper.

"There is no one. I scanned the area when we stopped." His hand tenderly slides up my calf, petting me lightly, soothing me.

"It sounded like screaming. I saw shadowy shapes out of the corners of my eyes and green orbs of light all on their own," I stutter out.

His hand goes still on my leg, helmet tilting to study me or maybe check my heart rate. I can see my terrified ghostly expression in his visor. He opens my bag and unwraps the rag that holds the stones. I can't follow his train of thought, just watch him quickly undo the covering. When they are fully unraveled and in plain view, I hear him exhale in relief.

"Do you think it is a creature in the forest?" I ask.

"I do not know. When did it start?" He fusses with the strap of my bag, wrapping it around me and moving my hair out of the way to prevent pulling.

"I half woke up from some nightmares last night, and I can still hear them. Like waking up while it was happening made a tether and now it's spilling out."

"What was the nightmare?" he says, sitting back into a squat with

286

his forearms resting on his knees.

"I'm not sure. It was sounds, feelings mostly. I had the terrible thought for a moment it was the creature in the cave."

"The Albright." 99 leans in a little, like he is trying to understand. I feel the blood drain from my cheeks at the sound of its name.

"What of the green orbs," he asks.

I pause. "Oh . . . I'm not sure."

His fists tighten ever so slightly, like he isn't satisfied with my answer for some reason. I can tell he is trying to block his mind's eye from me as he turns away, looking out into the forest. It's cold and final, so different from his tender demeanor moments ago.

"What? Say what you are thinking." I get to my feet in a sloppy, dizzy mess and he reaches for me, offering help.

He stands, puffing out a large exhale, like he doesn't want to answer. "You can ask anything of me. I will protect and defend you. I cannot do that if you keep things from me."

I feel myself recoil at the pivot in his words. I can tell he regrets it from the way he reaches out and then lets his hand fall.

"I keep things from you?" An eerie calm falls over me. I can feel my body ready itself for defense or attack if need be.

"The green light, Ferren. I saw you in the field that day I came back. You said you did not know what it was, if it was even from you. I understand if you felt like you had to lie before, but now . . ."

I stare at him with my jaw open and get the sudden urge to start running away into the forest, to get home, to get away from him. How did we get here from my nightmare?

He still thinks I am a liar. There's no benefit of the doubt, even now.

"And when you see how easily I can conjure it, will I go down the mountain the same way I came up it—in cuffs?"

"Ferren."

"What? I have never kept anything from you. I should have listened to my highest priestess when she said Viathans hated us, thought so poorly of us, that I would not be safe if you knew what I was. Admit it. Admit your people's hatred," I say, knowing that I am losing myself to the tiny doubtful thoughts I have been trying to keep at bay about us.

He steps back but his gaze on me does not waver. "I will not lie to you and tell you my home views the temple fondly," he says steady and plain.

"I am from the temple, 99. Me. That is why you do not trust me. You can't think of any other reason for the green light other than deceit. You accused me . . . again," I say and feel my heart breaking.

He nods his head slowly, reaching out to hold me steady by my elbows. "I'm sorry I questioned you again, Ferren. But I do not care that you are a priestess."

"But you would prefer if I wasn't?" I say, lifting my chin in defiance.

"There are things in your world I am uncertain of." His hand slides up my arm, squeezing my soft bicep like he can't let go. "But there are things I know for sure."

I ignore the insinuation of him caring about me, spoken in a mysterious riddle.

"When Vickers called me a religious fanatic, did a part of you agree with him? He said you would hate me when you found out," I counter directly.

Again, he shakes his helmet, slow and controlled. "Not even then. And I have known fanatics; you are not one." His voice is eerily serious, a soft demand for me to truly listen to him. "I never hated you. And if you want to see more evidence, please look for yourself." He softly grasps my hand and presses it to the temple of his helmet.

I snatch it back before he sends me anything. I do believe him, and I don't need to see into his mind's eye to know he is telling me the truth. He apologized for questioning me again about the green light, but he didn't just question me. He implied that I lied to him about it, jumping right to that conclusion. I refuse to look into his mind to find the apology. If he wants my forgiveness, he will have to ask for it himself.

I cross my arms and stare out into the forest. Everything is calm—no insects, no shadows, no screaming. The feeling of dread has subsided, like the forest wanted my acknowledgment and now it will leave me alone.

"I'd like to keep walking, Commander."

CHAPTER TWENTY NINE

M y stomach sinks to the forest floor when I see where we are camping for the night: the same circle-shaped rock structure we stayed at the first night in the forest—when I had to sleep in cuffs, using hot rocks to keep warm. But at least it means we are close, that we should be back to the ship by sometime tomorrow.

I just about collapse onto the ground when I see 99 unloading the bags from his back. We have not spoken since our fight earlier. I ran through our conversation over and over in my head, almost wanting to probe further about some things he said but not wanting to break my silence. He has annoyingly given me space but still made sure I was ok.

"We are stopping for the night. First Son could have more scouts in the area. I know you are anxious to get back, but there is a present threat we need to be wary of. We need to focus on keeping you and the stones safe—"

I wave a hand at him to wrap it up as I chug my water and remove my boots. For the first time since I've known him, 99 is talking too much. I rest my feet on the ground and rub them. The moss layer provided a nice soft cushion while hiking, but of course, I chose to stomp around the forest angrily on the day we passed it.

99 watches me, like he isn't sure where to sit or what to say. "You should eat," he says, then he starts digging through the bags with a newfound purpose.

He pulls out one of the wraps of bread and then digs farther for the sweeter things Calliape packed. The gesture isn't lost on me, but I'm still fuming. He sets them on the rock next to me and holds up a blanket to wrap around my shoulders without asking if I'm cold. I bring the blanket close to me and munch on the food as he gathers a small bundle of twigs from the forest floor.

The spot where we made our fire is eerily still present, untouched with black scorched wood. 99 crouches down next to it, placing the twigs in formation. He strikes his fire starter, creating a spark. Seeing the alternative for making fire makes me think of the night we left the torch in the forest when the creature mimicked me. I get a chill and bring the blanket up in a close tuck.

Bending down, he lifts his helmet just high enough to blow on the ember. The sight of his lips makes me swallow hard. The scruff of his chin is illuminated for a brief second, then the flash of light smothers out. Seeing that small fraction of his face, how hard he is trying to make me comfortable, twists my insides. I probably wouldn't have been so harsh if I could see his facial expressions, but the helmet censors most emotions, likely by design.

Another ember falls into the leafy debris and twigs as he strikes, leaning forward, puckering his lips into a blowing shape, but he isn't quick enough. I know he won't fully take off his helmet with the possibility of danger, so I scoot closer and lean down, wanting to be helpful. He stops striking the steel like I've surprised him then, as if he realizes my intention, strikes it faster, creating a large orange spark that rolls into the dead foliage. I cup my hands and blow gently, enticing the embers to glow brightly and catch. I peer up to see if he is watching me and of course he is. I almost feel a little embarrassed but that gets washed away when the fire takes a strong hold.

He stares at me intently still, holding the fire starter in his hand as if stunned. "Thank you," he says, adding to the modest flames steadily growing until it roars.

"Can you radio August to come closer, to pick us up?" I ask, letting the blanket fall to my sides at the increased temperature.

"Anything we say could be intercepted. Someone, anyone could hear us, and if they were closer to us than August—"

"They would kill us before he got here?"

"Yes. I don't want to take the risk," he says, placing a large log on the fire.

99 stays on the other side of the camp, looking out into the forest. He glances over at me as I position myself on the blanket. I hope I can just sleep to make the time go by faster, that the vivid nightmares don't terrorize me again. I lie down in a huff and watch as he turns his helmet slowly away, guarding our camp.

Mother's womb . . . he actually looks sad.

I wonder if the fight is on his mind too, but he isn't saying anything to me if it is. The orange and red flames reflect off the somewhat shiny parts of his metal armor, making him look deadly and inhuman. But I can tell he isn't himself. His broodiness has an undercurrent of something else. I take in a large inhale and look out into the trees, trying to look anywhere else but in his direction. When my eyes inevitably roam back to him, his head is tilted toward me, posture alert.

"Did you hear something again?"

I shake my head no.

I study him, trying to figure out what looks different. His shoulders look tired, and I haven't seen him eat or sleep very much since we left, now that I think of it. Even though his will power is stronger than mine, he must be exhausted.

"Do you want me to take watch?"

He shakes his head.

"I can't sleep anyway. And I'm perfectly capable of looking around the forest, maybe not as broody as you though," I tease.

With a huff, he stands from his guard post on the other side of the fire. I try not to smile that I have made a small crack in the tension between us.

"Oh, ok? Do we switch?" I sit up, surprised, as he makes his way right next to me.

With another labored huff, he descends to the ground on his side, facing away. "No, stay right there. Wake me if you see or hear anything, even if you don't think it's real."

He breathes deeply, his massive form coming up higher from the ground than I expected. It's silent again and I realize I don't really want or am capable of keeping a look out as well as he. I glance out into the forest, trying to see if anything looks odd, but it's just darkness around us, only a blown-out orange glow flickering off the trees and rocks surrounding our camp. But just after that, utter darkness. The forest is completely silent, still, not even the insects singing, just as Selene said it would be while traveling with the stones in our possession—like a silent respect as we pass through.

I find myself roaming the lines of 99's body more than I keep watch for the enemy. He is just out of reach, and I'm tempted to extend an arm and brush my hand over his shoulder.

A small dead branch falls from the treetops within the glow of our camp. I watch as it stutters down, hitting other branches. The noise is amplified by the silent backdrop of the forest.

99 reaches to his hip, withdrawing a gun, aiming it at the noise. He relaxes his elbow a little when the small stick falls to the ground and places his weapon back in his belt.

"You are supposed to be sleeping. I will let you know if I see any other suspicious twigs, promise," I say.

It's silent for a long time. I can tell he isn't sleeping, most likely watching out into the forest on that side. The fact that he is doing it next to me feels comforting. I am tempted to press into his mind's eye to see what he is thinking but right now, it feels like an unfair advantage. Sometimes, he is very easy to read, small movements giving away little hints at emotion, but right now, it's different.

I lean forward and throw another log on the fire, making hot flurries float up into the air.

"Are you cold?" he mutters.

"A little."

"I will get more wood," he says with a sad, hopeful tone.

"No, it's ok."

The fire crackling fills the long silent pause between us.

"August, at the watering hole, he apologized to you," 99 says, breaking the silence.

I lean into his space a little, trying to hear his low and hesitant voice. I wait for him to say more but he doesn't, like he wants me to fill in the blanks.

"He did . . . ," I say, ushering him to continue.

"I should have as well, or at any time, but I did not."

He rolls to his back, placing a forearm under his head and the other on his stomach. Our hips touch just a little, the fraction of contact making me crave being closer. He's so long, I have the look over my shoulder as I warm my hands closer to the fire. I'm not sure what to say, but the feeling of him this close to me again smooths out any jagged anger I had.

"I am sorry I cuffed you when we climbed the mountain. That I did not believe you. That there have been times that I didn't protect you properly. I am sorry, Ferren."

Has he been trying to string an apology together since we arrived at camp? I feel a warm wave flow over me as he tucks his chin to the armor on his chest, watching for a response, waiting for me to say something.

"Thank you. I am sorry too."

I feel a gloved knuckle run down my arm, which in return sends a shiver up my spine. If there is anything I've learned about 99, it is that he tries to do the best thing he can in the moment, but sometimes circumstances complicate those choices. Even the decisions I hated, I can still wrap my head around them. I may not fully agree with some, but it feels safe to know that they are thought through and that he truly doesn't want to hurt me.

I bump my side into the leg he has bent at the knee next to me. "I have no idea what the light is. I had never seen it before that day on the ship, but I understand, 99. I was a stranger and you were protecting your friend and the mission. I can't be too mad about that."

"And you know what it is now? In the grass, I saw . . ." He pauses, making such an effort to use careful words. "Will you explain it to me."

"I do not know exactly, the more time I practiced with Calliape, the more I could control it. But who knows? Maybe once we leave Frith, it will stay behind, like a strange phenomenon," I say, looking up at a rising ember in the air.

"I never hated you for being a priestess."

"Ok."

"No. I need you to know that," he says, deadly serious.

"I believe you, 99."

"I want you to know that the fact we are from different worlds is not lost on me, but you can talk to me. I am not good at . . ." He sighs deeply. "I will listen."

I put my chin to my shoulder and smile down at him and how hard he is trying. He runs a hand down my back, letting me know he meant what he said.

"I just keep coming back to thinking we are finally returning, that we have what we came for, but I won't feel like it's real until we are back in the Estate. Part of me wants to run straight to the temple and complete the task I started, to ascend at all costs, forgetting all about this world, what I have seen. That part of me feels so cold."

"Duty can be cold."

He is giving me more credit than I am due. The duty he is bound to on his world is much more honor driven; mine is more based on a promise to ascend.

"Have you ever . . . The things you have to do, as a commander, do they make you feel cold?"

"Yes, often, and more recently."

"Oh."

I feel him sit up next to me, pressing closer as he rests his forearms on bent armored knees. "I have lost family to extreme beliefs. First Son recruiters came to my family's village. I was away and duty forbade me from doing much to help," he confesses, hanging his head a little.

"I'm sorry." My stomach does a little flip at the small crack in his mysterious air—a small glimpse into his world outside of this bubble.

"Can I ask about them?"

"You may."

I don't know what to say or where to start. He must sense my hesitation because he takes my hand, calming the frenzy of questions.

"My younger brother joined First Son's followers. My mother couldn't bear the thought of him leaving . . . so she went with him, leaving my father."

"Do you see your father?"

He inhales deeply. Maybe I have offended him, but he looks at our joined hands like he is thinking of what to say.

"You may ask me anything, but some things are difficult to answer." He touches my face and I can feel him reaching out a tether.

He doesn't want to answer me with words, I realize, so I snag the connection and fall in. He sends me images of his mother's face, of the last time he saw his brother. Their house and his father are not as clear, and some parts are even blurry, like he can't remember. He shows me the time he visits with his father, how broken he seems. I can feel his thoughts get less intentional and more like a stream of consciousness, but I stay in tune. His mind drifts from his family to August's, how large and loving his is in comparison—all his sisters and their families inviting 99 over and how odd he feels around them. His love for August and excitement to see him again. I open my eyes to disconnect, and he gives my hand a squeeze, like he knows what it feels like when we are tethered and the moment we disconnect now.

"Tell me of yours," he whispers.

"There is not much to say. I do not know my mother or father. It is not the same, but I felt your pain for losing your brother. I feel something like that every time I think of my sister. We are . . . estranged."

In the long pause, I feel him reaching out again, inviting me to show him if I can't find the words, but the images I pass along are even more painful. I can't show him my mother. I never knew her face, only a hurried description from Leema of what she remembers as a child.

I send him images of Leema that always end with her expression as she leaves, the heartbreak on her face from trying to express why she has to go, how even then she was trying not to be cruel. 99's amber light embraces me from within, cushioning those memories. I hear him sigh deeply and I know he must understand the feeling of losing someone in this way, knowing they are out there but not able to reach them, the desperate ache that it leaves.

"The Highest is the closest thing I have to family, I suppose."

He watches me play with the trim on his gloved hand. "I promise you, I will protect you, even when we get back."

"Protect me when we get back?" I say, a little confused.

Every time we even touch on the topic of the Estate now, my body reacts so harshly. He isn't saying anything wrong, but I clench a fist at my side, trying to let those feelings fall away, but they are deeply rooted. I stare into his visor so close next to me. We are from different worlds, different beliefs. I always feel so raw at the thought of him thinking of mine poorly, but then I realize we are still tethered, our connection so effortless, I forgot to break it before I brought up Crixa. He must have felt every emotion my body has assigned to her: the desperate longing for a mother figure, her selective attentions, and her harsh, sometimes violent punishments for me.

He places a knuckle under my chin when I cast my eyes down in embarrassment, a small instruction to look at him again.

"You are mine to protect."

Any last bit of prickly feeling fades away at hearing those words and their sincerity. Whatever happens, he will be there for me. I can't help but wonder if he thought about how whatever this is between us will work when we return.

His words ring in my ears again, and I swear he casts a tethering net so wide that mine automatically reaches out in response, beckoning him to say it again. I want to hear him say it in this connected way, so that not even the silent forest would be permitted to hear the intimacy. He whispers into my mind without hesitation.

"You are mine to protect, Priestess."

CHAPTER THIRTY

The smallest sliver of light creeps in through the darkly barked trees, creating a ghostly view of the area around our camp. The fire is still going, so 99 must have been awake long after I fell asleep, guarding and making sure the fire was fed. I can't help but smile a little thinking of him taking care of me, an unexpected gentle side I only saw glimpses of with how he treats August.

The forest is eerie and silent, the pressure of expecting a sound almost torture. The anticipation of any noise makes my ears feel like they need to pop. If I couldn't hear the fire crackling and 99 moving around last night, I would have been driven mad.

My head feels clearer after our talk by the fire last night. 99 opened up to me in a way that was both surprising and heartbreaking. After seeing what happened to his family, his intensely protective nature makes a lot more sense. I had not quite realized what the amber light was every time he has let me in. Each time, it surrounds me in a coating of warmth, like a homecoming to a place I've never been before. That feeling was so foreign, I couldn't understand it was his response to my presence, of being inside and connected, until now.

I picture the way his shoulders always seem to drop in relief that someone can finally understand the things floating around in his head that he can't put into words. Seeing that vulnerable slice of him only makes me want to know more, to dive back into his mind's eye and explore every inch.

I can feel the instinct tugging at me to hook the tether, which seems to grow every time we indulge in it. It's addictive and calming being able to see his thoughts, feel things as deeply as he does. I know that depth is only possible because of how open he is willing to be with me. It's becoming clear how much I can trust him and how much he actually trusts me, even if our words can be careless. We may be from different worlds, but I do believe him when he says it doesn't matter because I've seen it.

I sit up and run my hands down my face, realizing I won't be able to fall back asleep. It's still just before dawn and too dark to start traveling again. I know 99 is somewhere close, on guard but not in view. I scan the nearby trees then grab my bag and a change of clothes. I'm half-dressed when I hear a rustling on the largest rock above me and look up to see him sitting casually on it, looking out into the forest. It takes me too long to level out of my shock at seeing him so close and looming. I pull down my top and adjust the hem, trying not to make any sudden movements.

"Blessed morning," I say, a little shy even though he has seen me naked already.

He slowly turns his helmeted head toward me like I've said something odd. "Blessed morning, Ferren."

We stare at each other for a long time, then I pat at my clothes, making sure I remembered to put them on and I'm not standing here half-dressed.

"Not quite time to head out."

"I know. I just—" I laugh nervously.

"Food is in my bag," he says.

I find it in a heap and dig through it, pulling out one of his beloved squares. I hear him jump down from the rock behind me in an elegant thud. It makes me suck in a breath for some reason. I take a bite, turning away from him, trying to hide my grossed-out face. I ran out of my food last night, eating it all in a fit of anxious nerves.

He paces toward me in the familiar determined swagger. I feel his rough glove on my chin, angling my head up to meet his visor. He holds it there, waiting.

"I'm fine, no nightmares last night."

It was a wild guess of what he was about to ask and to my surprise, I hear him exhale in relief. I didn't need to breech his thoughts to assume. It makes my stomach feel fluttery that I'm starting to understand how he communicates better. He speaks with his body, his silence, with the space he holds for me.

His thumb runs back and forth over my chin, a small gesture letting me know he is happy I'm ok, that he was worried.

"We should clean your bandages before we leave."

I nod with his hand still on my chin, looking up with doe eyes. "Yes, Commander," I tease.

He freezes then removes his hand quickly, like the moment is too much. I try not to laugh, but there is something about seeing him a little flustered. I lean against one of the larger boulders in the semicircular formation, almost as tall as me but round at the top, right at my shoulders.

"How long before we head out?" I say.

"Not long." He unloads the supplies to change my bandages.

"How far is the ship from here? I wasn't paying attention last time."

"Couple hours."

"Then we will be back on the ship . . . with August," I say. I'm probably giving away my train of thought.

He doesn't answer me, just rifles through the bag. It still feels a little off between us. It must be this damn camp. Last time we were here, I fantasized about killing him.

"I'm sorry I fell asleep when I was supposed to be on guard duty."

"You were never really on guard duty."

"99!" I throw the rest of my food square at him.

I see his shoulders rising and falling like he is pleased with his own joke.

"Then why are you extra sulky this morning?"

He gathers up the supplies and brings them over to my spot on the boulder. "I'm not . . . sulky. I'm thinking."

I reach out to touch his helmet, wanting to peek inside his thoughts. Maybe he just can't say them aloud. He always offers, so I assume it's fine. But then he snatches my wrist to stop me. I glare at him as he holds it away from his head. Now I really want to find out what he is thinking. I wish I could see through his visor at his expression. I have a feeling I would know exactly what it is.

"Be a good girl and turn around, Priestess," he says slowly, like it's his turn to make me flustered.

I pull my wrists back playfully and turn my back to him, leaning over the curve of the boulder a little to tease. I decide to take my top off completely and tuck my arms in front of my breasts so they don't touch the cold surface.

99 is utterly still behind me as I look over my shoulder.

"Well?" I say.

He presses into me as he reaches for the bandages. In silence, he removes the adhesive patch, the chill of the morning air replaced by his bare, hot fingers on my skin. I feel featherlight traces down my spine and have to fight the urge to arch toward him.

"Last night, when you apologized—" he says.

"Yes, for yelling at you."

"You had a right to be upset. I can handle you yelling at me," he says as he works on my back.

"A challenge?"

He huffs a laugh and gently smears cold paste on me which I'm assuming are the gross herbs Ruth gave him.

Challenging him makes me feel powerful, like I'm taking on someone who is feared and respected by all three worlds. At first, it was just pushing his buttons to get a reaction, but it soon changed into something else. He may be from Viathan, but he is not my enemy. We see First Mother through a different lens, but we see each other clearly.

"I am really glad I met you," I say softly.

He leans in and whispers, "As am I."

I feel a little heated at the pressure of his body pressed against mine. It doesn't help that I am naked from the hips up and his hands are so strong and warm compared to the air. I feel him press a new bandage over my wound, which is really just from the stitches now, and tenderly smooth it over with his calloused palm.

I look over my shoulder, thinking he will step away now that he is finished, but he stays there. I can tell he is stalling, smoothing the already adhered bandage again.

"Thank you."

"Of course."

He slowly backs away, leaving a cold spot where his body covered mine. I can't stand the thought of him pulling away completely and heading out again.

Not yet.

I rashly remove my arm from where I've been pinning it at my side. I reach back to stop him, it lands on an armored thigh, and he stills. I turn my head a little, trying to see him from the angle, hoping he understands my silent plea to stay and that he can tell by my touch what I can't put into words—a language he understands, a look, an exhale, subtle cues.

Of course he understands; he always does. His body crashes into me, pinning me to the boulder in front of us. I reach my hand up to the back of his armored neck. Every inch of my body is pressed into him, solid and unyielding.

His hands are on me, traveling over the soft curves of my body.

"Ferren." His voice is low and sultry.

His hands reach my breasts, and I arch back, exposing them to the cold air. The contrast in temperature makes heat pool between my thighs. I want him to cover me fully, fill my body with his warmth.

I can feel his hard cock pressing into my back, so I roll my hips back to make him groan. I move my hand up his thigh, making just enough space to find the full scope of him.

I suck in a breath as his hand travels down my belly to the waistband of my own, and I can feel him unraveling the string, loosening it to gain access. I want him in this way, pressed up against this rock. I need to feel his lips on my skin, need to see his face when he enters me.

I pull at the bottom of his helmet.

"No. Helmet stays on."

I am almost disappointed that I can't kiss him but quickly forget as his finger dips into my slick pussy. I cling to the back of his neck, knees buckling. I close my eyes and see amber light, an image he is sending me of plunging himself into me. I feel breathless at the sight of him showing me what he wants.

"Please," I pant as he fingers my entrance.

I move my hand back to his cock, wanting to give him the same pleasure, making him groan into my ear.

"Is this what you want, Priestess?"

"Yes," I moan out.

He pulls his hand out of my pants, taking my arms and placing them on the rock in front of me like a command to keep them there. "Hold on."

My pants are pulled down to my knees, the cold air making my skin prickle. I can hear him undoing his belt behind me, the end of it smacking my ass accidentally but still making me gasp.

He makes a satisfied sound and then leans in. "I will remember that for when we have more time."

I can tell he is smiling at the accidental revelation of spanking me. He pushes a flat palm on my back, making it arch, presenting me in an upward angle. I feel him glide the head of his cock down the cleft of my lower back through my ass. I try to angle my hips up more to accommodate our height difference, but the gap seems like a challenge in this position. It makes me a little shy that it's not going as smoothly as I thought, but then I feel him tap the side of my foot with his boot. I look down at it, realizing he wants me to stand on top to get myself high enough for him.

"Go on then," he whispers impatiently.

I step on one boot and then the other on my tiptoes. It makes me higher on the boulder, so I lean forward just as I realize the angle is perfect now. He presses into me slowly, and I close my eyes to savor the feeling of fullness. He exits and slowly thrusts in, making me gasp at the deeper feeling. His hand goes to mine, resting on the surface in front, as he leans his body down onto me, pressing in again and again, creating a rhythm, eliciting pants that become moans.

Every move I make, he follows. With every tilt of my hips, deeper arch of my back, he reacts in kind and groans low in his throat as I tell him how good he feels.

"I wanted to wait until we were on the ship to . . . fuck you, take my time with you." He groans into my ear as he pumps into me, holding my shoulder still as he fucks me. "You've tested my resolve every chance you've gotten, Priestess."

Then he is plunging impossibly deep, reaching to the front of my thighs to circle my clit, the callouses creating a beautiful friction that makes me cry out.

"Now I can't leave this forest without feeling you grip my cock with your hot cunt."

I practically scream a moan out at his words, surprised at how much its increasing the almost brutal sensation on my clit.

"Is this what you wanted . . . to be taken against a rock . . . by a Viathan commander?"

"Yes!"

Pleasure ripples through as he impales me with his cock, thick and stretching, reaching the deepest part of my channel. My walls clamp down on him when I'm on the verge of release.

His movements get harder and out of rhythm. He holds onto my shoulder and thrusts hard, banging his pelvis against my ass as he groans deeply. I sit back into him, the walls of my pussy holding him so tight, every muscle in my body pulsating as he draws out my orgasm. The new tightness makes him come with a growl, muffled in his mask, filling me with warm liquid, coating my insides, but he keeps driving up into me like he never wants it to end.

We both hunch forward over the round top of the rock.

I can feel him sending warm light into my mind's eye, soft and euphoric. I send my own back, letting him know how much I loved that. His head rests on my shoulder and we breathe in unison as the bright light of the day starts to peek through the trees. Beams illuminate specks of dust as we breathe into each other, recovering. Our hands are haloed by light on the rock in front of us. I'm still trying to catch my breath when I hear him shuffle behind me, our bodies still connected from the waist down. His gloved hand brushes back a piece of my hair, exposing the skin of my shoulder. I feel his lips press into me in a soft drawn-out kiss. I realize he has lifted his helmet just high enough to kiss me, breaking his rule to keep it on. I lean into the tenderness, and it's shocking and heartbreakingly sweet

CHAPTER THIRTY ONE

We step out of the dense tree line and breathe in the wild air, cool and fresh compared to the stagnant thickness in the forest. It's not quite the exact path we entered originally—we are higher up on a rockier ledge. The inky ward created the same eerie stillness as we exited its boundary. I can see the ship in the distance, nestled in the grassy field where we left it. I pick up speed with the excitement of seeing August, of sealing ourselves away for the journey home. The thought of seeing 99 without his helmet on when we get to the safety of the ship, and the promise of watching his expression as he fucks me, numbs any soreness in my legs from walking for hours again today.

But 99 puts an arm out, startling me to stop. His visor is fixed forward, posture deadly and alert. I look out at the ship again. There are smokey burn marks on the ground and dark streaks with large metal pieces scattered like something was torn apart.

"What happened here?" I say. I'm frantic thinking that August was attacked while we walked down the mountain.

"I don't know, but something else is off as well," he says.

I'm shocked that such a large battle happened while August was here alone. I can feel 99 stiffen with awareness like he does when he hears something, alert and ready to defend.

"We should stay low," he says.

Just then, a whooshing sound ripples from above, blotting out the sky, creating a breeze all on its own. A slow black sky ship comes into view and moves toward August's. This one is sharper, points jutting out of it, all reaching higher into the sky, like a terrible, horrifying pillar.

"99!"

He blocks me with his body even though we are well out of view, surrounded by saplings and boulders.

"That is the second. There is one already here," he says, pointing past August's ship where it is headed.

Movement catches my eye from behind the large pieces of metal. 99 points, letting me know he sees it too. It's August lying flat with a gun ready to fire, alone and in danger. Who knows how long he has been like this, defending and waiting for us, refusing to leave us behind and save himself.

Something across the field near the boundary of the forest moves in response to August's better position. Whatever made those marks on the side of the ship's wings is still out there.

"Looks like they are waiting for reinforcements," 99 whispers.

My whole body trembles, making me feel dizzy. The reality of this danger starts to finally materialize. It's not something sneaking up on me in the darkness; it's laid out before us in a field just as we are meant to be leaving. Our lives are not the only thing at stake. If First Son gets the stones, all life on the three worlds will be in danger.

"We need to leave before the second ship lands," he says.

I stare at the scene wide-eyed. When 99 calls my name with gritted teeth, I realize he has been calling it for some time, but I could not pull myself out of my racing thoughts.

"Ferren, you need to listen. Please, tell me you will listen. Tell me!" He grabs my shoulders to face him.

I jump a little at his raised voice, the urgency scaring me even more.

"Yes, yes. I'll listen to you."

"I'm going back in the forest for cover. You won't be able to see me—"

"You're leaving me?" I say, panicked.

"Listen. When you hear me firing, I want you to run as fast as you can toward the ship. Do you hear me?" He places a small gun in my hand, steadying it with both of his.

My eyes dart around and he shakes me a bit to answer.

"I won't let anything happen to you. I promise. Look at me, Ferren. I promise. You can do this. This is nothing for the priestess who defeated the Albright. Get to the ship. Get inside, shut the door, and wait for August to take off."

Before I can protest again, he lifts his helmet up to his strong nose and pulls me in, kissing me deeply. I press forward, trying to savor the kiss, make it last longer. But he rips away, darting off into the tree line.

I lose sight of him immediately within the darkness of the forest. I can feel the cold metal of the gun acclimating to my trembling hands. I don't know how to use it, and shame burrows a hole in my gut at the sight of it in my palm and my white knuckles clamped around it. I lean against a large boulder, sliding my back down until I've safely hidden myself. I hope I will be able to move when I hear firing. Right now, all I want to do is curl up and stay hidden forever. I can't even peek out over the rocks or bring myself to watch for any signs of danger. First Mother's stones feel heavier than they did before in my bag.

When you hear firing, start running.

How do I know it's his gun? What if I run too soon?

Get to the ship as fast as you can and leave with August.

Did he mean to leave without him? There is no way August and I are doing that. What if they come for the stones and 99 is still out there. *Would* August do that, leave without him?

A single shot echoes in the distance.

I cover my mouth, frozen but alert, not knowing if I should run. He said run when I hear gunshots, but that was a single one. Then, multiple shots rain out like the fireworks used during the Estate holidays, booming and sizzling all at once. My body takes over as if I'm lifted by my shoulders. I leap over the rocks, tiny trees scratching at my arms, pulling and begging me to stay where it's safe under their cover.

I break out into a sprint and my legs cramp, burning instantly.

The sound of weapons increases more rapidly in the cover of the woods.

Just run.

I hear men hollering, then more shots. I can't help but think of how many 99 faces alone out there.

August's ship seems so far away, even now that I have made it to the grassy field.

Run faster.

When I look toward the sound of firing again, the sight of four figures standing by the tree line almost sends me tumbling to the ground. Dark, shadowy forms watch me, determining the best moment to pounce. Then, they move slowly toward me as I weave through the long grass as fast as I can.

First Mother, help me.

I pump my arms, willing myself to somehow be faster. My lungs are heavy, like they are filled with mucus and blood all over again.

The men are running toward me now, full speed with drawn weapons. They know it's me. They know I have the stones. I can feel it. Their sights are locked in, aimed for me and the stones as they run.

A sob escapes me.

The ground is soft and uneven and a slow tremor runs through it, a soft rumble compared to the great quakes I'm used to.

I push my legs harder, my thighs screaming for rest.

Through distorted tears, I can see August by the ship. He is squared and authoritative, looking more like 99 than himself. I can tell he sees me when he steps forward, and a flush of relief washes over me, but I pump my legs harder to get to him. I just need to get to him.

He shoots in my direction and a light spits just past me from the barrel of his weapon. I stumble a little, trying to avoid his fire. Another zings past, then a grunt echoes behind me. He's shooting at the men. They must be so close now—just behind me.

My legs are about to give out as I sob again in pain.

Keep running, please. Bring the stones home. Get home for First Mother, for Crixa, for ascension.

Another shot zooms by my cheek. I can feel the heat of it making my steps waver. My eyes are fixed on August, but then another figure appears next to him, staring in my direction.

Then they disappear and my lungs are full of water. In the next second, I feel an intense pulling. Everything is blurry. The ground falls out from under my feet. My legs aren't moving.

But I *am* moving.

There's a sting from the air I can't release, stuck and stagnant.

I open my eyes to see I am up against the ship somehow, moved across the distance of the field to safety. I can see August's back as he shoots the next blast, killing the last dark figure. I gasp like I have been drowning.

Beautiful eyes peer down at me framed by curls, holding me steady as I recover.

Calliape.

She wipes my cheek as I wrap my head around seeing her here, but it doesn't matter. More tears quickly replace them.

"You were running too slow," she says with a half smile, and I realize she used her gift to bring me to the ship faster, to ensure I was safe. *She* was the person I saw standing next to August.

He smiles at me with that handsome grin and casually walks to us like he wasn't just in a shootout. I wrap my arms around his neck, squeezing with all my might.

"Alright, alright. Don't make Calliape jealous," he says through his charming laugh.

I fight tears when I see Calliape again over his shoulder. I'm overwhelmed that they are both here and we are ok.

August's forearm lights up in a glowing hue, and 99's voice comes from the small panel, grainy with static. He's alive.

"Do you have her?" he shouts.

"Get off the radio. There's another ship coming!" August says sharply.

99's voice rips out, angrier than I have ever heard it. "Do you fucking have her, August?"

August's eyes widen. "Affirmative, 99th Commander."

He's alive and breaking his own radio rule to make sure I got to the ship.

"They are landing. Get inside and take off," 99 says.

August turns slightly, like he doesn't want me to hear the instructions.

"Leave, I'll hold them off," 99 continues.

I storm over and grab August's wrist roughly. He smiles, knowing exactly the reason for my fury, then presses the button for me to speak and lets me scream into his forearm without a fight.

"No! Get your ass to the ship. We aren't leaving without you!"

August grins wider. "Missed you," he says to me.

There's a long static-filled pause as we wait for 99's reply.

"Standby." His voice is fuzzy and distorted.

I help Calliape strap into the seat behind mine in the cockpit. She looks really nervous, like I'm sure I did when they strapped me in for the first time.

"When did you get here?" I whisper, still confused she is on the ship.

Her eyes flick to August as he presses buttons that light up and come alive. I knew she was upset he did not come back to the village with 99, but was she upset enough to come down the mountain and say goodbye to him herself?

I hear the hatch close and the engines thrust as I finish clasping her buckles.

"I'm coming with you," she states.

"Of course you are," August interrupts before I can respond.

I hesitate, thinking of the complications that will happen if she comes with us. I had wished she would come back with us each time I talked about leaving, a wishful hope. But now, having her here, seeing her in the ship, I get a twist of excitement that takes my words from me.

August examines me over his shoulder, and I raise my eyebrows at his stern expression, realizing he thinks I mean to disagree.

"She comes with us," he says.

I'm almost offended by his tone. It's Calliape's choice, or maybe, technically, it's 99's. I'm not sure. All I know is that if Calliape says she wants to leave this place, I will make sure it happens, no matter the consequences.

"Are you sure you want to come with us? Cosima is . . . really different—"

"They saw her face. It's not safe for her here," August cuts in as he presses buttons on his control panel.

"Does Selene know?" I ask.

"Selene is not my keeper," Calliape says evenly.

"No, of course not. I didn't mean that," I say apologetically.

She nods her head and holds my hand, letting me know I did not offend her. Selene is hiding out on Frith for her own reasons. She asked me to keep her secret and I will, but Calliape should be free to go back if she chooses. She seeks answers, and she has said that plainly many times. Calliape is everything I wish I were: outwardly defiant in her actions, not just words. I can't help how happy I am that she is here, that she is coming back. I look over at August as he runs his hands over his face to hide his smile, but I couldn't hide mine if I tried.

"Alright, sit down, Ferren," August says, trying to transition back to his serious pilot behavior.

I tug on Calliape's straps and then take my seat, buckling only the strap at my waist, not wanting to secure myself just yet. Not when 99 is still out there. I can't get ready to leave until we are all inside.

"Let's go get him. No noble shit today, right?" he says to me.

"Right!"

The ship lurches and groans as it rises. The metal floor is stable and heavy under my boots, not the weightless feeling like I was expecting. The ship hovers over the ground, seeming to kiss the tops of the tall grass before slowly turning, facing the dark, expansive forest.

"We'll get as close as we can, but he's going to need to haul ass. That other ship is on the radar now," August says.

I look over my free shoulder, twisting to see Calliape. She's fisting the chest straps, then she closes her eyes slightly as the feeling of pressure in the cabin makes my ears pop. I wish I could reach back and touch her, smooth her nervous leg that she bounces at the knee uncontrollably.

The ship points to the shadowy exit in the forest, where the figures emerged, still leaving an echo behind at their camp.

August lands gently with a stutter. The panel in front of him beeps, the screen lighting up with a brighter glowing dot that ominously moves on its own.

"Insight." 99's voice crackles over the radio.

I look over at August, who answers the plain request without question. "Second ship has not landed."

There is a rustling behind me and the sound of metal buckles. I turn to see Calliape frantically pulling on her straps, trying to free herself.

"What are you doing?" I say, afraid she is having second thoughts already.

"Stay put, he's close. Stay strapped in!" August says.

I can hear the beeping from August's control panel become rapid, like every one of the dots is closing in on each other.

But Calliape rips the rest of her straps off. She's not just taking a breather from their restriction; she's leaving.

"I need to get outside!" she announces.

"What?" August says.

"Please, sit, it's okay. The straps are just until we get out of the thrusting part," I say.

"Not what it's called. Please, Calliape, love, sit back down!" August almost begs, not hiding the desperation in his voice.

I unbuckle myself in an effort to calm her back into her seat with pacifying palms raised so she doesn't panic.

"Fuck! Sit down, both of you!" August says, not able to take his eyes off the control panel as he adjusts buttons to prepare for another inevitable takeoff.

I make a downward pleading motion. "Calliape, please, this is the worst part. Please sit, it's almost over."

I know how scary being on the ship can be, the terrible pit it makes in your stomach as it moves. I can't blame her for the panic.

She bangs on the cockpit door, prying on it like she is determined to stay behind, but it's not safe out there right now. We can't let her go, as cruel as keeping her in here feels.

"I need to send a message to Selene," she says.

I shake my head, dumbfounded at her explanation of the sudden change. She doesn't want to leave? This panic is only to send a final message to Selene before we leave for Cosima?

"I just need to touch the ground. She will get a message sent to her through the roots, the leaves—she will hear it. I can't leave without saying goodbye. I owe her that much."

Calliape is coming with us, off her world, away from the life she has known, the one Selene made for her. She's right she needs to send a goodbye, to break away from her bound tether here.

"August, open the door," I say flatly.

"You're joking. We're going to take off again any minute!"

"August, please! Calliape gets to say goodbye," I demand.

In the next moment, the cockpit door whooshes open and Calliape runs out, feet pinging on the metal floor.

"Make it quick and be careful!" August calls out over the sounds of the beeping dots.

I run after her, struggling to keep up. She seems to know exactly where to go in the ship, down the stairs into the cargo hull, without any guessing. I can't help but think there is something more she isn't telling me with how effortlessly she moves, how in place she looked next to August when she folded the distance for me across the field. We took days to descend the mountain. She could have easily traveled down in that time, bending the soil to close the distance to spend time with August.

I breathe deeply as the door in front of us to the ramp slowly opens.

"Make it quick, ladies. Our 99th Commander is on the move." August's voice comes out of the panel's speaker.

The ramp door opens fully, thudding down into the grass-covered soil. The dark forest is right in front of us, closer than I assumed. August skirted right up to the tree line for 99 to exit the forest and get onto the ramp in the same step.

Calliape steps down, placing her hand deep into the short foliage that dances around the ship. In a blink, the greenery stops its movement, completely still for just a moment, then resumes its frantic sway from the ship's engine.

"Okay, that's good!" I call down from the top of the ramp, a little afraid to leave the threshold.

There are some distant sounds in the forest, unnatural even over the great hum of the ship.

"That's enough. Come on!"

Calliape does not answer me again, her palm pressed into the ground.

Either my voice doesn't carry far enough or she is, in fact, ignoring me. I reluctantly walk down and touch her shoulder. "Please. We need to go back to the cockpit!"

Loud gun fire breaks out in the trees right in front of us, capturing our attention in unison. I grab Calliape's arm, trying to pull her up the ramp.

"Let's go!"

"Wait," she says, pulling back to press her hand to the ground harder.

More shots and light dance in streaks between large trunks, and I see the grass still once more as she removes her fingertips.

As we climb the incline leading to the ship, August yells over the speaker, "He's almost here. Strap in down there. We are going to hover!"

I spot the first set of chairs before we reach the top, bolted to the wall by the hatch.

"August, we are in!" I scream, making sure both of us are over the yellow line of the still open door.

The ship lifts a little off the ground as we sit down in the pair of seats closest to the opening. I quickly buckle Calliape and then fasten my own as wind thrusts into the cargo bay and up around our hair.

I hold Calliape's hand and lean back, bracing myself.

The trees thrash angrily as more shooting cuts in over the loud thrusting of the ship.

Come on, 99. Come on.

"Almost here, get ready!" August says.

I squint hard into the dark trees and see him running, then stopping to shoot behind him. I wish I could help, that I could control my light better, but I don't know how to use it without hurting him too. I want to rip out of my straps as he reaches the opening and thuds his boots onto the hovering ramp, but his posture is aggressive and almost frightening. He's barely glancing at me as he enters, and he shoots out into the forest from the cargo opening.

Calliape lets go of my hand and covers her ears.

"Leave it open!" he shouts, voice filling the room.

"Copy," August says over the speaker.

He lifts us off the ground, as tall as the giant treetops next to us. Branches almost knock into the ramp as he maneuvers away from the boundary.

99 storms over to a locker, pulling out a gun almost as tall as I am. He sways a little with the ship to compensate, but everything else around us moves on its own.

"Do you see them on the radar?" 99 shouts.

"Affirmative."

"Skirt by!"

"Copy."

99 stands in the opening of the cargo bay as the whole ship lifts, latching his belt to the side of the wall. I watch in fascinated horror as he crouches on one leg, the giant barrel of the weapon on his shoulder.

The wind thrashes my hair into my eyes, making it painful to watch him. I squint as the ship cascades at the same height, traveling sideways across the tree line.

Then I see it through slitted lids: the giant black pillar-like ship after a bank of trees.

"Lock!"

"Locked."

The ship steadies in a continuous smooth line. There is a single breath of calm before I see 99's finger slide over a button on the weapon, body completely still like a statue in front of me.

A cracking sound splits across my eardrums and Calliape jumps, holding her palms tighter to her ears. The sound leaves a ringing behind and then a zoom across the sky like the lights that danced as

99 fought his way out of the forest. I close my eyes tightly just as the terrible sound of metal screeches and explodes in the distance.

He hit their ship.

Through my tousled hair, I see him stand and punch the hatch button with the side of his fist. The cargo bay calms, the deafening sound of wind dying to just the hum of the ship's inner workings.

"Welcome back, my friend. That should slow them down," August says as the familiar sensation of rising into the sky makes my insides feel heavy.

99 sits in a thud on the wall adjacent to me, legs spread, completely casual and not like he just blew up a sky ship. The confidence that we are out of danger allows me to take large, relieved breaths instead of the shallow, panicking sips of air I was surviving on.

He's locked on me now. I can tell he wants to get to me, but he is restraining like how he used to. It takes every ounce of willpower not to rip at my straps and run across the cargo hull and wrap my arms around him, to touch him and make sure he is ok, that he really made it. We both did.

Calliape's small whimper next to me snaps my attention away from his intense stare. She is still cradling her head with her eyes closed.

"Hey, it's ok. We made it," I say and try to gently coax her palms away from clutching her head so tightly.

A loud, airy sound makes my ears pop and then ring in a painful pitch.

99 sits upright and alert.

His casual position looks strained suddenly, like he would throw his body on us if he wasn't strapped in. I watch him as he presses the armor on his chest against the tight constraints, gloves going down to his side like he is trying to free himself.

322

My head fills with frantic thoughts then, suddenly, pinpoint focus as soon as I realize they aren't mine; they are 99's, our link tethering in desperation.

He floods me with amber light, holding me, protecting me.

The booming noise seems to fill the space, growing louder and more ear-shattering, like something terrible is on its way, closing in on us.

99 has one side of straps unfastened, grasping and pressing against the other in a ferocious pull. I know something awful is happening when the amber light turns almost sad, regretful, like he knows he won't be able to reach me in time.

CHAPTER THIRTY TWO

The side of the ship bows in like soft bread dough. The sound of a terrible metal groan fills the space then everything cuts out. My ears ring like I'm inside the bell tower, but it's not rhythmic, more of a continuous, painful toll.

The entire ship swings in the air. The lights cut out then red beams replace them all around us. The whole world shifts on its side and we start to spin. I can't find the words to pray to First Mother, to beg her to save us. I try to press back against the seat but I sway in every direction the ship moves.

August's voice cuts over the ringing in my head, yelling nonsense and instructing us to hold on.

Then the floor under us steadies. We aren't spinning anymore, but we are getting higher, faster and rougher than the last time we took off.

Alarms blare warnings throughout the entire ship, tolling and beeping in red flashes. We are launching into the sky and about to break apart. I know we need to get away from the other sky ships, but we aren't safe if we are in pieces.

The lights cut and come back on with their normal hue, the alarm stops, and my feet feel firmer on the floor. There is a huge black scorch mark on the wall, like whatever hit us on the outside almost made its way in.

I grip the straps of my seat, panting with relief that it's over. But I hear August's voice a little clearer now that the alarms have stopped.

"Prepare for jump."

My stomach is in my throat. I thought we had jumped already and were in between worlds by now. I close my eyes and wait for it to be over. I don't want to see the black spot on the wall and worry that it will crumble, sucking us out into the space between.

The ship angles and climbs . . . and climbs. I try to focus on breathing.

In and out. That's all I need to do right now.

Breathe in and out and ignore the woozy feeling in my gut.

Finally, the ship levels out again, the pressure around my face subsiding. A soft almost pleasant chime breaks my concentration. My eyes take a minute to adjust, but I see 99 ripping at the last of his buckles, flinging them back like he is an animal breaking free of chains. He bounds toward me and squats in front of my knees, gripping my thighs. I feel like I am in a daze that I can't find my way out of. It's not quite like the hallucinating sickness from before but it's close, like it could turn to that if we keep going at the same rapid rate into the cold sky above Frith.

He rips off his helmet, making me dazed in another way from his pained and searching expression. I feel his hand holding onto my legs, his thumb sliding back and forth in comfort.

"Are you alright?" he says.

I want to answer, to nod, but I can only stare down at him for a reason I am unsure of. I am trapped in a trance, clawing to get out of the shock.

I feel him pull closer to me, cupping my cheeks. "Ferren?" His eyes flick all around my face, his lips are parted, and the lines on his forehead furrow with worry.

I can feel my head moving between his palms; I am nodding. I see his eyes glance to my side.

Calliape.

I break from his hands and my daze all at once. I grasp for her, turning to touch her like I couldn't before when the pressure of the wind and spinning pinned me.

"I'm ok," she says, unclicking her restraints.

99's focus is only on me, his gloved hand tracing down my collarbone and shoulder, checking me over with his touch.

"That was very foolish, to be on the hatch like that," he says.

I find his forearm and run my hand up it, grounding myself to him. I don't care if he disapproves. I'd do it again for Calliape. We made it, we are in the space between, and the ship didn't break apart. I can't help but smile a little at his serious expression. It instantly softens, the subtle lines around his eyes hinting at a genuine smile. I watch his face as he carefully unfastens the buckles and straps holding me down.

Calliape rises from her seat, holding the wall for support.

"Are you sure you are ok?" I ask her.

She is steady on her feet but her pupils look blown out. She nods. "You?"

"I think so. I got sick the first time we took off. Maybe you should sit back down."

"I am not sick, but my ears are still ringing."

August's footsteps echo his fast tread as he comes into the hull, looking at each of us, assessing if anyone is injured. His brow noticeably softens, like he missed seeing us all together, then he flashes his boyish smile.

"Oh, good. The helmet's already off. Now get over here and let me kiss you," August says with open arms. They embrace with slaps on the back and a long, knowing gaze before breaking their hug. Their bond always fascinates me. It makes me want to know them both more and to have such a long history together like they do.

"Nice flying, how bad is the damage?" 99 asks.

August's eyes are on Calliape as he answers, "Mostly superficial. Won't know until we dig into that panel."

"Stones?"

August throws a thumb over his shoulder toward the front of the ship. "Locker. Safe."

99 pats him on the shoulder, leaving him to stare at Calliape in peace, then turns to the weapons locker, placing the guns on his waistband and knives from his boots inside.

I watch as August approaches Calliape with hands orbiting, like he wants to check her for injuries but awkwardly places them on his hips instead. She seems calmer and more at peace with him next to her now. It feels like I'm almost spying as they whisper to each other. Their sweet nearness all but confirms my suspicion that Calliape was here with him while 99 and I descended the mountain.

I climb up out of the cargo bay, hoping I can calm my nerves with something warm to drink. The moment I enter the mess hall, I hear 99 behind me.

"Are you in any pain?" He presses a flat palm on my chest.

"It felt heavy when I was running, burns still, but I am fine."

His hand travels up the side of my neck then cups my jaw, forcing me to look at him. His pupils dilate slightly, and he holds onto me like he can't let go. He looks so troubled, devastated even, searching each of my features to make sure I am really here.

"I thought you did not make it to the ship. I thought they caught you," he says in a controlled tone, like he is holding back a well of emotion, wanting to wrap me in a protective embrace. "I saw you running, and then . . . you were gone," he whispers as if it's too awful to say.

His kiss is so deep, it's almost painful, and he cradles the back of my neck like someone is trying to take me from him.

"I made it. We are safe," I say breathlessly as we break away from the too overwhelming contact.

"I don't know what I would have done if you didn't," he says gently, touching his forehead to mine, pulling me to press against his body harder, like he is fighting a feral urge that will break free if we are not connected.

"You have me, 99." I cup his scruffy chin, feeling him press into it, the touch instantly soothing the frenzy inside him. I whisper it again and he closes his eyes, the worry lines between his brows smoothing.

Seeing him fight to control his distraught feelings breaks my heart. I hold his hand to my lips, pressing a kiss into his palm, and his eyes open again, more peaceful and serene. His thumb brushes my bottom lip as he watches me. I want to scream at him for telling August to take off, for thinking I could leave him there. But for right now, I just want him to hold me.

August loudly enters the mess hall, making me jump like I've been caught by an elder past hours. But 99 does not waver. He holds me until he decides to let go, not from August's intrusion or the awkward silence that follows.

"Sorry, I'll need help with that panel," August says, clearing his throat and looking down, trying to hide an enormous grin at the sight of us.

I know my face is red by the way it's burning, like the sun has scorched it.

"I, um, should check on Calliape. How is she?" I ask.

"She's good," August says, pretending to buff invisible dirt from the metal wall, still unable to fully look at us without smiling.

"Why is she here?" 99 says flatly.

Both August and I snap our heads to him, at the tone of voice talking about someone as important as she.

"She wanted to leave Frith, and we want her here," I say. He can be angry if he likes, but it's a little late when we are traveling between worlds to voice an opposing opinion.

99 pauses, eyes lingering on me in contemplation. He moves his hands to his hips, waiting for August to chime in.

But to my surprise, August does not have anything else to add, no cute remark to smooth out 99's abrasive edge to the situation. He just stands there, watching 99 with intense eyes. I realize that is his answer. Her being here is not a circumstance for him to joke about. He is serious and willing to defend it against his commander if necessary—the first time I have seen him even hint at defiance.

99's posture softens; he notices it too. If August is willing to stand his ground in a way that is so unlike him, it must be for good reason. 99 nods, a quick acknowledgement that he will not press any further, but not as his commander, as his friend.

I lie facing the wall in the pilot's quarters, the bed I used to think was awful now feeling amazing. My hair is still a little wet from my scorching hot shower. The hum of the ship envelops me in a warm, safe cocoon. I left the lights at the floor's edges, not wanting to be in complete darkness just in case I couldn't handle that after what happened in the cave. The sounds of the inner workings of the ship are comforting now compared to the lack of all noise while we traveled through the forest.

I hear footsteps and then a whooshing of the door opening, making my heart jump a little. I know it's 99 without even turning to look. I wondered if he would sleep in the mess hall or in here with me. Not knowing is the only thing that has kept me awake, waiting for the answer, and now I have it.

I can feel him walking toward the bed slowly. Then, to my surprise, he ungracefully plops his body down, making mine bounce up a bit. He adjusts himself next to me, like we always sleep like this and have never slept apart. It feels familiar and safe as he pulls me in until my back is against his bare chest. I feel his heavy arm wrap around my waist and his breath in my hair. A silly giddiness flutters in my stomach, and I have to turn toward him.

He groans as if I woke him up from a deep sleep but lifts his arm so I can freely turn. I can see a soft glow of light on his pale skin. His arm returns to my waist, pulling me in once again.

He is calm and still. Not the kind of calm in the forest when he was alert, this is different. He is relaxed. No one is hunting us right now, and no creature is lurking in the forest. He probably hasn't slept fully in days.

I press my hand to the side of his face and in response, his hand slides up my sides to the back of my neck as he presses a sweet kiss to my lips. Then he pulls me impossibly close, and I rest my head on his chest and feel him lazily stroking my hair.

"You smell so clean," I say.

All his familiar smell and sexy musk is gone. He only faintly smells like himself, most of it masked by soap.

"I don't think I like it," I confess with a pout.

His chest ripples under my cheek as he laughs, a sleepy, breathy sound.

I watch Calliape and August across from me at breakfast, their legs touching lightly, and she does not pull away. 99 assured me August was making sure she was comfortable before I gave into sleep last night. I knew she would be ok with him. He made me feel safe and welcome within minutes of boarding the ship.

But 99 is scowling in their direction. He hasn't warmed up to the idea of a new passenger. I caught the tail end of a spat between the three of them when I came in this morning. It ended in Calliape reminding him how she traveled across the field to save me and if he took a minute longer, she would have had to save him too. That must have been how August felt watching 99 and me bicker: anxiety inducing but highly entertaining. I'm not worried about Calliape at all. She can hold her own against 99's abrasiveness.

Most of the day is spent watching August and 99 work on the damaged part of the ship and chatting with Calliape. We exchange versions of common prayers, something we tried to do many times in the village but were always worried Selene could hear.

At times, Calliape likes to sit and think in silence for long periods. I enjoy just sitting with her, being next to someone like me. We have an unspoken rhythm with each other. I can tell when she wants to be alone, and she can tell when I need to pour out into conversation. She's from Frith, and there is no status or stations there, but I know if she were born on Cosima, she would climb quickly. Even though she is much more skilled in her gifts, it feels like we are in tune with each other.

Thea has always been a good friend, but I have never been able to truly know her as fully in friendship as I have been able to with Calliape. It almost makes me sad and guilty for feeling so close to her in such a short period of time, like I am disrespecting my friendship to Thea somehow.

August asks to see my scars a few times throughout the day but stops when 99 glares at him. Calliape must have told him about how quickly I healed because he knew they were scars and not open wounds anymore. I wonder what else they spoke about in her time with him before we got here, if she told him about my light, that I practiced controlling it.

99 checks in on me frequently through the day to see if I have rested or if my little wounds from the stitches need attention. Sometimes, he just sends me amber light, which is a shock because he is in the cargo hull an entire level below. I have been able to reach out to him at long distances, but the tether he sends out for me seems to be getting longer and stronger.

Our dinner together feels so natural, each of us taking care of one another, getting items the other needs, so in tune like the families I saw on Frith. I'm so happy I can barely eat the food August proudly prepared.

After our meal, August is sitting on some palettes in the corner of the mess hall, and I watch him steal a glance at Calliape as she flips through my small prayer book.

As I pass, he pats the spot next to him, an invitation to sit away from the others. I climb up and bump him with my shoulder. I've missed spending time with him.

"Calliape told me about . . ."

I look at his expression; his face is serious. I can feel mine blanche a little at what he may be talking about.

"She told me about your light. You know, most of the things I've heard are ghost stories about scary priestesses, tales Viathan parents tell their children so they would behave," he jokes.

"That's awful. Is that why you were so scared of me when you found out what I was."

August barks a laugh. "Uh, yes!"

"You're not scared of me anymore though, right?"

"No, of course not."

I laugh a little and fuss with my hair, crossing my knees in front of me.

August tucks the piece that keeps falling behind my ear, a sweet, affectionate gesture, as he smiles at me.

"I am not a very good pilot, August, so please don't make me throw you out of the airlock." 99's tired, husky voice cracks across the mess hall.

August slowly lowers his hand. We both turn our heads to see 99 staring possessively at us over the data pad he holds. August chuckles and sits back with pleading, raised hands.

His flirting is innocent. When he touches me, it's the same as when Calliape does—soft and friendly. It's nothing like how 99 touches me, fiery and at times stolen. I watch him for a minute from across the room and have a sudden urge to sit in his lap as he taps buttons on the control panel, concentrating on First Mother knows what.

"You and 99?" August whispers

He grins a little and raises his eyebrows in insinuation. I suddenly feel a little flustered, like I did when he caught us sharing a private moment before. But then his teasing grin turns into a sweet smile that makes its way to the tiny lines around his eyes. I can't help but giggle a little and shush him when he does the same.

"I am not surprised. Don't worry, I've got my sights on someone too, but it does seem like we have the same type," he says with a flick of his chin, indicating I should look across the room.

Calliape and 99 are both sitting reclined in their chairs with crossed arms, content in their solitude. I can't contain the howl of a laugh that escapes me and August follows, laughing so hard, he nearly falls off the palette.

CHAPTER THIRTY THREE

The cockpit is dark and quiet. If I close my eyes, it almost feels like the Estate's temple after everyone is gone for the night. The screeching metal noises below drove me to seek the silence in the top of the ship as 99 and August fix the rest of the damaged wall. Seeing the black spot only reminds me that we are not fully out of danger, an uneasy feeling that I can't shake. Normally, I would use this time to pray alone, but it feels weird praying on the metal floor after being able to with the soil beneath me for so long.

Even when 99 told me the damage was a little more extensive than they thought, it felt useless to pray to First Mother, like she wouldn't be able to hear me out here between worlds anyway.

Instead, as an experiment of sorts, I decide to test the link that seems to always be outstretched, waiting for me to snag it. I bring my legs up into my chair and close my eyes. I feel myself slither down the corridor, almost feeling the cold walls, maneuvering down to the cargo hull, straight into 99's mind with no friction.

I see a mess of wires on the floor and August's body halfway in the wall. He huffs and throws discarded metal from the hole. Then, I feel a strange stutter in my concentration, like I have been bumped into, and a rolling feeling of amusement from 99's thoughts. Either he knows I am in here or he is finding August's tantrum funny.

Warm amber light caresses me, making my lips tingle.

I can't see out of his eyes anymore, just his thoughts. Images flash in front of me, sweet and welcoming, but then slowly, more heated memories make their way in. I see my own face crinkled with pleasure in the tent our first night together, then a memory of him standing behind me and accidentally spanking me with his belt. Another wave of rolling amusement crashes into me.

I know without a doubt he knows I am in his head. I can't help but smile and squeeze my thighs together at the memories.

"Quit smiling! Look at this thing. It's completely fucked." August's voice is muffled, like he is speaking underwater.

I open my eyes and blink, trying to adjust to the darkness of the cockpit again. 99 is so open, he knows when I slither in now, and I've been caught peeking inside. The salacious thrill of being able to see images through his point of view has me anxious for him to finish whatever they are doing. I close my eyes, sinking into the headrest to remember the sexy memory he teased me with.

When I open my lids again, 99 is standing in the middle of the cockpit, watching me. I gasp, expecting him to still be halfway in the wall with August. I cross my arms a little, realizing how hard my nipples are.

He steps farther into the room without a word, face serious or mad, I can't tell.

"Is everything ok?" I ask as I stand, moving around the cockpit chairs to meet him.

He nods.

"August looked pretty upset about the damage," I say, taking a step back as he slowly approaches.

He steps forward, the light from the control panel hitting his face. Oh, he is definitely not mad. I step back again, seeing the darkness of his gaze. He looks hungry, like he wants to devour me. I feel a little flustered, stepping back into my suite's door and pressing my back hard into it.

His arms box me in, resting above my head.

"I was just waiting up for you. I couldn't sleep," I whisper.

"Shame," he says, and his lip curls up slightly.

He presses the door button, I feel my support whoosh away, and his other hand quickly comes down to replace it. He guides me into the room backwards, running a hand up my arm softly.

"I could feel you," he says, voice so low and husky, every step deliberately directing me. "I could tell you were in here listening, watching." He pulls my hand to his temple, pressing my palm to it.

I bite my lip at how warm his skin feels against it. His eyes are heavy lidded and looking down at me intensely.

"You're fun to spy on. All sorts of things come up, interesting thoughts."

A hum vibrates low in his throat as I trace my finger down his neck, planting my hand on his hard chest.

"Like on Frith, when you were out scouting. I wondered where you were so I reached out. I've never done that so far, but your thoughts were so loud, they called out to me. So vivid."

His head tilts, brows furrowing a little, and I know he wants me to continue.

"You were under a tree and . . ." I send a flash into his mind of the memory of the daydream he had of us, what I saw. I know he sees it when his breath hitches, then a devious smile crosses his face. He studies me, eyes roaming over my mouth, before pressing into me with a deep, steady kiss. I wrap my arms around him and surrender.

The door closes behind us in a puff of air, then his hand returns to my hip, pushing me to walk backward. He lays me down on the mattress, still brushing his tongue around mine. I sink into the bed, the weight of his body pressing into mine loosening every tense muscle in my body from the journey. I move my legs around him, wanting him closer to me.

I tug at his shirt, pulling it up his back. He tears away from our kiss, taking it up over his head and exposing his hard stomach. When he comes back down, he nips at my neck, making me cling to him in a gasp when he grazes my skin with his teeth.

"Did you mean what you said, Priestess?"

I run my fingers through his hair, pulling his head closer so he won't stop. He bites down a little then soothes it with a slow lick.

"What did I say?" I ask breathlessly, rolling my hips up, seeking out the press of him between my legs.

"That I . . . have you." He nuzzles into the spot just below my ear, sending a shiver straight down to my pussy.

"Yes . . . every time I felt you squeeze my hand."

He grips my breast firmly in his fist as he bites down on my skin. I gasp at the dual sensation.

"You have me, 99. I am yours," I whisper.

He sits up on his elbow to meet my eyes, his expression a little shocked, like he wasn't quite expecting me to phrase it in that way.

I feel a little foolish for the vulnerable declaration, but then amber light bursts from the cracks and floods me. I close my eyes and let it fill the space, like seeing candlelight through closed lids.

Lips crash onto mine feverishly.

We rip at each other, trying to get closer.

He pulls away with a feral sound, pulling at the ties on his pants. I watch and slowly pull my night dress up my hips, making him fumble over his strings. I slip it up over my head and then lie back onto the mattress, staring up at him.

Wild pupils flick down my body.

His pants are not fully off before he impatiently comes back down in another all-consuming kiss. I dig my heels into his ass and pull at his waistline, trying to free all of him. He reaches down, tugging at them in the frenzy.

He kisses between my breasts, and then his tongue circles around my pebbled nipple, tasting the darker flesh.

Leaning to one side, he reaches down between my spread thighs and runs the head of his cock in a slow drag up the seam of my pussy. He hisses through clenched teeth in my ear, trying to go slow and restrain himself. When he reaches the top, I let out a whimper and roll my hips. With a breathy groan, he runs himself down to my entrance, teasing at the scorching wetness.

I tilt my head, seeking out the explicit view between us to see his length fully. In the forest, I felt his cock as he filled me, but now in our room, I want to see all of him.

I gasp when I see his full length as his hand moves the head up and down my clit, slicking it. I have to stop my eyes from rolling back as he groans, moving in small thrusts as I watch.

99 must see the pleasure mixed with concern on my face at finally seeing how large he is because I notice an amused smile hint at his lips at my reaction.

"You took me so well in the forest. You can handle it, Priestess."

I tilt my hips up in encouragement, wanting him to fill every bit of me with his throbbing cock. He slowly sheaths himself, his full weight now on me.

The breath is stolen from both our lungs at the overwhelming pleasure. He seems to pause, waiting to see if the gasp that escaped me was in pain. When I bite my lip and clench on the stretching feeling, he slowly settles, plunging even farther into my core. The sound that it elicits is guttural and undignified for sure, but he growls in response and looks at me like it's the most beautiful thing he has ever heard.

The thrusting rhythm he starts is slow and controlled, as if he's unsure if he can be with me without holding back. But I know his thoughts are feral. I can feel them crashing into mine, unable to hide themselves. I bite his shoulder, making him start to thrust more powerfully into me.

"Harder, as hard as you want," I say with a raspy voice, digging into his corded forearms.

Instead of pounding into me, he lifts me up from the mattress and adjusts my legs around his waist, sitting on his knees. I can't help the moan he creates as he starts to pump up into me.

"Say you're mine," he chokes out.

But I can't speak. I can barely breathe as he impales me, holding me in his giant arms.

"Say it," he says with each thrust.

I sit my full weight on him, to feel him deeper. He fists the sides of my soft hips, using them to move me up and down with each thrust.

"Say. It. Priestess. Say you're mine."

"I-I am yours!" I say between moans, clinging to his shoulders.

I watch his pained expression of pleasure, and being able to see him like this without the helmet is almost too much. His kiss is like a branding as his cock pounds up into me harder.

I can feel myself clenching around him, not able to stop the waves of euphoric pulses. He makes a vicious sound, holding me in place, watching me ride out my release.

Then, his thrusting gets shaky, and he buries his face into my neck, his groans turning to deep breathy whimpers of his own as he fills my pussy with his hot cum.

We cling to each other in place, breathing in tandem as we come back down. He slides out of me as we lie back on the mattress. He tucks me into his side, and I run my hand up the hard lines of his torso and nestle into him. The smell on his skin is more like himself, like it was when we had to snuggle for warmth in the forest.

We both stare up at the ceiling in silence as our breaths even out.

"What is it?" he whispers finally.

"Nothing, just thinking," I say and laugh a little. I can't stop thinking of his reaction when I said I was his, how he asked me to say it over and over and how much I meant it.

"Hmm, do you need to go pray, or are you mine for the rest of the night?"

I suddenly feel a little guilty for not wanting to pray at all, but I can't deny how disconnected I feel to it, and not just because I'm too comfortable and sore between my legs to get up. I am so close to finishing what I started, and now I can't even pray anymore. I want to be present in this moment and to not have to go within. To feel the world completely and all at once. Before it was so loud, praying was a comfort. I feel myself changing, shifting around inside.

"You were always so kind with that, making sure I had a place and time."

He huffs. "You look very pretty bent over praying. Kindness was not the only motivation truthfully."

I practically snort as I laugh and smack his arm.

He grabs my hand and kisses my knuckles. "The first time, it did take me by surprise. I've never seen a priestess pray like that before."

"But there are priestesses on Viathan," I say, confused, knowing Cosima has outreach temples all over his world, some there for generations.

"Yes, but that's not how—they aren't so formal."

I prop my head up on my elbow. "How do they pray then?"

"I'm not sure, smaller, maybe, more spontaneous."

Spontaneous prayer was something I noticed on Frith. Selene and Calliape would pray on a whim, even for just a second, no setup, nothing formal. I press my hand to his scruffy cheek and seep into his mind's eye with no effort at all.

Images flash and stutter incoherently then steady: August touching a charm around his neck and whispering, a woman I recognize as 99's mom from his thoughts before holding a baby and looking up thankfully at the sky and smiling, images of 99 whispering pleas to himself in the forest as he watches me run to the ship, his father sleeping in a pew in a temple room. They're real and raw prayers to First Mother, nothing formal about them. I can imagine how silly it must have looked when he saw me praying the first time.

I feel him stroke down my arm and pull myself out of his mind's eye.

"No, just different."

He must have felt the shift in my thoughts, the still present worry of how he views that part of me. Our connection is so strong and effortless now. I know things will need to be decided when we return and I have ascended. All I know for now is that I can't be without him.

CHAPTER THIRTY FOUR

The last day on the ship is spent in anxious excitement. August does repairs and sits in his chair most of the day. He tells me he always catches himself going slower on the way home, once the job is done and the initial sense of adventure has worn off. He flirts with Calliape, who just smiles and gives him sass or ignores him entirely. He likes both reactions, it seems.

We spend hours going over the plan for when we arrive, what we will say and how Calliape will stay on the ship with August until 99 can make sure it's safe. I tell them how the welcome party may be much larger now that we have the stones. The entire Estate may want to greet us when we arrive and pay their respects to Mary.

I know we are getting closer when I hear August and 99 reporting on the communicator to the beacon on Viathan. They tell the person on the other end there's been a casualty: Vickers. They effortlessly say he sustained injuries in the forest and succumbed to the wounds. That's not what happened at all, of course. 99 killed him. I'm almost uncomfortable at how okay I am with that, but Vickers was a bad person. Who knows how this would have gone if he didn't find out my secret. Would he have ruined our chances? Would he have gotten us killed?

They send a message to Cosima, an update on our arrival, the status of the stones—that Mary has passed. 99 tries his best to say it as formally to the beacon as a commander is expected without hurting me. They are hoping the message reaches them, that Cosima has repaired the beacon to prepare for our return.

When it is time to strap in, August calmly announces it over the ship's speakers, his tone intentionally steady, like he isn't trying to incite a panic. But I am suddenly overwhelmed with anxiety.

From here, I leave the comfort of the warm humming ship and am thrust back into my life in the Estate. I am excited to be home, but it seems to be happening quicker than I thought. The stones will be returned, and First Mother will finally see my devotion and come to me. I'll be a high priestess, and after the great conjunction year, 99 and I will have to make some decisions. I'm fairly certain we are thinking the same things, especially since he's practically declared me his in a way which is possessive and assertive. Normally, I'd hate that sort of thing, but I know not to look into the schematics of how he is phrasing it. I feel it, what was in his head and the way he won't let me out of his sight for more than a couple of minutes, even on the ship. I can tell he's not going to just drop me off and leave.

As I strap in, 99 comes over to check the tightness, making sure I'm secure, crouching in front of me. I stare at him as he adjusts my restraints, placing a hand on his, making his expression soften. This is it. From here, things change, but I'm determined for some to stay constant. He stands and brushes a thumb over my lips.

"You okay? Did you get all buckled in?" I crane my neck to look at Calliape behind me.

She smiles at me nervously. "I think so."

I point to a buckle she's missed, making her huff to herself. Then

I wait until August is fiddling with his controls to check her again but can't see them all from this angle. When I look over at 99, he nods, knowing exactly what I was thinking, confirming she is strapped in and safe. He must have been watching her carefully as well. As much as he doesn't want her on the ship, he knows that August and I do.

She smiles at me sheepishly. I can tell she is nervous because she gets really quiet, like a less extreme version of 99, when something is on her mind.

"I'm so happy you get to see my home now, Calliape."

Her shoulders relax, then she reaches out for my hand with grippy fingers. I strain to reach, our fingertips touching to the first knuckle. We can only hold the grip for a moment and let go in an exhaled laugh.

August's landing was even, smoother than the last time, or maybe my mind was too preoccupied. The loud, airy noises of the ship's descent cuts out at the last thump of meeting the ground. Then I hear a loud chiming, ringing in the distance outside.

"What is that?" Calliape asks.

My throat feels a little restricted, like if I am not careful, the emotions I am holding back will fill the space.

"It's the bell," I say.

The last time I heard it ring so frantically, I was in the library with Thea and Mary, petrified that the Viathans had arrived.

I watch 99 go over the plan one last time with the others in a daze, anxiety turning to a dizzying, internalized panic. He places my bag over my shoulders and attaches his normal number of weapons on his belt, a sight that no longer shocks me. He opens the compartment where the stones are kept safely, holding it in a bundle. August and

Calliape do not say goodbye to me, knowing we will see each other soon, but I still ache to embrace them both before the ramp door is open and I'm swept away by the Estate's strong current.

Calliape leaves to hide herself away in the pilot's suite. August has been instructed to help with Mary, reassuring me he will take care of her while she is removed from cold storage.

99 lightly bumps my shoulder with his, distracting me from the anxiety swimming in my gut. We stand at the top of the cargo ramp as the mechanical sound of the door hinge commences. I nervously nod and fake a smile.

"You will see Calliape as soon as it quiets down. She's safe on the ship," he says.

"It's not that, just nerves."

He grips my hand, squeezing it twice. A warm flush encompasses my body as I look up at him, and even through the dark visor, I can tell his expression is tender. It calms me until he breaks his clasp, needing to give the illusion he is a stoic Viathan commander.

Somehow, this seems more intimidating than leaving, than stepping into the dark forests or sleeping in the cold. Daylight cracks through first, then wind whips inside with heat and dust, materializing the feeling of home. The ramp descends to the ground with a final thump, letting in the louder toll of the bell tower.

99 takes the first step down, and I follow at his side, trying to stay pressed against him.

Crixa, Lord Hollis, and a few guardsmen walk toward us down the path of the sky ship docking area. They break away from a larger group of temple members and guards who have come to see our arrival. This time, August has landed us in the appropriate spot, not in an Estate courtyard, just outside it in a small docking station.

I stare at the group in front of us. They look foreign to me, and even Crixa's face isn't like I remember it. I feel a little underdressed as I see the flowing veils and temple gowns. I search each face, looking for a familiar one as we step off the ramp.

Crixa strides forward, crossing the distance in a long slender pace, beaming with arms extended for me. She's not who I'm looking for, but I'm still excited. She embraces me stiffly then holds onto my shoulders, looking me over.

"Ferren, you've returned." She looks me over for a long time. "Mary," she says in a knowing tone.

But her face falls as guardsmen make their way past us, entering the bottom of the ship. I hold my breath and realize they are retrieving her body from cold storage, just like 99 said they would if they got our message through the beacon.

She links arms with me to watch as they carry a long metal coffin down the ramp and past us. August stands at the top of the ramp, nodding once to 99, then presses the button to close it, sealing him and Calliape inside like it's completely natural.

Mary's coffin reaches the group of temple members, disappearing into them. Crixa hums like she is unfazed by the morbid display of Mary entering the ship alive but exiting it in a box. She smiles down at me, patting my arm like she is excited to see me, but it just seems a little too cold after seeing Mary like that.

Lord Hollis steps closer as we cross the dirt opening and gestures for two guards to come forward. They lift a large, wooden, carved box with the depictions of the First Birth on it.

"I am here on behalf of Emperor Matthias. We thank you for your service and the sacrifice of your crew, 99th Commander," he says.

99 nods his helmet slowly.

"The stones," Lord Hollis says expectantly, opening the box.

Crixa gets a stern look on her face and stiffens at hearing the word mentioned by him.

99 lifts the ratty cloth we have kept them in and roughly sets them down, making the guards brace to keep the box straight.

Lord Hollis looks at 99, appalled at his roughness.

"They're wrapped," 99 explains.

Crixa practically cranes her neck to see their resting spot as Lord Hollis adjusts them inside and shuts it. I can tell she is not happy Emperor Matthias sent him to hold the stones.

We walk up the dirt path toward the Estate, Crixa's arm still intertwined with mine. People lean out of their windows and watch, looking curious and happy even, but they remain silent as the guards stay on the outside of the group, an eerie border. I notice an angry man stand and begin to shout incoherent things at us. Two of the guards hit him and drag him away. He must be a drunk, but it still makes me nervous. I check over my shoulder to make sure 99 is still just behind me.

I lean into Crixa. She is calm and poised as we walk the short distance from the landing yard outside the Estate. Our pace is painful, and I want to break away and run up the path, but everyone around me is slow and orderly. I've never noticed how torturous it is to walk this calmly when you want to desperately get somewhere. I remind myself that I'm home, that I'm not running through the forest and fields of Frith anymore. I am expected to be poised. If I want to be a high priestess, there are rules and expectations I need to embody now more than ever. The weight of even remembering them is hard on my lungs. I have to actively force myself to breathe or I will choke.

Just get to the Estate, return the stones, ascend, everything will be as it should, and maybe I will be able to take in air without thinking about it again.

We reach the great room of the Estate and Crixa breaks off from her tight hold at my side. "Take Priestess Ferren to her chambers," she says low to a group of high priestesses walking with us.

Chambers?

99 said we would have to debrief with the emperor and that he would do most of the talking if I was uncomfortable. That he would explain in further detail about Vickers and the attack from First Son and how we got the stones. We went over in detail what I should and shouldn't say—no commands, just suggestions, ones I plan on heeding.

I feel a mixture of feeling left out and relief when I realize I won't be attending the meeting. It's a harsh reminder that, here in the Estate, I am not a pivotal member like I was with August and 99 on the ship. I got used to them wanting to hear my thoughts and opinions. Now, I am being taken to my chambers while the others talk of more important matters.

I notice 99 looking at me, not joining the rest of the group as they trail up the stairs, as if he is waiting to see if I will say anything. I know he is expecting me not to take this, but this is normal. I need to be on my best behavior. I can't let anything get in the way of my ascension.

I bow my head to Crixa as she slinks away, then I lightly nod to 99, letting him know it's alright.

He balls his fists, his massive shoulders rising in a silent, frustrated breath, then he turns to reluctantly leave with the group. I know it is killing him to leave me as he glances back over his shoulder, but pushing the subject with me would only draw attention to what has happened between us. He disappears around a banister to the council meeting I am not permitted to attend.

My part in this is over. I am home now.

CHAPTER THIRTY FIVE

The gaggle of high priestesses surrounds me, corralling me in the opposite direction. I start to panic, but I am being held in place as I walk with the priestesses, high and elder. I recognize some of them as even showing me outright disdain in the past, now displaying soft expressions in excitement and almost adoration. It's enraging. I want to say something out loud, but I can't think of anything clever. It's not me they are excited for; it's the stones. I could be anyone or anything, a piece of furniture that they guide along to its correct room.

"This way, blessed priestess."

They usher me down corridors where elder priestesses live and some of the more talented members of the temple. We arrive at a large wooden door and when they open it, I am shocked to see a giant-sized bed chamber with an adjoining room. My small room couldn't even house the bed from this one. It's empty and strange. Some of my things are laid out on the vanity, so this must be where I am staying.

I turn to say thank you but an elder priestess is already shutting the door, encasing me in the ornate room by myself. I look around at the opulence of the fabric and the doughy bed. I feel odd and out of place here. I would have rather stayed in my old, familiar room. I guess I will just wait here until 99 or Crixa comes to get me after their meeting, which makes me feel a little panicked at that thought.

The adjoining room is set with trays of food and a screened off area in the corner, where the feet of a claw-foot tub are revealed at the bottom. I scour the rooms one last time before stripping off my clothes and sinking into the hot water. I stay in the warm cocoon for as long as the water is steamy.

The massive wardrobe is carved and painted with planetary orbs and stars, the dark navy paint chipped a little in the corners. I open it, hoping they have moved my clothes here as well, but it's lined with a row of fancy temple gowns and veils. Only one or two dresses have a more casual look, but all of them are black, a stinging reminder of my station. Even in this opulent room, with food trays and expensive fabrics, I am still just a priestess.

This is temporary, I remind myself, *until I have ascended.*

I sift through and find a loose-fitting temple gown. It's almost as fancy as some of Thea's. There is a robe and nightgown, but I am hoping having a temple gown and veil on will help ground me here faster. My head is still spinning, but the familiar feeling of the veil in my hair is a discomfort I will learn to ignore once more. The silken fabric almost feels slimy compared to the rough clothes I've been wearing since I left.

I wonder if the council meeting is over, if 99 has left the Estate and is back on the ship. It's very strange being away from them in this empty room. I stare at the lumpy bed covered in ornate pillows and throw blankets. The headboard goes up the wall and reverse waterfalls to the ceiling in a ridiculous canopy. I might have to sleep on the floor if it's too soft. The contrast of being in this room compared to where I was just the night before is maddening. I am an impostor living and breathing in the dreams I once had. It feels unnatural for me to be here, but the urge to ascend still tugs on me, so I know I am still me, just a little rougher now—with some new skills.

The feeling of burning in my palms makes them itchy, and I pace back and forth, soothing the skin. The openness of the giant room starts to seem smaller than my room on the ship, like it's suffocating me. I start to scratch at my palms frantically, digging my nails in between my fingers until they feel raw.

I can't stay in here. I can't wait anymore. They can't just lock me up in a fancy room and conduct business with the stones on their own. I was part of it. I retrieved the stones on my own, with my light to help and protect me. I deserve to be there when they are placed in the temple, when they speak of what happened on Frith. First Mother's stones are here now because of me.

Before I realize it, I'm standing in the hallway outside my new room. I look down both hall directions, trying to get my bearings. I'm not brave enough to go barge into an ongoing council meeting, but I would bet my life the stones have been taken to the temple by now.

I walk briskly down a hall that I think may lead me there. I'm unfamiliar with this part of the Estate, but luckily, it's a late hour, so no one is out walking around.

I get to a corridor that looks familiar and pick up speed when I know for sure I'm on my way to the temple. I pass a few guards, who give me strange looks, but in this part of the Estate, they ask fewer questions.

I finally get to the temple and see there are four guards at the entrance. I slowly walk up to the door, glancing at each of them. The one closest to the entry steps forward and looks me over. The temple has never been guarded before, but he steps in front of me, blocking my way and making my blood boil.

"How dare you block my path into the temple."

"No one is permitted inside."

How is this possible? How is a guard able to tell me that I cannot go into my own temple. I stare daggers at him, but he does not waver.

"We are only following orders," a younger one chimes in from behind the one closest to me.

"You will let me inside. I won't ask again."

"No one is permitted inside."

"Let her pass," a calm, flat voice says from the now cracked temple door. Crixa is in the entrance, holding the door open for me to enter.

The men move in formation off to the sides, making an aisle for me. I glare at them as I walk in, marching halfway up the aisle before I turn to face her. "I've never been denied entry to a temple before. What is this?"

"I asked them to station there to protect the stones. Don't be offended if not all the guards know who you are, blessed priestess," she mocks.

Blessed priestess, a name that I've noticed some calling me since I've returned.

"That's not what I was implying. I do not expect—"

She takes a seat in the front row, admiring the statue of First Mother. I take a deep breath, sitting next to her when she pats the wooden pew.

"The 99th Commander told us that you were invaluable to the retrieval party, praised your knowledge of Frith. I am very proud of you, Ferren. You represented Cosima well, stepped in when you needed to. I had no doubt you would make sure they sent their stone here."

"Thank you, Highest." I feel all the air billow out of my chest.

"He also told me you had an injury—" she says in an exhale. "That you had to recover for a few days in a Frith village?"

I nod my head, not knowing how much he told her, how good of a lie he weaved according to our plan. I'm afraid to say anything to undo it.

"They made me put green mush on my cut," I say lightly.

"Any other things I should know? I would like to hear it from you, not a Viathan"

Other things like my hands emit green light? Those kinds of things?

"I wish to forget most of it truthfully. I'm just so grateful to be home," I say, hoping it appeases her. I can feel her examining the side of my face as I stare up at the statue of First Mother.

"I am even more happy that you are proud of me," I say, and she gives me a tight smile.

It's not a lie. I *am* happy she is proud of me. It just isn't as high on my mind as some other things anymore.

We sit in silence for a long time, watching the incense float around the statue. I have the urge to fill the void with my words, but I'm afraid I will slip about something I'm supposed to be keeping to myself. Subject changes are her specialty when she is avoiding a topic, so that would be very obvious to her if I changed directions. Instead, I decide just to breathe deeply and take in the familiar smells of the temple that I have missed.

"I want to show you something." She stands abruptly.

I watch her walk to the altar beneath First Mother's statue, pulling back the velvet cloth to reveal Cosima's stone, rough and untouched, coming directly from the birth lands to this temple during the war with First Son. I have to actively steady my breath at the sight.

"You have retrieved First Mother's stones, convinced Frith to house theirs here for the conjunction once more. That is no small feat." Crixa waves her hand, beckoning me to come closer.

She points to a wooden box as I approach with careful steps. I recognize it from when we landed and 99 practically threw the stones inside, to everyone's horror. I smile a little at that. The box is surrounded by dozens of tall candles. She opens it and pets the contents inside lovingly.

"Our First Mother's stones, back where they belong. Would you like to place them on the altar?" she asks.

My neck turns so fast, I make myself dizzy. "Me?"

"Yes, Ferren. I think you have earned it."

My heart swells. I have to stuff down the outburst of emotion. I still myself, trying to be poised, calm, and how she expects me to be, to embody a high priestess.

I nod my head slowly.

She turns and picks up the large wooden box and lifts her chin for me to stand closer to the altar. The chandelier above casts a spotlight on the velvet bed they are supposed to rest on, two indents lying empty, waiting to be filled. Cosima's stone is alone and broken.

Crixa presents the open box to me, the rags used to keep them safe still inside, preventing them from knocking together in my bag as we descended the mountain together. Crixa clears her throat and then juts her head slightly down, gesturing that I should reach in.

They look very different in this setting, rougher and smaller, more handled than the stone already on the altar. But I can see their clear-cut lines where they were broken apart and will fit together again.

"Priestess Ferren, will you honor us by completing the birthing stones' journey."

Crixa's expression is something I can't even describe, but something I know I have always been searching for. I can't look away from her. I just want to bask in this moment.

"Blessed First Mother . . . please find me worthy," I whisper.

Crixa nods lightly, reverting to her stern look.

My hands tremble as I reach into the opening, cupping the first stone. It's cold in my palms and I hold it gently, like an egg that could easily crack. My lips are dry from breathing out through my mouth, hoping it would ease my nerves. I rake my teeth over my flakey bottom lip as I hover my palms over the velvet nest, doing my best to align it with the other. The backs of my hands touch the soft fabric and I open them lightly, letting the stone wiggle into place.

I cradle the next one, the smallest of the three. It's porous with tiny holes and a dark-green shade in some spots. Moss, this is Frith's stone. I allow myself a small smile at the memory. It lies there with a gaping crack, not snapping into place like I assumed it would. The three pieces just lie next to the others peacefully.

Crixa closes the box in a snap, moving the symbolic candlesticks closer to each other, lighting each one with a strike of her long lighting stick.

My mind can't quite catch up to my body, like it is lagging behind, still in the forest of Frith with 99, warm next to the fire as we open up to each other. But I am here, and the stones are safe in the Estate. I've completed the task.

But I feel . . . nothing here. The ground does not tremble, light does not illuminate me or the stones, I don't go into a trance, and there is no vision of First Mother like others have said.

Nothing.

"You did very well, dear." Crixa can see my thoughts written all over my face. She pets my shoulder in the same pacifying way she does when I am unsure if I have set up correctly for a ritual. Then she dismisses me, once more reassuring I have met her standards with a genuine smile.

I should be ecstatic to have placed the stones, one step closer to ascension, but seeing them in their resting spots only reminds me of who I was with when they were retrieved. I feel a tug of my heart toward that direction, toward 99 and the others.

The feelings I thought would break free here, when I placed the stones, did not manifest. Instead they came alive in the forest, in the cave tunnels with 99, in small moments of subtle connection I was hesitant to give into and in the overwhelming tether we now share. The stones have been placed but all I want to do is get back to him. To feel with my whole heart, the way I only can when I am with him.

CHAPTER THIRTY SIX

"**W**here are you?"

I reach out to 99, hoping if I cast a tether wide enough, I can find him. He could still be deep within the Estate or back on the ship.

"Please, I need you. Where are you?"

"Are you alright?"

He sounds frantic, mistaking my desperation to get to him for danger. I sense a sweeping feeling of affection, like he is caressing my cheek, making me almost start running down the temple corridor, through a cloud of foggy incense, toward him.

"I am fine. I just want—need you."

I send him images of placing the stones and I get a prideful feeling in return. No words, just deep adoration and stoic joy.

"I am coming for you."

His words are thrilling, sending sparks down my spine. I answer his words with feelings of excitement and lusty suspense, thinking of him coming to find me.

"Are you in the Estate?"

He doesn't answer, but I can still feel him. His mind feels focused and unrelenting. Then, I catch a glimpse of his location, a hinting tease is all he gives me. I see stone walls, confirming he is still here, inside the Estate. He must hear my thoughts because I feel a low rumbling laugh. I lean into the feeling, seeking out the sensation, wanting to get lost in it.

I pick up the pace, looking over my shoulder as I turn down hallway after hallway. The candles are burning low now, making the stone corridors shadowy and haunted. I find my way to my room after a few missed turns and doubling back.

I glance around before I open my door and step inside. I should call out and let him know where my room is, but I can still feel the link between us, even if he is choosing to stay silent.

As I turn to face my now dimly lit room, I feel an arm pinning me back against the wooden door. I let out a gasp, raising my hands up to defend myself instinctively. My wrist is grabbed and held tightly in place. I catch the smell of 99, then the sight of him hovering over me. He was waiting for me in this ridiculous room, as anxious to get back to me as I was to him.

I let out a breathy laugh as he presses into my hips with his pelvis, his hand already free of his rough gloves, running up the column of my neck. His grip is tender but significant against my collarbone.

"Remove this," he commands.

I slink my free hand up to undo the veil from my hair, the sheer black fabric flowing to the ground in a pool at our feet.

His strong palm rests in the valley between my breasts, my low neckline revealing my chilled skin. My nipples pebble as he presses in closer, making me buck my hips into his. A deep groan vibrates in his throat as his knuckle travels from my chest down my stomach.

"And this," he instructs.

With my free hand, I pull on the single tie to my temple robe. It opens in a tiny sliver down my body. His fingers brush against the long seam, sliding down my abdomen, turning in an arch over my hip and then thigh.

He leans in, hardening his grip on my trapped hand above my head, then I feel fingertips caress the inside of my thigh, trailing up painfully slow. I press my head back against the door, wanting to rip his helmet off so he can kiss me.

"You are so beautiful, it is maddening," he says in a low, breathy voice.

I can't answer as he finally reaches the apex of my thighs, making me whimper and grind on his hand. He cups my pussy with his palm, fingers sliding in easily.

"When you left, I wanted to rip you back, have you in front of everyone so they know you are mine now," he says in a gravelly tone.

I pull him in by his waistband, feeling breathless, wanting him pressed harder against my entire body. My hips writhe, circling on his hand as he plunges into me again.

"Do I need to claim you here, so they know you are mine, Priestess?"

I nod shakily,

"No. I want your words." He pulls his finger from me, waiting for an answer.

"Yes," I pant right into his visor, my hot breath fogging it for a moment.

He plunges two fingers inside, stretching the walls of my entrance. I grab at his forearm, pulling it in to fuck me with his fingers deeper. He releases my wrist, using his now free hand to brace me by the shoulder, holding me still, plunging in over and over, agonizingly slow.

I tug on the base of his helmet, gasping as he works me. I want it off; I want to see his eyes watching me squirming on his palm. All it takes is a small press on the seam where it meets the metal of his neck armor for him to agree to the request. His fingers make a wet sound as he slides them out, needing both hands to remove it. I hold my frustrated breath and feel myself clench on nothing, missing the full sensation of his thick fingers.

He pulls it up, hair falling free and messy around his rugged face. He drops it to the ground a little less carefully and more hurried than any other time I have seen him remove it. His hooded eyes watch me as he runs a hand through his hair, brushing it back.

"I was afraid you would leave after the council meeting," I whisper.

He furrows a brow and lifts my chin with a knuckle. "I give you my word I will not leave you again. There is no reason to be afraid."

His voice sounds so sincere, so true, that even though we aren't tethered, I can feel his amber light without seeking it out.

This is how I wanted him: vulnerable and open. His rigid demeanor is wiped away as he starts to lose control with me again, but I have to fight to keep my thoughts from sinking back to the odd feeling gradually coming to the surface since I left the temple.

99 is not a distraction; he is more than a quick escapade with a guard to forget a difficult day in the temple. He truly cares about me. If I asked him to stop now so we could discuss what happened in the temple, I know he would without hesitation, without making me feel like I've ruined something.

"What is it?" he says and lowers his face to meet my eyes.

My expression is undoubtedly giving away my straying thoughts.

"I placed the stones myself. I thought I would feel . . . different," I say, almost laughing.

"Listen to me, Ferren."

He is trying so hard to comfort me that I can see it written all over his face. He's begging his mind to assemble the right words to say in this moment. It is heartbreaking and beautiful. I touch his face, pulling at his chin for him to kiss me, to tether to me. He attempts a few false starts and then presses his soft lips to mine, surrendering.

"You are perfect to me as you are now," he whispers, hovering over my lips.

99 does not care if I ascend, if I am a high priestess at all. The desire for that has not gone away, but the pressure that has felt so overwhelming in the past eases every time he speaks this way or reveals how he sees me.

I pull back, wanting to see his expression. His eyes have darkened again, and he fights me a little to fall apart with him in another kiss, but I place a hand on his chest to still him and let him know I am ok to continue. I pull at the sides on my dress, wiggling my shoulders from the soft sleeves. It falls to the floor, the chill of the night air on my skin. The heat of his eyes tracing down makes me forget about everything else.

"I am yours, 99, even here in the Estate. Take what is yours."

He growls deep in his chest before capturing my lips, kissing me deeply.

I tug at his belt frantically, his hard bulge desperate to be free.

His hands slide down to help me, slowing the pace like he wants to savor every moment. He licks at my tongue, his mouth slanted over mine making me feel dizzy at the slow pace. He then trails his tongue down my neck, nipping in slow motion, but I am determined to feel his hard skin against me, pulling at the armor as it clatters to the floor around us.

He tugs behind his back, pulling his tunic over his broad shoulders, and his lips come back down to kiss my forehead. He looks so different in the soft, pillowy room, a contrast with his hard lines and brooding nature.

I feel his hands reach around and cup my ass, squeezing it with a sly smile. Only our breaths sound in the room as we explore each other, not wanting to speak or open our minds to connect, just feel each other's skin, breathe in each other's scent.

I wrap my arms around his strong neck, kissing at his ear as I'm lifted from the stone floor. I circle my legs around him, aligning myself down to meet the head of his cock. The tip brushes up my wetness, and we both watch the space between ourselves as he rocks his hips to slide up and down, slicking himself, preparing to fill me.

I whimper and bite down on his shoulder, making him buck and slide in, stretching me.

He thrusts my back against the door, making it rattle with our movements. I gasp at the feel of him deeply seated inside me. I use my weight to slide down farther on his length between thrusts, little stolen movements between hard pumping. He groans into my neck with approval, the steady rhythm continuing to draw out cries that can't be held in. I tighten my thighs around him, seeking more friction as he rams into me.

Then, he hoists me up in a higher angle, and I hold onto the top of his shoulder for balance as he pumps upward. A smile teases the corner of his mouth as I clench around him with a throaty moan. He watches as his cock reaches deeper, the muscles of his pelvis brushing against my clit. Realization dawns on me for the reason of the new angle change, the friction hitting me at the top of my channel where he likes to hook his fingers and make me lose control.

My core feels scorching and I clench again, bearing down. He continues in smaller, deeper thrusts, fighting against the push of my incoming release. Corded forearms against my thighs hold me tightly, digging in and leaving a satisfying bruising feeling.

He slows slightly, shifting his weight.

I glance down at him stepping out of his pants, using his heel to remove his boots—now both of us are completely bare. I cling to him, savoring the small, less frantic movements as he sucks on my nipples, holding me so high on the door. I roll my hips again, missing the pump of his thrusts.

"Do not make me trip." He teases and smacks my ass, smothering the sting with a firm squeeze.

Then, he walks us to sit on the edge of the bed, still impaling me with his length. Before he can adjust himself back, I slowly roll my hips, making him groan and furrow the lines between his brow.

I do it again with a deeply circular hip roll, making his head fall back in a hitched breath.

He scoots us backward so I can move onto my knees on either side. I use his shoulder as a brace and tilt myself up and then roll back down his full length slowly. Slight surprise crosses his face, and he makes a noise I haven't heard yet: a throaty, unabandoned moan then a breathy huff as I push him back on the bed and position myself to ride him.

Hovering over the tip of his cock, I run my hands down his chest, reaching back till I touch his shaft, gripping it to guide him as I sink down fully. His eyes are dark, fingertips brushing over my thighs. I scoot up a little and brace my palms on his chest, drawing up his length and then slamming back down. His head pushes back into the mattress, expression dark and feral. My name comes out in a deep whimper of surprise as I bounce downward on him again, like the pleasure is almost too much.

I can feel his control slipping away as I ride him. I have never seen him quite so vulnerable-looking with his pleasure. I stutter my hips, clasping the head of his cock inside me and rolling back down to the hilt. His moan is deep, his light finger touches now gripping my hip roughly, trying to pull me down on him more. I interlace my fingers with his, thrusting down in a rhythmic bounce, making his brows wrinkle, mouth agape as he watches me with sultry eyes.

"I am yours too, Ferren," he whispers, holding my hips. "No matter what, I am yours and you are mine," he huffs out in sexy breaths.

Something breaks open, giving way to bright, blinding light crashing into my mind, blurring my vision. He sits up, capturing me in a kiss as we thrust in steady movements. He grips at my ass, pulling me harder, bouncing me on himself.

He reaches in between our bodies, fingertips gaining access to my clit in wet, rough circles. He rubs it as I clench down, riding in slamming unison.

"Come for me," he gasps, bucking up into me.

I feel myself tense and then fall into a spiraling oblivion, clenching and clinging to him as we both ride out the orgasm, listening to the vulgar sounds our bodies make as we pound into each other and the wet sound of his cum filling me to the brim.

My movements come to a slow roll and he holds me up, arms wrapped around my back now. Amber light dances in the corner of my vision, lazy and sweet.

This time felt different, like we connected and clung to each other in a permanent tether. The amber light meant something more this time, restrained and then all-encompassing. I run my hand over his shoulder to cup his face, his eyes flicking around mine, sweat beaded on his strong brow, his breathing still hard.

He smiles at me, a beautiful, sweet smile on this stoic man. The reality of what he sent me this time overcomes me and I can feel my eyes water.

He couldn't say it, so he sent it.

Love . . . He sent love.

CHAPTER THIRTY SEVEN

I stretch in the downy mattress and stare up at the canopy, throwing an arm over to the smooth spot where 99 slept next to me. I can hear him in the next room, polishing his armor like he does when he wants to busy himself.

The sweet sound of August's laughter floats in from the adjoining room, where I thought 99 was alone. I can't help the smile that crosses my face at thinking of them in there together. I stretch again and climb clumsily out of bed to find a robe.

Calliape is the first to come out, meeting me in the bedroom area with a bright smile.

"Morning," she says, her face lit up with even more of a glow than it had on Frith.

Mother's womb, she is beautiful. I grab her in a hug and then fuss over my hair. I probably look a mess after my long night with 99.

"When? How?" I stumble over my words, surprised they are in my room within the Estate.

"99th Commander came to get us, said you would probably want to see me," she says.

It warms my heart that he knew I would be missing them both.

"And August of course. He almost blew a hole through the stone walls trying to get here."

We both hunch in giggles, thinking of how August can be at times. The voices in the other room hush like our laughs have stunned them into silence. I see a strong hand press on the adjoining door, opening it farther. 99 pushes it open more to see us, giving me a sweet smile, half dressed in his armor again.

August sits on the frilly couch around some food trays, lifting his chin with suspicion at what we find funny.

"You placed the stones?" Calliape says in a hushed voice, leaning in.

I give her a flat smile and nod. She ducks her head, trying to find my gaze again, a question on her face.

"It's strange. I almost felt relief, like the tension is gone from anticipation, just like I've stepped through one door into another," I say, trailing off to look at the two Viathan men in the fancy sitting room.

"Ferren, I want you to know, that what you can do, it's not nothing. The light I have seen from your hands, how quickly you controlled it, and that—" She pokes at the spot where I was wounded from the back, the side with my troubled lung.

I pull my nightgown back to see it, wondering what I am missing.

"You did that," she states.

"No, Ruth did," I say, almost laughing.

"Ferren." Her face tilts down like I have said something ridiculous.

"That's impossible," I say.

"Why, because someone didn't say you could? How many high priestesses of old never ascended but used their gifts fully. Maybe First Mother never came to you because she had already given you all that she planned. Maybe everything is already there, inside, and you have just forgotten how to access it," she says, pointing to my heart.

I can't help but wonder how my life would be if I would have known Calliape sooner. If I would be different with her believing in me in this way from the beginning.

"Get in here, ladies, or I'm eating the rest of this sweet bread stuff," August interrupts from the other room.

Sugar bread, that bastard.

I smile at Calliape, taking in her stunning face. "I am so glad you are here, and you owe me details about . . ." I nudge my chin in August's direction, hoping she takes the hint.

"I am glad to be here too, and it's not what you're probably thinking," she whispers with a roll of her eyes.

We enter the adjoining room, and the food trays are a little mussed but still very full of breakfast items. I snatch up the remaining sugar bread from in front of August, making him laugh.

99 leans against the wall, and I run my fingers down his arm to cup his hand, my back turned to the others. His eyes light up at my simplest touch, sending shock waves through me.

"Did you sleep well?" I ask.

"Terrible." He raises my hand, pressing a kiss to my knuckles without breaking his intense stare.

I press my lips together, trying to hide my smile as I find a seat on the smaller pink couch across from Calliape and August. My robe drapes over the sides elegantly. I would have died for items of clothing like this a few weeks ago. Now, I just feel a little stuffy, seeing the others sitting around me with the same clothing they wore on Frith, harder and rougher against the fancy touches of the room. I miss the pants more than anything, I think. But none of them make me feel out of place or even comment on how different I may look to them now, and maybe I don't at all. The lack of pressure to be anything but *me* is a sigh of relief.

"I wish you all could stay in here with me. Calliape, I feel bad you're staying on the ship."

She finishes chewing on a big piece of pastry before speaking. August watches her mouth with glazed eyes.

"I am fine for now, really," she says, covering her still full mouth.

"All the temple business, veils and statues, gives me the creeps. No offense, Ferren," August cuts in and throws me a weak smile.

"I would love a tour, though, when things—I don't know—calm down?" she says.

"Safest on the ship for now," August replies.

Safest. Does August think Calliape is not safe? I feel my panic start to rise, thinking of the repercussions of her deciding to come with us.

"Safe? Why, did something happen?" I probe.

"I'm just saying, it's safer for Calliape on the ship right now," August says flippantly, making me panic more.

I look to 99 for a straightforward answer, to know for sure if something has changed.

"Nothing has happened, but better to keep out of sight. Precautions," he says flatly.

I feel my shoulders settle only slightly. It is safer. I know it is. The Estate and Crixa are paranoid of everyone, especially if they knew someone came back from Frith unexpectedly.

"It's safe. You are safe. Calliape is safe. Eat something, you are stressing me out," August says.

"I am sorry. I think I have some leftover worry from before. I can't shake it," I say.

"That's fine. You are allowed to worry about the people you love," Calliape says, coming over to sit next to me.

Love.

I feel a little prickle of embarrassment, like I've been found out, as if I've exposed my innermost thoughts. I look down at my lap, playing with my food, not wanting to look up and see 99 undoubtedly staring at me. I feel a little flush of nervousness, trying to get enough confidence to speak, but it has to be said even if it's not perfect. This I can say with full intention and meaning.

"Then . . . I *worry* about the three of you . . . very much," I say, feeling a little foolish as I slowly raise my eyes to Calliape's.

Hers are extra shiny when I meet them.

"And we *worry* about you too," August says a little more seriously than he has been all morning.

"So, so much," Calliape says, sniffling and reaching for my hands on my lap.

I feel a crash of amber waves flood into my mind, making me sway a little in my seat. I meet 99's eyes, and they are soft and full of affection. A small nod is all he can conjure. I can almost see an internal struggle to say something, but he doesn't have to. I can feel it. I send it back and he almost looks relieved, then a half grin creeps on the side of his full lips. He drops his head to hide it. From the outside, it looks like a single glance between us, but I am almost overcome by the pure emotion, the strong tether between us. It feels sweet, lusty, warm, and fiercely protective.

I am not unworthy when I am with them. They are in my life now and could care less if I'm a high priestess or not. They love me as I am. It's almost worrisome that I can't give enough back, but I am determined to try.

"Can we get back to breakfast before you make me and Ferren cry?" August says to Calliape.

I let out a watery laugh that breaks the serious moment.

Calliape squeezes my hand one last time before returning to the couch with August, who watches her as she slinks over. He makes room but somehow manages to be seated even closer to her than before.

I wipe at my eyes as 99 descends to the floor next to my knees. He places a forearm casually across my thighs, and I run my hand through the back of his hair as he tosses some savory food on a plate, reclining into me a little more.

"You are going to eat on the floor?" I ask him.

"Everything is very soft in here, too soft."

"Hopefully not *everything*," August says with a wicked look pointing back and forth between 99 and me, wiggling his brows dramatically.

Calliope chokes on her tea, setting it down in a clatter. I see the back of 99's head shake. All I can muster is throwing a piece of bread at August, instantly regretting it when he catches it and starts eating it with a wild grin.

CHAPTER THIRTY EIGHT

The Estate's grand hall overflows. I've never seen so many people crowded in, all dressed in fine fabrics and sparkly, large gold jewelry. Emperor Matthias, Lord Hollis, and Crixa all sit on the large, platformed dais, looking out at the mingling crowd, whispering to each other.

Crixa has stationed me off to the side with a few elder and high priestesses. I'm the only one in a black temple gown on the small platform, feeling on display as people walk past and gaze at me, murmuring to each other. The large windows behind me scorch the back of my black veil, making me even more uncomfortable.

I see a flash of white off to the side, a line of soft fabric. The Divine Mothers have entered the celebration. They walk stoically as the crowd parts, some waddling, heavy with child. Their gowns are airy and clean, a few in white veils, high priestesses who stay in the Temple of Divine Mothers until they give birth and then can go back to their posts. But most wear no veil. They are not divine, but they hope their child will be. I feel an ache in my heart thinking of my mother. It's a sharp slap to my senses, seeing them again and still not having ascended.

THE VIRIDIAN PRIESTESS

They walk in an elegant line, an elder priestess guiding at the front with a harsh expression and another at the back, keeping the pace. The women skim across the platform I'm standing on and to my surprise, each looks up at me and bows their head slightly. I notice they are not only being trailed by elders but also guards. Something that seemed very normal before now seems off. I notice the guards aren't really keeping the people away but more making sure the women are staying together.

"You look beautiful," a voice says. I turn my head, only taking a second to realize who is now next to me.

Thea.

She squeezes my hand, hidden under both our veils. It's a secret gesture, but it's not enough. I want to embrace my friend, truly hug her. She looks so elegant in her gray temple gown. The sheer fabric frames her face and lets the sparkle from her palm-sized earrings shine through. Her pouty lips are lightly colored in mauve pink to match her natural cheek hue. It takes everything I have not to break my obedient stance on the platform and greet her like I want to.

"I've missed you," I say, restrained.

"You too," she whispers, smiling then glancing around a little to see if we have attracted any harsh attention from the elders.

The last of the Divine Mothers glides past us, and I press my lips together as the elder priestess walks by, but she doesn't even glance in my direction, just keeps her eyes straight where the rest of the line is now greeting the emperor and Crixa on the dais.

Crixa purposefully leans in front of Lord Hollis, who is seated between her and the emperor, a show of dominance that always looks so petty but makes me laugh. They murmur as the women in white finish their bows, and then just as fast as they entered, the women are gone, guided back out the doors toward their temple.

The emperor stands and the room falls silent instantly leaving a ringing in my ears.

"Thank you all for coming. We are here to celebrate the successful retrieval of our First Mother's birthing stones. They can now rest in their proper home, united again, safe within the wards of our city, out of the grasp of those who seek to destroy them."

My eyes move around the crowd, and everyone's face is on Emperor Matthias, adoration in their expressions, hopeful and excited. The people look stranger standing still. The elaborateness of their jewelry and clothing looks odd without the elegant sway of their movements.

"May First Mother bless those who braved other worlds to bring the stones home, blessed priestess," he says.

One by one, the people in the crowd turn their heads to me and repeat the title without unison or order. It sounds grating and mechanical, and I want to shrivel down into my dress, into just a pool of fabric and crawl out of the room under toe as they continue to smile and gawk with a strange eerie glee in their eyes.

Emperor Matthias turns, holding out a beckoning hand to Crixa. "Highest Priestess, will you honor us further?" he says.

Crixa descends the dais, toward the large group of patrons who pull in closer, drawn to her presence. The ones closest to me linger their eyes and then slowly draw away in her direction.

Crixa raises her hands before she speaks, a subtle instruction for all to listen. "Through the years, with different leaders, the two stones have come and gone. Our neighboring worlds are free to take or leave their pieces of the birthing stone, but *our* stone stays constant. It stays safe in our city. And now, in the year of the great conjunction, when a new threat lingers, they rest in their rightful home until First Mother rises again. May she see our devotion. May she believe us no longer wicked."

The crowd pauses and then erupts in applause and cheers. Crixa is caught off guard with a little jump, the crowd more enthusiastic than her normal silent faithful types. She has clearly moved them—a speech from the highest priestess is an honor to hear. Crixa turns to Emperor Matthias when they continue with no sign of stopping.

They fall instantly silent again with a gesture of his hand.

The celebration turns into a feast. Large tables and trays are brought out and the crowd mingles around them. People stand with little plates, chatting along the edges of the grand room.

Crixa looped her arm through mine after her speech and pulled me up on the dais with Emperor Matthias and Lord Hollis. Both greeted me kindly but now ignore everyone but each other in their whispers.

I stand behind Crixa, watching the people below.

"Are you hungry, my dear?" Crixa says over her shoulder.

"No."

"Then why the face?" she asks.

"My feet hurt, I think."

She turns her torso to face me, her expression forcefully soft. I've been standing for hours and while my feet do hurt in my new stiff temple shoes, my thoughts are somewhere else, likely the reason for whatever face I am making.

"Come, let's get you some food." Crixa stands, tugging on my elbow to follow her. I'm reluctant to walk around. Having to brush up against or come eye to eye with one of the strange people here makes my stomach turn. They don't seem like faithful temple goers. They seem . . . I'm not sure. They were clearly moved by Crixa's words, but it's as if it were a new story to them, or one they hadn't heard in a long time. It's like they gave a small sliver of emotion and then went back to their prostrating and the judgmental looks they give each other.

As we weave throughout the people, no one talks to me directly, but they do whisper and smile, their strange glassy eyes on me like they think I am not someone who can be addressed directly.

Crixa pulls me to a long table of fruits and cheeses, the food maids around her looking nervous as she picks through it, not bothering to get a plate. They look at each other, silently questioning who will be the one to address the highest.

Without looking up, Crixa says to them, "Be dears and take some of this back to my chair, both of you."

They fly into action. My eyes connect with the shorter woman, who is about my age, and she just looks down like someone has yelled at her.

"What is it, Priestess Ferren?" Crixa says, her attention now on me.

She knows she will have to be stern with me to get me to say my true feelings as always with her.

"I just—I didn't know it was going to be like this," I say and follow after her as she glides down the long table, popping things in her mouth. She pauses, inclining an ear in my direction to continue.

"So overwhelming, such a big crowd, maybe. Who are these people? I've never seen them in any temple service."

"My dear, it's a momentous time. These are the wealthiest families in the city come to celebrate," she says, and I can already tell her patience is running low.

"I would have liked to speak with you before."

She hums in response as she glides down the table to the next section of food. It's a slow, agonizing chase, but I stay right next to her. She practically forced me to tell her what was on my mind and now she is withdrawing. I want to tell her how I felt when I placed the stones, how underwhelmed I was. On impulse, I grab her arm when she tries to walk to the next table.

"Stop!" I say, and then I instantly regret it.

She looks at the spot I grabbed her and then at me through her heavily wrinkled lids. I recoil my hand and bow my head. I've never grabbed her like that. I'm afraid to even apologize. Would she slap me in front of the patrons?

"I see the journey has made you a little rougher, my dear," she says with narrowed eyes, smoothing a hand over her arm.

"Highest Priestess, please, I feel like I'm drowning around all these people, like I'm being left in the dark," I plead.

"We did speak before, in the temple," she says, head tilted down.

"Yes, we spoke, but—"

"Please, dear, enjoy yourself. You have always needed so much praise. Look around—see that we celebrate your success."

Her words throw me in different directions, and I know it's intentional. I don't want praise; I want to be taken seriously. I glance around the room at the ridiculous people, at the celebration I didn't ask for. I'm not even entirely sure it's for me.

Someone dressed in a gown that looks like curtains walks by, bowing.

"Blessed priestess," she says.

I can only half smile a greeting. I turn to Crixa, who smiles at the patron. "Blessed evening," she says.

When that woman passes, Crixa studies me again. I dart my eyes around, trying not to look at her fully.

"Was there something troubling you about your journey?" She looks at me with suspicion.

"No, I suppose I am just overwhelmed after being gone for so long. Forgive me," I say quickly, thinking she is about to lead the conversation in a direction I can't come back from.

"Forgiven. I did miss you, dear," she says, stroking my cheek.

Her hand is cold, stiff, and boney. A gesture that would have made my day previously is now hard to find any warmth or comfort in. Crixa's crumbs of affection doled out and withheld to bend me to her now feels cold compared to the love I have felt from others. I take it anyway, knowing I am one of the rare few that have been on the receiving end of her attention.

"The temple ceremonies do not quite run as smoothly without you. Enjoy the spotlight, Ferren, and don't worry. You will be back in the library with your books in no time," she says and opens her arms for an embrace.

I lean in before truly realizing her words.

The small show of affection falls short, words that would be so comforting before now a striking blow. Back to the library, as someone else's assistant? Mary only took me in as hers because she knew I was waiting to ascend. Not a new post? Her hug feels stiff, like hugging a statue that doesn't quite wrap its arms around you, just a brace of thick stone.

She releases me with a smile that says all is well.

"Do you believe I will ascend?"

I prepare myself for an answer. I have never asked her fully, not so straightforward. But I need to know that she believes in me, that she misspoke and only meant I would go back to my old life until I ascended. But her face doesn't match that sentiment. I press my feet into the hard floor, grounding myself in hopes of lessening the blow that I know is coming.

"Desperation is not an appealing trait, Ferren, and you stink of it. Do you think First Mother would want that? No," she says flatly, trying to stay even in her tone with the patrons around us. But I can tell she's not happy with my question and my doubt.

I clench my fists at my sides, not breaking my gaze on her. Of course I'm desperate, and I'm not ashamed to admit it.

"You did say if I returned the stones, First Mother would show herself to me and find me worthy. Do you believe it will happen or not?"

"I said she *may*. She may today, tomorrow, or in this next instant. Or she *may* never."

"You guaranteed me."

"I made no such guarantee. You went to Frith to assist Mary, to show your devotion . . . You have and we thank you," she says, gesturing to the ridiculous crowd.

I wanted that sliver of hope, the reassurance, but Crixa snatched it away.

I watch her smile and greet a few more patrons who glide over. I clutch at the pang of betrayal in my chest as the reality of my situation spreads into my system, stunning every nerve ending.

"Ferren, try to compose yourself. The Estate has missed you, your spirit. Take solace in knowing you have proved yourself to all of them. However, sometimes what is miraculous to First Mother's children is not quite so miraculous to First Mother herself. It is something we need to remember going forward."

I can hear her giving up hope on me with every word. She holds my hand, smoothing the top, petting me like one of her caged weasels.

"There is no shame in a life of service to your sisters, your highest, preserving order for the next generation of high priestesses. You can serve First Mother in other ways. You could have a divine child. Your line could ascend through them."

I snap my hand back, appalled at the thought of my only purpose being a vessel. "Don't."

"My dear, we may need to look to the future."

When did she give up on me—a desperate priestess convinced to go to a poisonous planet on the promise of ascension.

"No, you said—"

"Enough." She pinches the bridge of her nose, exasperated. "You will handle this with grace. Not all those who are born divine are worthy of our First Mother's gifts, you know this. You will fulfill your duties to the Estate. We look to the future now."

"Is this what I am to you? A spectacle to parade around, the retriever of stones but not quite good enough. And to have a divine child who will serve you as well?"

"I do not want to see you in ceremony in my temple until further notice. You are clearly unwell, overcome with emotion."

I straighten, a new streak of anger blooming, a hatred I did not know starting to froth.

"The temple is not yours. You cannot keep me from it."

Crixa narrows her eyes in a way she does when she's about to delve out a punishment, but I don't care. I have nothing left to lose. I am sick of the word play, the manipulation, always being on guard and feeling like I am going to be found out for something I don't know that I've done. I am different now. I've seen people of Frith more powerful than some of the high priestesses I know here. Those people have never ascended, and I would never doubt their devotion, never think them unworthy. I am not the most devout. Calliape may be, and she has shown me a new way—a way that is becoming clearer, that I can't look away from.

"You cannot deny access to First Mother's love. You cannot contort it for your benefit to get me to do as you say and when questioned, you withhold all kindness," I grit out.

"What has happened to you? The Ferren I know would never speak so shamefully to her highest."

"If you think I am not worthy of her gifts . . . fine. But you will not keep me from her."

"You break my heart and blaspheme in the same breath," Crixa whispers.

"My Highest Priestess, I am realizing now that you haven't one for me to break."

"Get. Out." Crixa bares her teeth.

I know she wants to scream at me, but she won't, not in front of Emperor Matthias or her beloved rich families of Cosima. I brush past her with my head down, the few patrons within hearing distance watching me as I weave through the crowd. I have never seen Crixa so angry in such a composed way. It makes me feel sad but empowered and almost relieved to have gotten my thoughts out. I don't know where they came from or why they decided to come forth.

Yes, I do—from Calliape and the people who suddenly mean so much to me in such a short amount of time. It comes from the things I've seen in 99's mind's eye, the beautiful acts of devotion, spontaneous and wild.

There will most certainly be repercussions for the way I spoke to her, but for now, I just want to get back to the people who would never make me feel like this.

CHAPTER THIRTY NINE

I pant out breaths, walking on the uneven cobblestone, pushing forward and trying to get as far away from the celebration as possible. My smugness is now turning toward devastation. How can I face Crixa after this? How will I tell Thea she needs to finally cut our friendship loose because I won't have my stains affecting her.

Will I write to Leema, letting her know she was right, that she should stay away? That I'm sorry our mother gave her life for my divinity for nothing? How do I articulate that to her without breaking in half?

I rip my veil off, some of my long strands tearing out with it.

Crixa chose me, not because I was special but because I was invisible. She knew how desperate I was, how much I had to prove. That I was willing to do anything to win the favor of First Mother, go anywhere. She knew I was devout, but maybe she never truly believed I would ascend. It was just something to hang over my head out of reach. She used my devotion and twisted my desperation.

My legs don't move fast enough. I lift my gown up and start to sprint, huffing out air, not caring who sees as I exit the Estate. They can try to stop me, but I won't let them.

I see August in the distance as I get close to the landing area. He works on the side of the ship, Calliape handing him metal items with a smile. My heart lurches and I stumble a little at the sight of them. I calm my gait, trying not to trip, the destination in sight. I try to push into 99's mind's eye to see if he is close, but my head is too cloudy to concentrate. I get to the open ramp when Calliape sees me, saying my name in surprise, then worry crosses her face.

August shoots up from his workstation, but I walk past. I am glad to see them but I need 99 more right now.

"Is he in here?" I say and climb the ramp with lifted fabric bunched in my hands. I enter the ship before either of them can collect an answer. I bound through the cargo hull like I'm taking the ship by force.

I just need to get to him. My dress keeps falling to the floor, but I push forward, carrying it with me. I get to the mess hall and there he is.

He sits relaxed at the large table with his feet up, looking at a data pad. He lifts his eyes to me where I stand in the doorway in silence. I see the realization cross his face, and he jumps to his feet, letting the sensitive equipment fall to the floor. He crosses the room in an instant, letting me crash into him. He holds me and I collapse into his embrace, letting it consume me, exhausted from running and mind worn out from Crixa.

I cling to him, pressing my face into his solid chest. He says nothing, just runs his hand down my hair and sways lightly, holding me up. I send images of the events in the grand hall, and he relaxes slightly but still holds me tight. I feel his mind's eye open and the sliver of light trickle out to reach for our link, sending me love and comfort without words.

99 holds me long after my breath steadies, holding space for me to

fall apart if I need to. Calliape and August enter with worry on their faces, knowing something has happened. We sit at the large mess hall table together, and they listen as I tell them aloud about what Crixa said, the events of the Estate party. Saying the words doesn't quite cover my internal feelings and emotions attached. Only 99 saw those through our tether, a more vivid picture through that connection we share.

Calliape holds my hands, running a soothing thumb over the nailbeds I've bitten down too far during the party.

"How can I just go back to the way it was, to translate books like nothing has happened? Will the highest even let me back in the Estate after what I said to her?" I say to Calliape but mean it for everyone in the room.

99 glances over his shoulder from where he now stands in front of the tea machine, making sure August sees the thought written on his face.

August shifts in his seat in response.

Calliape reassures me, but I can't keep my eyes off the two men. I can read 99's nonverbal cues now, a necessary adaptation from being around him for so long.

Calliape has stopped midsentence to observe the two as well. They are hiding something, neither of them wanting to say what they are both thinking. I know it won't be 99. I can tell he is restraining because of how upset I am.

August bounces his leg anxiously, as if something is bubbling at the surface. So, I turn my attention his way. He is more likely to break.

"What is it?" I say as plainly as I can.

99 sighs deeply and sets the steamy mug in front of me.

I do not take my eyes off my target. "August?"

"We have been—talking," he says carefully.

"This is not the time," 99 cuts in, sitting down next to me in a huff, scooting my chair between his parted legs in a protective barrier.

"It may be the best time, my friend," August says right to 99.

"If it's bad news, I'd rather hear it now," I say, starting to panic.

"No, nothing bad," 99 whispers to me, stroking a knuckle down my arm.

August watches 99's affection toward me before starting again. "We want you to . . . all of us of course . . . Calliape is coming to Viathan. We have to get back and . . . well, maybe you don't have to face any of that."

I listen to August stammer over his words. It's endearing, but my attention is pulled by 99 next to me.

"Come back with us," 99 says over August's struggle to articulate. His expression is soft and unguarded, and it's shocking to see out in the open and not in the privacy of just the two of us.

I draw back, trying to conceal my surprise, but my mouth gapes at the complicated invitation. Go back with them, to Viathan? How long? Do they mean forever or just a visit? My flustered thoughts must be showing on my face because 99 won't meet my eyes now. He takes my hand, looking hard at it in a plea.

"When?" I ask.

"Whenever you are ready, now or after the conjunction," August says.

"No, now," 99 says in a flat tone.

"Now?"

He presses into our link and I enter his mind's eye, and he's sending me happy images of all four of us and the two of us alone. Feelings of freedom, acceptance, and patience overload my head. I close my eyes, leaning into the warm light of his promising thoughts, of how it would be if I followed them to their home. But in doing so,

I would have to leave mine, and that snaps my eyes open.

99 holds my chin. "I can make you happy, Ferren. No more of this."

I try to mull over how that would work, but my thoughts are swimming around and I can't keep one tied down long enough to work through it logically.

"But I can't just leave the Estate. My life is here. If I leave, what will that mean for me?"

"Your life could be on Viathan, with us. With me. Fuck the Estate. They do not deserve you. You are not yourself when you're here," he says, his voice growing desperate.

The vulnerability in his tone is the only thing making me not lash out at his statement. I feel him throw a mental hook out for our link, and I open for him to send images, more eloquently put than his words. He shows me a fierce version of myself that I don't recognize in the forest of Frith and in the cave with the Albright. Then he shows me my obedient hunched shoulders as he turns to leave and go to the council meeting, how much I bowed my head when we first met, and my lost eyes when he saw me in my temple gown after I placed the stones.

I squeeze his hand, letting him know I understand what he is trying to say as his shoulders relax.

99 sees me in a way that I am not or maybe just can't see for myself, when desperation manifests into courage and not cowering in a temple or begging for attention from Crixa. I'm starting to like that version of me better, and seeing it through the eyes of someone I love eases any worry I have about not being good enough or worthy.

"Someone I love," I repeat in my head and hear 99's breath hitch like he heard it too.

I knew I would have to face something like this soon with him.

He has not held back his feelings and intention, even with how mysterious he can be. If I did go with them to Viathan, would I be running away? Solidifying that things didn't work here? Giving up, turning my back on my life, my faith?

"There are temples on Viathan. I will sit with you all day watching you pray, if that is what it takes," he says as if he can read my thoughts.

I can't stop the smile on my face. Would running away be so bad? The thought is almost like a pressure coming to a head, my ears popping. It's a relief to the hopes that have fallen flat and the constant fighting for something that may never happen.

"Can I leave? Would they even let me?" I say meekly.

99 leans in, getting a deadly look on his face. "You don't worry about that part."

The seriousness of his tone heats my insides as I remember how he said he would protect me that night in our camp.

"Maybe you need some time to think on it. It's a big decision, but know we all want you with us. You and Calliape," August says, throwing a sweet smile her way.

"I can't lie and say the idea of spending more time with you in another place doesn't sound wonderful, but yes, think about it. And Ferren, you can be faithful anywhere," Calliape says.

I watch 99's face. There is a look of almost grief on it, but he quickly wipes it away in favor of a more stoic mask. I can't help but feel a little guilty for not having an answer for him right away.

"Maybe after everything settles, you can come back to Frith with me for a while too, stay on more pleasant terms," Calliape says.

99 pushes my tea in front of me, pulling my attention back to the question he poses. "If you prefer Frith, then we will go there. I do not care."

I can tell he is trying to be calm, but he is clearly on the verge of breaking off into angry begging. It's sweet and somehow makes the decision to go with them easier, if that's what I decide.

He gets really close to me and whispers, "And if you want to live on this ship and orbit the moon, we will, but we will have to deal with August."

My heart hurts that I don't have an answer for him, but I need time. It feels right but goes against everything in my life that I have worked for. But that was my old life. I have worked for the thing I wanted, did all I could. Going forward and moving past constantly striving for that feels like I'm floating in the space between the worlds unanchored.

I watch August recline on the back legs of his chair, balancing as he stares at the back of Calliape's head.

"Are you ok, Ferren? You are looking pale," he chimes in.

I nod, but I'm not. I'm overwhelmed by the events of the day and the question from the three of them that needs an answer—one that I am starting to already sway in one direction. The pressure of making a decision is replaced by the anxiety of the unknown.

"I'm sorry. I think I need to lie down for a bit. Can I stay on the ship tonight?" I ask, wanting to buy myself more time but still wanting them all close to me.

"You do not need to ask to stay where you already belong, Ferren." 99 runs his thumb up and down my skin in a small act of reassurance.

What have I done to deserve so much care and patience, space to be raw and messy without judgment? Years of being pent up in favor of strictness has left me unrefined in showing my emotions, but they haven't made me feel guilty for any of them. They deserve someone more stable, but they chose me. They love me, and they want me to come back with them.

THE VIRIDIAN PRIESTESS

99 holds me tightly in our dark room like I will float away if he lets go. I can guess what is in his thoughts without looking into his mind's eye. I know he wants me to leave with him. His whole body almost vibrates from restraining panic and fierce protectiveness, trying to not scare me away.

I can't pretend that what has happened between us isn't significant. That the people I consider friends and even family aren't important. My thoughts race nonsensically, and some stick, some I let pass by. But the one I keep coming back to is leaving with 99, and I think I know my answer.

CHAPTER FORTY

I try slipping out of the ship before dawn unnoticed but run into Calliape in the mess hall. She makes me convince her I am well enough to leave. I tell her I have to visit the temple before I make any decisions, and her shoulders finally relax like she understands, not able to argue against another step closer to leaving with them.

The last strand of pink sky clings to the horizon when I make my way back to my room to dress, promising to come back and pack up only the most important keepsakes: a few books, my favorite veil, and old letters from Leema. My whole life fits into a small purse. Everything else belongs to the Estate and they can have it. Something has been torn apart in me and put back together differently. It's impossible to ignore the pull to leave now, a sense of urgency that I can't shake.

Sunbeams streak through the taller peaks of the Estate as I walk toward the temple. A deep, hollow ache fills me, and I feel a tug on my heart for 99, August, and Calliape. I don't feel the intense need to plead to First Mother in the stone temple. It's replaced with the homesick feeling of wanting to be with the three of them, of sitting in a field with Calliape completely at peace or being on the ship with

August and 99 in its warm hum. Crixa is no longer my encouraging refuge. I cannot go back to the way things were.

I continue through the courtyard toward the temple, I have to go one last time. If I am going to do this, I must say goodbye properly, close this chapter. I cannot leave it unconcluded. If I am not good enough, then fine. I will beg to be cut loose.

I may never ascend, not in the way of the temple. Maybe First Mother already gave me all my gifts, hidden away, waiting for me to find them like Calliape said. Or maybe First Mother will not show herself to me because I came to her on Frith, in that forest, in the field and in the cave with the Albright, amongst her first children. Whatever happens, I have to make peace with it. If I am going with them, then I need to leave with my whole heart, not leaving trails of hope and unanswered questions behind me. They deserve my full devotion. If Crixa does not have a need for it, then I will take it elsewhere.

"First Mother, please, will you hear me?" I whisper and close my eyes for a moment.

The stones in the courtyard are rough and uneven, and I stumble and fall to my knees on the hard ground. My palms sting from catching myself, and then I hear a familiar sound—rustling leaves whispering at my side in the courtyard. I hear it again and look up at the giant tree in the center of the wall-lined courtyard. Its sparse leaves shimmy at the top of its branches. The roots serpent in and out of buckling stones. They look like they were once all flat and cut squarely, but the tree has made them uneven and jut up in different angles. The tree is huge, but it isn't thriving. It doesn't look like the ones on Frith, how lush and green they were, the bark a rich brown. The bark on this one is chipped and bleached, and the roots look white and smooth like the banisters in the grand hall.

I pull myself up, peer around the square courtyard, and see the roots pushing out and gathering at the edges like they want to crawl up the walls and free themselves. Under the roots, there is nothing, no connection; it's contained and trapped. The open air keeps it in place, and it can grow up, but the leaves are so few because there is no room to thrive below.

I place my hand on a misplaced stone next to me, its shape square. The ones around it are different shades of tan, cut from different stones and fit together in a pattern that is pleasing but not natural. I place my ear to it, thinking of what Selene told me about confused stones.

It's humming nonsensically.

I knew the moment I placed the sacred stones and felt nothing that something was wrong. No, not wrong . . . different. I felt more power in a field with my feet in the grass than I did placing the three worlds' most sacred items on an altar in a temple made of confused, murmuring stones. And here, against this tree, is the closest I have felt to First Mother since I returned home.

A strong, booming chime of bells vibrates inside my ears, calling the faithful to the temple. It begins at a frantic but intentional interval as the ground trembles under my feet. I wait for it to subside then push forward out of the courtyard, toward my temple with the hard stone floor. At one time, I would crave the pain under my knees and feet. I would let them dig into my skin for hours as I bowed my head in desperation, but now I know I do not need to suffer to show my love, to show I am good enough. Anyone who asks that kind of devotion does not deserve it.

The doors to the temple are lined with guardsmen who move aside as soon as they see me. Other priestesses are filling the temple and mingling as the bells continue to call them in. The rows of pews are sporadically filled by gray-dressed women. I spot Thea sitting close to the aisle alone, seeing her high pink cheekbones, and can't help but smile as I make my way to her.

She looks at me, making her cerulean eyes light up.

I encourage her to scoot for me to sit on the pew as other high priestess start to settle in, and she looks confused but makes room.

"Ferren, what are you doing?" she whispers nervously.

"I'm only staying for a moment. I needed to see you."

The bell toll dies down and the faithful take their seats. I feel a hastiness roll over me. I should not have come. I knew it would be crowded when I heard the bell. I won't be able to say goodbye to Thea and my temple unnoticed like I intended. There could be real consequences for this. Crixa said she did not want to see me here. Normally, a few days would go by and she would call me to her office for punishment, but there is no time for that now. This was a mistake.

"Ferren?" Thea says, looking at me like she almost knows what is happening.

"Know that you are so special to me. You were kind when you did not have to be," I say in a frantic whisper.

"Do not do this. Please." Her face is more stern than I have ever seen it.

The room falls into a familiar hush, and I know Crixa has entered. I suddenly realize my choice of seating, a black spot in a sea of gray veils.

I turn my head as she walks down the aisle with a few elder priestesses. I know I stick out; a few other women are staring at me. I scoot away from Thea, unrealistically hoping that a few inches will keep any punishment away from her.

The ground tremors lightly as the highest priestess stops short of my pew. A thick, expectant silence falls over the room, adding to the ringing in my ears.

I turn to see her meeting my eyes in a downward angle. Her face looks unfamiliar, like any affection and tolerance of me never existed. The scrutiny of her stare has a visceral reaction on my body. I feel like a child being scolded by their schoolteacher.

I stand on shaky knees without asking my body, moving to the aisle. She does not move aside to let me pass easily. She makes it a spectacle that she will not fully enter the temple when I am in the high-priestess section. She wants me in my place or, more than likely, not in here at all.

I pull a small string of bravery to walk to my section, hoping to just get through this ceremony now that I am here. I cast my eyes down in a bow, a strategic gesture of obedience, but she grabs my arm as I pass. Her eyes look angry and bloodshot when I look up, my jaw falling slack at the sharp pain on my elbow. Her brows furrow as she scans me, likely thinking I am making a statement, sitting beyond my station. And maybe I am unintentionally—something I would have never dared before.

"Do not make a scene." She says the words sharp and biting, close to my face. I can feel wet droplets hit my cheek as she speaks, emphasizing her command. "You bring shame to this temple."

Shame? I jerk my arm away roughly and step back.

"Take. Your. Place. Priestess," she continues.

I will sit with the other priestesses. I am not ashamed. No matter how high of a priestess Crixa is, she can't keep me from my First Mother. I answer to her and her alone.

I turn my back and walk up the aisle, eyes focused ahead on the altar. I can feel others' stares burning into my face and judgmental whispers from either side of the pews. The altar is set for a ritual, more elaborate than a common ceremony. Candles sit in gold, ornate holders, every color and texture of velvet cloth the temple has draped on elegant folds. With another step, I see the velvet placement for the birthing stones and realization dawns on me. They are holding the final ceremony for the birthing stones. I feel a stab of betrayal that I would have missed this if I did not show up today. Crixa was willing to kick me out of the most important ceremony the temple can have.

But then I see the wooden box that 99 put the Frith and Viathan stones in when we arrived, the one I saw that night when Crixa asked me to do the honor of placing them. The velvet bed is missing the two I placed. Only Cosima's lies in its spot. Crixa put the stones I placed back into the box like it never happened.

I spin slowly to face her, my vision a thin line between my lids. Her expression is self-righteous. This is her punishment for my defiance, the deepest disrespect, a slap in my face. She's erasing my greatest honor like it never happened, like she never thought me worthy for even a second.

I take a step down back into the aisle, glancing around at the faces turning from judgment to shock.

Crixa smooths the front of her gown and begins her slow ascent up the aisle, no longer waiting for me to take my place. No, she can't let this gesture be simple; she needs to drive it home. I brace myself, fighting tears, feeling small and exposed before the other temple members. Crixa comes to my side, her back to the shocked congregation I'm still facing. She bows to the altar and looks at me sidelong in inspection.

I hear some more murmurs and the loud boots of Lord Hollis entering the temple before stopping short in the aisle at our spectacle. He looks odd here. Normally, a ceremony is reserved for the priestess order, but this one is different. The birthing stones are being placed, a great honor, and it's not mine.

"The emperor will be here any moment. You may stay if you

behave," Crixa whispers to me, eyes on First Mother.

I grit my teeth. "Did you ever believe me worthy . . . my highest?"

"Always so desperate for approval."

"You used my desperation, used me."

"You disappoint me at every turn, even as we speak."

Her words thrash into me, but the cuts are not deep. I have made my peace with the way she views me, so there is nothing she can say about me that will make me falter.

"So disappointing, even your sister had to flee the city to get away from the shame," she spits.

She steps forward, breaking away from the small contact our shoulders made when she leaned in to whisper, making sure I heard her.

I feel my chest taking a deep heavy breath as a white-hot feeling falls over me, making the silky fabric of my veil feel like fire on my skin. My shoulders hunch the heavier I breathe as I take in her words. I turn to face her but her back is all I see, her pointy shoulders alarming. She kneels, ignoring me and focusing on First Mother's statue as if her words were not a calculated hurt.

"Crixa!" I scream, baring my teeth, a blurry line at the bottom of my vision spilling over.

I hear some gasps at the sound of her given name used so harshly.

She does not flinch. She is calm because she has won. Her punishment has landed, and she will begin plotting her next for this outburst.

No more.

The candles flicker lightly, like a breeze has come in through the tightly sealed windows. I feel myself losing control again as the edges of my vision tunnels like it did in the Albright's cave, when I was cornered and my desperation manifested in a different way.

A thin green line all around the stone room runs down from the ceiling, then a strobe flashes as I lift my chin. I know her eyes are closed, I know she is praying to First Mother, but she will answer me. I hear more gasps as I raise my hand, the thin lines of light concentrating in my palm and then slinking up my fingers like great green serpents.

She will see what I am now; they all will.

My wrist is suddenly restricted with a wrapping cuff. Lord Hollis has me and with a swipe over my fingertips, the green flames are gone, extinguished.

I meet his eyes in horror, snapped out of my rage.

"Mine for now," he says with a slimy half smile.

His grip is painful, but I'm too confused to pull from it. My fingertips stick up like dead, broken branches, with no light, no green tendrils.

"Highest Priestess?" he inquires.

"Remove her," she says nonchalantly over her shoulder.

I jerk from his grasp as he pulls me. Guards come to either side, grabbing at my elbows.

"No!" I jerk ineffectively as they pull me down the aisle. "No! You can't! Crixa! You can't keep me from First Mother! This is not your temple!"

I dig my heels in the floor, but my ankles twist unnaturally as I'm dragged along.

"You lying bitch! You cannot kick me out of this temple!"

Thea stands as we pass, the only one looking at me.

Do not say anything, Thea. Please, sit back down. I shake my head at her frantically. Her lip trembles but she sits and bows her head like the others.

As we get to the open doors, I crane my neck to look one last time at my temple, at the stoic statue of First Mother in a field of bowed, veiled heads.

"Forgive me, First Mother. Please, forgive me."

CHAPTER FORTY ONE

T he floor in my room shakes as if all three worlds are being rolled around. The bells in all the temples have been chiming slowly all day, letting Cosima know the stones have been placed, that the ceremony has been completed by the highest priestess.

I sit in the window seat, looking out at the city, and rub at the red and angry marks on my knuckles. My angry explosion on the chamber's thick door after the guards threw me inside has left the skin already bruising. All my rage needed to go somewhere, it was snuffed out at its peak by Lord Hollis.

He gladly flexed his gift in the temple, stealing mine away, but it's temporary. I've seen him do the bidding of Emperor Matthias before to other divine men or a priestess who needed to be punished. It never lasts long, and I can already feel it seeping back to me.

I've tried to reach out to 99 through our link, to let him know where I am, but it's broken. Lord Hollis took everything.

I probe at it to test my strength.

They must be worried—an entire day has gone by. 99's fierce protectiveness is not the kind that waits patiently. I wish I had told him I wanted to leave with him. I wish I had woken him up and said yes, I'm coming with you. But I knew if I told him I needed to say goodbye to Thea and the temple, he would have tried to stop me.

I knew it was a risk, but I never could have predicted how far Crixa would go to prove her point.

"*99, please hear me.*" I try again.

"*We are here, Ferren.*" His voice comes in soft but crisp.

I reach out, closing my eyes tightly. It's like pressing a heavy temple door but it opens a crack as the last of Lord Hollis's gift gives mine back.

"*Where are you? I'm—*" I say frantically.

I hear a scuffle outside my door and stand from my window seat across the room. Boots hit stone floors like the guards posted outside my door are running to battle with a loud shuffling and muffled masculine screech just down the hall.

Then nothing. Silence.

I hear strong footfalls on the floor leading up to my room. The metal lock on the door clicks, the handle turning as it opens painfully slowly, and then 99 is standing tall with his full armor and helmet spattered in blood.

"I am here," he answers aloud softly.

The only thing I can muster is an extended hand, a plea to take me with him, out of this room, this Estate.

He stands just inside the room, shutting it behind him. He crosses in strong strides toward me, and I feel myself crumbling. Then, he rips his helmet off his head and crashes into me, cupping my face in a deep kiss. I cry as he kisses me, clinging to him and steadying my breath.

A gust of wind blows my hair next to us, and I hear August's voice. 99 ignores him for just a moment longer, holding either side of my face, eyes darting around. I finally register that Calliape used her gift to bring herself and August into my room undetected.

"You have to come with us now, Ferren," August says.

"I went looking for you after we hadn't heard for hours—we all did. I heard women in veils talking about what happened," Calliape says.

My attention snaps to her. "What were they saying?"

"It does not matter. I do not think it's safe, not in a place that locks you away like this," she says.

"We need to get going. The other guards will come," August says.

99 is quiet, his hands slipping down my sides, back to his own. His fists are in a ball, clenching and flexing. I run my hand down his forearm and his fists relax as I cup them, holding them tightly.

"I should have told you this morning. I came to say goodbye to a friend, to the temple one last time. I'm sorry. I thought I needed one last, final answer from First Mother. I decided last night that I'm coming to Viathan with you."

I hear all the air from his body expel, like he was holding it since they first asked me to come with them. His eyes drop like he can't bear looking into mine without losing his composure, but I feel him squeeze my hand twice.

"They won't get away with treating you like this. When we get back to Viathan, we'll intervene. You will be kept safe," he says, but his eyes express so much more.

A chill runs up my spine knowing another world's government will need to be involved to make sure I can stay, that I am safe and that the Estate cannot make me return. Reality sets in, but there is no turning back. They have killed guards to get to me. I have blasphemed in the temple and the highest priestess cast me out. I have to do this. I have to leave my world.

I nod once, enough answer to make him place his helmet back on like he is getting ready to fight to get us out.

"No guns, we do this as quietly as possible," 99 says.

Calliape stands next to me with drawn back shoulders. She doesn't seem phased by the promise of more violence, looking like she fits perfectly with the Viathans. I pull at the pins that painfully bind my veil to my hair and let it fall at my feet then try to square my shoulders like hers, willing myself a fraction of their bravery.

"I don't want you out of my sight. Stay close. Do you understand?" 99 says bluntly.

I do not argue. I know he needs to be straightforward, even more than normal, and I don't care. He can try to use nicer words later. I just want to be out of the stale air of the Estate and boarding the ship.

99 slowly opens the door and peeks out, holding a thick serrated knife like all he has to do is bend his arm to kill someone. Then he gestures over his shoulder and exits.

August withdraws a long knife and follows but leaves in the opposite direction. After a moment, he leans back into the doorway with a flick of his fingers for us to come out.

Calliape and I stay in between August and 99 at the front. We walk briskly down the hallways, stopping when 99 raises his hand to check out an open doorway.

My heart is racing, and I feel like I'm being chased.

Calliape puts her hand on my shoulder, sensing my anxiety rising as we sneak through the long corridors. I don't know if she can fight, but she looks just as deadly as the others.

I feel helpless as we scurry through the Estate. I want to sprint to the ship as fast as I can, but 99 keeps our steps steady and measured. The air in the Estate isn't the cheery kind after a celebration; it's thick and oppressive.

We cross out into the wide hallway balcony before the large staircase into the grand room.

We are almost out.

We run down the stairs, my feet descending in a frenzy, knowing exactly where to step, no time to trip.

99 stops us at the base of the stairs to look around. He pauses for a long time, longer than he has before, and then I hear the footsteps coming toward us. He turns and I can feel his panic even though I can't see his face.

"Calliape, take her!"

I turn to Calliape, and she reaches for me, wanting to fold the distance from here to the ship, to safety. But her face turns ghostly gray and her eyes saucer as she is picked off the ground and flung across the room in a gasp.

"Where do you think you are going, Ferren?" Crixa's voice is low and all-consuming in the grand hall.

"Calliape!" I scream, running to her lifeless body.

I hear clanging metal and grunting—a fight has broken out behind me—but I need to see if Calliape is alive. I stop short as Crixa blocks my path with a deadly smirk as she circles me, keeping a distance between us.

99 comes into view, and he has a guard in a bear hug from behind. With a quick slash of his arm, blood sprays in a puddle for the guard to fall into. I can't see August, but I know he is fighting too. There are so many guards and so much noise.

Crixa is slowly closing in on me, rotating around me and making sure my attention is on her.

"You were so young when I noticed your potential, so much riding on your shoulders, so much to live up to," she says.

"You wanted a puppet, someone to do your bidding, to control. No more, Crixa. You can't have me."

She laughs. "I do not want you, but you will serve the temple. You will do your duty somewhere horrible. I will make sure of it. You owe the Estate years of wasted resources and that debt will be paid. The temple owns you."

August's lean body crashes into a pillar to my side. I wince at the sound, wanting to help, but I don't know how. He steadies himself and attacks two guards at once, fueled by a feral rage. They push out of my view.

I glance back and see bodies on the ground, guards dead all around 99. I hear a high-pitched sound coming from what looks like a gun, but it spits out a dancing web of light and encompasses a guard's whole body. He convulses and then drops.

"Stop this, Ferren. Tell them you are staying and this can all stop. It's not too late for them. Tell them to leave, Ferren, that you are not worth all of this. Live out your days in peace here, worshiping and serving as First Mother intended."

I can see Calliape's chest moving, her arm coming up to touch her head.

No, it is too late. I can't stay; too much damage has been done. I trust 99 and August, and I know they will get out with Calliape. I will let Crixa kill me before she can stop them from leaving. And if I can't leave, maybe they still can. First Mother has not shown herself to me, but I am divine. I do not need permission anymore.

The fighting stifles out and I see August with Calliape, cradling her with a look of anguish on his face.

99 is in a crouch with the last guard in the room. Others will come but for now, it's just one guard and the highest between us and freedom.

I have to do something.

"First Mother may not bring anymore gifts, but the power of my second mother's sacrifice is inside me."

She blurts out a hysterical laugh, covering it with her pointy fingertips.

It does nothing but make my rage flare, and I take three bounding steps toward her. Just as I'm about to come into her space, she casts up a hand, black peppery smoke shooting out and wrapping around my throat. I feel my eyes bulge at the restriction, and I claw at the smoke coiled around my airway, pushing me back away from her.

Her eyes are wild as she lifts her cupped hand slightly, making me rise to my toes. "You have no power. I took pity on you. You will fall to my feet and beg my forgiveness."

I choke for air, my toes losing placement on the stone floor, dancing suspended, finding no footing.

99 slashes the last guard down and bounds toward us.

Crixa doesn't take her eyes off me as she extends a glassy gray ring around us, encapsulating me with her.

He stops at the edge, watching me, stalking the orb's boundary, looking for a way to get in. I watch him through blurry eyes. He nods once at me, not in permission but in an acknowledgment that he is with me, that whatever I need to do, he has me.

"Please . . . forgive . . . me," I croak out.

She drops me and I fall to the hard ground in a hunched pile, feeling the bruising floor on my knees, like a disheveled prayer pose.

I hear her feet walk toward me slowly.

"Forgive me, First Mother," I say.

Her steps stop at my words.

"For *I* am wicked," I say, raising my head. "I have forgotten the magic within me. I have looked elsewhere for my power. I have forgotten your unconditional love. I have forgotten that when I close my eyes, you are with me," I say, eyes falling shut.

Crixa lifts my chin with her boney finger, making me look upon her amused face. "I was there when your mama died. She cried out for your sister. In the end, she wanted her child, not the daughter that would kill her for nothing. My, my, the regret on her face when she realized," Crixa says, closing in on my ear to whisper.

The skin where her fingers touch burns white hot, my vision tunneling onto her face. My chest once again rises and falls as if I am hyperventilating.

Crixa's brows furrow for just a split second, and it's enough for me to press forward. I've made a crack in her composure, a hairline fracture in her stone defenses, and now my light will slither in and break it apart.

Crixa's expression is confused as I stand. She thought I would crumble, fall to her feet at the mention of Leema, of my mother, but she doesn't know what she has done. Green light flickers in her gray peppery orb. She looks around it with narrow eyes and wrings her hands in confusion. No, not confusion, fear.

She is scared.

I step forward, panting and gazing at her through heavy lids. I see her eyes dart to the side to check her defenses around us, and I lunge for her.

She throws up a hand to stop me, and I skid back faintly but push forward against her current.

"So, First Mother has come to you after all? A pity gift?"

"No, Crixa, she has not." I push harder.

Dozens of guards come into the grand room, down the staircase, and I can see August and 99 fighting again, outnumbered two to twenty. Their movements are in slow motion through the hazy bubble.

99's large physique takes two men at a time, cutting them down and throwing their bodies over his shoulders, broken and bloody.

Beams of light from Viathan weapons bounce off our orb in

glowing streaks.

This has to end now.

"Ferren," Crixa whispers.

I don't want to hear what she has to say. I let the green light take me over and fill me. The orb changes from smokey to a shiny emerald light around us, keeping everyone else out and us in.

My hands reach out to my sides, and I'm screaming without any noise. I can feel the vibration in my throat, but no sounds escape me. I push it out harder and harder, screaming my light, reverberating it around me.

Crixa steps back as far as she can without running into the perimeter.

Sharp lines of light twine around my body. It's not from any sun or moon, but from within me, glowing and the deepest green.

The churning feeling within me breaks, and the entire space is filled with a brilliant beam. My body breaks apart piece by piece. I feel every hair on my head rip, my skin peeling back, my bones breaking. Ligaments separate and stretch as I am lifted into the deep viridian light around me.

Crixa recoils away from tendrils snaking and swirling in our bubble.

Then, it's silent.

I stop the vibration in my throat and take a deep, strong inhale, filling my lungs completely. As I exhale, the green light rolls, twirling into a fog that bursts out of the bubble and sweeps out into the grand room, filling it, cutting down Crixa and the guardsmen with an explosive force blowing out to do my bidding.

There is a small push back of peppery smoke, then nothing.

I drop to the floor the moment the green light shuts off, like blowing out a candle.

Then it is still, and strong arms are lifting me, cradling me safely. My stomach drops with nausea as my head tilts back, and I let the darkness take me. I've done what I needed to do, and they can get out now.

I hear a whooshing, swirling sound; it's unnatural and mechanical. I open my eyes a sliver and see only a small blue line of light on the floor. Warm fingertips brush over my forehead, smoothing my hair.

The sound of breaking bones and heavy wind echoes in my pounding head. My lungs feel spiced and tired. I smell pepper in my nose.

Calliape—where is she?

I remember the guards' bodies rolling into mangled balls as green waves exploded outward. I remember them screaming, the squelching sounds their bodies made, then an eerie, utter silence.

What did I do to ensure our safety?

"Shhh."

"99?"

I smell him next to me, feel his warm amber light all around me, caressing me from the inside out.

"I have you, Ferren. We are going home."

AUTHORS NOTE

Hello Dear Reader!

Thank you for reading The Viridian Priestess. This truly was a story of my heart and I found myself healing along with Ferren. If you enjoyed this book and would like to know how Priestess Ferren will adjust to her new life on the planet Viathan, then please sign up for my newsletter!

Be the first to hear when book two of Ferren's and 99's love story continues.

ABOUT THE AUTHOR

Katrina Calandra is a romance author with a passion for writing spicy love stories. Originally a screenwriter, she has found her true calling in writing romance novels. Her little Aquarius heart has a soft spot for heroes who look like they could kill you but are really cinnamon rolls for their heroines. When she isn't lost in a sci-fi romance book, she is practicing tarot or plotting her next series. Katrina lives in a sleepy town in Upstate New York with her two feline familiars Sookie and Jupiter.

katrinacalandra.com

Printed in Great Britain
by Amazon